STC[illegible]
AMBITION

By Robyn Nyx

2023

Praise for
Robyn Nyx's work

Let Love Be Enough

"Nyx's debut is an entertaining thriller with two well-realized heroines. But readers who can handle the gory content will find it well balanced by plenty of romance and copious amounts of sex, as well as a solid cast of supporting characters and some insightful handling of contemporary social issues." Publishers Weekly

"If you are a sucker for fast paced, gritty crime thrillers that will make you neglect your household chores and read way past your bedtime, well fellow book lover, this is certainly the story for you." The Lesbian Review

The Extractor Trilogy

"Nyx balances the task of developing emotionally complex characters and creating a plot that is well paced and full of action on a grand scale. The story is captivating, and the best part is that it's the first in a fantastic trilogy." The Lesbian Review

"I genuinely couldn't have predicted what did happen though, and urge everyone to read this trilogy if not for the imaginative story, then for the intensity of how people's actions affect not only their own lives but the lives and feelings of others. So good! Robyn has perfectly captured all that moral uncertainty between doing the right thing legally and then doing the right thing morally." LesBiReviewed

"The redemptive power of love is a huge take-away from this book. There were more than a few times where I found myself on the verge of tears while reading some of Landry's conversations with her best friend Delaney." Victoria Thomas

Music City Dreamers

"Fans of the show Nashville will love Music City Dreamers by Robyn Nyx, for its angsty drama involving megastars and aspiring singers, songwriters and record executives. This is also not the stereotypical Nashville of bros and whiskey you often see on CMT." NPR

"I really enjoyed this story and I am so glad Ms Nyx made this foray

into lesbian romance. She has captured the passion and intense emotions of the two women, as well as weaving a fascinating story." Kitty Kat's Book Blog

The Golden Trinity

"Ms. Nyx tells an awesome story with real characters, and that to my mind is the goal of a good book." Lesbian Reading Room

"What an excellent book and I demolished it in one go! I had such a great time reading Uncharted and would be happy to pick it up again tomorrow. The pace was perfect and felt like I was on the adventure with Chase and Rayne. For the last 30% of this book, my heart was in my chest with all the excitement." Les Rêveur

The Copper Scroll

"Holy hotness, batman!! Chase and Rayne's sexual and emotional chemistry flows onto the page. This isn't an experience you want to miss. Just make sure you read the first book before this one. It's just going to make the experience all the better. This book really is jam-packed with action, adventure, and romance. I really hope this isn't the end of the 'The Chase Stinsen' books because I am not ready to let these characters go just yet." Les Rêveur

"Nyx has the ability to get you into the heads of her characters, and Chase and Rayne are no exception; and I loved that she showed us that not everything in life is always black and white. I've already re-read it twice. I thought The Golden Trinity was good, it had my heart racing, and I was awash with adrenaline in places, but The Copper Scroll surpasses it. I'm just waiting for Book 3 and the film series." The Lesbian Review

Dead Pretty

"The relationship between CJ and Dak is really cute and wholesome even though it's really sexually charged, it takes a lot of talent to create that balance." The Lesbian Review

"A fantastic combination of crime and love story twisted together in a well balanced flow. Nyx's writing is power and beautiful." The Hyperactive Bookwork

"Robyn Nyx is a wordsmith that takes you on a roller coaster ride of emotions and drops you off at a HEA, but only after you've bitten your nails down to the quick." Mayra Luria

LesFic Eclectic Volume One

Robyn Nyx has put together a fantastic collection, and brought to us some amazing new talent as well as stories from some of our already loved and established authors in the genre. Engaging readers with new writers is always fantastic, and the new writers included in the Lesfic Eclectic are all absolutely brilliant." LesBiReviewed

LesFic Eclectic Volume Two

"I have read the seasoned writers before such as Anna Larner, Robyn Nyx, Brey Willows, Jenn Matthews and Anne Shade as always blew me away with their storytelling. A little something for everyone is the tagline across the cover, and I couldn't agree more. I highly recommend grabbing a copy of Lesfic Eclectic, a bottle of vino and taking one story at a time." Les Rêveur

LesFic Eclectic Volume Three

"Having read the previous two volumes, I wondered if volume three would still achieve the same delightfulness as its counterparts but, truth be told, it's the most magical one yet." Queer Literary Loft

By the author

Let Love Be Enough

Dead Pretty

Music City Dreamers

The Chase Stinsen Adventures

The Golden Trinity (Book One)

The Copper Scroll (Book Two)

The Extractor Trilogy

Escape in Time (Book One)

Change in Time (Book Two)

Death in Time (Book Three)

Edited by Robyn Nyx

LesFic Eclectic Volume One

LesFic Eclectic Volume Two

LesFic Eclectic Volume Three

STOLEN AMBITION

By Robyn Nyx

2023

BUTTERWORTH
BOOKS

This trade paperback is published by Butterworth Books, UK

CATALOGING INFORMATION
ISBN: 978-1-915009-32-6
CREDITS
Editor: Victoria Villaseñor
Cover Design: Nicci Robinson
Production Design: Global Wordsmiths

Acknowledgements

A huge thank you to my beautiful and talented wife, Victoria Villaseñor. I'm so incredibly glad that I get to trust my words to your sharply tuned editor's scalpel. I'd like to thank our Global Wordsmiths' proofer, Margaret Burris, who works really hard to polish our words to perfection. A big thank you goes to my dedicated team of ARC readers for their encouraging and enthusiastic reviews and for taking the time to read my words. Your early love of my books settles the ever-present panic of every new release.

And as always, thanks to my readers, new and old; your support means the world to me. I loved writing this story; if you like even half as much, I'll be one happy author. I love to hear from you, so please stay in touch via the channels below:

Facebook: facebook.com/RobynNyxAuthor
Instagram: Instagram.com/Robyn_Nyx
TikTok: tiktok.com/@robynnyx_author
Website: robynnyx.com

And one last note; it's a deliberate thing that Luca is often referred to in the masculine with regard to terms like hermano :-)

Dedication

For my wife, Brey, who helped
realise my own ambitions.
I *see you* every day.

Prologue

Seventeen years ago

THE BEEPING OF THE blood pressure machine, the sterile, acrid smell of disinfectant, the sour taste of imminent death...it became white noise as Marissa Vargas allowed herself to fall into her meandering thoughts.

It wasn't supposed to happen this way. Her mamita, her greatest supporter, her rock. She should be here forever. Or if not forever, the next fifty years or so. Selfish, yes, but Marissa couldn't face the rest of her life here with *him*, not without the strength of her madre beside her. She'd seen something she couldn't unsee, and it had colored the lens she saw life through. No longer rosy. Now blood red. And without the protection of her mamita, what else would she be exposed to? Her best friend, Arturo, had been pulled into it all. He'd repeated mechanically that he'd "come of age," his eyes glazed over, his hands trembling, his gentle face spotted with the blood of someone he'd been forced to deal with in relation to her father's enormous marijuana plantation. Her papá had ripped away Arturo's innocence two nights ago, and she'd felt him slip farther from her like the inevitability of passing time.

And now, this. If she'd known this was coming, she would've cherished the time that came before it so much more. The time that was to come? The point after which everything would be different for her? That she was to face alone, isolated in a mansion that may as well be a prison, luxury wrapped around her like barbed wire. "*You will have options, mija. Only stay here if you want to.*" Somehow her mamita's assertion seemed so much harder to believe now. With her mamita at her side, anything was possible. But without her? Marissa was rudderless, floating on the sea of destiny that led inexorably toward her father's legacy. There were no siblings, making her the singular heir to a birthright that couldn't be more wrong. Now that Arturo had been initiated, she was sure it wouldn't be long before her father called her forward, and her ambition to study law would be roundly dismissed.

What would become of the legacy her madre had left in Marissa's mind? She looked around her room. She'd read many of the texts on the expansive bookshelves. From Rulfo to Bellatin, Alice Walker to Kate Chopin, Shakespeare to the Brontë sisters, and Italo Calvino to Elena Ferrante. Her madre had ensured Marissa inherited her own love of the written word with her exuberant and passionate readings until Marissa could read for herself. But even the beautiful words on those thousands of pages couldn't adequately define the swirl of dark emotions ravaging her now. And as her padre pulled her into the business she wanted no part of, would her mind palace be ravaged and ruined by the cruelty of her actions? Would the books she'd read and the lessons she'd learned from them disappear one by one, to be replaced by darkness and savagery?

"Mija."

Her mamá's weak voice echoed distantly in her mind. She was still here, for now. Marissa returned to the bed, took her pale hand and sat beside her. "Mamá."

"Promise me you'll follow your heart. Don't let anyone steal your ambitions from you," she said, the words disjointed and slow to emerge.

Marissa took an ice chip from the glass on the bedside table and offered it to her mamá's lips. "You taught me not to lie, Mamá." She couldn't make a promise that was beyond her ability to keep. She wouldn't tell an untruth to the most important person in her world. *Not even if that promise means peace? Not even if she needs it to pass to the other side?* Marissa was no longer convinced the other side existed. Her faith had faltered, and she was in no place to pander to it.

Her mamá's lips twitched as if she were trying to smile. She'd always said she loved Marissa's unswerving honesty and commitment to truth and justice. She'd said that's why her daughter would make a perfect lawyer. But without her mamá pushing for Marissa's freedom, her papá would have no restraint and no moral compass. He would have only his greed and desire for expansion, for more. Always more. Her mamá had reined that in for over twenty years but unchecked, her papá would become the Mr. Hyde monster she had read about in a Robert Louis Stevenson book.

"You can do anything, mija. You will find a way."

Marissa sighed deeply. "It will be too hard, Mamá. I'm not strong enough."

Her mamá's eyes fluttered lightly, showing her pain, and she sucked in a shallow breath. "You will be, mija. You will be everything you need to be, I know it."

The acid burn of a grief yet to be fully realized assailed Marissa's eyes. "What if I fail?"

Her mamá managed a smile this time. "You have never failed, my love. But if you do, learn from it and grow. We are not our failures, mija. We are defined by our ability to keep moving forward despite those failures. You can define yourself outside the realms of this family fortress. You will be so much more than your father's daughter."

Her mamá coughed and clutched her hand to her chest, the effort of her speech taking its toll. Marissa wanted to tell her mamá not to speak, to save her energy, but what would be the point? To slip away in silence? And Marissa would never hear her mamá's voice again, not for real. She had phone recordings of many of their conversations; she'd started doing that at thirteen, when she'd realized she wanted to pour over their discussions, to glean every minutia of knowledge and not miss any nuance of her mamá's near-perfect English.

But she'd never be able to watch her lips form the words, watch the skin around her eyes crinkle when she laughed, watch her emotions dance in her expressive eyes. This was her last chance. These were her mamá's final moments.

"Promise me."

Marissa registered her mamá's light fading. Her eyelids flickered as though she were trying to keep them open until she heard Marissa's pledge. She swallowed against the rising ball of grief in her throat. Was she the woman her mamá believed her to be? Could she be all that they'd talked about? Her mamá nodded slowly, as if reading her thoughts. The red-hot fire of molten steel shot through Marissa's veins, fortifying her resolve. "I promise, Mamá. I promise."

Chapter One

IT WASN'T THE FIRST rejection letter Luca Romero had received, but it might be the last. Maybe this was the sign that she should finally give up on her dream. The walls of the small basement space she called home were plastered with evidence that the world didn't want her, wasn't ready for her, didn't like the way she wrote. Ray Bradbury said that most writers would publish something before their walls were full. Maybe with a bigger room, she could be one of the writers he spoke of. If she stood in the center of her section of the basement, she could touch her pancake-flat pillow with one hand and reach the two-ring electric cooker with the other. She had a roof over her head though. She should be grateful that her boss, Oscar, let her stay here as part of her "employment package."

Luca swung her legs off the bed and rose, looking for an empty area on the rough, gray concrete walls. She was running out of space and still, her manuscripts remained only on the hard drive of an ancient desktop that was barely capable of running Word and Google, and never both at the same time. Loading pages with images or videos was all but impossible. It had been stored in the basement, along with a whole load of other crap she'd had to clear out before she could turn it into something habitable. Oscar had said the computer was a piece of shit—one step away from dial-up internet and floppy disks—but it was better than having all her words on paper. Paper could be burned or soaked through, her words lost forever. At least with this old thing, she had her stories on the hard drive. She tapped the dirty cream-colored casing of the machine affectionately. If she ever *did* get published, the first thing she bought would be a sleek, silver MacBook Air. One of those with the fingerprint recognition keyboard, then she'd finally own something that was worth having. Something that was really hers that no one else could touch.

She pinned the thick paper stock to the wall and reread it. *Not a good fit. We wish you luck. Not quite what we're looking for*. Blah, blah, blah. They all had the same, pseudo-polite way of telling her to fuck off. Had any of the places she'd sent the first book of the trilogy to even read it? Read a chapter? A word? Did they get to the end of her query letter before they dismissed her as unworthy? She believed to the last fiber of her soul that she'd written a good story. And so did Veronica. She said she'd read it if Luca wrote it. Her writing mentor and biggest champion's words kept her going, even with the lessening space on the walls.

Her cell vibrated and began its annoying song to remind her that she had a bar shift. Throwing cocktails, flipping and juggling bottles, refilling the snacks. It wasn't the life she'd imagined building when she'd been abandoned all those years ago, but then who would? Veronica had filled her head with a world Luca could never be part of. She spoke of travel, and education, and dreams, but those were privileges an American girl could believe in, not a golfilla like her. Ambitions, like hope, were a dangerous thing, and maybe it was time for Luca to let go of both and accept her fate.

Chapter Two

CASEY SOTO TRACED HER tongue along the red and yellow fire trail leading from the number nine pool ball tattoo on the woman's hip. "Do you play?" she asked.

"Aren't we playing now?"

"Sure we are, Hayley, but–"

"Kayleigh."

"Sure we are, Kayleigh." Casey nibbled Kayleigh's freshly tanned skin then pressed her finger lightly to the professionally inked creation. What she would give for that kind of artistry. She glanced at the crude markings on her own hands and forearms. One day she'd have them all redone by one of the top tattooists in the world. "But I meant pool. Do you play pool?"

"No," she said. "Why would you think that?"

Wasn't it obvious? Casey hadn't expected Kayleigh to be so dumb, even with a few lines of coke up her nose. "This doesn't mean anything?"

Kayleigh propped herself up on her elbows and looked down at the tattoo in question. "I guess it means it's a really fast ball. Like, so fast, it leaves a path of fire." She flopped back onto the bed. "Tattoos don't have to mean anything. They can just be pretty."

Casey sighed a breath of disappointment between Kayleigh's legs. Sometimes the price of nights away from the shitty room she shared with her work buddy was almost too high. Her own ink might be lacking in quality, but they meant *something*. Casey shoved the distraction away and settled between Kayleigh's thighs. If Kayleigh didn't make another sound, other than to scream out a few orgasms, Casey could enjoy the rest of the night. A couple of hours of sex and a peaceful night's sleep on a thick, expensive mattress. The sex and money were always worth putting up with women who, given a choice, she wouldn't consider entertaining.

But Kayleigh *had* bought Casey's entire week of product. Vargas would be impressed she was coming back for more before she was due.

If she could keep this up, she could approach him about moving up the food chain soon. He needed loyal people close to him, and with no other way of funding her plan to escape to LA, getting deeper into the only game in town was her only play.

"Harder."

Casey tuned in briefly to Kayleigh's command and focused on enjoying what she was doing. Fucking the tourists was a perk and a requirement of the job. It made it easier to sell more. These women came to San Lucas for drugs and sex; if they could get both at the same time, they were more likely to keep coming back. And each sale put Casey a few dollars closer to her dream. Kayleigh was a new customer, but Casey could tell she was looking for familiarity in her search for weekend-vacation oblivion. She'd return again and again if her needs were serviced right the first time.

She slipped her finger inside Kayleigh, who writhed and bucked beneath her and whispered in a language she didn't understand. She pushed in harder, irritated that even when she was doing something she knew damn well she was exceptional at, she could still be made to feel stupid. The least Kayleigh could do was moan in Spanish.

"Más rápida," Kayleigh whispered as if she'd read Casey's mind.

She smirked. That she could do, faster than a freight train and as long they needed. It was one of the main reasons Casey spent as much time working out as she could. She almost always wore tank tops or shirts with no sleeves so these women could see they'd get exactly what they wanted for however long they wanted it. Her hands and arms were the first things they checked out once they realized she was a woman. It didn't matter that she wasn't that handsome. Rugged and rough got her laid.

She watched the muscles in her forearm as she pumped in and out, hard and fast like Kayleigh wanted. When the women didn't really do anything for her, concentrating on herself was enough to keep her interested. It was just another workout, except she was essentially getting paid for it.

Kayleigh said something else in the other language—was it French? Whatever it was, Casey had heard enough. She pulled out, flipped her over, and pressed her face into the bed before going back in with her other hand. She didn't want uneven biceps any more than she wanted a farmer's tan. And this way, she wouldn't hear whatever language Kayleigh was speaking.

She flipped her thoughts to Marissa. Beautiful, classy, educated Marissa. She could speak any language, and Casey would be hypnotized rather than hateful. If Vargas knew about her desire for his daughter, he'd probably string her up from the Canyon Bridge by her intestines. Marissa was a woman worth that kind of risk, and she was part of Casey's escape plan.

She just didn't know it yet.

Chapter Three

THE GENTLE, RHYTHMIC RAPPING on her door disturbed Marissa from her studies. Arturo still used the secret knocks, even after all these years. She didn't call out. She carefully replaced the cap on her pen and laid it on the desk in its velvet-lined cradle. She'd barely had time to wrap the lace around her leather journal before a different coded knock sounded. She closed her eyes and let out a short breath, irritated that she knew what it meant. So much had changed since the days of them running around the house, playing cops and robbers. Now Arturo played a dangerous game for real.

"I don't have time right now. I'm reading case files." She looked at the door. He'd be leaning on the solid oak now, wanting to bang his head against it. She never did anything he asked for without a little fight, which drove him insane, but it made her feel somewhat in control of her life. She pushed up from her chair. It wouldn't be long before she was *fully* in control of her life and Arturo of his. Knowing that meant she could enjoy their little charades more than when they'd been displays of useless defiance.

She opened the door and glared at him. "Arturo."

"Marissa." He lowered his eyes slightly, as he always did when he greeted her. "Your father requests your presence."

She arched her eyebrow. "Tell him I'm busy." Answering to his agenda wasn't on her schedule today. She didn't care that Arturo's code warned her that her father was in one of his less-friendly moods. Whether or not one of his government officials were doing his bidding wasn't her concern.

"Please, Marissa."

His gentle and soulful eyes pleaded far better than any words that might come from his mouth. If he returned alone, *he* would pay a price, not her. She looked back at the pile of books she wanted to get through before she left her father's distastefully decorated, pretend palace forever. This space, her sanctuary, would be the only thing she would miss. After her mamá's death, her father could no longer stand to be in this room, whereas Marissa wanted to be nowhere else. Her most-treasured childhood memories were created here, so many hours spent with her mamá, snuggled up in her arms, reading texts in Spanish, Italian, and English. She'd moved in the same week of her mamá's funeral, desperate to feel close to her though she was gone forever.

And this was also the only room in the house she could guarantee her father would never enter. Hence Arturo coming to get her. "Is this for business or his pleasure? Never mind," she said before Arturo had the chance to respond. He couldn't speak freely within these walls. Their childhood code continued to serve a useful purpose. "Let's go." She closed the door behind her, but Arturo didn't move.

He glanced at her feet. "Shoes?"

"I'm inside, Arturo. I don't need shoes."

He rolled his eyes and sighed deeply. "Your father expects heels, Marissa. You know this."

"And that's why I will go barefoot." She led the way along the stone floor of the long corridor then paused at the top of the giant, double staircase to wipe the gloss from her lips with the back of her hand. He expected makeup too. She pulled the scrunchy from her wrist, scraped her wavy hair back from her face and tied it up in a severe ponytail. Another expectation she wouldn't fulfill today.

His office door was closed. Briefly, she considered walking straight in. This was supposed to be her house too. But she would already be pushing his patience with her general appearance, and she didn't particularly want to fight with him. If it were left to her, she wouldn't see him at all, let alone spend time arguing.

Arturo stepped around her and rapped on the door, saving her from a longer discussion with herself.

"Come."

One word and her stomach knotted. Being around her father was as bad for her physically as it was mentally. Arturo motioned for her to enter before him. The wood warmed her feet. Since she hadn't stepped onto plastic sheeting, she assumed he hadn't called her to witness the more unsavory part of his business. There seemed to be infinite rolls of sheeting in the store cupboard, as if he was working his way through every government official in every state in Mexico.

She suppressed a smile when she registered the fleeting disappointment that flickered across his eyes as he took in her appearance. He glanced over her shoulder at Arturo, and her joy was short lived when he clenched his jaw and tilted his head almost imperceptibly. For Arturo, she should've worn heels at least. Her impending freedom was making her careless and cocky. She would have to rein that in for the next few weeks.

"I'd like you to meet Oscar Valle Espinosa from Guaymas," her father said. "He's come a long way to meet you."

She barely glanced at the man. Smart suit, slicked hair, veiled menace. A carbon copy of every other man he'd paraded before her. And that same expression of distaste for her obvious independence was obvious in his dark, narrowed eyes. "Then he's wasted his time." She was in no mood for more of her father's fantasy talk about marrying her to another family to further his legacy—*her* legacy, he would insist.

"Arturo," her father said. "Escort our guest to the library." He nodded toward Espinosa. "We will talk later."

Espinosa straightened, and Marissa noted the briefest flicker of irritation at the casual dismissal. He focused his cruel eyes on her as he passed and seemed to fight to suppress a sneer. She smiled politely at him and tried to disguise her complete lack of interest, which was ridiculous considering her response to his presence. She'd been as dismissive as her father, and that bothered her. "Thank you for visiting. I'm sorry my father wasted your time."

He sneered. "You are a daughter with no respect for her padre. I have dodged a bullet."

He was gone before she had time to respond, and Arturo closed the door quickly. A slight quirk of his eyebrow pleaded with her to be more careful.

"If you won't marry Arturo, at least consider Oscar. This business was built on the deep ties of blood, friendship, marriage, and community, Marissa."

She turned back toward him. "*Was* being the key word, Papá. Those days are a distant echo of a past you refuse to release. There is no loyalty anymore. Even in families."

He shot her an almost startled look before his expression darkened, and he resumed his usual emotionless mask. "When I'm gone, you want to run this business alone?"

"I don't want to run this business at all, Papá." She dropped into a large wingback chair by the arched stained-glass window that he'd had removed from his boyhood church. It was the one thing she loved about his otherwise intensely macho décor. The heads of black bear, cougar, mountain lions, Bighorn sheep. So much death mixed with dark wood and deep, blood-red leather upholstery. The one hint of his humanity was the gold-framed photograph of him with Marissa and her mamá when she was seven, which was also probably the last time Marissa had genuinely smiled at him or been glad to be in his company. Once she'd graduated from typically childish books and her mamá began sharing *real* books with true villains and questions of morality and ethics, Marissa became increasingly aware of the kind of man her father was. And she became increasingly sure she didn't like it.

"Why do you continue to fight me, mija?" He came over and sat in the matching chair opposite her. "Have I not been patient with you? I have never been disappointed that your mamá, Dios bendiga su alma," he said, crossing his chest, "gave me you and not a boy."

He opened the wooden humidor on the table between them, selected a cigar, and went through the motions. She considered joining him, but for all that it might annoy him, she wasn't interested in giving herself cancer. "So I should think myself fortunate that you love me, even though I was born a girl?"

He puffed a white plume of thick, curling smoke out toward the window and shook his head. "You twist my words, mija. I have loved you as much as I would have loved a boy—more, perhaps—and I've indulged your desires and allowed you to go to law school when I considered you were old enough, but you have family duties. It's time to put aside your selfish ambitions and learn what I do so you can take over when the time comes."

Allowed. God, she hated that word and its connotations of control, just as she hated the very concept that women should seek permission from men at all. She would *not* be considered inferior to any man, even her padre. She would be no one's object nor pawn. When she finally got away from here to start her new life, she would be in control, and no one would *allow* her to do anything.

"Why are my ambitions more selfish than your insistence that I learn a business I have no interest in?" she asked, trying to keep her tone calm and even. "And an illegal business at that. I want to *help* people with the law. You want me to use the law to benefit your illegal dealings." She glanced across at her mamá's image on his giant desk. Never once did her mother raise her voice with him, and yet she always got her way. "Isn't this simply a case of us wanting different things for me?" she asked softly. It would be so much easier if he would simply give her his blessing to leave. "You speak of loyalty, and you have several lieutenants who would die for you, families who have worked for you and your father before you for decades. People who understand the drug business and want to be part of that world. Why not consider choosing one of them?" She would not–could not–suggest he form his own alliance with another family through marriage. No one could replace her mamá, and despite everything, she was sure he felt the same.

He took another long pull on his cigar and released a series of circular smoke rings. "Perhaps there is a compromise, princesa. Marry Arturo and allow him to run the elements of the business you do not care for. You can run your law practice and occasionally help out Arturo if and when he needs it."

Marissa closed her eyes and pinched the bridge of her nose. Why had she thought that he would really listen to what she was saying? His compromise was no compromise at all. It was the same offer with recycled and reordered words. She didn't bother to respond to the Arturo part. They'd gone over it many times before. "It's not my law practice, Papá, it's yours." *Bought to keep ears on me and control me*. "You wouldn't let me find my own way."

"You're complaining that you didn't have to scrape and fight like a dog at a second-rate law office?" He tapped his cigar onto the edge of an ashtray, and a long stick of gnarled ash crumbled and fell. "I cannot win with you. Why are you not grateful for all that I do for you?"

She put her hands on the arms of the chair, ready to leave, but his raised hand stopped her, and she sank back. "I'm not being ungrateful, Papá. I just want to go my own way. I thought you would be proud of me for that. Mamá would've been."

Her father grabbed the ashtray and dashed it toward the stained-glass window. Marissa watched its progress in slow motion as it hurtled through the air. She waited for the almighty crash of metal against glass and the inevitable collapse of its centuries' old artistic beauty.

"Do not ever presume to tell me what your mamá would think, or say, or feel."

His roared words were accompanied by a cacophony of noise as the window shattered and fell outward onto the marble-tiled terrace. She pushed herself against the back of the armchair, trying to make herself as small as possible. Her heart hammered against her chest, and fear wrapped around her throat, making it hard to breathe. She was a frightened five-year-old child again, and the speed with which the transformation took place only hardened her resolve to leave this place and her toxic father before she was forever entangled in the roots of his family tree.

Chapter Four

LUCA MIXED THE FIFTH Cabo cocktail in ninety minutes for Annie, a pretty American tourist in her late forties. For someone so small, she sure could handle her liquor. Luca was tempted to reduce the tequila measure but had a feeling Annie would notice. For once, she seemed to be getting more attention than Casey, who had tried her charms on Annie with no success. It didn't keep her from throwing out her lines and smart comments, but Annie seemed unimpressed and consistently waited to finish the last dregs of her drink just as Casey was serving another customer and Luca was free.

She didn't mind the unusual reversal, but she was nowhere near as slick as her colleague when it came to romancing the tourists, encouraging them to drink more than they should and gleaning US dollars for tips instead of pesos. She didn't want to be responsible for anyone not being in a fit state to make good decisions, especially when they were on vacation. And regardless of Annie's apparently unquenchable thirst, she was a surprisingly good conversationalist. While the average barfly would dump all their problems, pop psychology, and politics, Annie encouraged her to talk and genuinely appeared to listen. As she ordered her fifth cocktail, Annie had somehow managed to get Luca to open up about her author ambitions.

"I think this has to be my last attempt at it for a while." Luca pulled a glass from the freezer and poured Annie's drink. "I'm not built to take this kind of sustained rejection."

"I'm not sure anyone is." Annie smiled gently. "Tell me about your book."

Luca launched into her elevator pitch, honed after hours and hours of watching tutorials and workshops on the subject, and writing plenty of query letters.

"And it's a trilogy? You've already written all three?"

Luca nodded. "And designed the tattoo I want of the sisters' wings."

"That sounds fantastic. I love the idea of the Fury sisters looking for love while they're busy saving the world." Annie took a large drink.

Luca half-smiled. "I'm glad to hear someone does."

Casey slapped her hard on the back. "Hey, I love it too, hermanito."

Luca shrugged her off. She was no one's little *anything*. She would've cursed, but she took her professionalism seriously and wasn't about to risk upsetting Annie or anyone else within earshot.

Annie frowned. "You look about the same size to me."

"We are *not* the same size in anything but sneakers." Casey flexed her arm.

Her boulder-like shoulders and baseball-sized biceps often seemed to be the things that impressed the tourists, even the men. Casey wasn't particularly discerning; Luca had seen her go back to the hotel rooms of a fair share of gay guys too. Thankfully, she never brought anyone back to their shared space. It was the one rule they had, though it rarely applied to Luca.

Annie tilted her head to see Luca beyond Casey's showy display and rolled her eyes. "Is she always like this?"

Casey scoffed and dropped her arm. "Always in amazing shape? Yes, I am."

She grabbed a cloth and wiped down the bar as if that's what she'd come over to do in the first place. Another woman drew her attention, and she was gone.

"She's a lot to take," Annie said. "Do you work together all the time?"

"Work and live together. I don't get much of a break." Luca glanced at Casey, already in full swing with the new turista. "She's okay. You get used to her." Luca had done more than get used to Casey; she'd come to see her as her only friend. With the way she'd grown up and no family that she knew of, she hadn't gotten a lot of practice at trusting people. But after four years of sharing the same air, if she had to say she trusted anyone, it would be Casey.

Annie ran the pineapple garnish around the rim of her glass then sucked on her slender finger. "She called you her brother, but are you *together*, together?"

Luca chuckled. "Dios mío, no. We both appreciate more feminine women."

"I had to ask." Annie finished her drink and pushed the glass toward

Luca. "Make me something special and tell me more about your latest attempt to become a published author."

"Do you like mojitos?"

"Honey, I like all hard liquor, but yes, I like mojitos. Especially the mint ones."

"Okay, I've got you, and this is with tequila instead of rum." Luca took a Collins glass from the freezer and added mint, brown sugar, and lime. While she muddled them for slightly longer than usual to release plenty of mint, she talked about her last submission. "I'd gotten paranoid about the American agents turning me down because of my name, so I decided to submit with a pseudonym instead, and one that didn't reveal my gender. I left my real name out altogether."

"And you think it's going to make a difference?"

Luca shrugged. "I hope so because it's the only thing I can change. I'm not sure that people are even reading it. I guess my writing could be really bad, but I've taken a lot of English and writing classes. It's amazing how generous people are with their knowledge online." She put the crushed ice and rest of the ingredients into a cocktail shaker, did the business, and poured it into Annie's glass, then topped it with 7-Up and garnished it with a sprig of mint. "One mojito diablo."

Annie raised it to her lips and took a small sip. She closed her eyes briefly and murmured appreciatively. "If you write even half as well as you mix cocktails, you'll be published soon enough. When did you submit it?"

Luca bit her lip. In publishing world terms, she'd committed a cardinal sin. It had taken nearly twenty rejections for her to bend the rules, but she'd been desperate. "I queried this agent seven weeks ago, four months after my other live submission, so technically, I had multiple submissions."

"And from the look on your face, that's bad form?"

Luca nodded. "They ask you not to do it, but the process can take months. It's so frustrating."

Annie waved her hand. "Then they probably expect people to do it. How likely is it for authors to get multiple offers at the same time anyway?"

"Judging by the responses I keep getting, not likely at all. I'd be happy to get just one offer."

Annie took another sip of her cocktail and sighed deeply. "So good." She raised the glass. "Here's to you celebrating getting an agent and a publishing deal before my vacation ends."

Luca laughed. "I love your confidence. Maybe you can leave that with me instead of a tip at the end of your night."

Annie wagged her finger. "No negativity from you, please. Put your request out into the Universe, and the Universe will provide. It's amazing how many times that's worked for me. I've been traveling the world for decades, trusting that whatever I need will make itself known to me at some point, and it always has."

Luca struggled not to laugh out loud. She'd never heard such horseshit in her life. If something *was* out there in the cosmos dealing out the good stuff, it had selective deafness when it came to what Luca wanted. "You believe that?" she asked.

"I believe in energy, and good energy attracts more good energy. That comes in many forms."

"So on the flip side, if all you get is bad shit happening to you, it's because you have bad energy and deserve it?" Casey bumped Luca's shoulder.

Annie raised her eyebrows, her expression cool. "Have you just described your life?"

Casey whacked her bar towel into her palm. "That's cold, lady."

She turned quickly and went to the far end of the bar where another tourist was waiting and clearly happy to receive Casey's attention. Luca heard her mutter, "You know nothing about me." After that burn, Luca figured Casey wouldn't be back again. She was resilient and persistent, but Annie's retort felt a bit too sharp even for Casey to deflect.

A group of young American guys descended on the bar. Luca, grateful to escape the awkward atmosphere, excused herself and dealt with them all. It took less time than she'd hoped since all they wanted was a bottle of tequila and six glasses, and Annie was already tapping her empty glass. "What would you like?"

"Same again," she said. "And sorry... I'm not normally mean like that, but she's the kind of sexually aggressive person that rubs me the wrong way. I didn't mean to offend you."

Luca smiled. "It's okay. She'll bounce back."

"Will you take my advice?" Annie asked after a short silence.

Luca set to mixing another specialist mojito. "About asking the Universe to publish me?" She winked and muddled the mint into the glass. "Sure."

Annie didn't look convinced. "Do it now."

Luca chuckled. "Mean *and* bossy—you're a walking ice queen trope."

She furrowed her brow. "Ice queen? Sometimes. But what on Earth is a trope? Did you just insult me?"

"Not at all. Ice queen tropes are super popular. If I ever wrote a romance, you'd make a good ice queen, that's all." Luca averted her gaze from the intensity of Annie's and continued mixing the mojito.

Annie held her hands out over the bar. "Come on. Let's ask the Universe together."

Luca poured Annie's drink. "Seriously?"

She tapped her knuckles on the wood. "Seriously. What have you got to lose if it's your last attempt anyway?"

Luca blew out a breath. Annie was right. It wouldn't cost her anything. "Bien." She took Annie's hands. They were warm and soft, and Luca imagined how they'd feel running over her body. "What now?"

"Tell the Universe what you want."

Luca wrinkled her nose. "Out loud?" She looked around and caught Casey's disapproving expression but ignored it.

"Out loud." Annie squeezed her hands. "And mean it. No half-hearted whispering nonsense. Say it like you really want it."

"Please, Mx., Ms., or Mr. Universe, I really want my book out in the world. Help me get published!" She shouted the last sentence and everyone within earshot looked at her. She loosed her hands from Annie and held them up. "Sólo estamos locos."

Annie gave a small smile. "We're not crazy. You'll be thanking me soon enough."

"I'll do more than thank you if it works."

Annie wiggled her eyebrows, and Luca half-regretted the clumsy pseudo-come on. The other half was just shy. It had been a while since she'd gone back to a customer's hotel. But she had needs, and Annie was sexy in that college professor kind of way. An older couple signaled for her attention, and she went to serve them. As she was throwing bottles and glasses and generally impressing them, she laughed at herself for what she'd just done. As if the Universe could make her dreams come true. She was the only one who could do that. Why should she expect a publishing contract to drop into her hands? There were millions of people out there wanting the same thing, and plenty of them were probably far more talented than she was. But she wanted it so bad. Maybe the

Universe would figure it owed her a favor after the cards it dealt in her childhood. Her stomach tingled with the possibility of what achieving her dreams might feel like. She couldn't imagine. She didn't want to *imagine*, she wanted to experience it.

The couple tipped her a ten-dollar bill for the show, and she stuffed it in the pocket of her cargo shorts.

"Do you have your phone in those?" Annie asked, gesturing to Luca's shorts.

"Yeah. Do you need me to call you a cab?" Luca acknowledged the small stab of disappointment that Annie might be leaving without her.

"No, silly. I want you to check your email."

Luca pulled out her cell and placed it on the bar between them. "You think the Universe works that quickly?" Maybe it'd be better if Annie *did* leave. She might not be outwardly drunk, but what she was saying made no sense. Casey would be good with taking advantage of this situation, but Luca had more respect for women. "Sure you don't need a cab?"

"Sure I'm sure." She indicated the hotel a few buildings away. "I'm only there. Maybe you'll walk me back to my room when you finish your shift," Annie whispered.

"I don't finish for another six hours... Unless you're happy to wait?" What the hell. Luca wasn't about to push away the offer of some easy sex and a night in a bed where metal springs didn't dig into her back.

Annie tapped her long fingernails on the screen of Luca's phone. She clenched at the thought of Annie dragging those nails down her back.

"I'll wait if you check your phone."

Luca shook her head but unlocked it with her passcode. She opened the mail app and began to scroll. Daily writing tips, author newsletters, and Amazon emails filled her inbox.

But one email address stood out from the rest—that and its subject line, Book Submission. Dread formed a leaden ball that settled in the pit of her stomach. A response so soon had to be more bad news. They probably hadn't even bothered to read it. Maybe it was the lesbian content as much as her gender or nationality. She'd always judged authors who'd changed the sexuality of their characters so they sold more, and she didn't want to compromise her integrity, even to fulfill her dream. People like her needed to see themselves in books. It was one thing to use a pseudonym to get a foot in the door, another thing entirely to change a book's protagonists to suit a heterosexual market.

"What is it?" Annie asked. "Is it from your agent?"

Luca managed to laugh. "*My* agent? Maldito, I wish I had your positivity." She locked the phone and slipped it back in her shorts. It'd wait. No need to get depressed and bum out the customers.

"What did it say?"

Luca picked up a towel and wiped down the bar. "Same as usual, I expect. 'Thanks for submitting. No thank you.' All rejection letters are pretty much the same."

"You didn't read it?"

"Nah, no need." Luca sidestepped to serve the next customer while Casey continued to charm the woman at the opposite end of the bar. It took a while since he wanted ten different cocktails, but Luca was grateful for the reprieve. She had a feeling Annie wouldn't heed the hint that she didn't want to continue their conversation about her failed writing career. She rubbed a chunk of lime around the rim of a highball glass as she realized what she'd promised herself. This agent had been her final hope, but there'd been a part of her that had remained optimistic, a part of her that didn't want to contemplate letting her dream go. Would giving up on it be easy? Maybe it would if she accepted that it had been way too unrealistic to begin with. Luca would never sell drugs like Casey, but there were other things she could concentrate on. Maybe she could talk to Oscar about working her way up the ladder, or she could learn to be a chef. She wasn't pretty or anywhere near feminine enough to be allowed on the reception desk or even to clean the rooms, but she could work in the kitchen. She'd spent plenty of time in the orphanage's kitchen, chopping and preparing food and helping the woman whose name she'd never known because she insisted on everyone calling her Abuela. She'd been kind too, just like the abuela Luca had often dreamed she had somewhere out there, an abuela who would've taught her how to become an independent woman.

She finished the last of the drinks, took payment, and pocketed the tip, trying not to show her disappointment that it was in pesos.

"Your bottle handling is impressive," Annie said, "but do you want to be doing that forever?" She tapped her watch. "Your time is running out. It is for everyone."

"Jesús, that's not dark at all."

Annie shook her head. "You're still young. The sooner you realize that your spins around the sun go faster than you think, the more you can get out of your life." She gestured to Luca's pocket. "Even if that is a rejection, so what? It's not about how many times you fall, it's about how many times you get back up. If you want something bad enough, you have to be prepared to work hard for it, and you have to take the knockbacks."

Luca grinned. "Are you a life coach?"

"I'm serious." She tapped her nails on the wooden bar. "For every one person who succeeds by pure luck, a thousand get to the same place through sheer hard work and commitment." She tilted her head slightly. "And a million don't get there at all. Of course, it's easier to be a quitter. Is that what you are?"

Luca clenched her jaw and bristled. She was beginning to wish for a regular barfly who only talked about themselves. "No." She kept her answer brief to keep from saying something that could get her fired, and then she'd be homeless as well as hopeless.

"Come on," Annie said gently. "I know people, and I see you've got something. Something that's better than serving drunken tourists for the rest of your life." She nodded toward Casey. "*She's* someone who could only ever fly on the wings of someone like you," she whispered. "She thinks she's made for far greater things, but she'll be eternally disappointed. Don't make the mistake of thinking you're anything like her." Annie held up her hands. "I know she's your friend, but I say what I see. And you're wasting your life here... Check that email. The Universe has your back this time."

Luca looked beyond Annie, over the horizon and toward the clear, bluebird sky. What Annie said had echoes of Veronica's many motivational talks. She'd been the only person who'd ever had any kind of belief in her. But Veronica knew who Luca was and had read her teenage scribblings. Annie had drawn conclusions from a couple of hours of conversation.

But that didn't mean she was wrong. Some people were able to read others, see something in them that they couldn't or wouldn't see in themselves, good and bad. Luca softened and pulled her phone from her pocket again. She unlocked it and slid it across the bar. "You read it."

Annie shook her head and pushed it back toward Luca. "You're in control of your own destiny. No one else."

Luca sighed and snatched up her phone. She flicked open the email and began to read.

The phone became a concrete weight, and it slipped out of her hand. It bounced on the rubberized floor and settled face up. Luca stared down at it, disbelieving.

It couldn't be. She blinked hard once and then again before retrieving her cell to reread the opening paragraph.

We would like to represent you...

"Fucking hell."

Chapter Five

FAITH, LOYALTY, AND ADORATION. That's why her mamá had said the Mexican sunflower was her favorite. They had always seemed too common to garner her appreciation, and when Marissa had learned they had been the flowers of her father's courtship, she liked them even less. Perhaps he hadn't known, but she suspected he would have been happy with what they meant. He expected loyalty and admiration from his wife and daughter and took every opportunity to remind them why he deserved it.

Whenever she brought flowers for her mamá, they were birds of paradise. Signifying beauty and excellence, Marissa thought them a far more worthy flower. She clutched a bouquet close to her chest and walked slowly toward the mausoleum where her mamá had been buried, though she tried to look everywhere but at the giant structure ahead. With its sleek lines and bulletproof glass, a/c and plush leather couches, it could easily have passed as one of her father's satellite offices. She despised him for that. Even at her mamá's shrine, she couldn't get away from his business.

She passed rows and rows of rainbow pastel, three-tiered shrines topped with crosses and wished she could stop at any one of them instead of the monstrosity he'd created. Her mamá deserved a colorful and dignified place to rest, not this ugly, modern creation. But as always, his needs were of far more importance than anyone else's, even those of his wife. Marissa had been too young to challenge him, but she had asked why the mausoleum was so different from everyone else's. He'd insisted that he was honoring her memory by creating something as unique as her mamá had been, and Marissa had vaguely believed him. But as the years passed, her original doubts resurfaced, and she realized he'd created something to keep himself safe, not to worship his wife.

It didn't take long for her white leather pumps to be covered in red dust from the sand-covered ground, but she didn't care. Her mamá loved to see her in white shoes, boots, or sandals, and she never wanted to disappoint her. But she would have to disappoint her soon. El Día de los Muertos was fast approaching, and it would be Marissa's last chance to communicate when the veil thinned. And then? She would be gone.

She heard Arturo's footsteps seconds before he was by her side. Her father wouldn't let her go anywhere alone, but Arturo was the least intrusive option of the people he trusted. He would soon reevaluate that when Arturo disappeared along with her.

"I'm sorry, Marissa. When I told him where you were going, he insisted."

He held aloft such an ostentatiously large presentation of Mexican sunflowers that she could barely see him.

"I suppose I should be thankful that he didn't insist on accompanying me," she said and resumed her slow pace.

Arturo scoffed. "I think he knows better than that."

She shook her head. "Then you think wrong. He only cares for his own feelings and his business. If he'd wanted to come with me, nothing would've stopped him."

Arturo lightly bumped Marissa's shoulder as he walked beside her. "Soon we won't have to think of him at all."

She smiled widely, a sudden lightness in her step at Arturo's words. Then caution took over, and she stopped and looked around. "You *are* alone, aren't you?"

He frowned and gave her the same expression he'd been giving her his whole life when he believed she was being dumb. "I'm not an idiot. You honestly think I would speak so freely if we weren't?"

Marissa still scanned the area. "No. But sometimes he sends extra people out to sit at a distance. You know that. And they have the equipment to hear everything."

"Trust me. He's too busy trying to expand his empire. Espinosa has stuck around even after you snubbed him. Your father is hopeful they can work something out without a marriage bond."

"Still. Say nothing more until we're inside." Marissa quickened her pace. She unlocked the thick, glass door, and Arturo pulled it open. Once inside, she flicked on the central switch that controlled the array of scrambling units dotted around the mausoleum. They were the singular security installation she approved of.

Arturo closed the door and locked it behind them. She despised the precautions, wishing that rival cartels and government agencies respected this one location and that any attacks or moves here were considered out of bounds. But they weren't. Her father had often told the story of how the Rubio clan in Michoacán were all but wiped out at the funeral of the leader's son. His visceral and bloody descriptions were meant to serve as a warning that they all needed to be careful. What it had actually done was strengthen her desire to leave him and all he represented behind. He'd also used it as an excuse to build her mamá's resting place this way instead of following her wishes to have something simple and bright.

"I'll be here," Arturo said and sat in one of the tan suede sofas in the anteroom.

Marissa nodded and walked into the larger area at the rear of the building. She laid the flowers on the shrine and lit the scattered candles before she knelt on a soft, multi-colored cushion a foot away from the many images of her mamá, each of them set in a twenty-four karat gold frame.

"I miss you," she said. They were always the first three words of her visits here. The three words that were *supposed* to be the most important words anyone could say were something she hadn't said to another soul since her mamá had died. Her father said them to her often but followed them up with actions that made the words meaningless, made them something rote that he said because he thought they would get him what he wanted.

Well, Marissa wanted something now. She wanted to be free of him. Free of him forever. "I have to leave you, Mamá. I need to get out of this place and find my own way. You told me to follow my heart and my ambitions, but they'll take me away from here, away from you." Her sorrow at the knowledge that she would never again be this close to her mamá pushed for attention, creating tears that swelled until her eyes could no longer hold them. They coursed down her cheeks and fell onto the photo she was holding so that it looked as though her mamá was crying too.

She laid the frame on a nearby cushion and pulled a Kleenex from her purse to wipe the glass. As she did, her tears flowed freely and formed a small sea of sorrow on the rose quartz marbled floor. "I need your help. I need your strength. I fear if I stay longer that I'll become inextricably intertwined in the vines of his vile and vicious operation." Marissa replaced the photo on the shrine and closed her eyes. Images of what she envisioned her father did in his office invaded, and she snapped her eyes open. She glanced over her shoulder but couldn't see Arturo. He too had suffered. He had been in that room, had witnessed—even participated in—her father's machinations.

"Was he a different man when you married him? He's changed even more since you died, and I find it harder every day to find an iota of decency in him." It was difficult not to regret her lineage sometimes. Her mamá had regaled her with the story of their courtship and how they met. She sometimes thought her mamá romanticized it purely for her benefit, but her eyes had sparkled, and she'd almost crackled with passionate energy whenever she spoke of it. That kind of connection couldn't be faked. "How did he drift so far from the man you fell in love with?"

She shuddered, thinking of Espinosa with his slicked back hair and dark, shark-like eyes. He was her father's kindred spirit; there was nothing in his eyes, in his heart, or his soul that anyone could fall in love with. Whatever her mamá had seen in her father was absent in Espinosa. "I won't marry a man to form alliances that serve his drug business..." She pushed up from her knees, took one of her favorite photos from the table and held it to her chest. She had only kept one secret from her mamá since she'd passed away, and perhaps now was the time to unburden herself. The number of visits she had left were finite, and she didn't want to leave with something so profound still unsaid between them. Her truth hadn't fully revealed itself while her mamá was still alive, though she wished with all her heart that it had. Instead, she'd held it inside all these years, furtively exploring it and only to a limited degree. She held the photo away and traced her fingers along her mamá's face through the glass. "I won't marry any man. Ever. My heart aches for a softer love, for the soul of a woman."

The flames of the candles flickered momentarily and then grew stronger, burned brighter. There was no wind in the building, no reason for a breeze. Marissa had been encumbered by her own failure to admit her truest self. She had carried its oppression like the weight of a dead body on her shoulders, but the faltering flames felt like a message. Her mamá heard her and the candles continued to burn... Her mamá continued to love her despite her confession. It was as if she could breathe again. Her body felt lighter, like she could walk on air. With her mamá's love, even without her presence, she could and would follow her heart.

"I'll push for my dreams, Mamá. I promise I *will* make you proud."

When she returned, Arturo hadn't moved. She appreciated that he hadn't made use of the specially imported Gaggia coffee machine even though coffee was his not-so-secret addiction. Couches and coffee made the area business-like and took away from the precious space it was supposed to be.

"Are you okay?" Arturo moved to stand but she waved him to stay seated.

"Better than ever." She smiled. The sense of her mamá's presence swirled around the room, comforting and buoying her.

He ran his hand through his hair lightly, something he did when his nerves overtook his calm exterior. Her father had no idea of the turmoil that swarmed beneath Arturo's surface. Hopefully, he never would.

"Are we still a green light?"

The reason for his anxiety became clear, like the fog lifting off the coast, where the Sea of Cortez meets the Pacific Ocean. "We are." She sat beside him and patted his knee gently. "We'll soon be free of this hell."

He swallowed so hard she heard the muscles of his Adam's apple crunch against his throat.

"Every day, I lose my grasp on another piece of the man I want to be," he whispered.

She glanced out the windows across the cemetery. She expected to see a member of her father's security team, but no shadowy figures marred the pretty pastels of the shrines. She didn't want to discuss this here, but it was their only truly safe space. "It's only temporary, Arturo. As soon as we're in Spain, you'll forget all about this place and everything you've seen here."

"What about the things I've done?"

Tears welled in his gentle, brown eyes. He was too soft for this world. She'd thought he would have already drowned in the blood of his unwilling crimes, but over the years, his strength had surprised her. Lately though, his fragility simmered too close to discovery. They had to get out of this toxic environment before it poisoned them irreversibly.

"Distance and time will wash our souls clean, primo. This will all be a distant, nightmarish memory that will fade like a painted wooden box in a sunlit window."

"I hope you're right. I can't take much more."

"I know." She took his hand and squeezed. "You're at capacity, I understand. But it's only a few weeks until November. After I've had one last chance to be close to Mamá, we'll slip away in the chaos of the crowds, and we'll be on our way to Europe before he's even realized we're gone."

He sighed heavily. "And then we can both be the people we were born to be."

"We'll have the freedom we've always dreamed of." Unlike her, Arturo had been unable to explore his own difference. The macho, misogynistic world in which they existed had forced him to keep his nature well hidden. They had been each other's cover for years, but Marissa had drawn the line at a marriage of convenience. She'd promised her mamá she would follow her heart wherever it led her.

And it was leading her away from everything she'd ever known.

She couldn't wait.

Chapter Six

CASEY PULLED DOWN THE last metal shutter at the front of the bar, and Luca snapped a padlock into position to secure it for the night.

"Hermano, can you believe this is finally happening?" Luca bumped her shoulder into Casey's as they headed off the beach toward their place.

"Sure I can." The lie rolled off Casey's tongue with the practiced ease of every untruth she told. She draped her arm over Luca's shoulder and tugged her in for a bro hug. "You've worked hard on your book; you deserve it." Not anything like as hard as she'd worked. She'd started on the bottom rung of the Vargas cartel and had been slaving her guts out for years, only for her feet to still be within easy reach of the ground. So, no, Luca didn't deserve it, but she said what was expected.

"It's a trilogy," Luca said.

"What?" She had to work hard to keep the sneer from her tone. She didn't care if it was one book or fifty, how difficult could it be? Casey had been in their basement apartment while Luca tapped on that ancient keyboard so loudly it sounded like the building had angry termites, and it looked easy. She didn't sweat or struggle. She just sat there for hours and hours, more interested in interacting with a machine than with people. It was little wonder she hardly got laid.

"It's not just one book, it's three. So far." Luca shrugged Casey's arm off and jumped up on a nearby wall. "If this agent can get this trilogy published—and she says she's certain she can—I'll be able to write all the time."

Luca twirled on the wall, and Casey rolled her eyes, wishing Luca would twist her ankle and fall. That'd be more entertaining than listening to her drone on about her *agent*. She sounded so pretentious, Casey wanted to punch her in the nose and bust up her handsome face. Good looks and now, good luck. Where was Casey's slice of the American pie? She wanted out of this life too. It wasn't fair that words held more power than damn hard graft, that words were going to make Luca's life better while Casey would be left in this dead-end job, selling twenty dollar wraps to ungrateful tourists and trying to scrape up enough tips to pay a coyote to get her into the States.

Unless Marissa finally stopped denying their connection and succumbed to her desires. She hadn't been by this week, but it was the week of her madre's death, so Casey wasn't surprised. She'd be back at the bar soon enough, and Casey would continue to chip away at the walls Marissa had erected to keep her safe from more pain. She and Arturo, the guard who was never more than twenty feet away from her, were there too often for it to be anything else other than her need to see Casey. She just needed time and encouragement, and Casey had plenty of both.

"Wouldn't that be great?"

"What?" Casey unlocked the door to their place and tuned back into Luca's droning and gloating.

"Me writing instead of having to tend bar anymore."

Luca had the decency to look apologetic when Casey glanced at her.

"Neither of us wanted to do this forever, did we?" Luca asked. "You've got dreams, and you'll get there, Casey, I know you will."

Casey looked away and clenched her jaw. She headed for the rusty fridge and a cold beer. Her brain needed numbing if Luca had more to say.

"Then you'll be able to stop working for Vargas." Luca took the beer from Casey's hand, opened it, and gave it back. "You'll open that bar on Venice Beach, and I'll have a table there where I come to write every day. It'll be perfect." Luca whistled and grinned. "You'll be able to score all the women you want, all the time. You'll be like catnip to those LA women."

"I get all the women I want here." Casey took a long pull of beer before she took another bottle from the fridge and handed it to Luca.

Luca snorted and clinked her bottle to Casey's. "Not *all* the time."

Casey shook her head. "You're talking about that skank you were chatting up all afternoon? I was never interested in her."

"You fooled both of us then." Luca uncapped her beer and sank onto her bed.

"She was way too...*American* for me." Casey sat on Luca's rickety writing chair and laughed. "But you seemed interested enough. Or was it just the tips you were working so hard for? I don't think I've ever seen you throw so many cocktails for one person in such a short space of time."

Luca laughed and took a long slug of her beer. "I don't think I've ever seen anyone drink that much and stay sober."

"I think she was playing sober. She was a mean drunk." Casey averted her gaze from Luca's sympathetic expression. She didn't want pity. But that woman's barb about her having bad energy and deserving bad shit was a little too close to the bone. Who was she to think she had any idea who Casey was and what she'd been through? Stupid American tourists dropping into her country to get fucked up should have more respect for the people here helping them have a good time. She'd been tempted to reach over the bar and knock her off her stool. But she needed this job for its easy access to customers for her primary job. Which reminded her, she needed to drop by the Vargas estate and get more product for the rest of the week.

Luca continued to talk about the email she'd gotten and how exciting it was. She was testing Casey's restraint too. That got her thinking whether she'd be able to take Luca in a fist fight. It didn't take her long to decide it wouldn't be much of a competition. Luca was soft in her head and body. Casey glanced at her arms and tensed them. Ripped enough that she could model for a statue, and hard enough that it'd be made of marble. Casey didn't see why she and Luca had sometimes been mistaken for sisters.

As Luca continued about finally getting her chance, Casey drifted to how she should be the one getting the break. She would appreciate it far more than Luca, who'd probably fuck it up one way or another. She'd be back here in less than six months, broke and begging Oscar for her job back. She should just let Casey go in her place. Luca could concentrate on writing and keeping the words flowing, and Casey could charm all the money-people and keep the dollars and the deals rolling in. She could be Luca's personal assistant and be paid a percentage of her earnings. Luca was a dreamer; she didn't have the business brains or killer instinct she needed to stay afloat in the cutthroat world that was America. It didn't matter whether it was publishing or drugs, all business operated the same, and Luca would drown in weeks. Casey was certain of it.

She glanced at Luca and narrowed her eyes. What if she just went *instead* of Luca? Pretended to *be* Luca and assumed her identity. How hard could that be? The books were already written, and the agent loved them. All Casey would have to do was sell Luca, sell herself. And she'd been doing that every day for years in one way or another. Luca had needed a friend when she first came into town, and Casey had fulfilled that role. Didn't she owe Casey for that? Luca would never have finished one book, let alone three, without her support.

And the agent hadn't seen Luca. Hell, she'd given a pen name, so the agent didn't know her real name yet. How easy would it be to show up in LA and say *she* was the author? She could stay as Casey Soto and not even have to get a fake passport. All she needed was access to Luca's emails and the original manuscript. Of course, having an agent didn't mean anything yet, right? The book hadn't actually been sold to any publisher, so was she jumping the gun thinking this way? She mentally shook her head. Better to have everything in place in case the big day came along. Then she'd be ready to make her move.

She emptied her beer, got up, and took two more from the fridge. Luca's innocent smile as she handed her a bottle almost made Casey feel guilty for considering this course of action.

Almost..

Casey had to look after herself, since she'd been shown time and again that no one else wanted the job. And as much as she'd enjoyed Luca's friendship and company over these past few years, her goal remained unchanged. Get out of here and live the life she should be living. She was meant for bigger and better things, and this was her opportunity.

She clinked her bottle to Luca's. "Here's to an amazing new life," Casey said.

"I should stop re-reading this email." Luca dropped her phone beside her. "I was on the verge of giving up, Casey," she said softly. "But it's happening. It's really happening." She bounced up from the bed. "I should call now and accept her offer. Yeah. I'll call now."

"Whoa." Casey held up her hand. "Take a beat, mijo. You don't want to seem too eager, and," she tapped her watch, "I doubt she'll be in the office. It's two a.m. in LA."

Luca smacked her forehead. "Ah, estúpido, claro esta! But you really think I should play hardball?"

"Definitely." Casey punched Luca's upper arm. "Give me your phone. Let me show you."

Damn, this was so easy, it wasn't funny. Luca dropped back down beside her and unlocked her phone. *1421735. Fuck.* Who had a seven-digit lock code? Casey repeated it in her head over and over, trying to commit it to memory.

Luca passed her cell over. "What are you going to do?"

"Show you how to respond professionally."

"I need to see it before you press send."

Casey pulled Luca into a side bro hug. "Relax. Of course you'll see it. And you can hit send." She opened the mail app.

Luca pointed to the inbox named t.l.graves@gmail.com. "That's my pseudonym. That's where the email is."

Casey smiled at Luca's enthusiasm, which again *almost* made her question what she was thinking. She hadn't decided she was definitely doing anything yet; she'd sleep on it and make her decision in the morning. She was always more lucid after eight hours and a good breakfast. But it didn't hurt to make some preparations and delay Luca's forward motion. She typed out a professional-sounding response, thanking the agent, Alyssa Dawes, for her interest and explaining that she'd have her lawyer look over the contract and get back to her by the end of the week. She handed the phone back.

"I don't have a lawyer," Luca said.

"Then you better get one. If you don't, they'll treat you like the barrio trash you are." Casey thought of Marissa Vargas, not for the first time today, as usual, but for the first time in that capacity. She had no idea what area of law she specialized in, but she'd be able to advise on a contract. And her father could help Casey with the final problem in the plan she was vaguely formulating: what to do with Luca. Because she wouldn't just roll over and let Casey take her dream away, that went without saying. For a price, probably a piece of the action, Vargas would solve that issue in an instant. As the local cartel head with the largest marijuana plantation in this area of Mexico, he was always on the lookout for opportunities. And then, if and when the money came in, they'd both be happy. But what if the money never came in? What if the agent didn't sell the book to anyone? It would all be for nothing.

"The only lawyer I know is Marissa Vargas, and I don't think she even knows I exist," Luca said. "I had one long conversation with her over a year ago, and I only ever see her at a distance when she comes to the bar because you always provide table service."

Casey couldn't help but grin when she thought about servicing Marissa *on* the table. That would give her something to think about while she took care of herself tonight. But what was that about a long conversation with Marissa? Casey didn't think Luca had the cojones to talk to someone like Marissa. And she shouldn't be talking to her anyway. She tamped down the rage that flared within. She had nothing to worry about. Luca would soon be out of commission. "I told you who she is and who her father is. Someone like that should never have to go to a bar to get her own drinks, but I could talk to her for you."

Luca shook her head slowly. "I don't know... I probably couldn't afford her services."

"Nope. You definitely can't, even with the dollars you've got stashed under your mattress." Casey finished her beer and got another one. "But she's a really kind person. She's always taking care of other people, like the unpaid workers on her father's plantation. You could promise to pay her once you got money from your publishing deal."

Luca looked hopeful, and her puppy dog expression would've melted most hearts. But Casey wasn't most people, and she knew what happened to stray dogs around here. If she showed a hint of compassion or vulnerability, she'd be done for.

"You think she'd do that even though she doesn't know me?"

"Let me arrange something and see what I can do." Getting Luca to the Vargas compound would be easier than she thought, and he always wanted more free laborers. It wasn't like Casey wanted Luca's death on her conscience, so this seemed like a perfect solution. And it had presented itself without Casey doing much at all, almost like it was fated. Bringing Marissa into the picture too might give Casey the opportunity to show her what an amazing life they could have together.

Casey clinked her bottle to Luca's. "¡Salud!"

Luca's grin grew wider. "¡Salud! Gracias, Casey. I don't know what I'd do without you."

Casey took a long pull on her beer. *I guess you're gonna find out soon enough.*

Chapter Seven

LUCA PUSHED HER MATTRESS against the wall and edged out one of the five rolls of American dollars she'd been saving since she moved to San Lucas. She wrapped the notes from last night around it and replaced it, careful not to rip the precious paper between the metal springs. She was going to need every cent she'd collected to visit LA and meet with her agent. She yanked the bed back into position, dropped into her writing chair, and picked up her cell. If she stared at it long enough, maybe Casey would text or call sooner. She'd gone to speak with Marissa and had said she'd get in touch when she had news.

That was four hours ago. In bad traffic, Casey said the journey to the Vargas place took forty-five minutes. What was taking so long? Likely, Marissa wasn't interested in helping her. Why should she? After the one-off, heart-to-heart conversation they'd shared that long afternoon, Marissa had kept her distance, and Luca didn't blame her, though she did feel sorry for her. They'd talked about dreams, and ambitions, and Marissa's family expectations. Marissa had seemed lost and alone, and she had no one to talk to. At the time, Luca had no idea who she was, but the next time she showed up, Casey had been all too eager to fill in the gaps.

The Vargas cartel sounded as terrifying as any other, which was why Luca had never wanted anything to do with Casey's side hustle. She'd seen the bodies hanging from the bridge, examples to anyone who crossed them. She didn't care how much money Casey made, it wasn't worth the risk. She would love to talk more to Marissa, but she'd only managed smiles and hesitant waves across the beach while Casey took care of her every need. It was for the best. Even if Marissa was gay, which she probably wasn't, befriending the daughter of a drug lord wasn't a sensible course of action.

But, damn, Marissa haunted her dreams and her fantasies. And it wasn't *just* because she was the archetypal femme, all killer heels, red-hot lipstick, and luscious, long hair. It was her energy and aura, her kindness. It didn't surprise Luca at all that Marissa helped the people who were essentially slaves on her father's compound. She'd heard bad things about their living conditions, and Marissa's involvement seemed sweet, though she wondered what difference she could really make.

Yep, Marissa Vargas was Luca's dream woman, but she'd been content to worship her at a distance. If Casey did manage to get her to help Luca with the agent's contract though, she wasn't sure how she was supposed to act. Pretend that they had never spoken? As she'd consumed more alcohol, Marissa had told Luca things she probably wouldn't want her father to know. She hoped Marissa knew that she could trust her. It had been over a year since that conversation, and she hadn't betrayed Marissa's confidence. Maybe that would score her some points and make Marissa more likely to help.

Her phone buzzed, and Luca opened the text.

I'll be back in thirty minutes. Wait in the parking lot. She wants to talk to you before she agrees to help.

Luca's body lightened, as if helium had been pumped into her veins. Another step closer to her dream.

I'll be there. Do I bring anything? A bottle of wine?

A huge bouquet of flowers and the finest chocolates from La Laguna. That's what she wanted to bring.

She can buy the best wine in the world, cabrón. Any wine you could afford would offend her.

Casey was right. She had nothing to offer Marissa other than eternal gratitude and a promise of payment once...if...she was published. And a shoulder to lean on. If everything went well and Luca made as much money as she hoped to, this could be the start of a more equal relationship where she *did* have something to offer Marissa.

She looked down at herself. "Mierda." Cargo shorts and a wrinkled *Love is Love* sleep shirt wouldn't impress anyone. Panic rose, and heat spread down her back when she suddenly realized that Marissa's decision might not be solely her own, and Luca might have to speak to her father too. She sprang up from the bed and went to her makeshift closet, essentially a hole in the wall with an old curtain taped to the pipework above it. Luca pushed her other hung clothes to the far side to get at the only truly decent item of clothing she owned. The designer plaid linen shirt had been a final parting gift from Veronica, but Luca had never worn it. She pulled off the two taped plastic bags protecting it and held it up to her chest. Veronica had said she'd bought it two sizes too big at the time for Luca to grow into it, so she just had to hope she hadn't missed that window of opportunity. Not for the first time, she wished she had the discipline to develop a body like Casey's. When she was a full-time writer, she'd get a gym membership and work on that. All she could manage now was bench-pressing rough concrete blocks and doing pull-ups on the pipework when she wasn't working or writing.

She quickly undressed and had a cold shower to wash off the funk of sleep. She should've gotten ready much earlier but part of her had believed that Marissa would simply say no. She also hadn't wanted to jinx it by being fully prepared. She dried off, pulled on some underwear, her best pair of jeans, and cleanest sneakers. They weren't much to brag about, but she hoped the shirt would keep anyone from looking too closely. She sprayed some deodorant, and then used a little on her neck and wrists. When she had money, she'd take the time to find an aftershave that suited her, something woody like one of those advertised by bare-chested, shredded guys on beaches and in deserts.

She unbuttoned the shirt almost reverently. She'd been keeping this for a special occasion, but her life hadn't presented her with one. Until now. And if Marissa agreed to help, this would be her lucky shirt that she'd wear to any important meeting from then on. She pulled it on and sighed at the softness of the material caressing her skin. Pure luxury.

Her phone buzzed.

Where the fuck are you?

Damn, Casey was early. She tapped out a response, checked her hair in the broken piece of mirror glued to the wall, and dashed out of the basement, fastening her shirt as she went.

Casey smacked her palm on the rusted hood of her car. "You don't keep Marissa waiting, hermano. Come on."

She got back in the driver's seat, and Luca jumped in. When Casey was in a mood and her temper flared hot, Luca knew better than to challenge her. "Sorry. I had to change into something half decent, and my options were limited."

Casey gave her a sideways glance and raised her eyebrow. "Nice shirt. It's the one you've been saving, right?"

"Yep. I figured it was worth pulling out of the bag for this meeting."

Casey snorted. "You'll need to pull your charm out of the bag too if you want their help. Vargas wants to speak to you before he'll let you anywhere near Marissa."

"What?" A chill ran through her despite the hundred-degree heat and no A/C in Casey's clunker. "I don't want to owe him *anything*. You told me all about the people working off their debts on his land; I can't be a part of that." She shifted in her seat, wanting to be anywhere but on her way to see the head of one of the most violent cartels in Mexican history. Maybe if the next stop lights were on red, she could jump out of the car and head straight back to the hotel. There were other lawyers. She could use some of her savings to buy their time.

Casey punched Luca's thigh hard. "Relax, will you? Your agreement will be with Marissa, not Vargas. He just wants to make sure you're the real deal and not loco. He has to be careful in his business, and he doesn't know you at all. He has to be sure you won't kidnap Marissa to get to him, or some stupid shit like that." She punched Luca's arm. "Don't make me look bad. If you pull out now, Vargas will think you're on someone else's payroll, and he'll come after both of us."

"Jesus, quit punching me, will you? I'm not comfortable in this area like you are." She tapped her foot repeatedly, her anxiety out of control. "And what do you mean, he'd come after us? For not showing up to a meeting I never wanted? That's fucked up, hermano."

Casey banged her hand against the steering wheel. "Fuck, Luca, calm the fuck down. This is how it works. Be cool, and everything will work out just the way it needs to." She sighed heavily. "Look, I'm sorry. I should've realized that Vargas would want to speak to you, and then I could've prepared you for it," she said. "But there's nothing to worry about. He's just looking after his own interests and the safety of his only child. You can understand that, can't you?"

Luca blinked and turned to face the window. Sure, she could understand that. She'd never experienced it, but she'd wanted to. Until she gave up worrying about why no one cared for her and started caring for herself. And she knew Casey had much the same story. She had parents, but they were so neglectful, she may as well not have had any. They were too busy running drugs for Vargas to be concerned about *their* only child. God only knew where they were now. Casey never said, and Luca never asked.

Which was why they stuck together, why they'd been drawn to each other as if they were blood. She slowed her foot tapping and took a deep breath. She had no reason to panic. Casey knew these people. She wouldn't lead Luca into something volatile and dangerous. And Vargas was just acting the way any father who cared about his daughter would. Her memory flicked back to her conversation with Marissa though, and she'd had little praise for his paternal instincts. She'd been convinced he was far more interested in his business activities than his fatherly ones.

"I'm sorry. You're right," Luca said. "I'm just so close to my dream, I'm being crazy. What you're saying makes perfect sense. Are you sure I shouldn't bring something? It feels disrespectful showing up empty-handed."

Casey shook her head. "You're all he needs to see. Answer his questions, stay calm, and don't act weird. And I'll—we'll be out of there in no time." She gave Luca's shoulder a shove. "I've seen the way you look at Marissa; you'd walk over hot coals to talk to her, so a quick chat with her father is nothing. Right?"

Luca swallowed. She thought she'd been discreet about her crush. "Hey, you're the one who waits on her every whim. I've seen the way *you* look at her." She'd had plenty of opportunities to witness Casey with hundreds of women, but there was something different about the way she was with Marissa. And if either of them had a chance with her, it was Casey. She was already in the family business, and she was charming and slick.

"You don't know what you're talking about. I'm attentive to all our customers. That's why I get more dollars than you do."

Casey's response was a little too sharp and instant to be believable, but Luca wasn't about to call her out since she'd already pushed her patience. "Okay, I get it." She still would've liked to have shown up with a box of cigars or a bottle of good wine, but Casey was right that she couldn't afford anything that would impress Marissa or her father. She just had to channel Casey's charm and promise she'd come through with payment as soon as she was published. How hard could that be?

They drove the rest of the way in relative silence, punctuated only by Casey's expletives at "dumb tourists" who shouldn't be on their road. Luca had learned early on in their friendship that Casey took a while to come down after she'd rocketed to the moon with her temper, so she stayed quiet.

They'd been out of the main city for a few miles before Casey took a left down a dirt road that looked like it didn't lead to anything. About a hundred yards in, she stopped the car at a huge black gate that looked like a military sentry station. Three guys with machine guns in their hands and pistols and machetes on their belts stood on guard, faces bland, their eyes constantly in motion. Luca bet they practiced their menacing glares in the mirror each morning before they left for work.

"Get out of the car slowly with your hands showing," Casey said as she did the same.

Luca's heart thudded against her chest, threatening to explode and kill her before these three thugs had the chance to. She climbed out of the passenger seat at the speed of a sloth after smoking a joint, keeping her hands palm out and above her head once she'd managed to get the door open with her elbow.

"Mr. Vargas is expecting us," Casey said. "This is Luca Romero, and he's waiting to speak to her."

"¡Vale!" the one in the middle said after taking in every inch of Luca from the top of her flicked hair to her trainers. He didn't look impressed.

He nodded to one of the others, who pressed a button on a panel in the sentry booth, and the gate began to slide open. He waved his gun and motioned for them to get back in the car.

Luca kept her hands high, slid back into her seat, and closed the door. Casey, by contrast, practically jumped back in the car and slammed her door shut. Granted, she *had* to slam her door otherwise it didn't close, but it felt reckless under the circumstances. One wrong move and the three mercenaries could pepper the car with bullets. Luca really wished she'd just gotten out of the car when she'd thought about it. There were other lawyers in town, ones without sadistic and violent family. Lawyers who would just check the contract over in exchange for some of her savings. She squeezed her eyes shut and kept the words inside, knowing Casey would lose her shit altogether if Luca changed her mind now. She didn't usually ignore her gut, and Christ, it was screaming at her to run as far and as fast as she could, but she put it down to not being comfortable in this environment. Five minutes with Vargas, a nice conversation with Marissa, and they'd be out of here and back at the beach. And Luca could text the agent, ecstatically agree to become her client, and organize a trip to LA to talk about whatever came next.

"Well?" Casey asked.

"Huh?" Luca glanced at Casey and realized they were on the move again. She must've checked out while she was busy in her head.

"Are you ready?"

Luca shrugged and blew out a long breath. "I don't think I'll ever be ready for something like this, so we better just get it done before I lose what little courage I'm drawing on."

Casey shook her head. "I really don't know how you ever survived your orphanage. Those places either kill you or make you stronger."

Luca snorted. "Wow, thanks, hermano. It means a lot that you think so much of me."

Casey's expression was hard. "I'm just saying you're a bit too sensitive for this world, and it amazes me you've made it this far. You should've been born into a nice, sweet, supportive family with money."

Luca prickled at the insinuation she was too weak to take care of herself. "You don't have to be an aggressive bastard to get the things you want in life, you know."

"Yeah, you really do." Casey laughed, then tried to ruffle Luca's hair.

She ducked and shoved Casey's hand away. "Don't mess with the hair. I've got to look my best."

"For Marissa?" Casey laughed even harder. "The likes of you don't stand a chance with a sophisticated, intelligent woman like Marissa. You're fucking dreaming if you think your schoolboi crush is going to turn into something after this."

"And you think you do?" The words were out of her mouth before she'd even processed how they might land. But Casey was pushing buttons she had no business being anywhere near, and Luca only took so much before she pushed back. "Why do you have to be such an asshole sometimes?" she asked.

Casey's eyes narrowed. "Why do you have to be such an ungrateful little shit sometimes?"

Luca fell silent. Now she was really wishing she hadn't set foot in Casey's car, but as the Vargas mansion came into sight and the dirt track turned into smooth tarmac, there was no backing out now. And she didn't want to fight with Casey. "I'm sorry." She'd apologized to Casey more times today than she had in several years of friendship, and this one she didn't mean, but she was prepared to say anything to restore the peace right now.

"Good." Casey pulled into a space some distance away from the front entrance, killed the engine, and got out.

Luca followed, not wanting to spend a minute longer here than was necessary. Casey waved her toward the giant double doors where another two gorillas stood on guard.

"Soto," they said separately and stepped aside for Casey and Luca to enter.

Just inside, another guy stood up. He exchanged a small nod with Casey, eyeballed Luca, and then motioned for them to follow.

Luca tried not to stare, but her gaze was pulled this way and that from one spectacular piece of art to another, from one ornate golden treasure to the next. Every wall, surface, and space was filled with objects of wealth Luca couldn't even begin to imagine. It was clear why Casey's visits here motivated her to push more drugs, or product as she called it, as if that legitimized it somehow. It didn't. But knowing Casey's history and her desire for a better life, Luca could see how being around this luxury drove her to want more.

They were led along a warren of corridors, making Luca think the place was as big as the hotel she worked at. Marissa and her father must never be able to find each other. Her sneakers squeaked on the shined-to-reflection wooden floor, and Casey widened her eyes at her and shook her head. Luca shrugged. What was she supposed to do about it? The guy stopped abruptly, and Luca's footwear announced their arrival way before he could knock on the intricately carved door. Both he and Casey glared at her like she'd spat on their shoes.

A voice from within called out, and Luca followed Casey in. The guy who'd escorted them closed the door and stood in front of it. A sense of unease settled over Luca's shoulders, and she tensed involuntarily. *This is just how they do things*. She willed her muscles to relax, but they were playing deaf, and her whole body remained on high alert. Casey took a few steps in and stopped, then indicated for Luca to stand beside her. She placed her hands behind her back and gripped her wrist to keep them from shaking. Thirty feet into the room, Vargas sat behind a desk that would have filled her entire basement space. He seemed to be working on something and didn't look up. Luca took the opportunity to glance around the office; another two guys sat in large leather armchairs in front of a large window. The stained glass had been seriously damaged, and she could make out sheets of Perspex keeping it in place. She didn't envy someone have to fix that. With so many colors and the elaborate design, the repair would be painstaking.

A hand slapping hard onto wood brought her attention back to Vargas. He didn't stand and come around the desk, so Luca gave a little bow in lieu of a handshake, then felt instantly ludicrous.

"You're the writer?" he asked.

"Sí, señor." The confidence in her voice surprised her, and she couldn't suppress a smile. She *was* a writer, she'd gotten an agent, *and* she was close to a publishing deal.

"And the Americans want to make your books?"

His narrowed eyes and flat tone erased her smile. She shouldn't have listened to Casey. She should've just looked for a lawyer in the city. But then she wouldn't have gotten the chance to speak with Marissa again. That was worth a little uncomfortable interrogation. "I have an agent, señor. She's going to try to sell my book to a publisher, but she sounds confident that she can." If she didn't say much, she couldn't offend him, but she also wanted to be clear that there wasn't any money yet.

He beckoned her forward with an impatient wave of his hand. "Let me see this email offering you a contract."

Luca glanced at Casey, who frowned and nodded to the desk as if her hesitation would be taken as an affront. She mustered her courage and stepped toward the desk as she pulled her cell phone from her pocket. She flipped to the email from Alyssa Dawes, gently placed her phone on his desk, and took a step back.

After reading it, he nodded but didn't return her phone. "This looks legitimate. My colleague has made some calls; the Dawes, Rossi, and Decker agency is one of the top five literary agencies in America. They represent some of the most well-known authors out there. That makes your chances good, yes?"

Luca nodded. She knew that, of course. She'd done her homework. She was still getting used to the fact that her snowball of a query had made it through hell *and* hit the mark.

"And your manuscripts, where are they?"

Luca frowned and resisted the temptation to glance back at Casey. Why would he care where the manuscripts were? She didn't think lesbian furies and demi-gods would be his preferred bedtime reading. "They're on my computer in our apartment. And of course, the agent has them."

Casey gave a quiet snort behind her, presumably at Luca's description of their cramped basement as an apartment.

"And you've never met or spoken to Alyssa Dawes?"

Luca swallowed and shook her head. "I just need Ms. Vargas to look at the contract to make sure it's standard stuff. Then I'll see if she wants to meet in person or just call or something. Not all agents need to meet you in person to represent your work." Why he was asking such bizarre questions, she didn't know. She hoped Marissa would walk in and get things back on track.

There was a knock at the door, and Vargas nodded, his focus beyond Luca. She half-turned to see who else was coming in and came face-to-face with the guy who'd led them up here. At the same time, she felt a sharp pain in her neck and cold liquid exploded in her veins. The edges of her vision darkened, and she lost all feeling in every part of her body. As she slumped into the guy's arms, the door opened, and Marissa Vargas's dark brown eyes were the last thing she saw before her vision gave out completely.

Chapter Eight

"PAPÁ? WHAT'S GOING ON here?" Marissa's heart dropped as she saw Luca fall into Diego's arms. What had he injected her with? And why? Had her father found out about her conversation with Luca? It had been a year, and she'd been careful ever since, though she couldn't resist returning to the bar. That damn Casey Soto always got in the way, so convinced she was charming when she was anything but. Marissa sucked in a breath and steeled herself for battle.

"Business, mija, business."

Her father's response was all kinds of cold and distance she'd rarely experienced. He hadn't quite been the same since their last meeting. She glanced at the window he'd done his best to destroy; it had been the one thing in this dark and deathly space she and her mamá had liked. Perhaps he was as devastated by what he'd done as she was, though she doubted it.

"Luca has no part in your business." She tried to slam the door behind her, but Teo thwarted her by catching it and clicking it closed quietly. Marissa glared at Casey. "Does she?"

"Casey brought us an opportunity, and I accepted," her father said. "Your expertise is needed. I want you to be involved."

"I don't want–"

"¡Espere!" Her father held up his hand. "Leave us."

Rafael stood and Marissa watched, helpless, as he and Diego lifted Luca and carried her out of the office. Casey and Teo followed without a word, and she was left alone with her father. He came around from his desk and took a seat by the desecrated window. He beckoned her to join him, and his expression made it clear he would tolerate no disobedience. She hesitated for the briefest of moments; choosing the right battles was an essential part of her existence in this palatial prison.

"Sit." He waved his hand impatiently at the chair opposite him.

Her faltering steps betrayed her, and she did as directed. She held no power here, and they both knew it.

"It's time to stop your immature rebellion, Marissa, and take your place in the hierarchy. You are my chosen. You are my blood. And you will act appropriately from now on. Your mamá would have expected it, as I do."

She suppressed a scoff of laughter. He had no knowledge of the conversations they'd had about her *choosing* her own destiny, making her own legacy, following her heart. Her mamá had no expectations of her other than she should *not* fall into the role he had designated for her. But she and Arturo were close to their escape. Playing along would be the most prudent course of action. "If you want me to be part of this, are you going to explain why Diego just rendered Luca Romero unconscious?" she asked, maintaining a hint of disdain. "As far as I was aware, she has nothing to do with...our business." The words were like acid in her throat and burned just as painfully. "It's my understanding that Casey tried unsuccessfully to recruit her when she first got into town."

Her father selected a Cohiba from the tabletop humidor, clipped and lit it, then blew out a plume of gray smoke. "You're correct, mija, and I'm thrilled to hear that you know these things. It gives me hope that you won't fight me all the way to my grave."

"And Casey has never seemed like she had the caliber to bring you an opportunity of *any* kind." She was already in deeper than she wanted, but it seemed like her initial concerns were unfounded. Unless he was toying with her like a killer whale did with a cornered seal, he knew nothing of her tenuous connection to Luca.

"Again, your instincts are impeccable, mija, and you show me why you are my natural successor. This business runs through your veins as naturally as your lifeblood."

He took another long suck of his cigar, and the burning embers of its end faded to black. She ignored its potential metaphorical similarity to her dreams. *Play the game for a little while, and I'll have the rest of my life to myself.* She repeated that over and over while she waited for him to speak.

"Casey Soto is nothing. *But* her bartending colleague has just been offered a contract with one of the top literary agents in the United States." He took another puff and emitted a cloud of smoke as if he were producing a magic trick. "I've been informed that strong book sales could lead to movie deals, where the *real* money is."

Marissa frowned. "You want to go into the movie business?"

He laughed and shook his head. "Of course not. But Soto is offering a slice of the action with very little input or outlay from us if the books are sold."

She balked internally at the ease in which he used the collective term. She was giving him everything he wanted, and he seemed to be unperturbed by her sudden change of direction, as if her capitulation was inevitable. "When something sounds too good to be true—"

"I know, I know." He waved her caution away. "Which is why I want you to look over the writer's contract. And keep an eye on Soto. She's going to ask to meet the agent in person, and it's her intention to relocate there."

"I don't understand. Why is Casey going to LA when it's Luca's contract?"

Her father tapped the long stem of burnt cigar into an ashtray. "*That's* the opportunity. She's going to assume the writer's identity, and I need you to help her wring every cent out of the deal. Make sure the agent knows it's in her best interest to find someone to publish the books and bring money in."

Realization of Casey's plan sickened her. Marissa had assumed they were friends as well as colleagues. Casey had said they shared an apartment. She almost dared not ask the question. "And what happens to Luca?"

He gave a wide, thin-lipped smile that dripped with malevolent intent. "She labors for us in the fields, in case she's needed in the future. You don't kill the cow until it stops producing milk."

Marissa swallowed the bile that rose in her throat. Had Casey asked him to *kill* Luca? Soft, sweet Luca, who had shown nothing but gentle kindness when Marissa had emptied her troubled heart and mind to her at the bar—she didn't deserve this. *Nobody* deserved this. She'd always thought Soto was unpleasant and obnoxious, but Marissa would never have thought her capable of such a wicked plot.

"I see." And she did. She saw her father for what he was, someone who would destroy an innocent person to serve his own greed. Whatever compassion and love her mamá saw in him once had long been chased away by his seemingly endless ambitions. Luca's spirit would be broken by the situation she would wake to after the drugs wore off. "Are we in trouble?" If he wanted her involved, maybe he'd be open to her suggestions.

He raised his eyebrow. "Meaning?"

"Do we *need* the money from Casey's scam? Do we need this opportunity? It could take years for the agent to sell the book, if she even does. How long do we support Casey just for the potential of money that might never come in? Or might be a smaller amount than you're getting elsewhere in the business?" She stretched the fingers of her right hand and pretended to concentrate on her nails. It was easier than looking at him.

"We can never have enough money, mija. And I can wait."

She should've expected that response. "Most of your laborers are working off a debt. They're here because they owe you something. If the policía raided the compound tomorrow, you wouldn't be brought up on kidnapping charges, because everyone would agree they should be here." She shrugged her shoulders. "But Luca is a victim, and Soto will be committing fraud in America. Do you really want to risk a potential visit from the FBI?"

Her father laughed hard, so hard that he had to put his cigar down and clutch his chest. She'd never wished him dead, but a heart attack would certainly solve her problems, and Luca's. She waited out his unusual fit of mirth and glanced out the window. Rafael and Diego dumped Luca onto the back seat of one of the compound's golf carts and began the relatively long drive to the barn housing her father's laborers. She'd wake with a headache and a very different reality to the one she'd started the day with. Marissa would've loved to have shared Luca's excitement with her. She'd talked about her writing and her dreams for a short time when they'd spoken—Marissa had dominated much of the conversation with her troubles—and her enthusiasm and passion were so all-consuming that Marissa had found herself wanting to help Luca make her dreams come true.

"Marissa."

Her father's voice permeated her thoughts, and she turned back to face him. "Yes?"

"Do you not see the joke in your concern?" he asked, still chuckling a little.

"I don't see the joke in any of this, Papá. And I don't see why you would risk anything at all for one of your low-level runners."

"The Americans won't care about a Mexican screwing over another Mexican. And the Soto family have worked for me for decades. I don't know the writer at all. I don't understand why you would have a problem with this."

"Her name is Luca Romero," Marissa said, irritated by his use of her profession instead of her name. "And it's not about Luca and Casey; they could make it a way to attack you."

He waved his hand and shook his head. She hated that expression of dismissiveness, the curl of his lip, the wrinkle of his nose as if there was a three-day-dead rat under it.

"There has only been a small exchange of emails," he said and retrieved his cigar. "*Luca* used a different name when she contacted the agency, so in a way, she was already committing a fraud of sorts. No one knows who T.L. Graves is yet. She could be you. Hell, it could be me for all the agent knows. Once Soto shows up in LA, *she* is T.L. Graves."

She sighed. He wasn't to be dissuaded from his current course of action. Arturo's warning voice popped into her head. *"She's not your concern, hermana."* She knew that. She didn't owe Luca anything. But she also didn't want to see her dreams destroyed. Or maybe it was her own dreams she was thinking about, and she was making Luca's problem her own. Which it wasn't. She didn't need any attention focused on her that might result in their plan being foiled.

"What exactly is it you want me to do?" she asked.

He motioned to a small stack of printed papers on his desk. "That's the agency contract. Put your degree to good use and see that it checks out. Soto is the apple that has fallen away from the tree. I fear she doesn't have the integrity of her family, and I don't fully trust her to hold her side of the deal without consequences present in the back of her mind—"

"I won't babysit her."

He held up his hand and patted the air. "I'm not asking that of you. But if there are any meetings or developments that might change the scope of our investment, I will want you to go to LA and ensure the negotiations are to our benefit."

Marissa twisted her mamá's ring on her middle finger. He was offering her freedom for the first time. She and Arturo could flee to Spain from LA. It would be one less border to negotiate without the threat of her father's influence. They would still wait until after she had visited with her mamá, but they could be out from under his rule at the first opportunity after the second of November. But Luca would pay for Marissa's opportunity with lifelong captivity, even death if she outlived her usefulness. Didn't such a trade mean Marissa was her father's daughter and no better than him?

He leaned over the low table between them and placed his hand on her knee. "There's no need to be scared, mija. Your mamá will always be with you, keeping you safe, and I will send Teo with you."

She struggled to stay calm. "Why Teo? I always travel with Arturo."

He squeezed her knee gently before sitting back. "They will both accompany you. We cannot be too careful. America is a dangerous place."

She laughed, though not as effusively as her father had. There was no danger she wouldn't be happy to face if it secured her freedom. "Arturo has managed to keep me from harm here. I'm sure he would cope in LA."

He shook his head. "I understand. You don't want to stand out in the company of two men. Okay. Teo will be your only escort. I need Arturo here to continue his preparation. If you will not marry to strengthen the business, Arturo is the only man I will trust to be your number one. But he is not yet ready. He needs to be close to the daily grind to complete his education."

Marissa twisted her ring faster, fighting to stay grounded. *This changes nothing*. The whisper of a favorable chance to escape was gone, that was all. She and Arturo would simply stick to their original plan. Still, she shouldn't let it go quite so easily. "I'm not as comfortable with Teo, Papá. If the sojourns are only short, surely you can spare Arturo."

Her father grumbled something inaudible. "You are your mother's daughter, mija, wrapping me around your finger so easily. Teo has visited America many times, and he understands their people, but I'll consider your request."

She gave him a full smile, one motivated by her nearing future away *from* him rather than any affection *for* him.

"That's not a promise, Marissa."

"I understand. Thank you, Papá." She glanced at Luca's contract on his desk. "I'll take that to my room and get started if you don't need me for anything else."

He reached across the table again and took her hands in his. "I always need you, mija. Without your mamá here, you are my guiding star."

His constantly evil behavior made his pretty words dissolve into ash like his cigar. Why did he constantly refer to her mamá and her shining light when he deliberately made his world so dark? "And you are mine."

He smiled widely. "I love when we are like this, Marissa. You are a whirlwind of passion and intelligence. This is why I want you to succeed me."

She gave his hands a squeeze and stood up slowly. If she had to take more of this, she would vomit on his alligator-skin shoes. She retrieved the papers and headed toward the door.

"Marissa."

She stopped and half-turned, her hand on the doorknob. She wanted to rush outside and take a lungful of clean, fresh air to rid herself of the toxic gases of his presence, but she held firm and waited. "Yes, Papá?"

"How do you know Luca Romero?"

The air left her body, and her legs threatened to fold beneath her. "I go to the Hacienda Medano for drinks sometimes."

He grunted. "Has she ever...approached you?"

His question was clear, and her heart thudded against her ribs, scared at what her response might reveal or what punishment it might result in for Luca. "I'm not sure I understand what you're asking, Papá. She serves drinks and says very little. Casey is the one who likes to charm her clientele, if that answers your question." Throwing *her* to the wolves was fair play after what she'd done to Luca. She held his gaze.

"I know all about Soto. She's harmless."

Marissa raised her eyebrow and pressed her lips together to hold back a response. Luca would disagree. Casey was in the process of stealing her ambition, her dreams, her *life*. Hardly harmless. "Is that all?" she asked, trying hard to keep the edge from her voice. Too much time spent in his orbit felt detrimental to her well-being.

He nodded. "Let me know what you think of the contract as soon as you can."

"Of course, Papá." She escaped into the corridor where Arturo waited. She had plenty to tell him, but she needed time to think while she went through Luca's paperwork. Poor, sweet Luca. The fates had forced her down an ugly, twisting path. But it was Luca's path, not hers. Marissa's road diverted from her father's just as Luca's smashed into it. That was her destiny, and while Marissa sympathized with her, there was nothing she could do. She had her own escape to conjure.

Chapter Nine

CASEY YANKED THE BATTERED mattress from Luca's bed and grinned at the five rolls of American dollars secured in the springs of the base. She carefully removed Luca's entire life savings and stacked them together before quickly counting it. Nearly three thousand dollars. Not too shabby. It'd be criminal to leave it for Oscar once he'd discovered they were both gone, and Luca didn't need it anymore. She wrapped a rubber band around the wad of notes and placed it alongside her own savings in the concealed compartment of her shoulder bag. Ten thousand dollars would keep her in a hotel while *her* agent went about selling *her* books. Hopefully the agent was right, and it wouldn't take long to sell the books. If it did...well, she'd disappear into LA, far away from any Vargas repercussions.

T.L. GRAVES WAS A weird name, but it didn't matter. As soon as she met the agent, Alyssa Dawes, everyone would know that she was T.L. Graves, and all the royalties, advances, and whatever else came with being a published author would be associated with her, Casey Soto. As if Luca Romero had never existed. As if Casey had written the trilogy. Not that she knew anything about the process, but there was always Google.

She lifted the hefty desktop tower and retrieved Luca's passport to give to Rafael before she left. Luca had been insanely excited when she'd earned enough to buy it. She'd seen it as a leap of faith. Casey had thought she was tempting fate, and she'd been right. She may as well burn it for what good it would do Luca, and Vargas probably only wanted it to make a fake passport for one of his drug mules. Casey left it on the desk and switched Luca's computer on. *BigDream* : she entered the password she'd seen Luca type in so many times. Casey made herself laugh with the thought that Luca's big dream had turned into an even bigger nightmare.

"Soto? Are you down here?" Rafael rapped on the door of the basement.

"Yeah. It's open. Come in."

Rafael had been distracted at reception by one of his regular conquests. That had been great news for Casey, giving her time to grab Luca's cash without him seeing it. He would've expected a cut and might have taken all of it, depending on his mood. He came down the stairs so heavily Casey thought he might fall through the rickety wooden steps. She pushed Luca's passport toward him. "For Señor Vargas, as requested."

Rafael opened and inspected it like he was at border patrol. "It's real."

"I said it was." She held back her sense of being offended by his inference that she might have lied and pushed in the new thumb drive for Luca's files. She copied everything from the individual manuscripts and character sheets to something called a book bible, intending to skim through them on the plane to LA and in her hotel for the next few days.

"Teo's waiting," Rafael said. "Are you going to be much longer?"

"I can be faster if you help."

"What do you need me to do?"

Casey gestured to the walls. "Rip everything down. I need to make it look like we left together." She didn't know if Oscar would care, but neither she nor Vargas needed anyone asking questions. She pointed to the curtained-off closet in the corner of the room. "There's a bag in there along with her clothes. Everything has to go."

Rafael nodded and set to work. Casey left the desperately slow machine to duplicate the files and went to her section of the basement to pack. She folded a small selection of her clothes into the canvas bag she'd just bought and zipped it closed then shoved everything else into a trash bag. The rags and fake labels she was ditching didn't suit her new author persona, and she intended to buy a whole new wardrobe when she got to LA.

She returned to the computer after the files had been transferred and switched the machine off, used a screwdriver to pry off the back, and pulled out the hard drive. She tossed that in the bag with her discarded clothes and handed it to Rafael, though why Vargas wanted all of Luca's possessions, she didn't know. "Now we're done."

Casey grabbed her bags and followed Rafael up the stairs. She pulled the basement door closed behind her without bothering to lock it. Her stomach rolled and bubbled with excitement as she got in the car with Teo to drive to the airport.

The life she was meant to live was finally beginning.

Chapter Ten

LUCA STIRRED SLOWLY AND became immediately aware of an intensely powerful throbbing in her head. She tried to open her eyes, but it was like her eyelids were glued together. She pressed her palms to the bed she was laying on, and the rough fabric of the blanket felt reassuringly familiar. She was safely tucked away in her basement bed after a bad nightmare. She really shouldn't try to keep up with Casey's drinking, but this hangover felt different, like her beer had been spiked. Casey knew Luca didn't touch anything harder than alcohol though, so if her drinks had been tampered with, it wouldn't have been by her.

Her eyes still refused to open, so she searched her mind for any memories of what had happened before she passed out. The nightmare had been so real—too real. She remembered celebrating at a bar on their way home, then emptying their fridge of all the beer. Had Casey gone out to get more? Luca couldn't recall. That's when her memories went soft and faded into the nightmare. It didn't take a genius to figure out it had been fueled by her insecurities around the email from Alyssa Dawes. *Alyssa Dawes. My agent.* She tried to smile, but it cracked her dry lips. She had an agent, and her dream was finally coming true.

Quiet, whispering voices drifted into earshot. That was nothing unusual since the basement was located adjacent to the laundry. She'd learned to filter it out so she could sleep and work through the noise. A hand pressed against her shoulder and rocked her roughly.

"You need to get up."

Luca frowned at the unfamiliar voice. Female, most likely, but not Casey's. Had Casey broken the rule and brought someone home? Or had Luca managed to hook up with someone in her intoxicated state? Had *she* broken their cardinal rule? Casey wouldn't let her forget it if that was the case. Either way, no one should be telling her to get up unless she'd ended up in someone else's bed.

Pinche estúpido. She'd scored and ended up in a bed just as uncomfortable as her own. Maybe she should get Casey to give her lessons; she always ended up in a luxury hotel or private villa.

She was shaken again, this time with more force. Luca managed to open her eyes. An older woman bent over her. Luca swallowed and tried hard to keep the surprise and disappointment from showing in her expression. The woman was at least two decades older than her. Damn, how much had she drunk last night?

"Quickly. Get up."

When the woman retreated and Luca's field of vision widened, she had the chance to take in her surroundings. None of it made sense. Had she ended up in a hostel? The haze over her eyes cleared, and she realized she was in a giant barn with rows upon rows of triple bunk beds. Women of various ages were lined up in front of the beds, as if ready for inspection. "Where am I?"

The old woman leaned in close again. "Hell. Get up."

Luca laughed at the woman's seriousness. This had to be Casey's doing. She'd gotten Luca totally wasted and left her in a women's shelter as a joke, a parting gift. Not that they'd be parting. Luca was going to ask Casey to come with her to LA. They could share a one-bedroom place until Alyssa sold Luca's books and the money started coming in. Hopefully. She couldn't wait to see Casey's face. She'd dreamed just as hard about getting out of this place and starting fresh to run her own bar. Venice Beach seemed like the perfect place for them both to start a new life.

Luca pushed up from the bed and tried to stand. Unsuccessfully. Her legs folded under her, and she fell to her knees. Soft dirt cushioned the impact. Now she was glad she wasn't back in the basement with its concrete floor.

The woman grasped at Luca's arm and tried to pull her up, again not gently. "You must stand, or we will all suffer."

Someone else grasped at Luca's other arm, and the two of them pulled her up. She leaned against the corner of the beds and wrapped her arm around a wooden post for support. What was this crazy woman talking about? Luca needed to get out of here. The novelty and amusement were quickly wearing off. "Is Casey here?" she asked.

"You must be quiet."

She'd had enough of this. Luca pushed away from the bed and began to walk toward the light at the far end of the barn, which she assumed was the door. She'd barely gone three steps when both her arms were grabbed again, and she was yanked backward.

"Are you trying to get us all whipped?" the old woman asked in a harsh, hushed whisper.

Luca pulled away. "What are you talking about? I have to go. I've got a plane to catch." After she'd spoken to Marissa Vargas and accepted her agent's offer, sure, but soon enough, she'd be on a plane to LA.

The old woman laughed. "In your dreams." She gestured around her. "You're not going anywhere for a long, long time. If ever. Most people die before they work off their debt."

"Debt? What are you–" Luca's legs dissolved beneath her, and she crumpled to the floor once more. Reality hit like a tsunami. There'd been no nightmare. Casey had brought her to the Vargas compound to meet with Marissa... Luca touched her neck; it was tender and bruised from where she'd been injected with something.

The woman helped her up again. "Please, chica, you must stand," she said gently.

Two armed men came in and walked up the narrow aisle between the beds, and every one of the women lowered their gaze. Luca pressed her palm to her forehead, trying to ease the incessant pounding of her brain against her skull.

"Are you eyeballing me?" one of them asked and stopped directly in front of her.

The other one tugged on his buddy's arm. "She's fresh in. Doesn't know the rules yet." He pointed to the ground. "Eyes down."

Luca nodded and did as instructed, realizing this insane situation had the potential to get much worse.

"Best learn quick, puta," the first one said and walked on.

Time slowed, and it was as if everyone held their breath while the two guards completed their circuit of the barn.

"Out in ten," one of them shouted as they left.

"Come," the older woman said. "We must eat and wash."

Dazed, Luca was caught up in the swathe of women as they moved to a small area at the front of the building. On a three-foot square table, there was a pile of small bread chunks and cheese. On another were squat wooden tumblers and pitchers of water. Luca watched as the women descended on the tables like locusts, and in seconds, it was all gone.

The older woman returned and pushed a cup and some food into Luca's hands. "Eat. Then we wash."

Luca chewed the stale-tasting offering while simultaneously pushing down the urge to throw up. This couldn't be happening. She allowed herself to be pulled around the side of the barn. Several jungle showers had been erected, and the women fell into line. Some filled the troughs with water and pulled them up to the top of the showers while others had stripped naked and stood underneath the slow trickles.

The older woman shoved Luca under one of the showers then filled the wooden pot from the giant metal container of translucent water. "Wash. Quickly."

Luca unbuttoned her special shirt and carefully placed it on a nearby bench against the barn wall. She took everything off but her shorts and washed with a small bar of soap beside the shower. When she was done, she looked around for a towel, but there was nothing but palm leaves.

Her self-appointed guardian nodded. "They're all we have."

When Luca had dressed, and her new friend had also washed, Luca touched her arm. "What's your name?"

She smiled. "Not that it really matters in here, but my name is Epifania. You can call me Epi. And yours?"

"Luca. Luca Romero."

Epi gave a small smile. "I'm pleased and not pleased to meet you, Luca Romero."

Luca ran her hand through her hair and shook off the last of the moisture. She felt the same. Waking up in her own bed would've been preferable to meeting Epi. "Thank you. For your kindness." Luca gave Epi's arm a gentle squeeze before letting go.

"You're welcome." She nodded toward a small dirt path beyond the barn. "Now, we work. Come."

The women filed along the path, whispering to each other though Luca couldn't imagine what they had to talk about. Maybe they were wondering how she'd come to be there. Luca was wondering that herself. How could Casey have done this? Had she gotten into debt with Vargas and had no choice but to—to what? Sell her best friend? Had Vargas kept Casey on the outside because she was worth more to him working the tourists than whatever Luca was being forced to do? Would she be released when Casey had fixed whatever she'd messed up?

Armed guards came into view at the end of the barn, but they weren't the same guys she'd met minutes ago. How many men did Vargas have on the compound? She looked around, trying not to be too obvious. There had been no signs of chains or locks on the barn doors. If she could get off the property, she could get back to her place, grab her passport and writing, and get the hell out of the country.

Epi tugged at Luca's shirt. "There is no escape," she said as if reading her mind. "The last person who tried..." She closed her eyes and shook her head. "They made an example of him to discourage anyone else from trying. It worked. That was nearly four years ago."

"You've been here for four years?"

Epi scoffed. "I've been here longer than that, child."

Luca didn't want to ask her next question, almost certain that the answer would frighten her senseless. "How...how long?"

"I stopped counting after seven years. When you go to rest tonight, look at the wood of your bunk more closely, and you'll see the scratches from women trying to mark their time." She shrugged. "Our years are controlled by Señor Vargas. You will drive yourself crazy if you think anything else."

The path grew narrower before opening out into rows and rows of cannabis trees taller than her. Epi took a muslin sheet from a pile at the edge of the field. Two guards were directing the women to particular walkways between the plant rows. Luca held her questions until she and Epi had been allocated their work, then she followed Epi along the row until they reached a skinny young man in a dirty tank top and khaki shorts.

Epi stopped a few plants short of him and unfolded her sheet onto the ground. She pointed to a plant with almost fully white buds. "These are the plants ready to harvest." She pulled a pair of shears from her pocket and began to sever the branch. "Next week, we will pick coca leaves on the other side of the compound."

Luca didn't want to think about spending tomorrow here, let alone next week. "Would you tell me why you're here?" Luca asked as she took the first stalk of buds from Epi and laid it on the sheet. Silence meant time to think, and she couldn't take the surreal turn her life had taken. Not yet. The coming despair had to be drowned out for the moment or she'd start screaming and never stop.

Epi's expression transformed in an instant, her seriousness overtaken by an obviously deep, abiding love. Her eyes brightened, and she smiled so genuinely that Luca was almost transported from this place of desperation and could imagine them sharing a coffee somewhere.

"My daughter was gifted with extraordinary talent. She could sculpt and paint the very essence of love into existence," Epi said quietly as she continued to work. "There was no way for her to share that if she stayed here." She looked beyond Luca in the direction of the main house. "I asked Señor Vargas to help us, and that help came at this price."

Luca couldn't vocalize an adequate response. She had no mother, but here was a mother who had sacrificed her freedom for her daughter. A dark jealousy competed with a total sense of awe for such an act of unconditional parental love. They worked in silence for a few moments before Luca asked, "Have you seen your daughter since you came here?"

Epi tapped her forehead and then her heart. "I see her every day."

The simplicity of the answer made Luca's heart tremble. It was all about perspective. Epi hadn't *seen* her daughter at all, but that was clearly okay because she was following her dreams. The thought of her own dreams intruded on her admiration of Epi, and a stark, contrasting rage wrapped around every nerve ending in Luca's body. Her talent had finally been recognized, but the rewards of that had been wrenched away from her before she'd had any time to enjoy it. Now she was stuck here with no knowledge of why or if there was any hope of her ever leaving.

"Why are *you* here?" Epi asked.

Luca puffed out her cheeks. "Damned if I know. I definitely trusted the wrong person."

"Meaning?" Epi indicated the branch she was cutting so that Luca took it before it fell. "We have to handle these carefully. The gross value from any damaged stock is added to our debt."

Vargas had these people completely trapped. "I've been alone all my life, but when I moved here, I thought I'd found some chosen family." She clenched her jaw as she recalled how easily Casey had duped her into coming here. When Marissa had entered her father's office, she'd looked surprised to see them. Luca was holding fast to that thought. She didn't want to believe that Marissa could have been involved in whatever had led to Luca's forced incarceration. From their intense conversation a year ago, Luca had come to realize that Marissa was in her own version of confinement.

"And what happened?"

Luca quickly retold the story of her history with Casey and what had happened the previous day. "So you can see why I'm not sure exactly what's going on."

Epi felled another branch and murmured something Luca didn't catch. "It sounds like your friend has never really been your friend. That kind of person is always looking out for themselves and only does things to help others when it serves their own desires."

That made sense. She'd offered to help with the agent's contract by putting Luca in touch with Marissa and had gotten something out of leaving Luca here, though she'd need some help figuring out what that was. "I thought I'd learned my lesson about hoping people cared about me." She looked away from Epi's curious gaze when her voice broke slightly. Learning a lesson didn't make it hurt any less.

"You should not close yourself off because of the actions of others, chica. That will only lead to more hurt."

Luca turned away and busied herself with making sure the branches were lined neatly. She was far from ready to hear any therapeutic bullshit. "Does anyone ever leave...alive?" It was a question she wasn't sure she wanted the answer to. But hope was all she had since everything else was out of her control. Her life at the hotel bar hadn't been stellar, but it was hers. She decided when she worked, when she wrote, when she ate. She'd only been conscious here an hour, but it was already clear she no longer had any autonomy. However, maybe her circumstances were different. She wasn't there because of any bargain she'd struck with Vargas. Maybe this was all short term, and the ordeal would be over soon.

Epi nodded. "Sometimes people are here for small debts, and they manage not to make any mistakes or add to their dues."

She would be one of those people. She didn't ask any further questions, like how many in how long? Numbers didn't matter. It was possible, and for now, that's all she needed to know. She wouldn't take Epi's advice on time though; she'd find a spot in her bunk and begin to mark her stay. And she'd talk to the guards and eventually get an audience with Vargas again so she could find out exactly what was going on.

She took another cut branch from Epi and laid it down with even more care. No damage. No mistakes. No additional debt. Then she'd get out of here and be back on track with her dream, just like Epi's daughter. Luca didn't believe her talent to be anything as grand as that, but the email from Alyssa Dawes had shown her that she had something of value to share with the world, and she was going to do everything in her power to get on with doing exactly that.

Chapter Eleven

ARTURO ARCHED HIS EYEBROW. "That looks like more than you usually bring."

Marissa pushed past him, took another chunk of cheese from the refrigerator, and balanced it on top of the bulging wicker hamper.

"You know you look like the evil queen with her basket of poisoned apples?" he asked.

She pulled the container from the marble countertop, choosing to ignore his comment and the accompanying twisted grin he always gave when he was being a smart ass. The basket was heavier than she'd anticipated, too full as Arturo had observed, and impossible to handle, so several of the items tumbled to the floor.

Arturo moved swiftly to retrieve them, almost bumping Marissa's head as she scooped up a bunch of grapes.

"Careful," she said and swatted his shoulder.

He frowned. "I'm trying to help."

She nodded toward a second hamper on a high shelf in the larder that she couldn't reach. "If you really want to assist me, get that down and put some of this food into it."

"You only had to ask."

Arturo easily reached the basket and helped her share the load across both baskets.

"Why so much today?" he asked.

Damn his persistent and observant nature, though it showed that he cared enough to see what she was doing. "There are nearly a hundred people in the barns, Arturo. This is just for the women."

He smiled again. "I know that. But it's still overloaded. Why?"

"I missed yesterday. I thought I could make up for it with extra today."

Arturo blew out a breath and leaned against the counter. "I don't think you have anything to make up for. They're grateful for anything you offer them."

"I don't want them to be grateful. They shouldn't even be here." She slammed her still quite full basket on the countertop. "I shouldn't have to do this."

"I know, hermana." He placed his hand on hers gently. "But your father has paid for many people to have new lives in America. Those debts have to be paid."

Marissa rolled her eyes and pulled her hand from under his. "I understand that. But they should be able to come and go from the compound as if this was normal work. They're prisoners, Arturo. Prisoners whose sentences are extended at Papá's will."

Arturo shrugged. "Most of these people don't have their own homes, you know that. Your father feeds them—"

"The bare minimum." She took a basket in each hand and strode from the kitchen, trying not to register the strain on her shoulders and arms from the weight. "And he adds it to their debt."

In his way, her father *had* helped lots of people build new lives across the border. He had made it possible for them to pursue the American dream. She wished it wasn't so. She wished there could be a Mexican dream, where the needs and desires and wants of her people were there for the taking in her own country. But in the absence of that possibility, her father offered a particularly high-priced alternative, and the relatives were the ones who paid it. He had found a way to feed on the misfortune of others, and she hated him for that. The vast profits from his drug empire could easily fund the relocation of a hundred people a year. He always talked of community—he'd poured hundreds of thousands into local government for schools—but he chose to monetize this desperation. His philanthropic logic created a dystopian nightmare.

Arturo came to her side. "Let me help you."

Facing the closed door and not wanting to put the baskets down in case she wasn't able to pick them back up again, she had no choice but to acquiesce. "Fine."

He opened the door then went to take the heavy hampers from her hands.

"No. I'll carry them to the cart." She shook her leg slightly and didn't hear or feel a metallic jangle. "I forgot the key."

"I'll get it," Arturo said.

She went outside, loaded up the golf cart, and slid into the driver's seat to wait for him to return.

He jogged back and handed her the key. "I assume you don't want me to come with you?"

Marissa smiled and shook her head. He asked every day even though her answer was always the same. "I'll be fine. And besides, you scare them." She regretted the throwaway comment the moment it hit his ears and transformed his expression from playful to pained. Unlike his colleagues, fear wasn't an emotion he ever sought to elicit from anyone. His response reinforced precisely why he needed to escape this place just as much as she did. "I'm teasing you. I just can't have serious conversations with them when they're all swooning over you... And the men are the worst," she whispered.

The corner of his mouth twitched, but the hurt remained.

He tapped his watch. "Don't forget you have the meeting with Señora Martinez at four."

She wasn't about to forget that. It was their last meeting before her first murder case began. She wasn't involved, but she knew the case just as well as the first and second chairs because she'd put in countless hours of research and interview time that had helped build the defense. She shuddered and every hair on her body stood on end. She was still struggling with the innocent until proven guilty concept when it was damn clear to everyone at the firm that their client had committed the crime. He was the kind of man that ended a life as easily as if he would stub out a cigar.

Marissa kicked the engine into action and pushed all thoughts of him away. When she and Arturo were in Spain, she'd start her own law practice and prosecute the guilty. "I'll be back in plenty of time." She motioned to her outfit of loose-fitting linen pants and tank top. "I need to change, and I have to be in the office by eleven anyway." She didn't want to take advantage of the fact that she worked at a firm owned by her father, but she had negotiated later start and finish times during the week so she could continue to do this every morning.

And today's trip was even more important because Luca Romero was one of the "workers." Marissa drove toward the barn accommodations as quickly as the engine would allow, wishing that her father had invested in quad bikes with more power than these sedate machines. Usually, of course, the steady pace of the cart was more than adequate, preferable even. A gentle ride amid the tranquility of the lush grounds often settled her warring mind and distanced her from the turmoil of her existence. At least until the barn came into view and she was reminded of what she was doing and why.

But today, she couldn't wait to get there, and she had no time to enjoy the scenery. She was being silly. She knew that too.

The women emerged from the barn when Marissa drew closer. They expected her around this time, and she didn't like to disappoint them or miss the slot. If she was late, they'd already be out at work, and she wouldn't be able to leave the food because it would spoil in the heat. She parked beside a wooden seat and climbed out. Epi, one of Marissa's favorites, was at the front of the group, and fate would have it that she was pulling Luca alongside her. Trust Epi to take it upon herself to befriend Luca and keep her safe.

"Hola, Señorita Vargas." Epi lifted one of the baskets and passed it to Gloria, then gave the second one to Romina.

"Hola, Epi. Cómo estás?"

"Bien. Y usted?" Epi smiled, and her sun-beaten skin wrinkled around her eyes. She was beginning to look older than she should.

Gloria and Romina hefted the spoils to two larger tables, and they dug in. Marissa ignored the nearby guards who shook their heads and laughed at her efforts. It was harder to ignore their hands moving to their weapons, prepped to shoot if they perceived she was in any danger. Her father's orders had been clear when he'd finally allowed her to bring food at all. He still wouldn't let her do the same for the men, but she knew that Epi organized what she brought so that they could filter some through for them.

Epi pulled Luca to her side. "This is the most important person here, Luca. Señorita Vargas, Luca has just joined us."

Joined us. It would've sounded almost normal had it not been for the way Luca flinched. "I know. I saw her being taken against her will." Marissa switched her focus to Luca. "I'm so sorry."

"Do you know why I'm here?" Luca asked.

Epi tugged Luca's arm. "Be respectful, chica."

Marissa touched Epi's forearm. "It's okay, Epi. Luca has every right to be angry. Please," she gestured toward the table, "take some food before it all disappears. I need to speak with Luca."

Epi narrowed her eyes slightly. "You know each other?"

Marissa nodded, impressed by Epi's intuition. She only hoped that Epi didn't pick up on the nature of her interest.

"As you wish." She pulled Luca to face her. "Control yourself, Luca. Señorita Vargas is our greatest ally here. Remember that."

Luca looked offended by the inference that she wouldn't be respectful. "Of course."

Marissa waited until Epi was out of earshot. "We should sit." She walked the few paces to the back of the cart and sat on the rear seat. Luca followed then seemed to hesitate, perhaps considering whether to sit on the bench, but she remained standing. Aware of the existing power imbalance already between them like an immovable boulder, Marissa stayed in her seat even though she wanted to be close enough to touch Luca, to comfort her. She couldn't tell her that everything would be all right—that wasn't in her control—but she could be a friendly face.

Luca clasped her hands together then rubbed at her wrists. Had the work begun to take a physical toll after just one day? Despite pleading with her father to help, Marissa hadn't been allowed to work, so she knew little of the strain other than what Epi and the others had told her. But she had a feeling they underplayed it; they just weren't built to complain.

"Tell me why I'm here. Please."

Marissa's heart would have folded in on itself if it were possible. Luca's pleading expression, the soft vulnerability in her eyes, her overall gentle nature, all of it made it virtually impossible not to pull Luca into her arms. Of all the people under her father's control, Luca deserved to be here the least. She hadn't done anything or *not* done something Marissa's father had asked of her. She hadn't bargained for some advantage for her family. Quite the opposite, Luca had managed to stay off her father's radar despite the activities of her "friend" Casey. And Marissa recalled that she had no family that she knew of. She'd even called Casey her chosen family. The bitter injustice of it all burned Marissa's throat as much as if the situation were her own. "You don't know what happened?"

Luca clenched her fist then wrapped her other hand around it. Marissa pressed herself back against the seat, acutely aware she didn't really know Luca or what she was capable of. Her father's guards stared harder, but she waved them away.

Luca opened her hands and held them up. "Sorry. I didn't mean to frighten you." She took a few steps back and put her hands behind her back. "I'm sorry. Please, don't go."

The softness in her expression returned, and Marissa chided herself for even thinking that Luca would strike her, no matter how angry she might be. No, they hadn't spent a long time together, and Marissa didn't know Luca at all, but she felt like she knew her soul. Kindness and empathy radiated from her; it had been one of the original reasons why Marissa had opened up and talked to her at the bar. It was one of the reasons Marissa had continued to go back to the bar, hoping to talk more but never getting the opportunity again—mainly because of Casey. And it was her main reason for making contact now. She wanted to get to know Luca in the limited time she had left at the compound.

"I'm not going anywhere," Marissa said and leaned forward.

"I'm frustrated and confused." Luca rubbed her hand over her mouth. "I don't know anything, no. Do you?"

Marissa took a deep breath. How was she supposed to break this to her gently? "Your friend Casey *isn't* your friend. She sold you out."

Luca dropped back onto the wooden bench as if the life had suddenly been drained from her. "What do you mean, sold me out? For what?"

"You'd just gotten an offer from an agent to represent you for the books you told me about, hadn't you?" She caught Luca's shy glance, as if she was surprised Marissa had remembered. She clearly had no idea that Marissa's repeated visits to the bar were all about trying to keep that promising conversation going.

"Yeah. I was going to accept it and arrange a meeting in LA." She half smiled. "I got my passport eighteen months ago so that I'd be ready to go as soon as I got an offer." She looked down and kicked at the ground. "It probably sounds stupid."

Marissa rose and sat beside Luca. She touched her shoulder gently. "No, it doesn't. It's optimism. It's a nice thing to have."

Luca let out a short breath. "It's something I've lost my grip on now. You know about my contract because Casey asked you to look at it for me, right?"

Marissa sighed at the depths of Casey's deceit. "No. I only know about it because my father told me to review it after I saw you being drugged and taken away. But I've read it now, yes."

Luca rubbed her temples then put her head in her hands and doubled over. Marissa placed her hand on Luca's back. She was hot, almost feverish, to the touch. Had she caught something already? Regular medical attention was another thing she was trying to convince her father to provide, currently to no avail.

"What does your father care about my contract?" Luca asked, her voice muffled from between her knees.

Marissa frowned. Was Luca really that naïve that she didn't think Casey was capable of executing such a devious plan? Or was she just deluding herself, not wanting to believe that someone she'd thought of as a good friend had sold her into a kind of slavery? "Casey made a deal with my father, Luca. He's agreed to keep you here..." She was reluctant to say forever. Her father had said she might outlive her usefulness. "He's going to keep you here while Casey goes to LA and–"

"Pretends to be me." Luca turned away and dry retched.

Relieved that Luca had put the pieces together for herself, Marissa winced at her obvious pain. "Yes. She's going to pay my father to keep you here. He's given her two months to secure a publishing deal."

Luca turned back to face her quickly. "And what if she doesn't? It doesn't always work that fast. Sometimes it takes years."

Marissa looked away briefly, unable to immediately dash the brightness of hope that glinted in Luca's beautifully expressive brown eyes. "Then she has to return to her usual job for him."

"Okay. But what about me?"

Marissa twirled her mother's ring on her finger. He hadn't expressed *that* part of his strategy to her outright, but she knew him well enough to know exactly what that would mean for Luca's future; she wouldn't have one. She'd be a loose end who could claim kidnapping, and that wouldn't do. "I don't know."

Luca looked at her. "Can you find out?"

Marissa hesitated. It was one thing to bring extra food to the barn but another entirely to spy on her father or draw out his intentions. And what if he confirmed that he would kill Luca? What then? Would Marissa rather not know that so she could leave this place forever with a clear conscience? Or would she forever wonder what had happened to the only woman since her mamá who'd really *heard* her when she spoke.

"I'm sorry. I shouldn't ask you to do that." Luca paced beside the cart. "How often do you bring the women these baskets?"

Grateful for the subject change, Marissa glanced across to the tables, now almost empty. Epi had chunks of cheese and bread beside her, most likely for Luca. The pockets of her dress also bulged with food stashed away for the men she'd see at the fields. The other women had done the same. "Usually every day."

"That's nice of you." Luca finally stopped pacing but didn't move any closer. "You told me you dreamed of escaping your life," she said. "Are you any closer to making that happen?"

An invisible hand squeezed at Marissa's throat, and she looked at the guards. They were too far away to have heard, and Luca had said it so quietly, it was barely a whisper. She got to her feet, willing herself to remember that she and Arturo had a plan, one she couldn't share with anyone. Especially someone she'd only met twice. She couldn't be drawn into Luca's plight, and she couldn't draw Luca into hers.

"I have to go to work." She walked around the vehicle and slipped into the driver's seat.

Epi rushed over and placed the empty hampers into the footwell. "Thank you, Señorita Vargas. This means so much to us."

Marissa squeezed her hand gently and smiled. "Same time tomorrow, Epi."

"You're an angel, just like your mamá."

As it always did, the mention of her mamá brought tears to her eyes, and she blinked them away. "I could try for the rest of my life and never be half as good as my mamá." She turned the ignition and set off down the dirt path back to her father's house. She didn't look back. She didn't want to see Luca's response to her abrupt departure. Whether it was anger or hurt, Marissa wouldn't be able to handle it. She'd wanted to see Luca, and though she'd known that she'd be affected by Luca's dire situation, Marissa *hadn't* anticipated the strong desire that challenged her to do something about it.

She drove the cart back as fast as its engine would allow, desperate to put distance between them. She was too close to freedom for this distraction, too near to her dreams to concern herself with anyone else's life but hers and Arturo's.

And yet... the enigmatic writer with whom she'd been craving a connection since they'd first met was now closer than ever, a literal captive audience. But she could do this; she could control herself. She owed it to the women to keep taking them extra food until she left forever. She probably had nothing to worry about, and Luca would keep her distance after the way Marissa had just left her.

She pulled the cart to a stop and rested her head against the steering wheel. "Please help me, Mamá," she whispered.

Chapter Twelve

CASEY HAD SEEN VENICE Beach in so many movies and TV shows, it almost seemed unreal. But now, as she stood facing the Pacific Ocean with her bare feet scrunched into the soft, hot sand, it came alive. Surfers rode the waves, twisting and turning, impossibly balanced on the roaring water beneath them. The iconic lifeguard huts jutted into the sky, staffed by wildly fit people ready to launch themselves into a sea rescue. The smell of fish tacos wafted in the air, interlaced with the familiar scent of weed. Behind her, skinny Hollywood wannabes in skimpy bikinis floated past on rollerblades, and the sidewalk was lined with a mix of jewelry stalls, artists, and fortune tellers.

She didn't need anyone to predict her future; she was making it happen. From the moment she'd caught the plane to LAX, her new reality began to settle in her mind and seep into her body. She'd never have to sell another bag of drugs to tourists looking for a quick, shallow escape from their meaningless existence. She'd never have to mix another cocktail for anyone but herself, and she wouldn't have to sleep with random people just for a comfortable night's rest.

She took another lungful of salty air before she turned back and walked to her waiting cab.

"Where to now?" the cab driver asked.

"Eden Rock Suites, West Hollywood."

He made an approving noise. "Nice choice."

She didn't respond. She'd had enough of making small talk with people she had no interest in, and he had nothing to offer her. If he'd been gay, she would've asked about the best bars to go to, but one of the first things he'd bored her with when she'd gotten in the car was a tale of his wife and his baby almost being born in the exact spot she was sitting. When he'd seen her reaction, he'd promised that he'd had it thoroughly cleaned. Still, she'd shifted to the opposite side of the car and sat behind him the rest of the way to the beach, making it difficult for him to catch her eye.

Casey opened Google Maps on her phone to check the route he was taking. Sure, she was starting a new life, one where she'd have plenty of money, but she wouldn't be taken advantage of like some stupid turista. One thing she hadn't really appreciated was the spread of the city. It was over ten miles from the beach to WeHo. It never seemed to take any time at all to get from one place to another in the movies. She watched his digital display keep turning and the fare increasing as they crawled along Venice Boulevard. How there could be a jam when there were five lanes of traffic was mind-blowing.

She let out a long breath, closed her eyes, and pushed back into the softness of the upholstery. There was no rush. She had a meeting scheduled with Luca's—no, her—agent tomorrow afternoon, but the rest of the day and night were all hers to explore a fresh playground. Her stomach rumbled, reminding her that she hadn't eaten anything since yesterday. She'd been too wired to have breakfast before taking Luca to Vargas and too desperate to get here to have anything on the plane. She decided she'd ask the hotel concierge for a restaurant recommendation and to hell with the expense. Or maybe get ridiculous room service and drink twenty-dollar miniatures from the bar fridge.

She craved company though. It had been so long since she'd cruised a bar for someone she was attracted to rather than someone who had a luxury hotel room that she'd almost forgotten what it felt like. And she needed the practice if she was going to successfully seduce Marissa when she visited. She was already halfway there, Casey was certain of that. She'd seen the longing in Marissa's eyes. She'd probably do anything to secure a one-way ticket from her father's clutches. It was clear she wanted out of that life just as much as Casey had, and she now had the means to offer Marissa that escape.

Casey drifted away from the frustration of the traffic and allowed herself to slip into a fantasy of how their life would be. She was lowering herself into the pool at their hilltop mansion when the cab driver coughed loudly.

"Eden Rock Suites," he said before popping the trunk and getting out. He retrieved her canvas bag and held it out to her.

Her worldly possessions contained in one thirty-pound backpack and the bag she had strapped over her shoulder. "Thanks, man." It wouldn't be long before she had a walk-in closet, crammed full of tailored suits, bright button-down shirts, and designer jeans, and she'd have a whole wall dedicated to Converse shoes and boots.

"Have a nice day," he said and got back in his car.

Casey turned to the hotel, and the doorperson let her in.

"Welcome to Eden Rock Suites."

She nodded and entered. A guy carrying her bag. Another guy opening doors for her. She could get used to this. A gorgeous redhead smiled widely at her as she approached the front desk.

"Welcome to your home away from home."

Casey tilted her head. "I hope not."

The redhead looked puzzled but continued with her well-practiced spiel. "My name is Anastasia. If you need *anything* to make your stay with us more comfortable, please call me, and I'll arrange whatever it is you need."

Casey raised her eyebrows. Was everyone programmed to be this flirtatious, or did she mean it? There was only one way to find out for sure. She placed her hands on the desk between them and leaned in a little. "Anything?"

Anastasia's lips twitched, and she gave a self-assured smile that came with a quick once over. "Anything." She held Casey's gaze for a long moment before returning her attention to her booking screen. "I can see that you've booked a junior suite, but I'm going to upgrade you to a terrace suite on the top floor." She made a few entries on her keyboard, then looked at Casey again. "Just the one bag?"

Casey nodded. "I have some shopping to do. I need a whole new wardrobe."

"Fasi, could you take the desk for me?" Anastasia called over her shoulder without taking her eyes from Casey.

An equally attractive brunette emerged from the back office. Was everyone in this city off-the-charts hot? Maybe they kept the regular-looking people working behind the scenes to maintain the façade. Until they were in her room and Anastasia was naked, Casey would continue to believe she was misinterpreting the situation or in a waking fantasy.

Anastasia held a card key to a black machine until the red light on it turned green. "I'll be thirty minutes, Fasi. I'm giving Ms. Soto a tour of the hotel."

"Sure, no problem."

Fasi smiled at Casey, but there were no sexual undertones playing on her lips or dancing in her eyes. So not everyone was an extra from *The L Word*.

Anastasia came around the desk. "If you'd like to follow me, I'll take you to your room to drop your luggage before I show you the rooftop tennis court, pool, and bar."

"You've got a tennis court on the roof?" Casey asked. She let Anastasia walk slightly in front of her so she could watch her form. "That doesn't sound like a good idea."

Anastasia called the elevator. "It's an enclosed court. Do you like to play?"

Casey followed her into the fully mirrored box, dropped her bag to the floor, and leaned against the back wall. "Yeah. But I'm not a fan of tennis."

Anastasia turned after the doors silently slid closed and stepped between Casey's open legs. Casey scanned the elevator for a camera.

Anastasia dragged her nail along Casey's cheek to her lips. "There's no CCTV, if that's what you're looking for. We take the privacy of our guests very seriously."

"Seems like you take the needs of your guests very seriously too." Casey sucked Anastasia's finger into her mouth and nibbled it lightly.

"We do." She placed her hand on Casey's chest then trailed down to her belt. "Why don't you tell me all about your needs, Ms. Soto?"

Casey wrapped her hand in Anastasia's soft hair and pulled her closer. She traced her tongue along Anastasia's collarbone and up her neck. "I've been traveling all day, and I need a shower."

Anastasia dropped her hand to Casey's crotch and squeezed firmly. "Then I should help you with that. You're probably very dirty and need help with all those hard-to-reach places."

Casey moaned when the heel of Anastasia's hand pressed against her hardening clit, and she pushed back against the pressure. Anastasia was having no trouble reaching her at all. It had been a long time since someone had wanted to touch her this way. Mostly, the tourists just wanted her to fuck their brains out, and then they'd fall unconscious, leaving Casey to service herself. Now that she thought about it, she couldn't remember the last time she'd had someone inside her, let alone a perfect woman like Anastasia. Flawlessly feminine and exactly her type. Casey took Anastasia's hand, paying attention to her nails. Not too long and expertly manicured. Probably wouldn't hurt more than was pleasurable.

"And when I'm clean, then what?"

"Then I think you need me to fuck you."

The elevator came to a halt, and the doors opened. Casey picked up her bag, and Anastasia pulled her into the corridor. She stopped at one of only three doors on the entire floor, pressed the key card to the lock panel, and pushed it open.

Casey had thought the junior suite would be huge, but this was something else. The short entryway opened into a giant living space with floor-to-ceiling windows from wall to wall. But she didn't have much time to appreciate the view before Anastasia pushed her against the wall and began to pull off her clothes.

Casey dropped her bags and let it happen. She was open to everything that could happen here, the place she'd dreamed of for almost two decades. A beautiful woman had decided she wanted Casey and was taking her. Yeah, this was exactly the kind of paradise city she'd hoped it would be.

Chapter Thirteen

LUCA USED THE BOTTOM of her tank top to wipe away the sweat before it got in her eyes. There was no real shelter from the merciless heat, and the more branches they cut down, the less protection they had. She and the rest of Vargas's army of workers had cleared one field already, and now they were working on their second. But with few breaks and only a small bucket of water to go around, Luca was beginning to feel faint. Every time she stood too quickly, blackness crept into the edges of her vision and a white shower of snowy dots blurred her sight completely for a few seconds.

"Are you okay, chica?" Epi grasped Luca's wrist to steady her.

Her eyes cleared, and she squinted at the bright blue sky. "Just dizzy. I'm okay now."

Epi's grip tightened. "Hold onto a tree for support but make sure it looks like you're still picking leaves."

Her meaning was clear: fall down on the job and suffer the consequences. As if to reiterate her concern, an old guy in the next row suddenly fell to the ground. Luca pushed through the bushes to get to him and dropped to her knees. She gently lifted his head and checked to make sure he hadn't landed on anything hard. She felt her shirt being tugged and looked over her shoulder. "What? He needs help."

Epi shook her head. "You can't help him."

Luca frowned. Of course she could help him. He probably just needed some water and a rest. He looked like he was sixty, and not a healthy sixty. More of a heavy-smoking and heavy-drinking kind of sixty. She pulled away from Epi and looked back to the fallen man. His eyelids were open, showing only the whites of his eyes, and he was a dead weight in her arms. But the steady rise and fall of his chest saved her the trouble of remembering the ratio of breaths to rib smashes. "Help me get him into some shade."

Before she could turn to Epi, Luca was grabbed under the arms and flung backward. She landed hard on her ass in the dirt.

"Get back to work," one of the guards leaned over her and yelled into her face before he stalked away. He kicked the old man in the ribs. "Get up."

When he didn't respond, the guard kicked him harder. Luca tried to scramble to her feet, but she was immediately tugged backward again.

"You can't help him now, Luca," Epi whispered.

Another guard ran up the pathway, and she recognized him as the one who'd kept her from being harassed on her first morning. At the other guy's instruction, he grabbed the old man by his ankles and began to drag him backward in the direction of the barn, clearly struggling. The unconscious man's head bounced over the uneven ground, doing his existing condition no good at all.

"We will not see him again," Epi whispered.

A wave of relief washed through Luca. "They'll let him go home because he's too ill to work anymore?"

Epi laughed quietly, but there was no humor in the sound. "No. They won't let him go home or everyone would pretend to be sick. If you cannot work, you are worth even less than nothing."

Luca waited for further explanation, but Epi went back to work, resignation clear in her expression. How many times had she seen something like this happen while she'd been imprisoned here? "And once someone is worth less than nothing?" she asked, already tiring of asking questions she didn't want to hear answered but also, *had* to have answered.

Before Epi responded, the first guard turned on Luca again and kicked her shoes. "Help him."

She held up her hands and nodded. "Okay, okay." She got to her feet and jogged the short distance to catch up with them. The guard stopped for a moment, allowing her to crouch and lift under the old man's arms to protect his head.

"Ready?" he asked.

She nodded but no, she wasn't ready for any of this. Sure, she'd helped Casey lift several tourists who'd passed out blind drunk, and they'd carried them to their hotel or to a cab, so it wasn't the dead weight or the heavy strain that troubled her. It was the complete lack of respect for human life that went against everything she believed in.

As they carried the old man down the pathway to a cart, she caught quick glances from workers on either side of her. Anger, desperate sadness, hopelessness. She saw those emotions and many more. But it was the loss of hope in their eyes that struck her like a kick to the gut. How long would it take to have her hope drained away when there was no obvious end or way to escape? She had to get out of here.

"Will you call a doctor or take him to the hospital?" Luca wanted to believe that Epi was wrong, and that the people who were genuinely too sick to work didn't suffer the fate she had intimated.

The guard looked beyond her toward his vicious colleague and shook his head, almost imperceptibly. "That's not how it works here."

She adjusted her grip under the old man's sweat-soaked armpits. The guard was rake thin, and he seemed to be letting Luca take most of the weight. "How does it work?"

He shook his head, again so slightly that Luca might've missed it if she wasn't looking hard enough, and he flicked a glance toward the other guard behind her. Now she got it. He didn't want to talk while that asshole could see him.

"Okay. I'll wait," she said. His reluctance comforted her, because it came with the notion that maybe not every guard on this prison-like compound was a cold, sadistic bastard. And she might be able to use that to her advantage.

She stayed silent the rest of the way and tried to keep her eyes focused on the man they were carrying, unwilling to handle the barrage of emotion from the onlooking workers. When they got to the cart, they hoisted him up and placed him gently onto the backseat. Luca glanced back toward Epi, but she was out of sight, as was the nasty guard. "So what will you do with him?"

"Get on the back and keep him from falling off," he said. "We'll talk on the way back to the barns."

He glanced around as if he was expecting another guard to emerge from behind a tree and punish him for talking to her. If some of the guards were this terrified, how were the workers supposed to handle it? She got down on her knees on the back platform and held the old man as best she could. The guard set off jerkily. She lost her balance, and the old guy nearly fell on her. She corrected herself and held on tighter. The man began to stir, and he looked at her, though his eyes rolled around like he was unable to focus properly. He muttered something she didn't catch, so she leaned closer. His murmurs continued, but even though she could now hear him, he wasn't making any sense. Disjointed words and broken sentences were all she could make out, and none of it seemed to go together. He was clearly delirious from dehydration. She hoped that's all it was. Some water and rest, and he could be back in the fields, proving his worth in a couple of days...if they gave him that opportunity. Epi's warning made it sound like they'd shoot him just as ruthlessly as if he were a race horse unable to run.

"We'll take him to the isolation area," the guard said after they'd been driving for a while.

Luca pulled away from the old man's incoherent rambling to hear the guard. He was speaking so quietly the hum of the engine almost drowned him out. "And you've got people there who will know what to do? People who will look after him and find out what's wrong."

"I wish that was how it is." He glanced over his shoulder. "That's what Señorita Vargas has been trying to achieve for a few years now, but Señor Vargas is stubborn. He would rather these people die as an example to the others than spend money helping them to recover."

"Will anyone be there to give him food and water?"

He shook his head. "No one is there. There'll be no help."

Luca took a deep breath to quell her rising anger. As if their shared situation wasn't dire enough, their keepers weren't prepared to help the sick. "How is he supposed to recover and get back to picking Vargas's fields for him?"

He shrugged. "Like I said, Vargas is more interested in discouraging others from falling ill. An old guy like this probably costs more to keep alive than he produces in the fields. Vargas doesn't really see you people as human beings. But it's not like he treats many of us much better."

Luca didn't respond and glanced down at the old man. He'd stopped mumbling, and his eyes were closed. His breaths had become shallow. She hated that this had happened, but it had given her the chance to speak to this guard. And his bubbling resentment of Vargas might mean he would help her when she finally figured out what she needed. She didn't know how she was going to get out of here, but she knew that she had to because she couldn't face a life without her freedom. "What's your name?"

He hesitated and looked around again. "De León. Jorge De León."

"Can I call you Jorge?"

"Only if you're sure there's no one else around." He stopped the cart and got out. "I heard what happened to you. Soto is ruthless, like a man."

Luca swallowed hard. She'd been so caught up with the old man's plight that she'd actually stopped thinking about her own situation and her supposed best friend for a while, probably for the first time since she'd woken from a drugged state and, with Marissa's help, realized what was happening. "Everyone can be ruthless. It's not just a man thing."

He shrugged. "Seems like we're better at it... Usually. But I think Señor Vargas is proud of Soto for her ambition, even if he doesn't like her much."

Luca clenched her jaw. "She stole *my* ambition. She doesn't have her own talent."

They maneuvered the old guy off the seat. Jorge pulled his neck bandana over his nose and shuffled back the short distance toward a small wooden building that she hadn't noticed before. She matched his slow pace easily.

"What's that for?" she asked, but her question was too late. He kicked open the door, and the stench of death and rotting flesh soared up her nostrils, making her gag.

"It's for this," he said, nodding into the building. "Sometimes they forget people are in here. They die, and no one moves them for a couple of days. Doesn't take long for the body to start decomposing in this heat."

There were no windows or openings, and the only light came through where slats in the wall had fallen away. The ground was covered in straw, and three dirty and torn blankets took up the majority of the floor space. They were gray with black stripes, but the muted colors failed to hide blood and puke stains all over them. Layered over the smell of dead flesh were those of other bodily fluids and excretions. She fought the overbearing urge to add her own vomit to the putrid collection and prayed for Jorge to move faster.

"Lay him here," Jorge said.

Movement caught her eye, and in the shafts of bright light, she saw rats patrolling the edges of the building. If the old man didn't have a disease, he probably soon would. "You said Señorita Vargas is trying to do something about this?" she asked after they'd positioned him on the closest blanket. When Jorge had mentioned Marissa's name, Luca's heart beat harder against her chest, but she'd tried to ignore the reaction. It didn't seem right that she could feel something positive when she was carrying an old man to a lonely and squalid death.

He ushered her out of the space, and she took a deep, cleansing breath, though she knew the smell would stick to her.

"The others say so. I've only been working on the compound for a year." He closed the door and dragged the rusty bolt across to lock it before pulling his makeshift mask down. "They say she tries to help the sick. She is a special woman."

His eyes lit up, and she smiled. It wasn't surprising that Marissa had the same effect on other people as she did on Luca. She'd only had to spend a few hours with her to recognize what a wonderful woman Marissa was. It had been clear then that her capacity for selflessness was huge, and Luca had seen it firsthand that morning. Until she'd stepped over a line she couldn't see, and Marissa abruptly left.

"How'd you end up here?" Luca asked.

"I ran a corner for Vargas, but I made a mistake." He gestured around him. "This is my punishment." His mouth twitched at the edge, but he didn't smile. "I was lucky. Señor Vargas doesn't tolerate failure. I've seen people beaten to death and hung from telephone wires for lesser mistakes."

Luca shuddered at the grotesque image that invaded her mind. "What did you do?"

Jorge shook his head. "It doesn't matter. What matters is that I need to keep my head down and do what I'm told so I can get out of here and back in the city." He glanced back at the isolation barn. "Away from this."

His words severed the thin thread of hope she'd had that Jorge might be willing and able to help her in some way. "Can I come here on my own time to help him?" she asked, hoping that she might run into Marissa so they could talk without the rest of the women and guards watching over them. Maybe Marissa could arrange for Luca to meet with Vargas. Casey was charming and a hustler, but she had no idea what she was doing. She couldn't write. She knew nothing about Luca's books or the characters that lived within those pages. She wouldn't be able to redraft a query letter, or handle edits, or reassure a publisher that she had so many more stories in her head. If Luca could persuade Vargas to bring Casey back so that she could go to LA and live the life she'd earned, she could pay her way out of the situation Casey had engineered. It would be more lucrative for Vargas in the long term. And it was obvious he was a man driven by greed. Negotiating a better deal would be in his selfish interest; why wouldn't he be interested? It wasn't fair, but if it got her out of this, then she'd do it.

"Are you loca? You want to go back in there?" Jorge frowned and pulled at his neck scarf. "You'll need something like this if you do."

"I know. But is it possible? Would it cause trouble for me?"

He scratched at his stubbly beard. "I don't think so, but–"

"You can tell that main guard that I'm trying to get the old guy back on his feet and working again." Luca looked deep into Jorge's eyes, imploring him to speak on her behalf. "Then he won't have to deal with getting rid of a dead body."

Jorge grunted. "Martinez gives the orders; he doesn't have to deal with the bodies." He tilted his head to the side. "But he does hate losing the workers to grave-digging."

Luca looked away, disgusted but not surprised. Of course they'd be expected to dispose of the bodies of their dead co-workers. Was that the unidentifiable expression she'd seen on some of the men's faces as they carried the old man to the car? The dreadful anticipation that they would be forced to bury one of their own? "Then you'll ask for me?"

Jorge shrugged. "Sure. But I don't know why you'd put yourself through that. Isn't your situation tough enough?"

"Maybe." She glanced back at the ramshackle wooden barn, still able to see the disgusting interior clearly in her mind. "But he's all alone and probably knows he's been locked up to die. There's always someone in the world in a worse state than me, and if I can do something to help that, then I will."

"You sound like Señorita Vargas." Jorge put his hand on her shoulder and gave Luca a gentle shove to guide her back to the cart.

"That's a good thing, right?" She sat in the passenger seat and waited while he came around to the driver's side.

"It should be, yeah. But around here, not so much. Caring about anything could get you killed." He set off back to the fields.

Human life clearly meant little to almost everyone within these grounds. But Marissa was different, and so was Luca. Would that mean Marissa might help her plead her case? She thought of the old guy back in the isolation barn. She couldn't end up like him. She wouldn't let that be her fate.

Chapter Fourteen

"HOW IS EVERYTHING, MARISSA? Are you happy?"

Marissa gave the most genuine smile she could manage. Raul Aguilar was her boss and the senior partner in the law firm. Aguilar's question wasn't directed at her, not really. He was asking if her father was happy, because no one in this city wanted the great Elvio Vargas unhappy. There were consequences to him *not* being happy.

"Happy in what way, Señor Aguilar?"

"Please, call me Raul. Happy in every way. With how everything is going."

He'd asked her to use his first name before, but anyone less than a partner had to address him formally, so she continued to do the same. Everyone in the office knew who she was and how she'd gotten there. It was humiliating. No one would dare voice their displeasure, but she could see it in their expressions no matter how hard they tried to disguise it. They treated her like royalty because fear was a powerful motivator. But they most definitely didn't think highly of her, and she couldn't blame them.

"I'm not happy about this case," she said and watched the color drain from his face.

"What do you mean? Has Moreno been working you too hard? Asking too much of you?"

She shook her head, though wasn't that what being a lawyer was all about? Working twenty-hour days to earn the respect of colleagues? To earn her place in the firm? Wasn't that what Moreno *should* be doing? "No, she hasn't, but I'm not happy about the client."

He sat back in his chair and nodded slowly. "You're having trouble with the 'innocent until proven guilty' concept?" He seemed almost amused.

"We all know he's guilty. He's practically admitted it." She tapped the graphic police photographs of the dead body frozen in a macabre pose. "He knows things about the murder that only the person who perpetrated the crime could know. He's not taking the case seriously. He's acting like it's a sure thing he'll be acquitted."

Aguilar narrowed his eyes briefly. He looked like he wanted to say something but felt that he couldn't. Marissa glanced out the window toward the harbor full of rich men's boats in the distance. The dirtbag client, Marín was probably on his way to his yacht now to drink tequila and have sex with any number of the women he paid to be ready to serve his every whim. Aguilar didn't have to say what was on his mind; his thoughts may as well have been in comic-strip bubbles above his head. He clearly couldn't understand how the daughter of one of the most prolifically violent drug lords in the country would be against representing Marín. The irony wasn't lost on her.

"We have a strong case, Marissa," he said. "The police made mistakes in the chain of custody and in their handling of the crime scene. Marín knows that, so he knows that it's highly likely we'll win his case." He twirled the gold Mont Blanc fountain pen in his fingers. "Winning cases like these are how we can afford pretty things like this." He pointed at her with it. "And you will too when you become a partner."

She ignored the mention of the partnership. If she were any other lawyer in the building the prospect of becoming a partner wouldn't be on the table yet. The inevitability of it was offensive. And if Aguilar wasn't one of her father's childhood friends, he would've thought so too. "So he should be allowed to get away with it on the basis of the police's incompetence? How is that justice?"

"It's for the court and the judge to dispense justice, Marissa. It's our job to win the case for our clients." He placed his pen beside the three other similarly expensive pens on his desk. "This firm has been built on the success of such cases. That's why your father invested in it."

Marissa weighed the options of her potential responses. She knew Aguilar reported directly to her father on her progress, but would he gloss over her disregard for his firm? Aguilar was a founding partner, clearly content with the path he'd taken that allowed him to spend thousands of pesos on fancy fountain pens and flashy cars. Did her distaste for their legacy of representing criminal gangs and impossibly rich men who believed they should be able to do exactly as they pleased, legal or not, irritate him? She hoped so. But she also had to remind herself that she wouldn't be here much longer and wouldn't have to buy into their willingness to sacrifice justice for extra zeroes on their retainer checks. There was no real need to rock the boat.

"My father didn't invest in this firm because of its reputation. He did it to provide this opportunity for me, and because he wants to cure me of my social conscience."

A flicker of anger crossed his eyes, but he recovered his dispassionate expression quickly. She was unreasonably happy that she'd gotten under his skin. If Arturo were by her side, he'd be kicking her shin and telling her to play the game for a little while longer. But if she did that, she dishonored the memory of her mamá, and nothing was worth that sacrifice. She'd promised she would make her proud, and this was the kind of conversation that would do exactly that and have her smiling down from heaven.

"You should be grateful your father cares about you enough to help shape your career." He leaned forward and smiled. "So many young women don't benefit from the kind of support your father gives you, Marissa."

His smile and backpedaling didn't disguise the contempt in his eyes, but she didn't want it to. Truly honest conversations were invariably limited to those with Arturo. Everyone else around her was too concerned with how their words and actions might be perceived by her father, making new friendships all but impossible to develop.

But her conversation with Luca had been honest, partly because Luca hadn't known who she was when they met but mostly because Luca didn't seem to have a disingenuous bone in her body, a quality Marissa hadn't experienced since her mamá was alive. Even Arturo lived in deceit, though that was from necessity rather than choice.

"Marissa?"

She looked up at Aguilar, realizing that their conversation had come to an abrupt halt. "My father is supporting me to serve his own agenda." She gathered her papers and stood. "If you'll excuse me, I have to get back to work." She turned at the door. "Thank you for checking in, Señor Aguilar. My father will appreciate it, I'm sure." She didn't wait to see how her words landed; he already knew he couldn't be complacent. *Everyone* was expendable and replaceable. Proving their worth to her father was a full-time occupation.

She checked in with Moreno before going to grab lunch. There was plenty of food in the office kitchen, but she wanted to make her monthly call to Carolina, her mamá's best friend. She wandered across the courtyard to the Virgin Mary fountain at its center and waved to Arturo, who was waiting in his car at the far end of the courtyard outside the office building. "Tía Carolina, qué tal?"

"Bien, bien," Carolina said. "Where are you? Are you sure it's safe?"

"I'm in the city. It's fine." Her mamá had wanted Carolina to play a far larger part in Marissa's life after she passed, but her father saw her presence as a threat and had forced her to leave the country. It was another thing to hate him for.

"Tell me."

Marissa smiled. She could always count on her tía to want a rundown of her life. She obliged, starting with the murder case and how every aspect of it went against every moral fiber in her body. What she really wanted to talk about was Luca, and it didn't take long to get there. When she'd finished telling Carolina about the injustice of it all, Carolina chuckled lightly.

"Oh, mija, your mamá would be so proud of the woman you have become."

Marissa sat on the wall of the fountain, and warmth flooded through her body. She dipped her fingers into the water, and its coolness caressed her skin. She closed her eyes and imagined it was the soothing touch of her mamá. "Do you really think so?"

"I know so, mija. You're always thinking of everyone else before yourself."

Marissa pulled her hand from the fountain and wiped it dry on her skirt, suddenly feeling unworthy of the imagined comfort. She wasn't putting Luca before her own needs. She was thinking of her, yes, but she'd already decided that she was unable to really help her if she wanted to stick to her plans with Arturo. She squeezed her eyes shut, praying for her mamá's guidance. Did her own happiness and freedom mean that she wasn't able to do *anything* for Luca?

She hadn't answered Luca when she'd asked for her assistance; she simply let her retract the request immediately. And when Luca had selflessly asked about Marissa's own desires to escape her father, she'd been cowardly and run away. No, she hadn't conducted herself in any way that warranted her mamá's pride. "I wish I could do more. I promised

Mamá I would make her proud, but I don't know if I can do enough to make a difference."

"Even small things can make a big difference, mija," Carolina said. "You bring those baskets to the workers every day. That's something your mamá would have done if she'd still been here."

Marissa scoffed. "Mamá wouldn't have let him exploit those people at all. She wouldn't need to bring food and soap, because he would still be paying people to work those fields like he did when she was alive." And then Luca would be following her dreams and living the life she'd earned instead of being imprisoned.

"You don't know that, mija. You put the weight of the world on your shoulders, and you're too young for that."

Marissa shook her head. She picked at a weed growing between the marble slabs of the fountain wall and scraped her nail polish. It should've bothered her, but she wanted her outward appearance to match the emerging ugliness inside. "No. There's no minimum age to begin caring for the people around you. He stopped paying the workers and began his slavery only a few years after Mamá died. Mamá would want me to stop him." Hot tears forced themselves to the back of her eyes, and she tipped her head back, trying to keep them from falling. "But I'm not strong enough, tía. I can't even get him to provide doctors for the sick. Mamá would be disappointed in me."

"Marissa, stop. Why are you being so hard on yourself? You've done so much for those people over the years, and you've fought your father every day to do that. You should be proud of that, and I know your mamá would be, no matter what you say."

Marissa sighed deeply and tried to gather herself. The sudden onset of self-pity had taken her by surprise, especially given that she was in public. She'd become used to keeping her emotions hidden so that she could battle her father. Within the four walls of her room was the only place she allowed them free rein. She knew the answer before she even asked herself what had changed. Luca Romero's presence on her father's compound had disturbed the steady equilibrium of her life and shifted her focus from her plans with Arturo. She needed to talk to him. She wanted to help Luca, more than she'd ever wanted to help any of the other imprisoned workers, and she had to find a way, or she might never forgive herself. There must be something she could do that wouldn't jeopardize her own bid for freedom.

"I don't understand my father," Marissa said, her reserve easing back into place. Part of her wanted to talk to Carolina about Luca, about why she felt so strongly that she had to help her, about the connection she was sure existed. But she couldn't. What she would sacrifice to have that conversation with her mamá instead. Anything in the world.

"Your father is a stain on humanity, and I don't know what Valentina ever saw in him, but I could never wish for her to not have met him or the world wouldn't have been blessed by you."

Her tía's words made her smile, despite the dilemma she faced. Carolina believed in her, just as her mamá had, and in a way, it was like a small piece of her mamá lived on in her best friend. That was both comforting and devastating. She wasn't alone in the world, but at the same time, she could never have more of her mamá than she'd already had. "Enough of me. Tell me what's happening in your life." Marissa shifted position and dipped her fingers back into the fountain, resolving to talk to Arturo. He would understand, she was sure. He had to.

Chapter Fifteen

CASEY STEPPED INTO A hazy smog that hid the autumn sun. She rolled her neck and put on sunglasses anyway to disguise her tired eyes. After an initial fast and furious fuck, Anastasia had returned to Casey's room once her shift had ended and picked up where they'd left off. Her first night in LA hadn't disappointed; she'd gotten very little sleep, but boy, it had been worth it. She gave a wide yawn that almost broke her jaw then focused on the white SUV parked in front of the hotel.

A woman in a black suit and white shirt stood beside the vehicle with the rear door open. "Ms. Graves," she said and gestured for her to get in. "I'm your driver. My name is Lou."

Given that she'd waited forty minutes for Casey to shower and dress, she seemed surprisingly laidback and unaffected. "Hey, Lou." Casey smiled and climbed into the back of the car. Lou closed the door gently. This was the kind of service Casey could get used to.

Lou got in and set off. "Help yourself to drinks and snacks." She pressed something on the dash, and a door slid open to reveal a fully stocked mini fridge in the center of the rear seat.

Casey looked over the contents and was immediately tempted by an ornate, blue glass bottle on the top shelf. A quick shot wouldn't hurt, and she had a pack of gum to freshen her breath and hide the smell of alcohol for her first meeting with her agent. She poured herself three fingers of the amber-colored liquor into a delicately bubbled tumbler. *My agent*. This whole situation was unreal, but with every minute that passed, she was settling into it. She'd done a horrible thing to get here, so not living life to its full potential would be an insult to Luca.

She took a hefty swig of the whiskey and briefly wondered how Luca was doing and if she'd even realized what Casey had done to her yet. Would she have worked it out if no one had told her? Probably not. Luca trusted her, which was stupid. One of the first things Casey had told Luca when they met was that she shouldn't trust anyone, and that she had to look out for herself because no one else in San Lucas would. Luca's life had been hard, and she'd spent it alone—she shouldn't have needed that warning.

But she didn't listen, and now she was paying the price while Casey reaped the rewards. It wasn't like Casey had planned this from the beginning. She'd been skeptical of Luca's ambitions and dreams. Who didn't want to escape their shit-ridden life of poverty? Casey had heard so many of her drug-running buddies talk about it, but no one had ever left. But when that email came in, and Luca shared it with her, Casey's own desperate desire to escape had taken over. She'd practically been on autopilot, barely thinking about the consequences and just focusing on her goal. How she got there was largely irrelevant. Who she hurt in the process was inevitable collateral damage.

She emptied the glass, relaxed back into the soft leather of her seat, and pushed away all thoughts of how Luca might be suffering on Vargas's compound. She didn't have the headspace for that. She had to concentrate on meeting Alyssa Dawes and selling herself as T.L. Graves, author of the Eternity Inc. series. She'd intended on skimming the books last night, but Anastasia's superior customer service had left her with no time. But Luca had subjected her to so many conversations about her books and characters that Casey could handle this initial meeting. Alyssa had read the books and wanted them, so Casey didn't really expect to have to talk about them much. She was more interested in how Alyssa would get them published.

Two months. Vargas hadn't given her long to make this happen, and there was no way she was heading back to Mexico with her tail between her legs. This was that rare once in a lifetime opportunity, and she wasn't about to waste it.

"Is this your first time in LA?" Lou asked.

"Yeah. Is it that obvious?"

Lou nodded. "You've got that wide-eyed look a lot of people have when they first get here. A lot of them end up working in bars and cafés waiting for their big break, but I hear you're already halfway there."

It seemed a little strange that the chauffeur would know her business, but she knew nothing about agents and how they worked. She had to let go of the mindset of how drug dealers operated and learn the ropes here. "I hope so. It's been a long time coming."

"I don't think you've got anything to worry about, Ms. Graves. Alyssa let me read your books when they came in—I'm playing with the idea of writing my own manuscript—and I loved them. It's like *American Gods* for lesbians! And your sarcastic humor is razor sharp."

"Thanks." She had no idea what the hell American Gods was, but Lou made it sound like it was a big deal. She pulled out her phone and googled it. What she read sounded weird and complicated.

"What inspired you to set the Eternity building in Santa Monica, out of all the cities in the States, or the world, even?"

"Come on, where else could it have been? That place is so recognizable and iconic for people all over the world, and it's been in almost all the movies that I grew up watching. I couldn't imagine setting it anywhere else." What kind of a name was Neil Gaiman? At least Luca had a decent pseudonym. She scrolled some pages and stopped at the one about that book being made into a three season TV series with a huge budget. If Alyssa got her a publishing deal, was it possible Luca's books could get the same kind of attention? Jesus.

Lou glanced in the rearview mirror and caught Casey's eye. "I can't believe this is really your first visit to LA. The way you described everything, it was like you'd grown up here and spent your childhood running barefoot along the Venice Beach sidewalks."

Casey thought back to the hours and hours of research Luca had done, all the googling and dropping the little figure onto the streets of Santa Monica. It had all been so time-consuming, though Casey had gotten excited when she'd seen Venice Beach, the place she'd always wanted to have her own bar. "It's all in the research, Lou. With Google Earth, and Google Maps, and all the videos that people post on YouTube and TikTok, it's easy to get a real sense of a place without ever having been there." Casey watched TikTok mainly for the thirst traps and huge amount of lesbian content, women stripping off their firefighting gear or doing quick changes into bondage gear. It had quickly overtaken Instagram to become her favorite method of peeking into a world she was desperate to become part of. And she'd taken a big drink of that world last night with Anastasia.

"Can I ask where you got the idea to base a trilogy on the three furies?" Lou asked.

Casey sighed. "Maybe later." When she'd actually read all three books and had run through all the conversations with Luca that she'd not fully tuned out of. There was probably something in her memory banks about Luca's inspiration. But she hoped Alyssa wouldn't be asking the same questions. "I didn't get much sleep last night, so it'd be great if I could close my eyes until we get to your office."

"Jet lag?"

Christ, why didn't she shut the fuck up? "Yeah, something like that." Casey removed her seatbelt and lay across the back seat, effectively ending the conversation. She closed her eyes. She *was* tired and a nap would be nice...

Someone shaking her shoulder woke her too soon from a very nice dream involving Marissa and Anastasia. She removed her sunglasses and opened her eyes to see Lou hovering over her.

"Jesus, you sleep like the dead," Lou said, releasing her shoulder. "We're here, and Alyssa is at the window if you want to give her a wave. You might want to straighten up a little before you get out of the car."

"Thanks." Casey looked down at herself. She made some minor adjustments, but it wasn't like she was going to a job interview. Writers weren't supposed to always be in a perfectly pressed suit, were they? She did need to go shopping though. Her wardrobe worked for her old life, not this one. Maybe Anastasia's customer service would extend to being her personal shopper.

She got out of the car and looked up. The skyscraper was forty floors at least, and the glass had a mirror effect. "Where is she?" Casey asked.

Lou laughed and closed the door. "I was just kidding. You wouldn't be able to see her if she was standing at the window. But you are late, so we should get you signed in and up to her office. Follow me."

Casey, seriously tempted to punch Lou in the back of the head for her irritating sense of humor, balled her fists and stuffed them in the pockets of her cargo pants. She took a quick look up and down the street, lined with similarly impressive buildings, and traced Lou's footsteps into the lobby. Three gorgeous women sat behind the desk receiving visitors, making Casey wonder if everyone in this town was movie star pretty, then she side-glanced at Lou and dismissed the idea. The sleek interior of the building was like nothing she'd ever seen before, far superior in design and elegance than even the best hotels back in San Lucas. Alyssa Dawes was clearly a big player to have offices here.

Lou signed her in and took her to the elevator. "The agency has the whole of the twenty-fifth floor." She leaned in when the doors opened and pressed the corresponding number. "Kate's expecting you. She'll be there to greet you and will take you to meet Alyssa—Ms. Dawes." She waited until Casey had stepped inside. "She's going to blow you away. Good luck. I'll be waiting down here to take you back to your hotel," she said as the doors closed.

Great. She couldn't wait. Maybe she'd walk back to the hotel and start to get to know the city instead of chancing another long journey with the chatty chauffeur. Until Casey was up to speed with Luca's books and had jotted down some of the shit she could remember Luca saying about her process and inspiration, it was better that she kept her interactions with nosey people to a minimum. Especially when those people were as annoying and bouncy as Lou.

The ride to the twenty-fifth floor took seconds, and when the doors opened, an average-looking woman smiled pleasantly at her.

"Ms. Graves?" she asked.

Casey stepped out of the elevator and shook her hand. "That's me."

"Welcome to Dawes, Rossi, and Decker. I'm Kate, Alyssa's personal assistant. If you'd like to follow me, I'll take you to a conference room."

"Thanks." Casey trailed alongside Kate and took in her surroundings. They passed several large offices, the walls of which were stacked with hundreds of books, and framed book covers covered the walls of the corridor.

Kate led her to a huge glass door at the end of the corridor and ushered her in. "Can I get you something to drink?"

Another glass of whatever smooth whiskey she'd had in Lou's SUV would be perfect, but she guessed that wasn't the kind of drink Kate expected her to ask for. "Black coffee, no sugar."

Kate gave a small nod before exiting quietly. She returned a few moments later and placed the cup on an agency coaster. "Alyssa will be with you shortly. She took a call since you weren't here on time."

Casey didn't miss the edge in Kate's voice though her expression betrayed no emotion. Maybe she should've said please when she ordered her drink. Or maybe she should've just been professional and arrived on time. It seemed like that might be important in a way it wasn't when she was a part-time bartender and drug-pusher. "I'm sorry I was late. I overslept. I only flew in yesterday and I've never flown before. I think the anticipation and a little bit of fear took it out of me." Appearing vulnerable occasionally was useful, even when it was a complete lie.

Kate's blank expression softened, and she smiled. "You've never flown before?"

"I've never even left my hometown," Casey said. "Driving to the airport was the furthest I'd gone until I got on the plane."

Kate raised her eyebrows. "Really?"

"Really. Can I tell you something?"

Kate nodded and took a step closer, clearly hooked and already forgiving Casey's behavior. "Of course. Anything."

Casey gestured around the plush meeting room. "This is all so overwhelming." She dug deep to channel Luca's pathetic innocence. "I never imagined that writing my books could lead to this." She turned full circle and laughed. "It's unreal, you know?"

Kate moved even closer and touched Casey's upper arm gently. "It's about to get very real, Ms. Graves. But we can help you cope with all of it. We're not your usual LA agency, out to make as much money as we can from authors and screenwriters and actors. We're as interested in the person as we are in what they write."

"That sounds amazing. All my friends said I had to be careful not to be taken for a ride." Casey gave her best version of Luca's awkward smile, the one she'd seen so many times when Luca was interested in a woman but too shy and self-doubting to do anything about it other than smile. She wasn't even sure it qualified as a smile. It was more of a squished-up grimace. Whatever it was, it hit the mark with Kate, and her expression turned sympathetic. She even tilted her head like she was looking at a beaten child.

"You're going to be really happy here, I guarantee it." Kate rubbed Casey's arm. "It'll soon feel like home."

She quashed a derisive laugh. What the hell did home feel like? If it was what she'd had as a child, she didn't want any part of it. People who'd had sweet, loving families threw around the word like it was easy to achieve and had no clue what someone like her had been through. But instead of risking alienating Kate again, Casey doubled down on her affected smile-grimace. "I hope so."

Kate's watch buzzed. She checked it and scrolled the message on the screen, but it was too small for Casey to see.

Kate sighed and looked reluctant to leave. "I have to attend to something. Will you be okay, or would you like something to read? Or I could turn on the TV." She pointed to the giant collection of nine screens that covered the end wall.

Casey turned to the view through the floor-to-ceiling windows. "I'm good with looking at this, thanks. It's going to take some getting used to." She was making herself nauseous with her performance but was also quietly amused at how easy it was to convince these people she was Luca. Innocent, unassuming Luca. It made Casey's skin itch like she was wearing a horse-hair suit.

"You're going to be fine, I promise." Kate gave her one last smile before leaving.

Casey stretched her arms and cracked her knuckles. Everything was going as smoothly as she'd hoped it would. She looked out across the city. Swarms of people looked like tiny ants on the sidewalk below, and the cars looked like toys. She realized she'd never been this high up in a building before and grinned. Everything felt perfect. She belonged here. Maybe Kate was right, and this place would soon feel like the home she'd never had.

The glass door swung open, and Casey jumped slightly.

"T.L. Graves," the woman said as she entered. "It's wonderful to finally meet the author of my favorite books of the decade. I'm Alyssa."

Casey walked swiftly back to greet her and held out her hand. Alyssa batted it away and drew her into a strong hug. Casey hadn't really had the time to picture what Alyssa might look like, but with everyone she'd met up until now, she might've expected her to be beautiful and in her mid-thirties. What she saw was a middle-aged woman with graying hair and a round, kind face. She looked like a caring mother: nurturing, sweet, and loving. The disconnect made her withdraw from the hug and take a step back.

"I'm really pleased to meet you, Alyssa," Casey said when she'd regained her composure.

"Before we sit and get to know each other," Alyssa motioned to a pile of paperwork on the glass table, "are you ready to sign a contract with me and let me help you become the most sought-after author in the Western Hemisphere?"

The woman was a whirlwind, and it was hard not to be swept up in her energy. Casey flicked through the stack of papers with no sense of purpose because she didn't understand any of the language. Marissa had approved the contract, and Vargas had given her two months to make this work. Hell, yes, she was ready. "Are you sure you can get me published?" She pictured the letters from publishers and agents Luca had pasted all over her walls. "I've had so many rejections."

Alyssa picked up the pen beside the paperwork and offered it to Casey. "Because you were on your way here to sign the contract, I got things moving even though it wasn't official yet. I've already got three of the big four in a bidding war for the book rights. By the end of this week, you'll have a publishing contract and worldwide distribution on the horizon."

Damn, this woman was impressive. Casey took the pen slowly, forcing herself not to snatch it. "By the end of this week?"

Alyssa patted the back of Casey's hand and nodded. "And that's not all. I have an agreement with the owner of FlatLine Studios, and he sees all the new manuscripts from authors I'm interested in representing. He wants a meeting to discuss purchasing the movie rights. Things *never* move this fast in publishing, but your books are a fantastic anomaly."

Casey raised her eyebrows and opened her mouth to say something but for once, she couldn't find the words. When she'd wondered about the possibility of a TV series, she hadn't given it serious thought. But a movie? That was almost beyond her understanding. How much more money would that mean? She wished that she'd just gotten rid of Luca herself, and then she wouldn't have to share any of this with Vargas. "That's... I can't thank you enough."

"I believe in you and your words, and a whole host of other people do as well." Alyssa pointed at the contract. "If that's enough to help you choose us to represent you, all you need to do is write your legal name and sign in all the blanks where the little stickies are and initial all the pages in the top corner—as long as you and your lawyer are happy with the terms."

Casey nodded slowly. "I had a lawyer friend check it over, and she said it was..." she searched for the legal term Marissa had used, "standard boilerplate or something like that. I'm just so excited that someone finally wants to publish it."

Alyssa leaned back in her chair, her expression honest and open. "I can tell you that all the agents you ever contacted are going to rue the day they ever rejected you. Your books are going to be huge." She touched Casey's arm as she began signing. "But are you sure your friend knows entertainment law? I don't want you signing a contract you don't understand and might not be happy with."

Casey smiled. Alyssa was the total opposite of everything she expected in a Hollywood agent. Her point of reference was movies, but still. Casey had been prepared to be surrounded by... well, by people like herself, people who would sacrifice their firstborn child for success. Luca wasn't her kid, but she was the closest she had to family. "I'm happy. Trust me, I'm happy." She flicked the papers over to the first marker and filled in the details.

Alyssa peered over her shoulder. "Casey Soto. That's a great name. Why use a pseudonym?"

Shit. Luca had been convinced her Mexican name had been a barrier, but Casey's first name was an American one she'd chosen and had changed legally. "I thought it might be more mysterious and intriguing. That's stupid, isn't it?"

"Of course not. There are lots of reasons to use a pen name, and that one is as good as any other." Alyssa poured herself some water while Casey worked her way through the contract. "I have one final piece of fabulous news."

What else could there be? "Okay."

"Have you heard of Elodie Fontaine?" Alyssa asked.

Alyssa's eyes twinkled, and her huge smile revealed perfectly straight, white teeth. Casey ran her tongue over her top teeth. She would soon be able to afford to have them straightened. With a bright new smile and a healthy checking account, Marissa wouldn't be able to resist her. "I've been living in Mexico, not under a rock," Casey said, and Alyssa frowned briefly, clearly puzzled at the change in her tone. So playing the role of herself wouldn't work here. She'd have to add more Luca to her performance, weak and needy. "I mean, who hasn't heard of her?" she asked, saccharine sweet. "*Night Deeds*, and *A Glass Heart's Requiem*. And she's amazing in the new 007 movie. You can't tell she's American, her British accent is so perfect."

"Then you'll be happy to hear that she's read your books and is interested in playing Caletho."

Casey rocked back in her chair. Was all this really happening? "Would I be able to meet her?" She knew Elodie had supposedly settled down with someone, but how could a woman *that* sexual be satisfied with one lover? Casey bet she still had plenty of onset affairs.

"If we negotiate a deal with FlatLine, you'll do more than meet her. Jules, the studio owner, and Elodie have already said they'd want you to write the screenplay if they get the rights. You'd be on set during filming every day for potential rewrites." Alyssa smiled and rubbed her hands together. "I said you were going to be huge, and I meant it. After I read the books, I started getting everyone whose opinion I trust to read them too. We're off and running in a way I haven't experienced in years. We still have edits and such to work through, but you're in the big game now."

Casey dropped the pen, and though Alyssa continued to speak, her words didn't reach Casey's ears. It was as if her senses disappeared from her body, and she was in a vacuum. Terror gripped her throat. She couldn't do edits. She couldn't write the screenplay. She didn't know the first thing about what it might take to turn Luca's hundreds of thousands of words into a two-hour movie. She'd be found out, and everything she'd hoped for, this amazing life she'd already settled into, would be taken away from her, and she would have no choice but to run as far away from Vargas as she could. Everything she'd worked to achieve would be gone. Selling out Luca would have been a waste of time.

No. She took a deep breath and focused. Luca was still alive. *She* could write the screenplay and do the edits. That had been the whole point of keeping her alive, right? She could be on the end of a phone at Vargas's compound for any rewrites during filming too. Alyssa's voice drifted back into her awareness as Casey began to form a new plan. Luca still had a purpose to serve. If Alyssa's enthusiasm was matched in dollars, there'd be more than enough to satisfy Vargas's greed. She wasn't about to let her dream go so easily. She couldn't. Marissa wouldn't want to be with a failure, and she was a big part of Casey's new life, even though she didn't know it yet.

But she would. And with Marissa by her side, she would be complete.

Chapter Sixteen

LUCA BACKED AWAY FROM the melee before she became completely overwhelmed. Each person was as hungry as the next, but the food they'd been given was barely enough for half of them to have a decent serving. She'd naively assumed Vargas would provide adequate supplies to keep his free workforce healthy. A few days in had disabused her of that notion. The same meager portions of rice and beans were handed out from their dwindling monthly supply, and when they weren't working, a trusted few of Epi's friends had to guard their rations to stop desperate women from stealing it for themselves.

"There are two types of people in here, chica. Those who want to look after everyone, and those who want to look after themselves."

Epi's words were easily applicable to the world outside their prison compound. If Casey had been here, she'd try to steal food to satisfy her own needs just as she'd stolen Luca's life. Luca was still angry with herself for being taken in by Casey's talk of chosen family and brotherhood. Being alone and relying only on herself had worked all her life. She'd made an exception with Casey, and it was now clear where trust led.

She sat on a bench and leaned back to watch the disappearing sunset over the blue fan palm trees. The sky looked bruised, much like her heart felt. Up to now, she'd always enjoyed being in the sun. The warmth of its touch on her skin was something she treasured. But after days of being exposed to endless hours without shade, its appeal was fading, and this time of day was rapidly becoming her favorite. It was also the only moment of rest from the constant cycle of sleep, work, eat. This was poverty and deprivation on a new level, and nothing was under her control.

She became aware of the faint smell of her stale sweat and headed for the shower. It might have the added benefit of taking her mind off her growling stomach. She filled the bucket, took off her tank top and shorts, and pulled the rope. The slow trickle of cool water hit the top of her head, and she closed her eyes and leaned against the wooden pole, enjoying the solitude and peace.

There was a small cough behind her, and she turned, expecting that Epi or maybe Gloria had come to check on her. She had no idea why they'd taken it upon themselves to look after her, but she was quietly grateful. That didn't mean she was about to start trusting any of them, but it did make her feel less isolated in her desperation.

Marissa. Luca turned away quickly. She'd just about gotten used to being near naked in front of the other women but being caught with only her briefs on by Marissa was a whole world away from her comfort zone. "I'm sorry. I won't be long," she said.

"No, no. I'm sorry. I didn't realize you'd be showering. I shouldn't have disturbed you."

"It's okay. I'm done." Luca glanced over her shoulder. Marissa looked flushed and embarrassed, but she also looked a little guilty, like she'd been caught doing something she shouldn't. How long had she been standing there before she made her presence known? Luca half-smiled and wondered if Marissa liked what she saw. Reality kicked in. Luca was kidding herself that someone like Marissa would have even a passing interest in her.

"Did you need something?" Luca secured the rope back to the post and realized she hadn't planned on showering so didn't have a towel. She grabbed her tank top and pulled it on with difficulty over her damp skin before turning to face Marissa.

"Nothing specific. I had some time—and some meat." Marissa raised a bag in the air. "I hope I haven't missed dinner."

Luca tugged on her shorts quickly and shook her head. "I'm not sure you'd call what's happening over there 'dinner,' but it's still in progress. It's too hectic for me, so I took a spa shower." She gestured to the rudimentary set-up, surprised at her own humor. She didn't want to get so comfortable here that it was okay to make jokes about the terrible conditions.

"How are you doing with everything?" Marissa asked and sat on one of the nearby benches.

Luca dropped onto one opposite. "Not great, but I'm surviving." She looked beyond Marissa to the isolation barn. "Unlike Cedro. He passed yesterday." Her attempts at nursing had failed. She couldn't get him to eat or drink anything, and his delirium had just gotten worse and worse. She hadn't been there to hear the last whisper of breath rattle from his mouth and for that, she felt she'd failed. No one should die alone.

"I'm sorry to hear that."

Luca noticed her twisting a ring on her finger and was struck with a jab of envy. When they'd spoken a year ago, Marissa hadn't mentioned anything about dating or love, and Luca hadn't noticed the ring, though she'd been too focused on her face. But it was clear from the way she touched the delicate band of jewelry that she cared deeply for the person who'd given it to her. As ridiculous as the thought was, Luca wanted to be that person. "One of the guards told me you're trying to get medical help for the workers here." She didn't want to say "for us" because she was nowhere near ready to accept that she was one of them.

Marissa raised her eyebrow. "They shouldn't have told you that."

Luca was glad she hadn't said who it was. Getting Jorge into trouble and kicked off this duty would narrow her options for escape even more, though they were already slim, and he'd seemed to avoid her since they'd brought Cedro to the isolation barn.

Marissa reached across the small gap between their benches and gently touched Luca's knee. "It's not a problem. I just didn't want Epi and everyone else to get their hopes up. I don't like to make promises I'm not certain I'll be able to keep."

Luca glanced at Marissa's hand on her leg, and she pulled it away. It didn't mean anything. "I get it. I won't say anything."

"Has Cedro been taken away?" Marissa asked.

Luca shook her head. "He was still there when I checked after coming back from the fields an hour ago." She closed her eyes briefly and tried to shake away the image of a dozen rats on his body gnawing at his wrinkled, sun-charred skin. And the smell that struck her nostrils was a thousand times worse than the stench of the isolation barn when she and Jorge had put Cedro in there.

"Is it the first time you've seen...a dead body?"

Luca opened her eyes. "Yeah. But I've got a feeling it won't be the last. Unless you manage to do something about it."

Marissa played with her ring again and glanced away. "Father can be incredibly stubborn. He doesn't want to acknowledge the possibility that spending the money on medicines and doctors would keep people alive and working for him." She raised her chin and her nostrils flared. "Once people are in these barns, they stop being people to him. I hate it."

"So do I."

Marissa rolled her eyes and touched Luca's knee again. "I'm sorry. You're suffering because of him. I should shut up about how it affects me when I get to live the way I do." She picked up her bag again and stood. "I should get this to Epi before it's too late."

Luca rose too and risked a small touch to Marissa's back before she walked away. "I don't want you to shut up. It's nice that you care at all."

Marissa turned and gave Luca an intense stare that almost melted her away. There were mere inches between them, and Luca could smell Marissa's sweetly perfumed scent. How easy it would be to slip her hand around Marissa's neck and pull her close, press her lips to Marissa's and show her what she felt, what she'd been feeling since they'd first talked on the beach for hours. Marissa's pupils dilated, and she bit her lip. Was this real, or was Luca dreaming all of it? It was foolish beyond belief to want the daughter of her captor.

A loud click caught Luca's attention and broke her focus. She glanced over Marissa's shoulder to see one of Vargas's henchmen standing fifty yards away. She hadn't spotted him before, but she should've expected his presence. Marissa never seemed to go anywhere unaccompanied. Luca took a step back, her hands in plain sight.

Marissa blinked. "Let's take this to Epi."

She led her back to the group around the corner. When they got closer to the open fire, Marissa made her way through the crowd to Epi. Luca followed, not because she was going to help cook, but because she wanted to stay close to Marissa. She'd spent almost a year waiting for another opportunity to talk to her again, and now Marissa was coming to her. It was far from ideal that it had taken Casey's betrayal to bring them together, but Luca wanted to make the most of a bad situation. Plus, Marissa was the only way Luca could get an audience with Vargas.

Gloria shifted to make room for Luca, and she took a seat within a few feet of the fire. Epi took the bag from Marissa and looked inside before she thanked her over and over. Luca was close enough to see Epi's eyes tear up, but she sniffed them back and didn't release them.

Epi beckoned Luca. "Come and chop this meat for the pot."

Luca didn't question why Epi would choose her for the task over the ten other women close by and simply joined them. She positioned herself on a flat rock and began to slice the flesh into the smallest chunks she could to make the most of it.

"Good, good. Perfect." Epi placed a large pot in front of Luca. "Put it in here when you've chopped it."

Luca fell into a kind of meditation as she sliced through the meat and listened to the intense conversation between Epi and Marissa. She was struck by how they spoke as equals when in reality, the power imbalance couldn't be any more pronounced. Occasionally, Luca would look up to locate Marissa's guard. He moved around, but he was never far away. He looked alert but not concerned, and Luca thought she could see a gentle kindness in his expression that was lacking in every other guard on the compound, even Jorge.

Marissa, however, never once took her attention from the deep discussion with Epi. She laughed, smiled, and gently touched Epi as though she was her abuela. She made it seem like they were just a group of women who'd chosen to come together and make dinner outside instead of Marissa being the daughter of the man who held their lives for ransom.

Luca finished the meat and gave the pot to Epi.

Marissa moved to a stone next to Luca. "Epi says that you're doing the work of three people in the fields. She's impressed."

Luca shrugged. "It's no big deal. I don't really do anything slowly." And she'd seen the way the guards beat anyone who didn't work as fast as they wanted them to. She didn't want to be on the receiving end of that wrath. "And if I'm working as fast as I can, all my concentration is on that instead of thinking about Casey in LA with *my* books and *my* agent."

Marissa edged close enough that Luca felt the warmth of her skin against her thighs, still cool from the shower.

"We should talk about that. But not here."

Luca thought of Epi's words about the two types of people she was surrounded by. Clearly, Marissa was aware of it too and didn't trust everyone who might overhear their conversation. "Can we go back to the benches and talk there?" If the opportunity to talk to Marissa about getting out of this place was now, she didn't want to let it pass her by. Vargas could rescind his permission allowing Marissa to visit them at any moment, and that would leave Luca adrift in her sea of misery and broken dreams.

Marissa nodded, and as she rose, took Luca's hand and pulled her to her feet. Luca glanced toward Marissa's guard, but he seemed unaffected by their closeness. Marissa didn't let go of Luca's hand as they wound their way back through the crowd of women too hungry to notice them, and Luca was unreasonably comforted by the continued contact. They sat on the benches, and Luca again chose to sit opposite Marissa, mainly so that she could stare at her while they talked.

"I want to help you," Marissa whispered. "But I'm not sure what I can do." She looked back in the direction of the chattering women. "And we have to be careful. Some of these women will use any information they can to trade with my father and shorten their time here." She tilted her head slightly. "I can't blame them. I can't even begin to imagine what you're all going through, and good people can be driven to do bad things in these conditions. But still, what we talk about must stay between just you and me."

"You don't trust Epi?" Luca asked, confused by their apparent closeness and this request to freeze her out.

"I do. But I don't want to involve her and risk anything happening to her because of it."

Luca's pulse raced. "Like what? What are you suggesting we do?" The possibility of an aided escape terrified her and gave her hope at the same time. If that was her only option though, she'd get on board with it because she couldn't face any kind of existence here.

"I don't know yet. But it's better that we don't pull anyone into this that doesn't need to be involved."

Luca flicked her eyes toward Marissa's ever-present guard, though he remained far enough away that he couldn't possibly hear their whispered conversation.

"Don't worry about Arturo." Marissa had clearly caught Luca's concern. "He's been my best friend since we were six years old." She looked over her shoulder and smiled.

Luca saw the deep affection Marissa had for him. "Does he work for you or for your father?"

"My father's been grooming him to help me run the business for years."

"But that's not what you want to do, is it?" Luca wanted to hear more about Marissa's plans and dreams. But when she'd tried to ask a couple of days ago, Marissa had promptly left without responding. Luca didn't want to lose their tenuous connection by prying into Marissa's personal life. She reasoned that Marissa had been open with her before. Why wouldn't she talk to her now, especially if Arturo was on her side?

"You remember?"

The intensity of Marissa's gaze made Luca feel like she was the only person in the world at that moment. She supposed Epi had the same experience when they'd been talking. Marissa seemed to have a natural talent for making people feel like they were her top priority, which Luca wanted to be, even if it was only to help her escape. "Of course I do. I don't have a lot of engaging, five-hour long conversations with intelligent and sober people." She wanted to say that it had been one of the best conversations of her whole life with the most beautiful woman she'd ever met, but that was stupid. "I had no idea who you were, and I think that's why you talked to me so openly. Now that my life has crashed into yours, I think that's why you practically ran away the other day when I mentioned it. Am I close to the truth?"

Marissa nibbled her bottom lip and didn't respond immediately. "You could be, though I think you're misremembering my sobriety. The alcohol got me talking, but your gentleness kept me there all afternoon."

Marissa's loneliness was so palpable, Luca could almost touch it. She wrapped her arms around herself to keep from pulling Marissa into an embrace she probably didn't want. Marissa needed a friend far more than she needed a lover. Not that Luca could ever truly be either, obviously. "You seemed so isolated."

Marissa looked down at her hand and twisted her ring. "My father has so much influence in this city, it's hard to know who to trust. Arturo is the only person who knows how unhappy I am here, and he shares that with me. Neither of us want this life, but we're trapped."

Luca's heart sank as she heard the subtext of what Marissa was saying; she and Arturo were more than just best friends, and they wanted to escape the clutches of her father to pursue a life together. The ring Marissa always played with was most likely a gift from him and a symbol of the life they dreamed of. "Have you told your father you don't want any part of the family business?"

Marissa leaned closer, then paused. "Repeatedly. But he still tries to marry me off to one drug lord or another every few months."

She placed her hand on Luca's knee and squeezed gently. Luca tensed. What she'd thought might be a tender touch was just Marissa being tactile and affectionate. Holding hands had been nothing more than a gesture of friendship. Luca resolved to push away her attraction and focus on getting to Vargas and renegotiating. She had more books in her head. Casey could only live on Luca's talent until the trilogy was published. Then her usefulness to Vargas would expire. But Luca could offer him a percentage of her earnings for more novels. She could only hope that his greed would outweigh any loyalty he felt toward Casey.

"But I shouldn't be going on about my situation when yours is so much worse." Marissa gave a sad smile and took her hand away.

Luca shrugged. "We're both trapped in different ways, and we don't need to compare. I do have a favor to ask you though, if you don't mind?"

"Go ahead."

"I need to talk to your father. I have to offer him a better deal than he's getting through Casey."

Marissa frowned. "You shouldn't try to bargain with him. You'll—"

"My life can't get any worse, Marissa. I have to try." Once again, Luca resisted the temptation to reach out for her. She'd only be torturing herself. "Will you help me?"

Marissa ran her hand through her hair. Luca had seen her do it so many times and always wondered what it might be like to run her own fingers through Marissa's long, dark curls. They looked so soft and bouncy to the touch. The thought of Marissa draping her hair over Luca's naked body made her shiver, and gooseflesh erupted all over her skin.

"I want to, I do, but—"

"Then please help me. You're my only hope of not rotting away here." Who said a little hope was a dangerous thing? There was also something incredibly powerful in it. Without hope, she may as well resign herself to this fate and fade away to nothingness, but she wouldn't do that. She wouldn't let Casey get away with stealing the life she'd earned. "Epi says you've visited the women here almost every day since your father fired his paid workers and brought in people who owed him money or favors. Why do you do it?"

"Because I hate what he's doing, and my mamita would hate it too."

Marissa's lip and chin trembled slightly, and she looked away. The urge to sit beside her and wrap her arms around her was strong, but Luca pressed her ass to the hard wooden bench and didn't move. She hated to upset Marissa by bringing up her mother, but Luca needed her to do more than bring them extra food. "You've been doing it for years, and nothing's changed. But you could change my life if you do this for me." Luca dropped from the bench and squatted in front of Marissa. "I'm begging you. I can't do this—I can't stand being kept here while Casey is in LA living my life." In her peripheral vision, she saw Arturo twitch as if he might come toward them, but he didn't move forward.

Marissa sighed deeply. "Please don't get on your knees." She stood and pulled Luca to her feet. "I'll talk to my father, but I can't make any promises."

Luca released her hands. It had been a while since she'd been with a woman, but that wasn't what this was about. Her connection with Marissa was deeper, more visceral than the need for physicality. But it wasn't reciprocated, and she had to put it out of her mind and concentrate on getting out of here. Was she making a mistake in trusting Marissa, someone she barely knew? She'd known Casey for years and thought she knew her well. This could turn out even worse if she was wrong. "I'm not asking you to promise anything, Marissa. I just need an audience with him, that's all. I know the rest is up to me."

Marissa nodded and glanced toward Arturo. He tilted his head slightly, and Luca registered his look of concern. No doubt he was wondering what Marissa had agreed to do after Luca had gotten to her knees. If she were in his position, and Marissa loved her like she clearly loved him, she would move mountains to get Marissa away from her father. He was slowly crushing her spirit and killing her, and Luca would do anything to stop that happening.

Marissa looked back at Luca. "I'll talk to my father in the morning, and I'll let you know as soon as I can if he agrees to meet with you." She placed her hand on Luca's shoulder. "I'll do my best, that I can promise. You don't deserve this, Luca. None of these women should be here, but at least they made a choice and got something from it for their family. You've been betrayed and stripped of everything."

Luca felt her own chin begin to tremble. The empathy in Marissa's eyes was too much to bear, as was the desire to press her face into Marissa's neck and draw strength from her comforting embrace. She drew an image of Casey to mind to refocus on her rage and imagined what she might do to her when or if they crossed paths again. "I'll wait. I trust you." Her choice of words surprised her, and she wasn't entirely certain she believed them. But she wasn't made of stone, and Marissa's actions spoke loudly.

Marissa looked at her searchingly. "How can you trust anyone after what Casey did to you?"

"Honestly, I don't know." Luca took a step back, and Marissa's hand dropped from her shoulder. Being this close to her was almost painful. "I'd never really trusted anyone before Casey, and I thought I'd never trust anyone again. But there's something about you, Marissa, something special. You're not like anyone I've ever met before."

Arturo's phone buzzed and illuminated where he stood. Luca was so engrossed in their conversation that she'd barely noticed the last of the daylight disappear.

"Marissa," he said. "It's time to go."

His voice was far gentler than Luca had imagined, but then she wouldn't have expected Marissa to get involved with some gruff and aggressive henchman-type. As he drew closer, she saw a soft kindness in his eyes that strangely pleased her. She couldn't stand the thought of Marissa with anyone who didn't cherish her.

Marissa looked between Arturo and Luca and seemed to hesitate. Did she want to stay? Luca was torn between wanting the same thing but also needing Marissa to leave. Her stomach grumbled loudly, and Luca clutched her hand to it, embarrassed at its volume.

"Sounds like you need something to eat," Marissa said and laughed.

Goddammit, why did she have to be so beautiful? And her smile... Luca could happily spend forever watching Marissa's face light up like that. "I guess so."

"I'll see you soon."

Luca nodded and began to back away. She pressed her hands together. "Thank you," she said and turned away. It took every fiber of her resolve not to turn back to see if Marissa was watching her leave, or if she'd already been tugged away by Arturo. And she didn't want to see him pull her into his arms either; she'd be tormented by that mental image all night anyway.

She turned the corner of the barn, and the scent of Epi's cooking flooded her nostrils, reminding her of the food the orphanage used to serve. Being here among all these women had dragged back many unpleasant memories from that time, memories she'd fought long and hard to suppress. She kicked out at the barn, and her foot went through the rotten wood. "¡Mierda!" She pulled it out and brushed away the blood from the light scratches on her leg. She'd never been a violent person, even when she'd been subjected to violence as a child, but her anger toward Casey was building with every second she was forced to spend in this decrepit, rat-infested compound. Luca had just said that she trusted Marissa, but really, how could she ever trust her own instincts again after being so easily duped by Casey?

She picked up her pace and headed toward the glowing fire. The evening had chilled considerably after the sun had set, making Luca shiver. The dancing flames promised a welcome heat. She'd get something to eat, go to bed, and pray to a god she didn't believe in to influence Vargas to meet her.

And she'd pray even harder to get her ever-present thoughts of Marissa out of her mind.

Chapter Seventeen

MARISSA'S ALARM WOKE HER from a dream she didn't want to emerge from. She'd only just gotten to the part where she was kissing Luca's naked skin as they showered together. She began to circle her clit. She closed her eyes and went back to the previous evening when she'd seen Luca almost naked. She'd guiltily watched her for a minute before making her presence known. She may have waited longer had it not been for Arturo's amused and questioning look. This time, she imagined they were alone, and Marissa took her time to kiss every inch of Luca's clear skin. She wasn't ripped or toned, but there was a strength about her physique that made Marissa imagine Luca carrying her upstairs to her bed, laying her down on the soft, silk sheets, and making love to her until she cried out for her to stop.

Arturo's coded knock jerked her from the fantasy.

"Go away."

"Your father wants to see you," he said, his voice muffled through the door.

She reluctantly withdrew her hand from between her legs and pushed off the covers. "And I want to see him, but not until I've showered, dressed, and had two cups of coffee."

"You handle the first two and if you open the door, you'll see that I've got your third demand covered. A fresh cup of vanilla and macadamia right here."

She sniffed the air for her favorite brew. "Are you lying? I can't smell it."

He tapped the door again. "This is seriously thick wood, Marissa. And when have I lied to you?"

She had to give him that, though he was often economical with details to protect them both. She didn't want to know what her father made him do, and he didn't want to relive his actions. "Leave it outside and tell Father I'll be there in an hour."

"He wants to see you now. Casey Soto is on the phone from LA."

Marissa jumped up from her bed, crossed the room, and pulled the door open. "She's on the phone now?"

Arturo looked startled then turned his head to stare down the corridor. "Um, yes. She's talking to him now." He thrust the breakfast tray toward her. "Clothes would be a really good next step."

Marissa gasped as she realized she was completely naked. She laughed and took the coffee. "Sorry," she whispered. "I forgot. It got unusually hot in here last night." Unusual because she couldn't remember the last time that she'd had a sexual dream about anyone real. "Tell Father I'll be there in five minutes." She pushed the door with her foot, and Arturo clicked it closed.

She threw on a pair of linen pants and a silk blouse, picked up the cup of coffee, and opened the door. Arturo waited in the corridor for her.

He narrowed his eyes. "Why the big rush?"

She walked past him and didn't make eye contact. He knew her too well for her to lie to his face. "It doesn't hurt to do as Father asks occasionally, does it?"

He caught up to her quickly. "Is your enthusiasm something to do with your new butch friend at the barns?"

"Would you call her butch?" Marissa stopped to take a sip of coffee but still didn't look at him. "And I have lots of friends at the barn."

"She's got short hair, wears baggy jeans, and has that indefinable swagger that seems to come from somewhere in her soul. Yes, I'd call her butch."

"I think you're stereotyping."

"And I think you're being evasive." Arturo caught her arm. "You have to be even more careful than before, Marissa," he whispered. "We're too close to our goal to risk getting involved with something you can't do anything about."

She stopped at the top of the staircase. "Maybe I can do something about it without affecting us. I want to talk to you about it, but not here."

"Marissa."

She ignored the caution and concern in his voice. "It's going to be fine, primo. Don't panic. Nothing has to change for us, I promise."

"You know I trust you, but—"

"There's no but if you trust me." Marissa pulled her arm away and continued to her father's office.

Arturo caught up with her. "You're right. I'm sorry," he whispered. "When do you want to talk?"

"Soon. Perhaps on our way to the office next week."

He shook his head. "The whole fleet has been bugged. It was a new directive from your father last week."

"Why didn't you tell me? Is this so he can spy on me?"

"No, it's not for you, I promise." He shrugged. "He seems to be getting more and more paranoid. You're rejecting all the families he wants to make alliances with, and he's concerned they're going to form an alliance and turn on him."

"And you didn't think to tell me about this?"

Arturo rolled his eyes. "There didn't seem much point. It's not as though you'll change your mind and marry the next guy he shoves in front of you, is it?"

"Of course not." She stopped again at the top of the corridor leading to her father's office. "Does he have genuine cause for concern?" If other families planned to move against him, she hoped it wouldn't be before they'd had the chance to escape.

"Maybe. It's hard to get solid information, and he has no real evidence. It's more of a feeling, and I haven't found or heard anything to prove his theories other than whispered threats. There's nothing different from the usual battles he has to fight daily."

"Is he losing his grip on reality?" she asked. "It can't be the pressure of the business. He's been doing this too long to be bothered by vague rumors."

He shook his head. "I don't know. But he's worried enough to have initiated an increase in security protocols, and that includes having all the vehicles fitted with listening devices."

Marissa held her fingers to her mouth. "And the house?" She and Arturo had been careful when and where they'd discussed their plans, but they often had whispered conversations like this.

"Clear. For now." He ran his hand across his stubbled chin. "But no one's safe."

She waited for more, but he seemed to have censored himself. "What do you mean?"

He swallowed hard, and she recognized the look in his eyes. She'd seen it too many times. He'd done so many things he couldn't forget, and she hoped that a new country and their fresh start might allow him to push away those memories to make room for new and happier ones.

"You don't want to know, Marissa. Trust me." He wrung his hands as if that might wipe away whatever he'd had to do with them.

Her throat tightened, and she could barely squeeze the question out. "Who?"

"Santiago."

Her knees almost gave way beneath her, and she had to steady herself against the wall. Santiago had been her mamita's trusted guard in much the same way as Arturo was Marissa's. He had also been with the family from the beginning, and he'd been like a father to Arturo. He reached out, and she allowed him to wrap his arms around her.

"When did this happen?" she whispered into the soft cotton of his shirt.

"Two days ago."

She heard the catch in his voice as he tried desperately to control his sorrow. Whatever fate her father had decided for Santiago, he'd forced Arturo to carry it out. His heart thudded against her ear, and her heart broke for him. How had he managed to hold himself together since? They hadn't spent much time together in the past couple of days because of her work and her visits to the barns, but she hated that he hadn't come to her. "Why didn't you tell me?"

"I couldn't... I can't talk about it. I can't think—"

She hugged him tighter and felt him fight the threat of heaving sobs.

He stepped back, his mask firmly back in place. "Please don't."

Marissa sighed and nodded. He couldn't be seen to show any emotion beyond the confines of his quarters or her room. Seeing him like this, seeing him lose pieces of his humanity and now his chosen family, ripped her apart. Now more than ever, especially if her father was losing control, they had to get out of here.

But first, she had to try to help Luca. "Let's go." She got to her father's office, knocked and entered without waiting to be beckoned. She left the door open and heard Arturo close it softly behind them.

"Ah, my beautiful daughter. Thank you for coming so quickly." He rose from behind the desk and came around to embrace her.

She allowed it but pulled away after the briefest of contact. "Arturo said Casey Soto called. Is there a problem?" Marissa so wished he would nod and say that he was sending someone to bring Soto back from LA.

That something had gone wrong, and he was releasing Luca.

"Far from it." He smiled widely before returning to his seat.

She noticed he was slightly unsteady on his feet. She thought she'd smelled alcohol, but she'd assumed it was on his clothes. Perhaps it had been his breath. She scanned the surface of his desk. A half-empty glass of dark liquid sat beside his cigar box.

"Sit."

She took a seat, trying hard to hide how eager she was to find out why Soto had called. She'd never shown any interest in his dealings before, so he'd be suspicious of her motives if she asked too many questions now. It was notable how quickly she'd responded to his summons, but he made no comment.

He pressed the screen of his cellphone. "Soto, are you still there?"

"Sí, señor."

Marissa clenched her jaw at the sound of Soto's voice almost as if Soto had wronged her and not Luca.

"Marissa is here. Tell us again why you're calling," her father said.

"My agent has sold the books to Simon & Schuster," Soto said.

My agent? The woman had no shame. She didn't have to continue her vile charade for their benefit. Her father looked at her like he was expecting her to show some excitement. She maintained a passive expression when what she wanted to do was reach down the phone and scratch Soto's eyes out.

"That's good news, Marissa, yes?" He patted a pile of papers at the edge of his desk. "This is the contract they're offering. It's better than we hoped for, but that's not the best of it. Soto, continue."

"Alyssa is in talks with FlatLine Studios for the movie rights to the books, and that's where I need your help, Marissa."

Marissa clenched her toes and fought against speaking her mind. Who was Soto to speak to her as if they were friends or even colleagues? Every time Soto had approached her at the bar when she'd gone there to seek out Luca, Marissa had made it clear she wanted nothing to do with her. Soto's persistence wasn't admirable; it was creepy and stalker-like. "I don't see how I can help with anything beyond the contract." She mentally reprimanded herself. She'd promised Luca that she'd help her. How better to do that than to stay on the inside of whatever this was? "Perhaps you could explain?"

Her father smiled at her addition. Was he so easily fooled to think that she suddenly cared about his business?

"The studio head and the actress who will play one of the lead characters want me to write the screenplay, and the publisher wants me to work on edits for the books," Soto said. "Obviously I have no idea how to do that. I know the books better now after reading them, but I can't do what they need me to do."

Marissa uncurled her toes and barely kept from smiling. They needed Luca. Everything would fall through without her. "I'm a lawyer, Casey. I can't write a screenplay or edit books either."

Soto laughed. "Sure, I know that. But Luca is still alive, isn't she? She can do it."

The throwaway nature of her question brought bile rushing to Marissa's throat. Soto's betrayal of Luca had been complete, but was it really so easy to think about her already being dead from her ordeal? "What makes you think Luca will agree to do this?"

Soto laughed even harder. "She doesn't have a choice. Your father has very persuasive ways of making people do what he wants."

That was probably the truest thing that had ever passed Soto's lips.

"And besides, she likes you. She'll do it if you ask her, and then Señor Vargas doesn't have to hurt her. Either way, she ends up doing what we need her to."

There was something about the way Soto said that Luca *liked* Marissa that was coded for her understanding only. Was it true? Did Luca like her in that way? If it was, she had to keep that information from her father. He had no tolerance for what he viewed as "against God." And she suspected that it wouldn't matter how much money he was making from this deal, if he found out Luca had feelings for Marissa, he'd kill her with his own hands.

"Don't sign anything. Marissa will be in touch when she lands."

Her father hung up, and Marissa stared at him. "When I land where?"

"I want you to go to LA and meet with her agent and the studio people. Make sure we get the best deal. Soto has ambition but she doesn't have the brains to pull this off, and I don't want her blowing it."

Her father's enthusiasm for what Marissa saw as only a side hustle confused her. Did his paranoia—if that's what it was—have him looking for a potential escape route? It wasn't like him to be so blasé about her being so far away. "You don't think that can be achieved without me going all the way to LA?"

He shook his head. "I don't. They're probably already thinking they can take advantage because Soto is one of us. We need to make a show of force."

She raised her eyebrow. "This isn't one of your cartel takeovers, Father. They're just agents and studio heads."

"Agents are sharks out for what they can get. And the studio will want to pay as little as they can to make maximum profit. Books and movies are drugs just like the ones we produce, and the business can be just as brutal."

There was so much wrong with that, Marissa didn't know where to start. She doubted there were many murders when studio executives didn't agree with each other, and she resented the use of "we." She had nothing to do with the production and wanted to say so, but thinking of her promise to try to help Luca, she schooled her response. "Exactly. The agent will want to squeeze as much as she can from the studio to maximize her cut. It was fifteen percent, wasn't it?" She remembered the details, of course, but she wanted to test his mental acuity. Arturo thought he might be losing it, and she wanted to know for certain.

"Something like that." He waved her away impatiently. "I want you there, Marissa," he said and placed his palms on the desk.

He didn't slam his hands down, but he may as well have. The darkness in his eyes tested her will to stay in place. She wasn't a little girl anymore, and yet he could return her to that state of mind with a simple look. God, she couldn't wait to get away from him. If she and Arturo didn't already have plans, she would've used the trip to LA to begin their escape. She'd said that she would help Luca though, and the sojourn to America was part of that. "What about my work? The court case begins in three days."

"I'll call Aguilar and let him know that I need you here for a while. He'll understand."

She didn't want to work that case anyway so pulling her off it was a bonus. "Then I'll go. You'll have to move Luca out of the barns. She'll need a laptop and a comfortable, quiet space to write. You can't expect her to keep working in the fields."

Her father held up his hands. "Of course I don't. But what would you suggest?"

"The old villa on the eastern side of the property." Marissa had spent many hours there after her mamita's death, reading the books they'd never gotten to enjoy together. It had given her much-needed distance from her father and was far enough away from his business dealings that she could almost forget what he did. "Does it still have running water and electricity?"

He motioned to Arturo. "Check how secure the east villa is. We can't have our new number one asset escaping."

Arturo confirmed the order and left. She missed his presence immediately. He made her feel safe in the unstable environment her father deliberately fostered. "I'll speak to Luca and get her settled in with everything she'll need."

"Do it quickly. I want you on a plane in the morning. And no internet, Marissa. When you get back, I want you to stay close to her. Make sure she's working as fast as possible. We don't want her to drag her feet once she's out of the barns and in a luxury house."

"The barn or the villa make no difference, Father. She's still your prisoner."

He grinned. "Yes, I suppose she is. And she's going to be a particularly lucrative one."

"Is that what this is all about? Money? Or is this the beginning of you diversifying your business interests?"

"I've always loved the movies, you know that." He leaned back in his chair and looked wistful. "And your madre loved books. This feels like something she would have done, if she were still alive."

How was she supposed to hold her tongue with such nonsense spewing from his mouth? Her mamita would never have allowed any of this to happen. When she died, so did his compassion, and he'd been growing steadily worse. This deal with Casey and taking Luca prisoner was an all-new low.

He laughed. "And the money is a welcome bonus. My accountant showed me the numbers for some popular books made into movies. With all the spin-offs, merchandise, and advertising opportunities, it's practically a license to print money." He sat up and took a cigar from the chestnut wood box on his desk. "If there's an opportunity to make easy money, who am I to pass it up?"

"Is everything okay with the family business, Father?" she asked. The picture Arturo had painted worried her more than she wanted to admit. Cartel-on-cartel violence escalated fast and was always drenched in blood.

He frowned as he lit his cigar and puffed away on it. "Why would you think it isn't?"

She couldn't say too much more without jeopardizing Arturo. She could never forgive herself if he fell foul of her father's temper and suffered the same fate as Santiago, whatever that was. It was clear from the haunted look in Arturo's eyes that it had been a violent end. "I thought you wanted me to show an interest?" she asked, injecting a little of the insolence he expected from her. "Forget I asked. Back to my impending journey to LA, I'd like Arturo to accompany me. I don't feel safe with anyone else. Will you allow that?"

He chewed on his cigar, as if considering the options. "Since you'll only be gone two days, I suppose so. But Teo will also be going with you. I can't risk anything happening to you."

Two days didn't give her much time to do anything other than fly, take the meeting with Soto, her agent, and the studio execs, and fly back out. But that was okay since it meant Luca wouldn't have to be alone for too long. "Is there a threat I should know about?" Was this the paranoia Arturo had mentioned?

"Nothing more than usual, mija."

He tapped his cigar into an ashtray and seemed to avoid her gaze. Maybe Arturo was right, and her father believed he could be under siege at any moment. It wasn't unheard of for cartels to target the vulnerable family members first. She'd take the extra protection. The last thing she wanted was to fall into the hands of her father's enemies. She needed business as usual in the next two weeks leading up to Día de los Muertos and her escape.

She stood and collected the publishing contract from her father's desk. "I'll take this to read on the plane."

"Be careful, Marissa. I don't know what I would do if I lost you too."

The usual hardness in his eyes wasn't visible, and his soft tone took her by surprise. It brought back memories of hearing him speak that way to her mamita when Marissa was young, and when he was still in touch with his humanity. The dull ache of that loss settled in her mind like a leaden weight, confusing her clarity on the path she'd committed to. One gentle sentence couldn't combat all the other evidence that he was beyond redemption, and yet she couldn't stop a tiny flame of hope from bursting into life.

Chapter Eighteen

"THE MEN ARE USUALLY the ones who bury our dead." Epi jutted her chin and placed her hands on her hips.

"It's okay, honestly." Luca was getting used to Epi's insistence on protecting her, despite it feeling incredibly strange, but she didn't want Epi to be punished for it.

"See, puta vieja? It's good for her to have another use."

Martinez didn't try to hide his sneer. Luca's skin crawled. Some of the prettier female workers exchanged favors with a couple of the more handsome guards for extra food and lighter work detail. Luca was quietly content that her presentation didn't even raise that possibility.

She grabbed a tank top from the washing she'd just finished and followed Martinez to the isolation barn where Ángel waited at the door. When she got closer, the look of abject resignation in his eyes stopped her progress. She didn't want to know how long he'd been here and how many of his friends he'd been forced to bury. She did know that she wasn't strong enough to withstand the same future.

Luca quickly tore her tank top into strips and created two makeshift bandanas. She wrapped one around her face and offered the second one to Ángel. He thanked her and opened the door. In the dim light, Luca barely recognized Cedro, still in the center of the room where she'd found him dead two days ago. The stench of death easily penetrated the thin cotton of her mask.

"You get his legs," Ángel said. "I'll take the other end."

She wasn't about to argue. The rats had taken their fill, and Luca had no desire to see that any closer. What was left of Cedro didn't weigh much, and they easily picked him up to place him on the wooden stretcher outside the door.

"Take the bottom end but face away," Ángel said. "We're walking that way."

"Thank you." Luca squatted down to pick up the handles, and they lifted the body. As they walked, she saw Marissa drive up in her cart across the field. *¡Mierda!* She was going to miss her.

"You won't be back in time," Ángel whispered. "But don't worry, Epi will always make sure there is something left for you."

She must've been staring, and he'd caught her. She wasn't worried about the food. She needed to see if Marissa had spoken to Vargas yet. "I know."

"And you'll need it after this."

She'd lost her appetite the moment Ángel had opened the door to the isolation barn. If her rising nausea was anything to go by, she wouldn't want to eat for a week.

She pulled her gaze from Marissa and the other women who gathered around her to remove the baskets of food from the golf cart. Luca would have to wait until tomorrow to talk with her unless Marissa made another surprise evening visit. Epi had commented that she'd never done that before, and that she suspected Marissa's compassion for Luca's situation had prompted it. Luca doubted that it would become a regular occurrence. She didn't know how Marissa found the time to visit them every day anyway, given her career. And surely she'd want to spend her evenings with Arturo. But if Marissa had been touched by Luca's plight, she'd take whatever help she could offer. The bigger life she'd dreamed of was out there, and she wanted it back.

Martinez guided them another half mile away from the barns. When they walked just beyond a line of trees, Luca nearly lost her footing and then blanched when she looked up. The clearing was full of rudimentary graves marked by small crosses that looked handmade. He pointed them toward an area where two shovels stood erect in the ground.

"Lay Cedro here while we dig," Ángel said.

She squatted and placed the stretcher carefully on the ground, before rising and massaging her palms where the rough wood had bitten into her skin.

"You'll get used to that." Ángel patted her on the shoulder. "We need to get this hole dug before the sun comes over those trees, otherwise we'll bake in the heat."

Luca pulled the shovels from the dirt and handed him one. "How many of these have you been forced to do?"

"Too many."

"Less talk, more work," Martinez said before he wandered over to a tree stump in the shade and lit a cigarette.

Luca followed Ángel as he walked to where the outline of the grave was already marked out.

He pointed to the opposite end. "You start over there. Eventually, we'll meet in the middle."

Luca drove the shovel into the ground and began a task she'd never imagined herself having to do. "How deep?"

"Deep," Ángel said. "Just dig and don't think about it."

Luca glanced over to Cedro's body. How could she not think about what they were doing? But if Ángel had buried so many of his friends here, maybe that was just his coping mechanism. "Do you normally have to do this alone?"

Ángel shook his head. "Cedro and I have been doing this together for fifteen years. We were some of the first workers Señor Vargas made deals with."

Luca snorted. "Deals? Is that how you really see it?"

"Yes. He gave us what we needed, and we agreed on a deal to pay for it."

Luca continued to dig, but she was morbidly fascinated by Ángel's weird kind of loyalty to Vargas. "You've been here fifteen years minimum then, so how long have you got left?"

Ángel gestured to the deepening grave. "Until you and someone else put me in the ground."

He still looked relatively healthy. She had no intention of being here until he died. "You made a deal with the devil for your life?"

He chuckled and threw another shovelful of dirt over his shoulder. "That's dramatic. But yes, the payment was working for Señor Vargas for the remainder of my life."

His laughter seemed totally out of place, unless he'd already been driven insane by digging graves and picking leaves for so long. She couldn't imagine ever finding an amusing side to this situation, but then she wasn't the one who'd made the deal to be here. "Can I ask what you've been paying for all these years?" Nothing warranted lifelong servitude. Vargas was abusing the trust of desperate people.

He smiled broadly. It was the same kind of smile she'd seen on Epi's face when she'd told Luca her story.

"My family's freedom. My wife, my two daughters, and my sister and her family. They are all living their American dream in California. Seven lives for mine seemed like a great deal when I made it, but now I'm not so sure. As the years have passed, Señor Vargas is not so generous, and people trade their lives for far less than I did." He jutted his chin at her while he continued to dig. "What about you? What's your 'deal with the devil?'"

"Two devils made a deal, and I'm their pawn." Luca sank her shovel into the ground with force, imagining Casey beneath it. What was happening to her? This betrayal had colored her soul, and she was struggling to find the light. She had to hold onto the hope that Marissa would be able to help, and she could get back on track.

Ángel frowned and stopped digging.

"Is there a problem over there?" Martinez shouted.

Luca held up her hand. "No problem. Just a big rock." She dropped to her knees and began to wrestle an imaginary boulder.

"Get on with it. I don't want to be out here all day."

When he turned away, Luca rose.

"Thank you," Ángel said. "He doesn't need a reason to be vicious with any of us."

"I guess it's one of the job requirements."

"What did you mean about being a pawn? You didn't make a deal?"

Luca shook her head and continued to channel her rage into their task as she relayed Casey's betrayal.

Ángel's deep frown brought out the lines in his leathery skin. "That doesn't sound like something that the Señor Vargas I know would do. Though I haven't seen him for a long, long time, and he was a different man when his wife was alive. He was destroyed by her death, but I thought he would recover."

"His daughter lost her mother, and she hasn't turned into an evil monster." Maybe monster was dramatic too, but it sounded more than appropriate.

"Ah, Señorita Vargas. She was always such a sweet girl."

Luca's mood turned instantly. "You knew Marissa as a child?"

He nodded. "I've known the Vargas family my whole life. I worked for Señor Vargas and his father until I became too old."

"Too old for what?"

He flexed his arm and laughed. "To be taken seriously as an enforcer."

Luca's opinion of Ángel faltered. He could easily be one of the people Epi had said to stay away from, someone only interested in themselves. She ran through what she'd said, hoping she hadn't given him anything he could use against her, or Epi, or even Marissa.

"Don't worry," he said, as if he'd read her expression. "I have no interest in reporting any of this back to men like him." He gestured toward Martinez. "And I wasn't like that. I wasn't even on security detail. I was just a driver for the family. That's how I knew Señorita Vargas."

Just as the conversation returned to something she wanted to talk about, Luca hit a real rock and stopped to focus on getting it out. Ángel helped, and after some time and effort, they finally freed it from the soil and tossed it beside the grave.

"You said Marissa was always sweet?" Luca wanted to know as much about her as possible. Even if she was with Arturo, it didn't have to stop Luca worshipping her from afar. She had little else to focus on.

She felt him pause and look at her, but she didn't meet his gaze and continued working.

"Why are you so interested in Marissa Vargas?"

"I'm curious, that's all. I'm a writer. I like to know how people come to be who they are, and it's unusual that someone so compassionate could exist in this kind of environment."

Ángel grunted as he shoveled. "Are you going to write a book about this?"

Luca wiped sweat from her brow. "If I ever get out, maybe I will."

"Look around. No one ever gets out."

There was a serious foreboding in his tone that scared her. "No one?" She looked at him, searching his expression for a sign that he was messing with her.

He shrugged. "Maybe a few. Over the years. But the people who end up here have cost Señor Vargas a lot of money. In the early years of this new system, he even sent monthly payments to our families. Debts like that are often for life." He looked back down at the ground and continued his work. "We know what we're signing up for when we seek his help."

"I didn't."

"So you *did* ask for help?"

"No. I told you. This is all Casey Soto's doing."

"Soto? That explains much. They are not a good family."

Luca wished someone had told her that four years ago. She would've kept her usual walls in place and not fallen for Casey's bullshit. "You know them too? You know a lot of people, Ángel."

"I've lived here all my life, and so did my father and his father before him.

You get to know the other families who do the same. It's hard for people to escape their family history or break out of family expectations. The Soto family have a certain reputation."

Luca slammed her shovel into the ground, again thinking about Casey being on the receiving end. "You're making excuses for what she's done to me?"

"Not an excuse, an explanation. What about your family? Who are they? Who are you?"

She didn't want a therapy session. She wanted to talk about Marissa. "I don't have one."

"Ah," he said. "Then you are not burdened with expectation or responsibility or tradition. You can be your own person and forge your own path. That's a good position to be in."

She hadn't thought of it like that before, and if she wasn't imprisoned in a drug cartel compound, she might appreciate the concept. But she was, so she couldn't. She worked in silence for a while, trying hard to concentrate on the action of digging and how it made her body feel instead of roaming around the depressing depths of her mind.

"Señorita Vargas is an amazing person, just like her mother was," Ángel said after a long period of quiet. "I feared she would lose herself when her mother died, but from what I've seen, the beauty of her mother moved into her soul, and she has become more amazing because of her loss."

Luca didn't respond in the hope that he would tell her more if she kept silent.

"They were barely apart, always talking and laughing. It was a wonderful sight. Always with their heads in books—ah, speak of an angel, and she will appear."

Luca jerked her head up and saw Marissa round the corner of the tree line. She dared to hope that she was the reason for Marissa's visit, but more likely, she was coming to pay her respects to Cedro. It seemed like something she'd done for every one of the people he and Ángel had buried here.

"Keep digging. He doesn't need an excuse, though he might behave while Senorita Vargas is here. If you're lucky."

Luca shifted her position so she could continue to shovel dirt and still see Marissa in her peripheral vision. She stopped the cart just short of

Martinez and began to chat with him. Luca couldn't imagine two more different people. What could they even be talking about? Luca noticed someone in the passenger seat, but she couldn't tell who it was from this distance.

Marissa got out of the cart and walked toward them, her male passenger a few paces behind her. Luca's heart pounded against her chest. She tried to convince herself that she was just anticipating positive news about meeting with Vargas, but it wasn't that. It was everything else about Marissa. The way she held herself as she walked, still managing to look glamorous and controlled despite the uneven ground. The way her eyes radiated more heat than the sun at high noon. The way her beauty within somehow managed to outshine her outer beauty, and the way she let everyone see both. Luca had lost count of the number of times she'd watched Marissa walk toward the bar and then away from her to a beach table. She never tired of enjoying Marissa's elegance and poise. She was unlike anyone Luca had ever met.

"Hi, Ángel, how are you?"

It was obvious Marissa was intentionally avoiding looking at Cedro's remains on the plank of wood. Instead, she seemed to focus solely on Ángel as though she weren't standing in a cemetery of broken dreams.

"As good as every other day, Señorita Vargas. Thank you for asking."

"I hear your family are doing very well with their restaurant, Ángel. I'm going to LA tomorrow, and Arturo is going to take me to see them."

Ángel dropped his shovel and clutched his hands to his chest. "Señorita Vargas, that would mean the world to me, and to my family."

"It will mean a lot to me too. I'm looking forward to seeing Camila again."

Marissa and Ángel continued to talk and reminisce, but all Luca could focus on was the bombshell that Marissa was going to LA with Arturo. Was this the opportunity they'd been waiting for, and Luca would never see Marissa again? She leaned on her shovel for support.

"Luca, I need you to come with me."

Marissa flashed her gorgeous smile, and Luca silently acknowledged that she'd go with her anywhere to keep seeing that smile. Marissa glanced behind her to where Cedro's covered body lay, and her smile disappeared. Luca climbed out of the half-dug grave and stepped back into Marissa's view. She'd probably seen far worse, but it was clear she hadn't been desensitized to the horror of death. Most people wouldn't have noticed, but Luca saw the light in Marissa's eyes dim a little. She walked over to Cedro's body, stayed a few moments, then returned.

"Has you father agreed to meet me?" Luca asked after she'd given Marissa the time she needed to refocus on why she'd driven out there.

Marissa pulled her gaze back to Luca. "I'll explain on the way to the barn. Ángel, Bruno is going to help you."

"Thank you, Señorita Vargas," Ángel said.

The guy hovering behind Marissa stepped forward and held out his hand. "Your shovel."

Luca handed it to him then shoved her hands in her pockets. "Why are we going to the barn?"

"Please, I'll explain everything as we drive." Marissa gestured to her cart.

Luca sensed her reluctance to talk further in front of Ángel and Bruno, so she followed Marissa, a few steps behind as he had. A little voice in the back of her mind wondered if it could be a trap, if she was trusting Marissa only to be walking willingly to her own death. With a deep breath, she shook off the thought.

"You don't have to walk behind me, Luca." Marissa slowed her pace until Luca caught up.

"I don't?" On an equality level, she didn't like it, but there were other advantages to walking behind someone that Luca had never appreciated until this moment.

"You don't. Come, get in. We don't have a lot of time."

Luca moved swiftly around to the passenger side of the cart and avoided eye contact with Martinez. She didn't want any trouble when she came back, especially not with him. She felt his stare bore into the back of her head but kept her eyes firmly focused on where she was going.

Marissa turned the vehicle around and headed toward the barns.

"You're killing me with the suspense, Marissa," Luca said when she couldn't wait any longer.

"I had the impression you were a patient person, Luca Romero." Marissa glanced at Luca and wiggled her eyebrows.

Her playfulness might've seemed out of place if it had come from anyone else, but somehow it was just about okay. In Marissa's company, Luca could almost forget where she was and imagine them driving up the coast to spend a day at Playa de los Amantes. "Normally I am. But there's this little thing with me being imprisoned against my will that's pushing my patience to its limits."

"I'm sorry, Luca. I was just—"

Luca touched Marissa's forearm then pulled back, aware the touch was inappropriate. "Hey, it's okay. I'm sorry. I can't seem to help the bitterness, but I'm trying."

Marissa half-smiled. "Ah, good. I shouldn't joke. This is your life and your future we're dealing with."

"Honestly, it's fine." Luca stuck her hands under her thighs to prevent any more spontaneous contact. "But since you've brought that up, what's this all about? Am I meeting with your father? Is that why you're taking me back to the barn, to clean myself up?"

"Things have developed since we last talked. I'm not taking you to meet my father, but I am getting you out of the barns and away from the fields."

Luca's heart jumped. "I'm free?" This was amazing. She thought the best she could hope for was to start negotiating with Vargas. Marissa had worked a miracle, and this nightmare was over. Luca wanted to hug her.

A few beats of silence passed, and Luca's excitement faltered.

Marissa stopped outside the women's barn, cut the engine, and turned to face Luca. "I'm sorry, I can't give you that."

The words landed on her unguarded sense of hope and flattened it like a boulder dropping on a coyote. Luca closed her eyes and put her head in her hands. Tears rose and fell. Tears she didn't want Marissa to see. Of course she wasn't free. Nothing could be that easy. She felt Marissa's hand on her back but didn't move. Sharing her emotions didn't come easy. She had never felt safe enough to show her vulnerabilities to anyone. But there was nowhere to run to here, no place she could let go without an audience.

"But I have got something I want to show you. It's not what you were hoping for, but it's far better than where you are now." Marissa rubbed Luca's back. "Please. I'll wait here while you collect your things. I'm taking you somewhere else."

Luca swung her legs out of the cart, keeping her back to Marissa and her weakness to herself. "I won't be long." The other items of clothing she'd been given would take seconds to pull together, and she'd use the rest of the time to calm down and gather herself. She walked quickly to the barn entrance and went in without looking back.

She got to her bunk and used the light sheet to wipe away her tears before wrapping her clothes in the bedding. She was especially careful with the button-down shirt she'd arrived in, which she'd folded neatly and used as a pillow. Maybe one day it wouldn't be tainted by her first experience of wearing it.

"You're leaving us."

The voice startled Luca and she turned quickly. "I don't know what's happening, Epi. I wanted to talk to Vargas, but Marissa's just told me to pack up. I don't know what's going on. Do you?"

Epi smiled and sat on the edge of Luca's bunk. "I know less than you, chica. But you can trust Marissa, you know that, don't you? She will do everything she can to help you if that's what she's promised."

"Trust is what got me here. Do you think she can turn things around?"

Epi shook her head. "I can't answer that. Marissa is keeping her secrets to protect the rest of us. But you don't belong here, Luca, so I hope that whatever is happening, you don't end up back with us." She moved closer and put her arm around Luca's shoulders. "I've enjoyed getting to know you, but I would like nothing more than to never see you again."

Luca laughed. "That's a strange way of saying goodbye, but I'll take it."

Epi handed her a small slip of paper. "This is the address for my family. If you get out and need a place to stay while you rebuild your life, my daughter will help you. Just tell her I sent you." She dropped her arm from Luca's shoulder. Tears welled in her eyes, and she gave Luca a larger, folded piece of paper. "And if you can, please give her this."

Luca took the letter and put both notes into her pocket. "I'd love to meet your daughter." She ached for Epi's loss and the sacrifice she'd made, and she wished that she could reunite them somehow. But that was just a fantasy. She couldn't secure her own freedom, let alone anyone else's.

"Come." Epi stood and wiped her eyes. "Marissa is waiting for you."

Comforted a little by Epi's strength of purpose, Luca rose and pulled her into a hug. "Thank you for everything." Spending time with Epi had gone some way to building her faith that some people could be good. She'd allowed herself to trust Epi, just a little, and she hadn't suffered as a result.

"You're welcome, chica." Epi broke away and gently pushed her toward the door. "Now, go."

She picked up her clothes and headed out. Marissa smiled brightly as Luca got in the passenger side of the cart, and the radiance of her light enlivened Luca's hope again. There was no meeting with Vargas yet, but Marissa was clearly excited about something, *and* Luca was out of the barns, so it couldn't be all bad.

Marissa drove away from the rickety buildings, and Luca didn't look back. She was done with looking back. There was nothing good there.

"You've got everything?"

Luca patted the pile of material on her lap. "I don't have much, but yeah, I've got everything." She hadn't had much back at her basement apartment either, and she expected they'd thrown away what they hadn't returned to her.

Marissa didn't respond, and they drove in silence. Luca fixed her gaze on the woods, half-looking for a potential escape route, but the number of guards placed along the perimeter they passed indicated that would be a longshot. She hadn't really expected anything less. Vargas had millions of pesos worth of drugs on the property which had to be protected. He needed to keep trespassers out and nearly one hundred indentured workers in.

The main house came into view, and memories of pulling up there flooded Luca's brain. Marissa turned away from the mansion and onto another a wide dirt track, and Luca released a breath of tension. *Where are you taking me?* She didn't voice the question. It was clear that Marissa had a plan to reveal whatever she'd arranged, and Luca didn't want to ruin that. Which was wildly out of place. Marissa wasn't driving her to a birthday surprise. And yet, there was something so natural about being beside her that almost made Luca forget the dire situation she was in.

About a half mile down the trail, Luca saw a small villa. "What's this?" she asked.

Marissa pulled up and stepped out elegantly. "This is where you're going to be staying from now on."

The building looked like it hadn't been used in a while but had still been looked after.

Marissa unlocked the door and pushed it open. "Come in."

Luca followed with her meager worldly possessions while she turned over the possibilities in her head. She dropped her makeshift bag on a chair and closed the door behind them. The scent of disinfectant indicated it had been cleaned recently, but the large bouquet of flowers that sat on the table in the living room competed for dominance with its own strong scent.

"Do you like them?" Marissa asked, gesturing to the flowers.

Luca shrugged. "Sure. They're pretty."

"I got them for you," Marissa said, looking straight at her.

Luca raised her eyebrows then laughed lightly. This must be one of those friend things she'd never experienced. "No one has ever bought flowers for me before. I've always wanted to have someone to buy them for though." She looked away, instantly regretting her words. Marissa had done something nice for her, something platonic. Luca needed to control herself and focus on the friendship that was being offered. Friendship was better than nothing.

"Maybe one day you could buy them for me." Marissa tapped the table then wandered away. "Let me show you something else."

Luca dismissed the gentle flirtation she thought she heard. Marissa was just being Marissa. That "one day" would never come if Luca couldn't get out of here. And Luca would want to buy flowers of love, like roses, not whatever flowers symbolized friendship, and she couldn't imagine that Arturo would be quite as laid-back as he'd appeared if Luca did that.

She sighed and followed after Marissa. "Where are you?"

"End of the corridor," she called.

Luca entered the room and gasped. It was a library and office, with shelves and shelves of books. A huge wooden desk sat in front of a similarly huge window overlooking a beautifully kept garden, and an elegant leather office chair was positioned at the desk. But it was what was *on* the desk that caught Luca's attention the most. A white box with the distinctive Apple logo on the side and a picture of a MacBook on the top. Unopened.

Marissa stood beside the desk, looking like she was playing El Papá Noel at an orphanage. "This is for you."

Luca ran her hand through her hair and blew out a long breath. None of this was making any sense, and it all felt so out of place. If she ignored *everything* else, this could easily be her fantasy. Coming home to Marissa, her eyes glistening with mischievousness and excitement, gifting her a brand-new laptop for her to write her next best-selling novel on. But this wasn't real. Maybe she'd passed out in the heat, and she was actually lying unconscious in the half-dug grave, and Ángel was trying to wake her up. Hell, maybe she was the one being buried.

"I don't understand what's happening, Marissa." She approached the desk and ran her finger over the smooth box. It *felt* real.

"Take a seat, and I'll tell you everything." Marissa sank into one of the giant armchairs in front of the fireplace.

Luca gave the MacBook box one last caress before she joined Marissa and sat on the edge of the chair beside her, not wanting her dirty and soiled clothes to leave a mess. She had a vision of a young Marissa with her madre, going through all these gorgeous books, one by one. They were so pristine, making Luca even more aware of how out of place she was in these surroundings. Even before this all happened, she wouldn't have been comfortable somewhere like this.

"Casey called today begging for more help."

Luca scoffed. "Help enjoying the life she stole from me? It's hard for me to feel sorry for her."

"And no one's asking you to. But it's your help she needs."

Luca gripped the arm of her chair so tightly, her fingers began to ache. "I think I've helped her enough, don't you?" She glanced back at the desk and the shiny, pristine box waiting to be unwrapped. "Is that what that's for? For me to help that cabrón keep up the charade of playing writer? You can't be serious, Marissa. I asked you for a meeting with your father to get out of here, and this is—what? A compromise or just a cruel joke?" She took a deep breath and remembered Epi saying that she could trust Marissa to come through on her promise. "I'm sorry. I know that none of this is your doing, and I'm not angry with you..." She released her grip on the armchair and rubbed her thumb into her palm. "I'm just angry with the situation, with your father, with Casey fucking Soto."

"I get that, Luca, I do," she said. "And you could be angry with me too. I'm the one here offering you the poisoned chalice."

Marissa's voice, gentle and soothing, was like balm on Luca's burning soul. She inched forward onto the edge of her seat and held out her hands. Luca stared at them for a long moment before holding out her own. When Marissa wrapped her hands over Luca's, all the tension in her body softened and she exhaled the rage within. "Then what am I doing here?"

"The rest of what I'm going to tell you is going to make you want to tear down my father's house with your bare hands, but I need you to see the long game, not just the short-term situation. Do you understand?"

"Not yet, but I'll hear you out." Twenty minutes ago, she'd been digging a grave in an unmarked cemetery, and now she was sitting in an air-conditioned room. It wasn't like she had anything to lose simply by listening to what Marissa had to say.

"Hollywood studios want to option your trilogy, and Elodie Fontaine wants to play Caletho."

"What the–"

Marissa held up her hand. "Please, let me get it all out, and then we'll talk."

"Sorry." Luca relaxed back into the chair, though she was on an emotional rollercoaster from just the opening sentence. Excitement at her books being made into movies. Thrilled by the thought that the awesome Elodie Fontaine could play Caletho, and she couldn't think of another American actress who'd be better. But an all-consuming rage that her dream was playing out without her in it overrode them all.

"Elodie, as you'll probably know, is one of the biggest and most powerful actors in Hollywood."

Marissa waited until Luca acknowledged that, yes, she knew exactly who she was talking about. How could she not? Luca had a type–personified by the woman sharing oxygen with her right now–and Elodie wasn't that; she was soft butch sexiness with a hard edge from her military experience. But still, there was a raw sexuality about her that made her incredibly attractive to almost anyone, including Luca.

"And as such, she makes a lot of the decisions on the movies she works on. She's even got her PGA mark, so she knows what she's doing on the production side. It's probably only a matter of time before she directs her first film."

Luca coughed at Marissa's off-topic aside.

"Right. Back to your books. Like I said, Elodie makes a lot of decisions, and she wants the author of the books to write the screenplay and be on set when they eventually begin shooting in case they want changes or rewrites. They think the author is Casey but obviously, she doesn't have the first clue about writing anything creative, let alone a script from a book, which I've read is quite the skill."

Marissa wasn't wrong. Truncating eighty-thousand words into a two-hour film of mostly dialogue and stage direction was hard. Luca had studied a few books on it and even played with some free scriptwriting software, more out of interest than any illusion that her books might ever become films. They weren't even close to being published at the time, so it really had been just for fun. But she'd enjoyed the challenge.

"That's where you come in, and that's why this is your new home."

Home. She'd never had a real home, and while this place was a beautiful house, it could never be a home while she was forced to stay within a golden cage. Though she could pretend almost gleefully if Marissa was staying here too. As long as Arturo didn't figure in the equation.

"Casey needs you to write the screenplay, and then she'll need you to be on call for any rewrites when they begin filming. There's also the edits on the books themselves, which apparently will be coming through soon too. I convinced my father that here would be the best place for you to do that." Marissa held out her hands. "That's everything. Now we can talk."

Luca nodded slowly, processing everything Marissa had told her. "I don't see the long game, Marissa, unless you're just talking about me not working in the fields or sleeping on a wafer-thin mattress and a solid wood base for the next six years or so *if* I can turn my trilogy into three movies. Often, several books are made into just one film. Which is it they're expecting? And do you know what depth the edits on the books themselves are going to be?" She thought there was a true trilogy in her books, but the studios might disagree and only want to fund one film.

"I can ask about that when I meet them tomorrow."

"That's what you're going to LA for?"

Marissa nodded. "To oversee negotiations on the final sum and the parameters of the contract."

The threat of Marissa leaving for good temporarily overtook her concerns for her own future. "Will you come back?"

Marissa frowned. "What do you mean?"

"Isn't something like this exactly what you and Arturo have been waiting for? You'd finally be away from your father. You could catch a plane to Europe, and he wouldn't be able to track you down." Nausea bubbled in her throat as she voiced her fears along with her words.

Marissa took a breath then looked around as if she were looking for the camera watching them. She leaned closer and whispered, "We have to be careful talking about that. My father is installing CCTV and bugs everywhere. Arturo has checked the villa, and for now, it's a safe place... But to answer your question, no," she whispered. "A few months ago, this might've been a great opportunity for us to escape, yes, but—I can trust you, can't I?"

"As much I can trust you. I'm literally putting my life in your hands, and I understand that you're doing exactly the same if you tell me anything else about you and Arturo."

Marissa twisted her ring over and over as she clearly considered Luca's response.

"Before you say anything though, will you tell me about your ring?" Luca reached out to touch the band around Marissa's finger but pulled back at the last moment. "Whenever you're in deep thought or nervous about something, you always play with it. As if it grounds you or gives you strength."

Marissa smiled softly and looked down at her hands. "It was my mamita's ring. It's like having a little piece of her still with me." Her voice broke slightly, and she began to cry. "This wouldn't have happened to you if she were still alive. And I should be able to stop it."

Luca sat on the arm of Marissa's chair and gently put her arms around her. She hoped Marissa would forgive her dirty, sweaty body and take comfort in her arms anyway. "None of this is your fault, Marissa. Please know that I don't blame you for any of it, and I'm grateful that you're trying this hard to help me."

Marissa leaned into Luca's chest. "Thank you. My tía says I take on too much, but I can't help it, not with you. All of this is beyond unfair." She pulled back and looked up at Luca. "But in answer to your original question, we've made other plans. And I wouldn't do that to you. I've made a promise to help you as much as I can, and I won't let you down on that. I'll continue to work on my father."

Not with you? Luca could almost believe there was something more than Marissa's altruistic nature at play. With the flowers and her words, it would be easy for Luca to think that Marissa had feelings for her. In a way, she was glad that Marissa had revealed her wish to escape and that she had seen Arturo, otherwise Luca might harbor a desperate hope that her attraction to Marissa was reciprocated. She glanced across to the desk again and the laptop taunted her. She got up from Marissa's chair, the proximity too much to bear. "I'd made a promise to myself that I'd buy a MacBook with my first royalty check or advance. I guess I'd be able to afford it if Casey hadn't betrayed me. You know, I had every intention of asking her to go with me. She didn't need to do any of this."

Marissa sighed deeply. "That would've been such a beautiful gesture, and one that shows what a wonderful person you are. But I fear even something so grand wouldn't have been enough for Casey. She's driven by greed, and she wanted it all. If she didn't, and if she knew you at all, she would've known that you'd take her with you."

"You think I'm a wonderful person? All I seem to do when you're around is yell at you."

"Look around–you've got damn good cause to yell." Marissa gestured to the desk. "I bought that for you. Are you going to open it?"

"I'm delaying the gratification," Luca said, and Marissa laughed. "Plus, you still haven't told me what the long game is. This place is great, and it's a massive improvement from the living conditions in the barn. But it's still not freedom. It's just a nicer prison." She ran her fingers over the box and imagined the keyboard beneath her fingers. She'd once touched an Apple MacBook that a woman at the beach bar had; compared to the clunky keyboard of her old desktop, it was like typing on silk.

"That's because I'm not really certain what the long game is yet," Marissa said. "But you're closer to the compound gates, and we can go for walks."

"We? Won't you be in LA?"

"I'll be back in two days, and then my father wants me to keep a close eye on you, so I'll be moving in to the second bedroom."

Luca kept her gaze fixed on the MacBook box. Marissa living in the same space would be torture, but she'd also love the chance to spend so much time with her. "What does Arturo think of that?"

Marissa frowned. "It has nothing to do with him. Why do you ask?"

She was being stupid. Of course Arturo wouldn't feel threatened by her. "No reason. I just thought he'd be involved."

Marissa shook her head. "He does my father's bidding and doesn't ask questions. Questioning my father gets you killed."

Luca's throat tightened. All she'd ever wanted was to write and be happy. She hated Casey for putting her here. "It's dangerous, I understand.

You're saying I have to be patient and wait for an opportunity to escape. You don't think there's any way I could talk to your father and work out a different deal with him? One that sees Casey back here and me in LA where I'm supposed to be? Wouldn't it make sense to just cut out the middle woman and send me to LA where I can still make him money?"

"I'm sorry, Luca, but I don't think so. He has history with the Soto family, and he doesn't know you at all. Casey's family are still here, which gives my father leverage. If you went to LA, he has no insurance that would stop you from simply disappearing. So yes, we have to be patient and be ready to act. Can you do that?"

Luca nodded. It was the first time *not* having a family had been an advantage. "I can try. I don't really have a choice, do I? It's that or death, isn't it?"

Marissa came over and pushed the MacBook toward Luca. "I can't wait any longer. Please open the box."

Luca raised her eyebrows. "What's your hurry? Is it a trick, and there's actually just a stack of plain paper and a pen in there?"

"Open it and find out." Marissa inched the box toward her some more.

"It's not wrapped. It really is just paper, isn't it?" Luca tore off the cellophane and lifted the lid to reveal a sleek, graphite MacBook. She peeled back the protective film and sighed deeply as she ran her fingers across the cool metal casing.

"Wow, Luca, it's a laptop, not a woman."

Luca's head snapped up, and heat rushed to her cheeks. "It's not just a laptop, it's a MacBook," she said, trying to recover from Marissa's casual reference to her sexuality. She couldn't remember talking about it with her before, but it wasn't as if she could hide it either. And Casey had hit on Marissa so often at the beach bar that she'd probably just made the correct assumption Luca was gay too.

Marissa grinned and raised her eyebrow, clearly amused at Luca's discomfort. "Turn it over."

Glad for the distraction, Luca carefully removed the Mac from its box and turned it over. Below the serial number was the inscription, *We live in the gaps between the stories*. Luca smiled. "That's beautiful. Thank you." There were plenty of other things she wanted to say, but she kept them to herself.

"It's Margaret Atwood—Oh, shit." She grimaced when Luca quickly set down the computer. "Not that, not you. Sorry." Marissa tapped her watch. "I've just noticed the time. I have a plane to catch."

It was probably for the best that she left now. The air had become charged with a possibility Luca knew was all in her head, but it was still hard to ignore. "Good luck on your trip and be careful. You're exactly Casey's type."

Marissa winked. "You don't have to worry about me. I know all about Casey Soto. She's been trying to charm me since the day we met. She's deluded. All those times she desperately tried to impress me she had no idea that I really just wanted to talk to you."

Luca gripped the back of the office chair for support. *What does that mean?*

Marissa walked away and stopped at the door. "Get settled in and start thinking about the screenplay. I'll get the answers to your questions while I'm there. Your Mac is already set up, and you'll have to save your work to the hard drive. My father won't allow internet access unless I'm here to keep an eye on you."

Luca's half-smile froze in place. There were so many flirtatious comebacks, things that would roll off Casey's tongue, but she could say nothing. Which was the most sensible thing to do. Luca was terrible at that game even if Marissa did want to play, which she didn't because she was with Arturo. "Safe journey, Marissa."

"Happy writing, Luca."

She turned and was gone. Luca heard the door close. When it locked, she was pulled from the strange limbo she felt suspended in every time Marissa was close. This was *still* a prison, and she was a long way from her freedom.

Chapter Nineteen

MARISSA SANK INTO THE seat beside Arturo and fastened her seatbelt. Teo nodded to them and took his seat four rows up at the front of the plane. The flight was almost fully booked, and the last-minute decision meant they were unable to be seated as a trio. Marissa insisted on Arturo sitting beside her, not just because she was far more comfortable in his company but also because she wanted to discuss the changing Luca situation with him.

They made small talk while the few remaining passengers boarded. Marissa wanted the engine noise to overpower the potential for their conversation to be heard by Teo.

When they were in the air, Arturo turned in his seat. "What's happening with Luca Romero, Marissa?" he said, his voice just above a whisper.

"What do you mean?" She knew exactly what he meant, but her instinctive tendency toward secrecy kicked in—as did her irritation that he knew her too well—and she answered on autopilot. "We're going to help Soto secure the best deal possible so Father makes more money." She didn't temper her distaste, and she didn't have to.

"That's not what I'm talking about, and you know it isn't. You're spending a lot of time with her."

"If you're talking about this morning, I had to get her set up in the villa before we left. It's best for us if we get ahead of whatever schedule Soto might already have agreed to on the delivery for the scripts and edits."

He pressed his lips together and shook his head slowly. "I'm talking about fresh-cut flowers, Egyptian cotton sheets, and engraved MacBooks worth sixty-thousand pesos."

Marissa held his gaze. "She needed to be comfortable and feel well looked after if we want her to do this for Father. Her only incentive to earn money for the woman who stole her life is to stay alive." She flicked her hand. "And the Mac wasn't that expensive. Pedro has a stock of them and gave me a favorable deal."

"What about the evening visit to share dinner with her?"

"You were there. It wasn't exactly intimate with fifty other women present, Arturo. What are you worried about?"

He tilted his head and looked at her, his expression incredulous. "You know what I'm worried about, Marissa. You've never looked at anyone the way you look at her."

She had no answer to that clichéd declaration. Now that she was finally getting to spend some time with Luca, even in unfavorable circumstances, their connection was as undeniable as she'd thought it would be. Though it seemed impossible after one conversation, Marissa *had* known she was attracted to Luca, and talking with her more had simply reinforced her belief. Her mamita had always taught her to trust her instincts, and she had no intention of ignoring that advice now. Surrounded by the threat of violence, and with Luca held there against her will all of that seemed to fade into the background when they were together. "What about the way I look at her?" Could Arturo see it only because he knew her so well, or had she been careless with her affection?

"Have you told her about our plans?" he asked, ignoring her petulant question.

She couldn't lie outright and look him in the eye, so she glanced down and tightened her seatbelt. "I haven't told her any details."

"But you *have* told her that we're planning to leave?"

His eyes bulged as he struggled to keep his voice quiet, making Marissa glad they were having this conversation here and not in Arturo's car where there would be no barrier to him raising his voice. He might not like what he had to do for her father, but it often proved impossible for him not to employ some of the bad habits he'd picked up.

"I trust her, Arturo."

He pressed his palm to his forehead as if he was trying to keep an explosion of curses inside. "Why? Why do you trust her? You don't know her. Look at the situation she's in, Marissa. She has nothing. And now you've given her information she could use to bargain her way to freedom. Did you think about that when you spilled our secret?"

His warning gave her pause but only for a moment. "She wouldn't do that to me, and especially not after Soto's betrayal."

"Can you hear yourself? Why *wouldn't* she do that to you? She doesn't owe you anything. And what if Soto's betrayal has made her rethink her own moral stance? If I was in her shoes, I'd do anything to get out of there. I wouldn't think twice about using that information if it helped me get out."

"You need to calm down, or I'm swapping seats with Teo." She stared at him until he broke eye contact. "And remember who you're talking to."

Arturo leaned back in his chair. "You're playing that card?"

"I'm not playing any card," she said, aware how her words had landed.

"It sounded a lot like a threat, and a lot like something your father would say."

"Now who's playing cards?" Marissa pressed the call button and ordered a white wine and a whiskey on ice when the flight attendant came to her. She remained silent until she'd gotten her drink and taken a long sip. "I was reminding you that you weren't talking to someone my father had sent you to lean on, Arturo, that's all. We've been friends a long time, but that doesn't give you the right to speak to me that way."

"I haven't spoken to you any way but honestly and logically." Arturo sighed. "I'm scared out of my mind, Marissa. We've been planning our escape for years, and now that it's so close, the thought of someone jeopardizing it is terrifying."

She placed her hand over his. "Me too. But I can't sit back and do nothing. I can't explain it and I don't know quite how it's happened, but Luca is special to me. She has been since she spent an afternoon listening to my hopes and fears—all of which she kept to herself even after Soto told her who I was."

"And are you special to her too?" he asked.

He was calmer now, his voice more even, and Marissa exhaled and relaxed back into her seat. She hadn't realized how tense the confrontation had made her. "I don't know the answer to that, and even though it's like we're in a weird bubble when we're together, it doesn't feel right just to ask her outright if she has feelings for me."

"Do you get any sense of attraction from her?"

She shrugged. "I thought so, but when I was there the other evening, she seemed to put up a wall between us."

Arturo chuckled. "The night I was fifty yards away from you?"

"Yes. Why would that matter?"

"For someone with such a high intelligence, you can be pretty dumb sometimes."

"Hey." She punched his shoulder lightly. "What are you talking about?"

"Have you told her that I'm gay?" he whispered.

"Of course not. That's your personal information to share, and it's not for me to out you to anyone."

He nodded. "Exactly right. And you've told her that we want to run away together, yes?"

"Yes. So?"

He raised his eyebrows, as if waiting for the lightbulb to go off in Marissa's mind. "You don't hear how all that sounds when you put it together?"

Marissa played the words back, and the penny dropped. "Luca thinks that we're a couple? Ew, that's so gross."

"Agreed." He wrinkled his nose like she was a bad smell under it. "You're like my sister, and even if I was into women, that would be all kinds of wrong. But if you think about it from Luca's perspective and just with the information she has, it would be easy to assume we were together."

"Again, ew."

Arturo shrugged. "It's what your father has wanted since we were old enough to have those kind of feelings. And it's what Santiago thought would happen too." He paused and half-smiled. "We were inseparable as children. If you weren't with your mamita, you were with me. People make assumptions based on societal norms, and nobody has any idea that both of us are far from normal." He bumped her shoulder and giggled.

"That giggle is definitely not normal, no." Marissa hadn't missed the flicker of sadness that crossed his eyes when Arturo had mentioned Santiago. They still hadn't talked about it, and Marissa knew that keeping grief locked inside only turned it bitter and hard. "Are you ready to talk about that yet?" she asked.

He looked away briefly. "Ask me that question when we're in Spain. I can't unlock any of this," he tapped the side of his head, "until we're safely away from your father and his reach. Unpacking everything I've done over the past seventeen years..." He blew out a long breath. "I don't even know what that's going to do to me, but I do know that I can't risk starting that process until we're free."

She squeezed his hand. "I understand. I won't ask again until we're relaxing on a beach in Europe. Circling back to my woman troubles then, you're saying that Luca thinks we're a thing, and because she's such a genuine person, she wouldn't make her feelings known to me out of respect for you."

Arturo laughed. "'Woman troubles?' I long for the day when I have man troubles to discuss with you. Anyway, she's probably keeping her feelings hidden more out of respect for your position and the fact that she might be murdered for making a move on you than anything to do with me, but yes, that might play a part too."

"I don't know how we're supposed to give each other any advice based on experience when we're playing for opposite teams." She smiled, feeling so much lighter now that she'd gotten everything out in the open with Arturo. She hated keeping secrets from him. Whatever was happening in her life, he would always be a part of it.

"What are you hoping to achieve for her though, Marissa? Regardless of feelings, what can you do for her before we leave?" He touched her arm and looked at her seriously. "We *are* still leaving on el Día de los Muertos, aren't we?"

"Of course we are." When the veil thinned, she wouldn't miss her last chance to be close to her mamita, to tell her she was leaving, and to thank her for accepting who she was. She couldn't help but think that her mamita would have gotten along so well with Luca; they would've loved each other. Maybe that's why she was so strongly drawn to her. She could feel her mamita's approval, even now.

"Is she coming with us?"

Marissa hadn't thought of that, but it couldn't be an option, could it? She and Arturo would have to hide in Spain while Luca had a lucrative author/screenwriter career to reclaim. The two were mutually exclusive. There could be no way, no happy ending for both of them. Unless Luca was willing to start over and write under a new pen name, far away from Mexico and Marissa's father. Whatever she was able to do for Luca, she had to accept that it might mean they could never be together. "I don't know yet. I want to find a way to exchange Luca for Casey so she can have her life back."

Arturo raised his glass. "Good luck with that."

She clinked her glass to his. "Whatever happens, primo, our plans won't change, I promise you that." And she meant it. She would do everything she could to help Luca, but she had an obligation to Arturo and to herself to get them out from under her father's clutches. The dice were rolling, and the game was on. With the spirit of her mamita pushing her forward, Marissa was sure she could outwit her father and win for them all.

Chapter Twenty

CASEY PULLED HER VARIOUS purchases from their branded shopping bags and laid them out on her bed. The bags alone were worth more than anything she'd ever bought, and she folded them up neatly.

"What are you doing with those?" Anastasia asked.

"Keeping them to use for something else." She put the bags on the dressing table and turned back to Anastasia, who looked amused. Beautifully naked and amused. "Why?"

"Because they're just bags. You'll get more when you buy more clothes. You should leave them by the door, and the maid service will take them away."

Casey shrugged. It made sense but seemed wasteful. But what did she care now that she had Luca's money to spend and a little more money in the bank?

"I hope your girl is going to appreciate the effort you're going to." Anastasia turned onto her back and parted her legs slightly. "Any chance before you get ready for your big meeting?"

Casey bit her lip, tempted by Anastasia's offer, then checked the time on her new smart watch. "I can't."

"Fine." Anastasia rolled out of bed.

Casey watched while she dressed, deciding that she had enough time to appreciate Anastasia's fine form. "I shouldn't enjoy you putting clothes on as much as I do."

Anastasia gave her a wicked smile. "As long as you enjoy taking them off more, we're good." She buttoned her blouse, slowly walking toward Casey as she did. "I'm on late tonight. Do you think you'll need my kind of evening room service?"

Casey slowly ran her finger between Anastasia's breasts. "I have other plans tonight. You know that. You arranged everything for me."

Anastasia kissed her hard. "And you know where I am if your plans change. I could always serve myself along with the fancy dinner."

"I'll keep that in mind, but I think my dinner date is too classy for a threesome."

"Her loss." Anastasia slapped Casey's butt and strutted out of the bedroom.

Casey waited until she was out of sight and the hotel door had closed before she turned back to the outfit she'd just bought with Anastasia's guidance. The suit was amazing, and when she'd tried it on, she knew she had to have it. The price was more than she'd expected, more than she'd spent on clothes in her life, but thanks to a discussion with her agent about the cost of staying in LA, the agency had just deposited a loan against the first installment of her advance in her checking account, and Casey was celebrating. She also liked the way Anastasia looked at her when she came out of the dressing room, like she wanted to devour her. It made her confident that Marissa would have the same reaction.

Anastasia had been a lot of fun to have around over the past few days, and between the marathon bouts of hard sex, she'd also been a great tour guide. Casey was starting to feel comfortable in LA. In a couple of days, she was moving into the apartment Alyssa had arranged for her, and then she could settle in for real. She grinned and stroked the soft cotton of the suit trousers. She couldn't have imagined a better scenario than the one playing out, and it'd get even better today when she saw Marissa again.

Vargas wanted to keep an eye on the financials, and that was okay with Casey, especially because he was sending Marissa. Casey wouldn't be here without his help, and with the new movie deal on the table, there'd be plenty to go around for everyone to be happy. Well, everyone except Luca, but at least she was getting to be a little part of it by writing the screenplay. She'd be putting words into the mouth of Elodie Fontaine. Casey laughed. She'd like to put more than words in her mouth.

She stripped off her tank and shorts and pulled on the new Calvin Klein boxers. God, they were soft on her skin. She'd almost be reluctant to let Marissa take them off. The shirt and suit felt just as great, and when she looked in the mirror, she saw the Casey she'd always known was there, desperate to get out. She'd been suave and charming her whole life—now she had the outfit to match. Marissa wouldn't be able to resist her.

Casey checked the time again then looked out the window. Lou was leaning against the side of her car, puffing away on her vape. Probably a fruit flavor. She'd bored Casey with the range of options she carried around with her—"One for every mood"—on a recent pick up. While Casey appreciated everything Alyssa was doing to welcome her to the agency, she wished they had more than one driver available. Lou didn't seem comfortable with silence and filled every second of it with dull facts and stories about people Casey had never even heard of, let alone cared about.

She headed to the bathroom, fixed her hair, and splashed her neck with the new cologne Anastasia had chosen. She took one last look in the mirror. *Irresistible*. Get the meeting out of the way and get Marissa back to her hotel room for a full-on seduction. Her dream life had fallen into place, and Marissa Vargas was the only missing piece. That would change tonight.

***

"You were amazing in there," Casey said. "I can't believe you got another two hundred thousand dollars out of them." She slid into the back seat of the car and closed her own door when neither Teo nor Arturo moved to do it for her. Marissa got in beside her, and her door was closed for her. Casey didn't care. With her share of the contract Marissa had just negotiated, she could pay someone to do it for her if she wanted. But Casey was already thinking about investments. She was confident that Marissa could get Luca to do anything she asked her to do, and even if she resisted, Vargas had other methods to force Luca's hand. But it didn't hurt to have a backup plan. Alyssa had already asked if she'd started her next book, because Luca had mentioned in her submission email that her next idea was a nine-book series on the muses, whatever the hell they were. But the money for nine books, based on what Casey had been promised would come through from sales, the movie deal, and all the merchandising, would be beyond what Casey had thought possible in her lifetime.

"I just did my job, Casey," Marissa said without looking at her.

Casey glanced at Marissa's bodyguards in the front. *That's* why Marissa was being so cool and distant. She clearly didn't want them to know her business. "Well, you're great at it. Your father will be impressed."

Marissa turned to look at her. "Do you think? What about your father?

Is he impressed with what you're doing?"

"He will be when I send some money his way." Casey winked. "We're a family of grifters, Marissa. This is what we do, and we're damn good at it."

"Mm. My father is easily impressed by anything that makes him money without him having to do much too," she whispered, her gaze fixed on the back of Teo's head.

Casey snorted. "This kind of con takes a lot of work. Trying not to be charming and having to channel a loser like Luca Romero is harder than you'd think."

Something flickered briefly across Marissa's eyes, but she didn't comment. She probably thought Luca was lame but was too classy to twist the knife.

"We should celebrate. Come up to my hotel room. The room service is amazing." Mostly due to Anastasia, but she didn't want to share Marissa on their first time. Maybe after a couple of hours, Anastasia joining wouldn't hurt—if Marissa turned out to be game for that. The night had the potential to be one of the best nights of their lives.

She saw Arturo's head shift slightly, and Marissa clearly caught his eye in the rearview mirror.

"This isn't a social visit, Casey," Marissa said and inspected her nails. "Father sent me to negotiate the movie deal, and I have to be on a plane home early tomorrow morning."

Fuck Arturo. Casey could see Marissa was uncomfortable with his oversight, but how was she supposed to get Marissa out from under his nose so they could spend some quality time together? "We'd be toasting the deal you made. That'd make it a business meal, wouldn't it?" She wiggled her eyebrows. "Rodríguez and Castillo can enjoy some downtime and go to a strip club."

Marissa laughed, but it didn't sound genuine.

Arturo turned this time and stared at Casey. "Señor Vargas would cut off my balls and feed them to me if I left his only daughter alone in America."

"She wouldn't be alone. She'd be with me. You can trust me to look after her." *In all the ways you'd want to look after her if you had a shot*. In the corner of her eye, Casey saw Marissa stiffen. She must hate how her father treated her like a fragile piece of glass when she was clearly strong enough to look after herself. As his right-hand man, Arturo was just an unpleasant extension of Vargas's authority over her. Casey bet Marissa wouldn't be sad to see Arturo die in a drive-by shooting. That might take her a little time to arrange by getting to know a powerful local gang, but it wasn't out of the realms of possibility. Marissa had said she would have to come again, and these two knuckle heads would be in tow. It'd be the perfect opportunity to kill them off and give Marissa the freedom she obviously craved. Yes, it'd be the end of this wild ride because that would mean her father not letting Marissa off the compound ever again if she returned, but damn, the reward in having a woman like her was worth it. And if Casey made the investments she'd been looking at, they'd be comfortable enough while she figured out the next big score. She could give Marissa the life she desired, the life she deserved away from Vargas.

Casey looked across at her again. Damn, she was hot. Casey could imagine the looks they'd get if Marissa was on her arm at the awards when Elodie Fontaine won her third Best Actor Oscar for playing Caletho in their movie. All those people who'd wish they could be her just to have a woman like Marissa on their arm. But she'd be hers. Marissa would be *her* woman.

"I have other plans," Marissa said. "I'm visiting one of the families Father has relocated."

"And I don't trust you at all, Soto."

Casey sneered at Arturo then refocused on Marissa. "What if I come with you?" she asked. She leaned closer. "I know you want to get out of this life as much I did, Marissa," she whispered. "Let me come with you, and we can talk about going to New York. We can get away from your father together."

Marissa's eyes blazed. That caught her attention.

"I can give you the life you're dreaming about, I promise."

Marissa was silent for a moment, and Casey made no attempt to fill it. She was offering Marissa her fantasy life; that would take some processing, some believing. She had to understand that Casey was her knight in shining Prada, and no one had ever been there for Marissa like Casey was now.

"Before I say yes to listening to what you've got to say, I have one question," she whispered.

"Shoot." Casey could almost smell the victory. Marissa would soon fall into her arms.

"Do you feel *any* guilt over what you did to Luca Romero?"

Casey looked deep into Marissa's eyes, searching for the motive behind her question. Marissa had a conscience, something Casey was unfamiliar with. Marissa *wanted* Casey to have remorse, to feel bad about what she'd done to her best friend. "Of course I do." She sighed deeply. "Every day I think about what I did to Luca to get here. I know I called her a loser earlier, but that's just me trying to stay on top of my guilt by convincing myself that what I did is okay." She ran her hand through her hair and glanced out the window. "But it isn't. None of what I've done is okay. And I could say that it's all I know, that it's what my family have raised me to be, but that's just an excuse. I'm my own person, and this was my decision, and I have to live with it."

Marissa's expression softened, and she nodded slowly.

Casey had her; she was falling for every bullshit line. "If I could go back in time, I wouldn't have done it." She tugged at her suit jacket. "All the expensive clothes and the fancy hotels can't take away my regret, and they can't replace the friendship I've thrown away." Now to seal the deal. "But I can't go back. Your father would kill me *after* he made me suffer for a very long time. I just hope that having to write the screenplay will get Luca out of the fields and back to doing the thing she loves the most, even if she isn't where she hoped she'd be." She took Marissa's hand gently. "Please. When you go home, please tell her I'm sorry. Please tell her that I wish I hadn't destroyed our friendship. Will you do that for me?"

And the Oscar goes to...

Chapter Twenty-One

THE SOUND OF THE key slamming into the front door lock made Luca jump. Her fingers had been flying on the keyboard now that she'd mastered the functions of the scriptwriting software Marissa had pre-loaded, and she was deep into writing Caletho and Nelese's first meeting. She looked at the time and leapt from her chair and headed out the office, hoping it was Marissa back early from her trip.

She had barely stepped through to the corridor when the door was pushed opened. Luca stopped as two men stood in the opening. She didn't recognize them, but the disappointment at them not being Marissa temporarily overrode the potential terror of what this visit might mean. "What do you want?" She heard the hint of fear and weakness in her voice and stood up straighter, expanding her chest with a deep breath.

"Señor Vargas wants to speak with you. Let's go."

This couldn't be good. Marissa had said he wouldn't meet with her, and there couldn't be a problem already. She'd only been working on the script for a day. What was he expecting? "I need to put shoes on."

"Quickly."

Luca nodded. She dropped into the chair against the wall and pulled her new sneakers on. Marissa had managed to guess her size correctly and choose something that she'd love to wear. These and the modest new selection of clothes Luca had found folded neatly in the bedroom closet were just another thing that reinforced what a thoughtful and caring person Marissa was. Another thing that made her wish everything was different, and that Luca could have a chance at showing Marissa they could be together. But that was just the stuff of fantasy, and she wasn't worthy of a woman like Marissa anyway.

She followed Vargas's heavies and got into the backseat of their SUV. They didn't say anything else to her on the relatively short journey to the main house, for which Luca was grateful. She had nothing to say to them other than, "Keep driving and get me out of here," but that plea would probably just make them laugh.

When she got out of the car, she was sandwiched between them to walk into the mansion. Her heart pounded against her ribs, and she took long, deep breaths to calm herself.

She was escorted into Vargas's office after they'd knocked and waited to be admitted, and Luca let out a sigh when she saw no sign of plastic sheeting on the floor. She hadn't expected this to be the kind of meeting she didn't survive, but Casey had told her enough about Vargas and his reputation for acting on a whim to be slightly concerned.

She scanned the office, but Marissa wasn't present. She was seated roughly in front of his desk, and the two of them stood inches behind her. He didn't look up from the papers on his desk, so Luca took the time to study him. His dead eyes flicked across the lines quickly, and she could see nothing in them but darkness. His nose was puckered and reddened, a sure sign of alcoholism, and his jowls hung looser than a hound dog's. His jaw tensed on and off, though she couldn't tell if that was a tick, or if he was annoyed by whatever he was reading. His hands and fingers looked rough and pudgy, and she shuddered at the unwanted thought of him touching Marissa's mamá.

There were pictures of Marissa and her mamá all over the villa, on tables and hung on the walls, and Luca had enjoyed looking at them all. It was a shrine of sorts, but with a relationship as powerfully positive as theirs clearly was, there was no reason Marissa would want to forget her mamá, regardless of how painful it was to be constantly reminded she was no longer here. Looking at Vargas now, it was clear that Marissa had gotten her outer beauty as well as her inner beauty from her mamá. From what Luca knew of Marissa and Vargas, Luca couldn't see what he'd contributed to making Marissa the wonderful human being she was. Although Marissa would also have learned how *not* to be through being around him.

"How are you finding your new accommodations?" he asked.

She hadn't seen that coming. What did he care about how comfortable she was or wasn't? "It's a very nice villa." When he didn't say anything, she added, "Thank you," in case that's what he was waiting for. But the words were like acid in her throat. She shouldn't be thanking him for anything.

"And are you comfortable?" He leaned back in his chair and steepled his fingers. "From what Soto tells me, your previous apartment at the hotel was very basic. It must be nice to sleep on a mattress thick enough that you don't feel the frame beneath it."

Luca nodded. "It is." Another expectant pause followed. "Thank you." She gritted her teeth the moment the words left her mouth again. She'd be in less pain if he'd chosen to torture her.

"And the refrigerator is full? You're not wanting for anything?"

She swallowed and shook her head slowly. Each of his calm and deliberate questions were like leeches on her skin, not painful as such, but out of place and uncomfortable. His blank expression and the way his eyes bored into hers with such dispassion gave her no indication of what might be coming, but she knew it was something unpleasant by the way her skin prickled and her hairs stood on end. "Everything is...perfect. Thank you." Her third expression of gratitude, and it wasn't getting any easier. Nothing was *perfect*. This evil man had taken away her freedom with no consideration for anything other than what he was gaining from it, and he wanted her to *thank him* for it? For stealing her ambitions, her life, her dream? *Fuck you*.

She offered a tight smile instead of the rage she wanted to unleash and waited for the next unnerving query.

"The Soto family have worked for me for years. Casey Soto is una cucaracha who thinks she's entitled to far more than she's worth."

He sneered and pulled a cigar from a box on his desk before he used a standing guillotine to slice off the tip. Luca imagined he'd sliced more than cigars with that piece of equipment.

"She thinks this is her big break. But she's just a blunt tool I'm using for easy profit."

Luca pushed herself back into the leather chair, and it creaked noisily. She wanted to pick it up and smash it across his smug face. As if sensing her anger, one of the men behind her placed his hands on her shoulders and pressed her into the chair.

Vargas came around to her side of the desk and fixed his hand around Luca's throat. "I'm allowing my daughter to handle your side of this operation." He squeezed, forcing her breath out. "But if you fuck with her, you will have me to answer to."

Luca suppressed a gag at the stale smell of his spittle and tried to swallow against the pressure of his hand around her neck. In response, Vargas tightened his grip, making her cough.

"You understand that you do not want to have a different kind of conversation with me, don't you?"

She tried to nod since there was no way she could speak, and he released her.

"Do you understand?"

Luca coughed again and put her hand to her throat. "Yes. I understand completely."

He patted her cheek firmly and smiled. "That's very good to hear, Luca." He pushed away from the desk and returned to his chair. He lit his cigar and blew a cloud of blue smoke in Luca's direction. "So, back to the villa and more writing for you, yes?"

Luca looked down at her hands. "Sí, señor."

Vargas jutted his chin, and his guys hauled Luca to her feet. "No delays, and no excuses. Deliver the screenplay to my daughter, and then we'll see what's next for you."

He waved her away, and they shoved her toward the door. She somehow managed to stay upright despite her legs wanting to fold beneath her. She swallowed against the rising urge to vomit and hurried back to their vehicle. The implied threat in his last words coupled with his blatant warning made being caged in the villa some kind of twisted solace. When the door closed and locked behind her, Luca leaned against it and slid to the floor. She wrapped her arms around herself and choked back tears. She wouldn't waste them on him. The only thing that gave her a hint of comfort was the knowledge that Marissa would soon return. Whatever strange bubble of protected isolation she brought with her, Luca didn't understand. But she couldn't wait to be back inside it.

***

The knock that came early that evening made Luca stiffen, but the door remained closed as Luca approached it. She peered through the side window and smiled widely when Marissa waved, her eyes bright and full of happiness. She held the door key up, and Luca nodded at the sweet gesture. Marissa entered the villa, wheeling a suitcase behind her.

"Have you come straight from the airport?" Luca asked.

"More or less. I dropped my overnight bag at the main house and got this." She continued down the hallway and into the second bedroom, with

Luca following behind. "I'd already packed it to save me time."

"It's good to see a friendly face." Luca stopped at the doorjamb. She subconsciously touched her neck and winced. It didn't hurt to speak, but her skin was seriously sore.

Marissa turned back to her after she'd lifted her suitcase on the bed. "Or any face, I'd imagine. You must've been lonely after the past week in the company of fifty other women."

"Oh, I've seen other faces while you've been gone, but none that I'd want to see again."

Marissa frowned and came closer. "Has something happened?" She gently pulled Luca's hand from her neck and gasped. "Who did that to you?"

"Your father took the time to explain the parameters of me staying here and to lay out what would happen if I didn't hold up my side of the deal in good time."

Marissa gently traced her fingers across Luca's neck, and she shivered. Goosebumps—the good kind—erupted all over her body, and the pain from Marissa touching her bruised skin was vastly outweighed by the pleasure that ignited through her body.

Marissa drew her fingers back quickly. "I'm sorry. Did I hurt you?"

Luca shook her head, instantly missing the softness of the connection. "I'm fine."

"My father did this personally?"

Luca nodded and noticed Marissa clench her jaw and flare her nostrils. She looked cute when she was angry, and Luca liked it even more because Marissa was angry on her behalf. She felt protected and cared for, two things she longed to do for Marissa. What she wouldn't give to turn their bubble into reality by being in Arturo's position and taking Marissa out of this toxic and damaging environment.

Marissa took Luca's hand. "Let's get some ice on it."

She didn't feel the need to tell Marissa that she'd already iced it, which was why the bruising was already out. Instead, she went to the kitchen and sat on the bar stool that Marissa pulled out. She watched as Marissa moved around the kitchen gracefully, collecting this and that and preparing an ice pack. She pushed away all thoughts of *why* they were here together and concentrated on the deep joy that resonated in her heart and mind at the simple action of being in the same space as Marissa.

Her bliss was interrupted when she remembered where Marissa had just returned from. "How did everything go in LA?"

Marissa let out a breath, then she tenderly applied the wrapped-up towel to Luca's neck. "Is that okay?" When Luca nodded, she took her hand and pressed it gently to the ice pack before checking her watch. "Keep that on for fifteen minutes if you can." Marissa went back to the fridge and began to gather ingredients. "I can see that all you've eaten is chips and an apple. I'm going to make you tacos al pastor. It's something my mamá always made me when I didn't feel well." She took a bottle from the fridge, opened it and pressed it into Luca's free hand. "And you might need this while I tell you what happened."

Luca took a long pull on the ice-cold beer and prepared herself for the story. Marissa chopped and fried while she retold the events in LA. Luca slammed her bottle hard on the counter when Marissa gave her the figure she'd managed to negotiate with FlatLine. Beer bubbled to the top of the bottle, and she stuck her mouth over it to stop it from overflowing. "That's crazy money for book options on an unknown, isn't it? How did you get so much?"

"It is, you're right. But the guy who owns the studio, Jules French, is an unusual cat in Hollywood. He's all about the process and ensuring everyone involved is paid what their contribution is worth. He said, 'I can't make this movie without this book, and I'm willing to pay you whatever you ask for as long as my team and I think it's reasonable.'"

Luca let out a short breath and bit her bottom lip. "I would've loved to have seen you in action." Powerful femme women were Luca's catnip. She'd roll over and let them tickle her soft underbelly any day of the week, and Marissa personified the kind of soft and subtle supremacy that drove Luca wild.

Marissa looked across at Luca and raised her eyebrow as she smiled, clearly amused. "It wasn't as impressive as it might sound. My *amazing* negotiation skills weren't employed because Señor French made it clear he was ready to pay whatever we asked for, so you would've been sorely disappointed, I think."

Luca bit the inside of her lip to stop the immediate response of *Nothing you could do would ever disappoint me*. "I doubt that."

In the moments of silence that followed, Luca's initial euphoria at the amount Marissa had secured dissipated into the hard realization that she would never see any of that money, and nausea turned her stomach, snuffing out her appetite despite the fabulous scent of Marissa's cooking. "Did Casey say anything about me? About what she's done to me?"

"She played up the regret and guilt, because she thought that's what I wanted to hear," Marissa said. "She didn't fool me for a second. The lies dripped from her mouth like honey from a beehive."

Luca clenched her jaw. She was stupid to have ever thought Casey had been a friend. "I've worked years for this, and everyone but me is benefiting."

Marissa dropped a tortilla into the hot oil and flipped it on both sides before gently folding in the sides with tongs. "I know that's how it is right now, Luca, but Casey has made a fatal error in judgment that we can exploit."

Luca almost laughed at Marissa's theatrics. How was it possible that she could feel so desperately out of control and exploited but so uplifted at the same time? "And what's that?"

"She seems to think that I'm into her."

Luca clenched her fist and quietly grumbled under her breath.

Marissa laughed lightly. "Was that a growl?"

"No," she said a little too quickly to be believable.

Marissa looked down her nose at Luca and raised her eyebrows. Luca glanced away, unable to bear the playful scrutiny.

"Are you lying to me?"

"No."

Marissa raised her eyebrows even higher.

"Okay, yes. It was a growl. So what?"

Marissa grinned, triumphant and clearly pleased with herself. "Why would you growl like a wolf?"

"Because Casey is an asshole. She thinks every woman is into her, even the straight ones like you. And that's really irritating." There. It was out, at least partially. No need to make Marissa uncomfortable by telling her that she envied every conversation Casey had ever had with her, or that Casey had teased her mercilessly for her pointless crush.

"I see." Marissa flipped out a perfectly shaped taco shell and slid another tortilla into the pan. "Well, because she thinks I'm interested in her, she told me all about a plan to go to New York with every cent that the book and movie deals have made after your agent's cut."

Luca dropped the ice pack onto the kitchen worktop. "Without paying your father his cut?"

Marissa smiled and nodded. "Without paying my father *anything*."

"Why would she risk that? She knows what he's capable of."

"Because she thinks she's in love with me, though I suspect I'd just be a previously unobtainable trophy girlfriend and winning me is the thrill she's seeking. Not actually *me*."

Luca silently agreed, but she also knew Casey was as much in love with Marissa as she could be when she loved herself so much.

"Loyalty is the most important thing to my father. If he believes Casey is planning to double cross him—"

"*And* steal his daughter."

"Then he'll act first and take Casey off the board. I'll let her know that he's onto her, and she'll have no choice but to run." Marissa smiled. "Leaving you to reclaim your life."

"Doesn't that mean you'll have to play along so Casey puts her plan in motion?" The thought of Casey anywhere near Marissa turned her stomach.

Marissa went to the refrigerator and pulled another beer out. "And you don't think I can do that because I'm straight?" She handed the bottle to Luca but didn't release it.

"I don't *want* you to do it. Casey should carry a health warning after all the people she's been with. I bet Arturo doesn't want you to do it either."

Marissa moved closer so that she was between Luca's legs. "Why else don't you want me to do it?"

Luca swallowed. The bottle in their hands was ice-cold but it was doing nothing to cool the raging heat in response to having Marissa close enough to smell her shampoo. "Because you don't know where she's been and who she's been with, not to mention that she's dangerous in her own way. You shouldn't go anywhere near her."

Marissa put her free hand on Luca's thigh. "And why wouldn't Arturo want me to do it?"

Luca's breath caught. If Marissa was preparing to fool Casey, she didn't need much practice. "Because I don't think he'd want someone else kissing you."

"Someone else?" Marissa whispered.

Back away or lean into the game? If Marissa needed to practice being a lesbian on someone, it may as well be Luca. But she was kidding herself. "Other than him, obviously." She adored Marissa for being willing to do this for her, but she'd bet money that Arturo wasn't happy about it.

Marissa removed her hand from Luca's thigh and ran her fingernail along Luca's cheekbone. Luca wriggled slightly in her seat. The urge to get away before she did something stupid competed with the urge for her to stay exactly where she was twisted her mind until she didn't know which way was up. Luca held her breath and waited to see how far Marissa was prepared to go.

"Other than him? You think I'm kissing Arturo?" Marissa inched even closer and wrapped her hand around the back of Luca's neck.

"I think you do more than kiss him if you're running away together." Though she didn't like to think about that at all. When she was thinking about Marissa, which was a lot, Arturo didn't feature in her scenarios at all. But thinking about him right now would be useful to keep herself under control.

"Because you think I'm straight?" Marissa played with Luca's hair and didn't break her gaze.

Luca closed her eyes and tried to concentrate on the conversation instead of all the insanely good feelings tearing around her body. How many times had she dreamed of being close enough to Marissa to kiss her?

The taste of Marissa's lips against her own jolted her back into focus. She opened her eyes, and Marissa stared deep into her soul. She pulled Luca into the kiss, and she could do nothing but respond to the moment she thought would never happen. She softened in Marissa's firm but tender grip, every fiber of her being dancing in absolute joy. Marissa parted Luca's lips with her tongue, and Luca exhaled as the feeling shot straight to her core. She throbbed hard against her shorts and kissed her back. She let go of the beer bottle and placed both hands on Marissa's hips, drawing their bodies together. Marissa's breasts pressed against her chest, and she moaned quietly into Marissa's mouth.

Reality tugged for her attention at the back of her mind, telling her this wasn't real, and that Marissa was showing Luca she was more than capable of playing along with Casey's plan. She'd proved her point. Luca pulled away reluctantly. "Okay, so you'll have no trouble fooling Casey into thinking you're into her if you do that."

Marissa's smile seemed slightly shy, but she didn't move away. "I'm not trying to fool you, Luca." She moved the wisp of hair that had fallen onto Luca's forehead. "I'm not straight, and the only time I've kissed Arturo was back when we were fifteen, and that only proved that I didn't like boys."

Luca opened her mouth to respond but paused as the puzzle pieces showed themselves in a new light. She didn't want to smash them together to make them fit, but it was really beginning to sound like Marissa was telling her that she had feelings for her. Was the picture she *wanted* to make also the picture that was right in front of her? "What are you saying, Marissa?"

Marissa sighed. "You still don't get it? I'm attracted to you, Luca Romero." She traced her finger along Luca's collarbone. "And I have been since we talked that day on the beach. Every time I came down to the bar, it was to see you. And every time, Casey got in the way, and you stayed in the background."

Luca's head was spinning and not from the alcohol. "I've wasted a year of conversations with you?"

"You could put it like that." She placed both hands on Luca's upper chest. "Or you could say we've missed out on a year of kisses like that one."

Luca blew out a long, slow breath. "I never thought for a second that you were gay, let alone that you might be interested in a gutter rat like me." She looked around. "And now we're here." Together but not together. "And you're leaving with Arturo soon."

Marissa glanced away. "That was the plan."

Luca took Marissa's hands in hers. "And it should stay that way." She couldn't believe she was saying the words. "I don't want to get in the way of your chance at freedom, Marissa. When we talked on the beach that first time, my heart ached for the pain you were in. You have to get away from your father and live your life, and there's no way I would ever want to mess that up."

"I think I can still do that and get you out of here."

Luca laughed gently. "You haven't told me the details, but I think that you're close to your escape time."

"Día de los Muertos," Marissa said. "I want to explain everything to my mamita when the veil thins."

"That's not enough time to run a con on anyone, so it's definitely not enough time to run one on someone like Casey." Luca kissed Marissa's knuckles. "And the money she needs to take you both to New York won't come in that quickly. That's not how publishing works."

The hopefulness in Marissa's expression fell away. "I suppose I hadn't thought about the specifics of it all."

"You promised that you'd help me, and you have." Luca gestured beyond Marissa to the office. "I'm doing what I love instead of picking leaves in the hot sun for hours. It's not where I hoped I'd be after finally getting a publishing deal, but it's better than thinking no one wants my words at all." It didn't feel better, of course, but there was no way she was voicing that to Marissa.

Luca rose from the stool and gently stepped Marissa back. "Let me help you with dinner, and you can tell me about your plans with Arturo."

Marissa nodded and said nothing. As Luca tried to find the plates and glasses, she dismissed the persistent niggle of her thoughts that this was what her life could've been like if she'd realized that Marissa was trying to get her attention.

She'd done the right thing. There was no way to guarantee Vargas would fall for Marissa's ruse, and Luca couldn't live with herself if she stood in the way of her happiness.

Even if that happiness had to be far, far away from her.

Chapter Twenty-Two

THE MOONLIGHT BURSTING THROUGH the blinds pulled Marissa from a light sleep. She muttered quietly to herself, wishing she'd pulled the drapes before she'd dropped into bed last night, when she'd been more than slightly buzzed on a couple of glasses of wine. The alcohol hadn't done what she'd hoped it would, which was numb her feelings. All of them. It had done the opposite, deepening her regret that she hadn't had the guts to approach Luca months ago. Then maybe none of this would be happening. They would be friends at the very least, and Luca would've been able to ask her for advice on the contract without Soto using her as bait.

Her cellphone buzzed on the bedside table. What did her boss want this early in the morning?

"Your father called me yesterday to let me know you were no longer available to work on the Marín case. I understand, of course, but I need you to come in to brief Ana so they can pick up where you were without causing too much inconvenience to Moreno."

Marissa rubbed sleep from her eyes and kickstarted her brain. "Sí, Señor Aguilar. I can come in this morning, if that works for you?" She couldn't wait to be rid of that case.

"Yes, Marissa, as soon as possible, please."

"You're already in the office?"

"Yes. There's been a development, so everyone who can help is being brought in." He sighed. "Your father's timing couldn't be worse, so I hope whatever you're dealing with is worth it. I'm sure he thinks it is, even if– Well, anyway. As soon as you can, Marissa."

Five a.m. would be extreme for Moreno, even with a big case looming, but for the senior partner, it was unheard of. She hadn't expected his little dig at her father either, which indicated he was feeling the pressure. "I'll be there in an hour." She hung up and sent a text to Arturo asking him to pick her up in twenty minutes. She was showered, dressed, and ready to go in fifteen minutes, so she headed to the kitchen for coffee to go.

The door to Luca's bedroom was slightly ajar. Marissa didn't try to resist a quick peek. If Luca was stirring, she could let her know she had to leave for a couple of hours but would be back for lunch. In the half-light cast by the setting moon, Marissa could make out Luca on the bed, naked but for the shorts Marissa had chosen and the sheet over her left thigh. Marissa stared for longer than was decent before she reluctantly turned back toward the kitchen. Their kiss had inflamed the desire that already surged through Marissa's veins. When she'd initiated it, she had every intention of taking Luca to bed, if she were willing.

But she hadn't been. She'd pulled away and returned to conversation, the physical pull between them set aside.

Reality, her father, external circumstance all conspired to keep them apart. For now. For the moment, she couldn't think of how to conquer the obstacles that sought to derail their connection, but she planned to talk to Arturo now and Luca when she returned to see if there was any way the three of them could escape the oppression of her father and still be together.

She quickly made a pot of coffee and wrote a note to Luca before she left the villa quietly. She made her regular run to the barns with a basket of food while Arturo waited. When she was done, she climbed into the passenger seat. "Are you clean?" she asked, their new code for whether or not the car was bugged.

"We are." He pulled down the interior light and tapped a small device with a red wire exposed. "I've disabled it for now, but I'll need to reactivate it halfway to your office in case your father listens to the recordings later."

"He's monitoring them himself?"

"I told you, his paranoia is getting worse and the people he trusts are getting fewer." He nudged her lightly and pulled away from the villa. "Did you confess your feelings to her?

She swatted his shoulder. "I didn't confess anything. She's not my priest."

Arturo laughed. "No. Nobody wants to sleep with their priest."

"That's not true though, is it? You had a thing for Father Juan when you were seventeen."

"This isn't about me. Did you tell her or not?"

"Yes." She touched her lips, remembering the passion and fire of

Luca's mouth on hers, and Arturo whistled.

"She feels the same, doesn't she? I knew it." He slapped the steering wheel and looked smug.

"Yes." She said nothing else as they approached the perimeter barrier. Arturo acknowledged the guards, and they opened the gates. When they were out onto the main street, Marissa tapped the listening device. "But we don't have time to talk about that if you have to switch this back on soon. We need to talk about how we're going to get her out of there."

Arturo glanced at her briefly before returning his gaze to the near-empty road, still too early for the morning rush to work. "Marissa..."

She waited for more, but it didn't come. "There's got to be some way to undermine Soto and get Luca where she belongs. Soto's plan to leave for New York has to be usable in some way."

Arturo frowned. "But that doesn't solve your problem, does it? She'd be in LA, and you'd be in Spain. Or do you think she'd give up her writing career for you?"

Marissa shook her head as a new plan began to form. "I don't want her giving up anything for me. I'm thinking longer term. My father will stop looking for me eventually, if he even tries to—"

"What makes you think he wouldn't try to get you back?"

"Because we were originally just going to disappear, and he wouldn't know whether I'd been taken or had left. But now that you've told me how his paranoia is growing, I think I should leave a letter, explain everything, and ask him to leave me alone to live my life."

Arturo laughed. "He'd send people for you, don't doubt that for a second. And what about me? Where do I fit into your new plan?"

"I say that I've taken you for protection, and that he should trust you to look after me."

He stayed silent for a while, clearly processing. "It won't work," he said eventually. "And I don't think it's a better idea than just leaving without a trace. If he thinks rival cartels or his enemies are to blame, he'll go looking there first, giving us more time to disappear."

"I know that, but I don't think we thought about the consequences of that for other people."

"You mean his enemies?" He looked at her, and she nodded. "That's commendable but a little naïve. They're at war anyway, Marissa, and there are casualties and collateral damage in any war."

"That may be, but I don't want to be responsible for adding to that bloodshed." She touched his forearm gently. "I can't even begin to know how you feel about all the things he's made you do, but don't lose sight of who you are now, Arturo. Not when we're this close to getting away from it all."

"And I won't," he said. "But for us to both to heal, we have to get away successfully and our best chance is to stick with our original plan." He tapped the clock display on the dash. "Time's up. And I won't be able to switch this off on our way back. We'll talk tonight." He pulled over and reconnected the wire.

They talked about nothing of consequence for the rest of the journey, so Marissa took the time to contemplate why her father was suddenly unraveling. By the time they got to the office, she still hadn't figured out any triggers for his behavior, other than his fears over her refusal to marry any of the other cartels' suitors. She said goodbye to Arturo and headed into the office. Maybe she didn't need answers. If everything went to plan, she wouldn't have to think about her father or his violent actions ever again.

***

Marissa knocked on the villa door and waited until Luca appeared at the window, then she unlocked the door and Luca pulled it open. "Hi."

"Hey," Luca said and stood in the doorway.

Marissa smiled. "Can I come in?"

"Oh, sorry. Of course." Luca moved out of the way and closed the door behind her. "You left early this morning."

Marissa bit her lip at the unasked question, but it didn't stop the smile she was trying to keep from forming.

"What's funny?" Luca asked.

"This. Us." Marissa gestured into the air. "You missed me this morning," she said and headed to the kitchen to make lunch.

"I didn't say I missed you."

"Then why are you following me?"

"Because I'm hungry, and you probably want to feed me something real."

"See what I mean?" Marissa pulled open the fridge to gather the ingredients for quesadillas. "What would you like me to make for you, husband?" She had no idea where this light banter originated and how Luca could seemingly ignore her situation, but she liked it, and judging by the grin on Luca's face, she was enjoying it too. And if it helped Luca as a coping mechanism, Marissa was happy to play along.

"You can make me anything you like. I trust you completely after yesterday's meal." Luca dropped onto a bar stool and rested her chin on her hands. "Thanks for the note. Did everything go okay?"

"As well as I thought it would. Aguilar wasn't happy about me leaving just as the case is about to start, but it was more than that. A new witness came forward yesterday, and they don't know who it is or what they've seen. The person is under protective custody, because they're worried Marín, the defendant, will somehow eliminate them."

"And that concern is warranted?" Luca asked.

"Completely. Marín has been in this position multiple times and has gotten away with it because they've destroyed evidence or murdered witnesses. It looked like he would be walking away this time too." Marissa laid the cheese in four small tortillas and folded them carefully. "I didn't want to be part of the legal team, but I had no choice. And criminals are the main source of clients, obviously."

"Why obviously?" Luca picked up some stray cheese, and Marissa tapped her hand. "Ow."

"I don't know how you've survived on your own as long as you have." Marissa laughed at the wounded expression on Luca's face. "'Obviously' because it's my father's firm. He bought it for me."

Luca rolled her eyes. "That's a hell of a gift."

"It was just another attempt to control me and keep me close by. Tied to his business." She placed the quesadillas in the large frying pan. "What do you know of your parents, Luca?" Other than a fleeting reference to an orphanage, Luca hadn't talked about her parents at all. "You don't have to talk about it if you don't want to."

Luca's expression grew serious, and she flicked at a crumb on the counter. "I don't mind talking about it with you."

Marissa flipped the tortillas then poured them both coffee. "Here. It's too early for alcohol."

Luca half smiled, but it was clear she'd already fallen into the memories of her childhood.

"Are you okay? There's no pressure to share, honestly."

Luca shrugged. "You've told me a lot about your familia. It's only fair that I do the same." She gave a short laugh. "Then you can decide if I'm still worth your time."

Marissa looked up from the pan and smiled, thinking Luca was joking, but she was staring intently at the counter and tracing the grain of the wood with her fingertip. "Of course you're worth my time. Why would you think you're not?"

Luca glanced up and met her gaze briefly. "Why wouldn't an amazing woman like you want to spend time with a poor kid from the barrio? Really?"

"The way you grew up isn't who you are. I like the person I get to talk to. I only care about your background to the extent that it helped create the wonderful, talented, creative woman you are." She plated the quesadillas, and Luca followed her to the kitchen table.

Luca took a bite of her food, closed her eyes, and exhaled noisily. "Mm. This is so good. If you ever get bored of being a lawyer wherever you're going, you could always open a restaurant or a roach coach."

Marissa smiled and watched Luca devour her first quesadilla before she started her own. Her mamá had always loved to feed the people she cared for, but Marissa hadn't seen the appeal until now.

Luca licked melted cheese from her fingers then took a slurp of coffee. She wiped the escaping liquid from her chin. "Sorry. I can be messy."

Marissa shook her head. "No need to apologize. I like messy. It means you're enjoying it." She dipped her piece into a cup of sour cream and continued to eat, hoping that Luca would pick up the conversation and fill the silence.

"I was at the Door of Faith Orphanage from the time I was three years old. I don't have solid memories of what went on before that time, but I have wispy silhouettes in my mind. I have a feeling that my parents cared for me but couldn't care for me, but it's nothing more than a hope, if that makes sense?"

Marissa nodded when Luca paused, clearly waiting for a response.

"People abandon their children all the time—that's why those places have to exist. But I don't know if I was left there because they were dirt poor, or if they thought I could have a better life without them. They could've been addicts or criminals, I just don't know because there were no records."

"At the orphanage?"

Luca nodded. "I sneaked into the office when I was thirteen, but my file was empty of anything other than the notes they'd made of my illnesses and vaccinations. So whoever left me didn't leave any way of me contacting them when I got old enough to care for myself. Probably just left me on the doorstep like an Amazon package."

Luca fell silent again, and Marissa waited before asking, "Were you well treated?"

"It was as good as you could hope it would be surrounded by eighty other hungry kids. There were fights and bullies, but that kind of thing just prepared me for real life."

"You don't seem like the fighting type, but you're built like one." Marissa recalled seeing Luca almost naked in the outdoor shower. She was sturdy and solid without being noticeably muscular or ripped. And her skin was unmarked by scars or tattoos, which was unusual. Marissa hadn't had the displeasure of seeing Casey naked, but the flesh she paraded to everyone—arms, legs, chest, and shoulders—were covered in crude ink and poor design.

"Thanks...I think." Luca laughed.

"It was a compliment. I don't like fighting, but I like... Well, I like the way you look. A lot."

Luca's cheeks flushed, and she dug into her second quesadilla. She put it down after a couple of bites and sipped her coffee. "I'm not a fighter. I got my ass kicked most days, but it toughened me up. I can take a beating and get up and walk away." She shrugged. "I can fight if I have to, but I prefer to talk my way out of a confrontation over throwing punches. I spent most of my time there reading and staying out of the way of trouble as much as I could. And when I was twelve, there was this American college kid who was studying composition theory at Cal State. Her name was Veronica. She started coming every year for the summer, and she changed my life."

Luca's face lit up, and Marissa registered a pang of jealousy. "Really? Don't tell me she was your first." She wanted to hear about Luca's life, but she wasn't sure she wanted to hear *everything*.

She laughed and shook her head. "I admit that I liked her that way for a while, but those feelings faded pretty quick. She helped me read, and instead of Bible study after school, we dove into the classics." Luca blew out a long breath and smiled gently. "She came back for five years, and they were the best five years of my life."

"Do you still keep in touch?" That seemed like the better question than any of the others that came to mind. What does she look like? Or did she like you that way? Or would you get together if you met her now?

"Here and there." Luca twisted her coffee mug in her hands. "I sent her my first book when I finished it, and she encouraged me to try to get it published. We haven't spoken in a while. In her last email, she said she was teaching in Venice." Luca gestured around the room. "Obviously I haven't been able to let her know that I got an agent, or that my books are going to be published and made into movies with the great Elodie Fontaine starring in them." She shrugged. "You know the pages in the front of books where the author thanks everyone?"

"The acknowledgments? Yes."

"I was going to dedicate the first one to Veronica. I think she would've liked that."

Marissa put her hand on Luca's shoulder. "Of course she would." She wanted to say that Luca would get the chance to do that with another book, maybe even this book if they could just figure out how to get Casey out of the picture. But she couldn't. Luca finished her lunch and rubbed her stomach. "Thank you for making those. They were the best quesadillas I've ever had."

"Another thing my mamá taught me to—" Marissa sighed. It was insensitive to talk about how her amazing her mamita was.

Luca narrowed her eyes. "Taught you to cook?" She placed her hand over Marissa's. "You don't have to do that. We all have different backgrounds. You shouldn't not talk about yours because you think it might upset me. I love hearing about you and your mamá, and it breaks my heart that she's not still here with you now."

Marissa laced her fingers with Luca's. "Okay. Thank you."

Luca rubbed the back of her neck and made such an adorable face that Marissa wanted to kiss her. She sighed deeply. "But it's hard for me to keep a positive perspective on life after all this has happened." She stroked Marissa's fingers still interlaced with hers. "You're helping with that. I'm still angry, and I think that I'd tear Casey to pieces if she walked in here right now, but with everything that's happened, it would take a saint not to react that way."

"I think you're handling it far better than I'd expect anyone to. And it's nice that we get to share moments like this." Marissa liked the feeling of their fingers entwined. Their hands were so different; Luca's were large and rough and dwarfed Marissa's. And of course, hers were soft and smooth because she'd never had to do a hard day of manual labor in her life. She drifted again to the image of Luca in the outdoor shower and imagined running her hands over Luca's wet body, and she let out a long sigh. "I think you're an amazing person, Luca. I can't even begin to imagine how it feels, and sorry isn't a big enough word, but I'm glad that it's given us this." She lifted their hands. "I would never have built up the courage to approach you at the bar before I left forever."

Luca smiled, but it looked full of sadness. Marissa didn't need to ask why. She felt it too. Fate had been cruel to show them the potential of a life together, along with the knowledge that it would be all but impossible to make it permanent. She wanted to talk more about that, but for now, she'd enjoy the moment.

"I should get back to writing." Luca gently separated her hand from Marissa's, got up, and kissed the top of Marissa's head. "I'm getting to the part when Caletho and Nelese have sex for the first time."

"Okay. I'll bring you more coffee in a moment. Would you mind if I sat in the office with you?"

"Thanks. And I don't mind it at all. I'd love you to be in the room with me if you're not going to be bored."

"I never get bored with a book in my hand. I'll read by the fireplace." Where she'd try not to think about them having sex while Luca was writing about it.

Chapter Twenty-Three

LUCA STARED BEYOND THE blinking cursor on the screen, her fingers hovering above the keyboard, and transported herself to Venice Beach. She closed her eyes and imagined the sun setting over the horizon of the ocean. Hues of pinks and oranges played in the dusky white clouds, and turquoise waves rippled gently onto the smooth golden sand as the water receded. Caletho wrapped her wings around Nelese, cocooning her in their safety and strength.

She opened her eyes and looked across at Marissa, huddled on a huge armchair with her feet tucked beneath her. *What I'd give to have those wings now.*

"What?" Marissa asked.

"Nothing."

"You were staring at me. What were you thinking about?"

Luca wrinkled her nose. "I was thinking that I'd like to have Caletho's wings so I could fly us both out of here."

Marissa smiled and nodded. "That would be perfect. Although, after you'd gotten me somewhere safe, you'd have to fly back for Arturo."

"Are you guys a package deal?" Luca asked, half-teasing but wondering how close they really were.

"Actually, yes, we are." Marissa closed her book and laid it on the table beside her. "We're familia. Arturo was always in the house as a kid, and Mamá took him under her wing while Santiago, who had unofficially adopted him, worked for my father."

"He's an orphan?"

"Yes. My father decided he was going to take young boys from the orphanage to create a little army of guards. He started with Arturo. I suppose it was a different version of what he eventually did with the workers and the barns. Mamá was so angry with him when she found out what he'd done, he was going to take Arturo back. But she wouldn't let him, and Santiago stepped in and asked if he could look after Arturo and raise him as his son. He was a good man, and he wasn't involved in the violent side of the business, so Mamá allowed it. I think she would've happily taken him on as her own if Santiago hadn't offered. Obviously, he left the orphanage kids alone after Mamá chastised him for it."

"That's a nice ending to a terrible beginning," Luca said. The story was further proof that Marissa was right; if her madre was still alive, Luca wouldn't be in this situation either. She wouldn't have allowed Vargas to ruin an innocent's life. She noticed Marissa's expression turn sad.

"It was a good middle but not such a nice ending. My father forced Arturo to kill Santiago a few days ago."

"Jesus. Why?"

Marissa shook her head and dabbed the corner of her eye. "Arturo says that my father thinks he has enemies trying to muscle in on his business. I don't know why he would suspect Santiago even if there are people plotting his downfall. He's been with my father from the very beginning."

"And Arturo did what your father told him to?" She couldn't help the disbelief in her tone. "How could he murder the man who raised him?"

"He didn't have a choice, Luca. If he hadn't done it, someone else would have and my father would have killed Arturo as well. And that would have left me alone in the world. I only hope that he was able to do it quickly and without suffering." Marissa closed her eyes briefly as if she were having to blink away an image of the dead man. "Please don't judge him. I can see it's destroyed a piece of his soul, and he's barely glued together right now. If I don't get him out of here soon, he's going to have to lose himself to save himself."

"What do you mean?" Luca asked.

"He'll have to disconnect from everything that makes him Arturo and forget who he is so he can continue to do my father's bidding. He's told me that his only other option would be to...kill himself. But I can't let either of those things happen."

"Has he talked about it?"

Marissa shook her head. "He's keeping it locked away until we're finally free. If he begins to process it, or any of the horrendous things my father has made him do, he'll disintegrate. I have to make sure he's in a safe place before he can begin to unpack the terror of the last seventeen years." Marissa shifted in her chair to fully face Luca. "Sorry, that probably hasn't helped you get in the right frame of mind to write your sex scene."

"No, it hasn't. But you've helped me understand you a little more, and anything that gives me a better understanding of you is great."

Marissa swapped chairs to the one in front of the desk. As inspiration, Marissa being that close would've worked well, but the way she stared at Luca made her more of a distraction and impossible to ignore.

"Okay, let's talk about sex." Marissa wiggled her eyebrows and leaned forward.

Luca tried to keep her eyes locked with Marissa's, but the deep V in the linen shirt Marissa wore revealed her skin, and it was too tempting to resist.

"Eyes front, Luca."

Luca nibbled the inside of her lip and looked back at her screen instead of seeing the knowing expression Marissa would no doubt be wearing. "I'm struggling with how to express what they're both feeling. In the book, this scene is in Nelese's point of view, but for the movie, I've got to get both characters' vulnerabilities and feelings across to the viewer." She wheeled her chair back and looked out the window. She missed the ocean and its view to nowhere and everywhere. The tall trees were beautiful, but they penned her in and acted like nature's barbed wire. "I don't have any internal thought or black space to play with. *Everything* they're feeling has to be in looks they exchange, the actions they take, and the expressions on their faces." She glanced back toward Marissa. "Did you read the manuscript?"

Marissa narrowed her eyes. "Is that a trick question? Is there a right and wrong answer?"

"No. Why would there be?"

"Well, you're the author, but you haven't given me a copy to read. If I say that I've read it, then it means that I've read it without your permission. And you might not be happy about that. Hence, it could be a trick question."

Luca laughed gently. "That's a lot of overthinking. Have you read it and don't want to tell me that you think it's bad?"

"No, of course not." Marissa rolled her eyes. "How could you think it was bad? Especially when you've had such positive responses from it?"

Luca shrugged. "I don't care what Hollywood thinks about it. I care what you think about it."

Marissa held up her hands. "Okay, okay, I've read it. I asked Pedro to attach your old hard drive to the machine I have in my room after he'd placed all the files on a thumb drive for my father."

Luca grinned. She liked the idea of Marissa guiltily reading her words. "Do you remember Caletho and Nelese having sex on the beach?"

Marissa flushed a gentle pink. "I may have re-read that scene a few times. Yes, I remember it. Why?"

Luca caught the edge of the desk and pulled herself back. "In that moment, there's massive desire. It's the first time they're going to let themselves go, let their real selves show, and unmask all their vulnerabilities and desires."

"Yes," Marissa said.

Her husky whisper made it difficult for Luca to concentrate on what she was trying to achieve on the screen. She was overtaken with the desire to let herself go, to see if they could have a first—and probably a last—time. "How do I get that onto the page with stage direction and dialogue? What can I give the actors to translate into that kind of desire?"

Marissa ran her tongue over her top lip and looked to the ceiling as if she were seriously considering how to answer. "What does desire like that look like? Show me."

Luca got up, came around the desk, and got to her knees in front of Marissa. It wasn't hard to emulate what Caletho and Nelese's desire felt like when she looked at Marissa. Beautiful, perfect Marissa, who Luca had desired since the moment she'd laid eyes on her. And that desire had only strengthened and grown after they'd spent this time together. Marissa, who Luca had watched and adored from a distance for almost a year, whose laugh filled her with light and whose voice soothed her soul. A woman so sweet and compassionate that it almost made Luca weep.

She channeled all that emotion, her longing, and what she'd thought had been unrequited attraction, and tried to put it into her expression.

Marissa ran her fingers along Luca's jaw. "That's what desire looks like," she whispered before she pressed her lips to Luca's.

Luca sighed deeply and gave herself to Marissa's kiss. She didn't want to think about all the reasons this wasn't a good idea. She didn't want to focus on the voice at the back of her mind, warning her that this would hurt more than it would feel good, that knowing how wonderful they were together would make their inevitable separation far harder.

She cupped Marissa's face in her hands and put all those feelings into her kiss. If this was going to be the one and only time she'd get to show Marissa how she felt and how much she adored her, then she'd better make it the best kiss in the world. Marissa wrapped her hand around the back of Luca's neck and pulled her in deeper.

Luca rose from her knees and pulled Marissa up. "Bedroom?" she asked. There was no bed of rose petals, but Luca wanted to take her time discovering Marissa's body on a soft mattress. She'd waited a long time for this. There was no way she was going to rush it, no way she wanted it to be quick sex on an uncomfortable desk.

Marissa nodded. "Yes." She took Luca's hand and led her to her bedroom. She placed her hand on Luca's chest. "Wait right there." She stepped back and began to take off her blouse slowly.

"Please." Luca moved forward and touched Marissa's wrist. "Please let me."

Marissa looked deep into her eyes, searching for what, Luca didn't know, but she waited for her permission.

"Why?" Marissa asked.

Luca played with a loose curl of Marissa's hair before she kissed her neck. "Because I want to remember every second, every sensation. I want to take it so slow, we're almost not moving. I want this memory to be perfect."

Marissa dropped her hands. "I'm all yours."

Luca swallowed against the choke of irony that rose in her throat. Marissa could never be all hers, not in reality. But in this moment, Marissa had allowed Luca the fantasy.

Luca took the hem of Marissa's blouse and lifted it over her skin. Her fingers skimmed the softness of Marissa's flesh, and a gentle vibration surged through Luca's fingers like an electrical current. She pulled it over Marissa's head, and her curls fell over her bare shoulders. Luca's breath caught as she cupped Marissa's breasts in her hands and dragged her thumb over her nipples.

She kissed Marissa's neck while she continued to play with her breasts. Marissa moaned, and sighed, and made noises Luca had never heard from the women she'd been with before but ones she wanted to hear for the rest of her life.

"I want to feel your skin on mine." Marissa tugged the front of Luca's tank top.

Luca raised her arms, and Marissa pulled her top off. "Nothing you haven't seen before," she said as Marissa dropped the clothing to the floor and grinned wickedly.

"This time you know I'm looking," Marissa said before she flicked Luca's nipple.

The sensation flamed through Luca's chest. "How long *were* you watching me before I turned around?"

Marissa gently pushed Luca back toward the bed. "Long enough to notice that you don't have a single tattoo."

The backs of Luca's legs touched the bed, and Marissa gave her a light shove so she tumbled onto the mattress. "I think I'm supposed to feel embarrassed..." She sat up and pulled Marissa closer.

"But instead?" Marissa ran her hands through Luca's hair.

"I feel seen." Luca reached around Marissa's waist and slowly unzipped her skirt. It fell to the floor, and Marissa stepped out of it and kicked it aside. She kissed Marissa's stomach and ran her fingertips along the band of Marissa's panties, teasing herself as much as Marissa. Luca had never considered herself an impatient person, and she was the one who wanted to take her time but touching Marissa and having her this close made her want to tear off what little clothing they were still wearing and plunge deep inside her, bringing them as close as they could possibly be.

Marissa slowly traced circles on Luca's shoulders. "I don't think I've ever touched a woman who didn't have tattoos."

Luca looked up into Marissa's eyes. "You don't like it?" Damn it. She wanted tattoos, lots of them, but she'd been waiting until she could afford to pay a real artist who knew what they were doing. She definitely hadn't wanted the kind of crappy graffiti Casey had scribbled all over her.

"It wouldn't matter if you were like this or if every inch of your skin was covered, I'd want you just the same." She lifted Luca's chin higher with the tip of her long fingernail and ran her tongue along Luca's bottom lip. "It's just unusual, that's all."

Luca sucked Marissa's tongue into her mouth and inched Marissa's panties down her hips. Marissa shimmied out of them, and the scent of her arousal hit Luca's senses. It was all she could do not to throw Marissa onto the bed and dive between her legs to taste her.

"Your turn," Marissa whispered.

Marissa pushed Luca's shoulder, and she relaxed back into the softness of the comforter. She put her feet on the edge of the bed and lifted her hips to push her clothes off.

Marissa batted her hands away. "Allow me."

Luca put her hands behind her head and lay back to watch. Marissa unbuttoned Luca's trousers and slowly pulled them off. Luca helped a little by lifting her ass off the bed, but mostly she enjoyed the unfamiliar sensation of being undressed by the most beautiful woman in the world.

Marissa tossed Luca's pants on the floor and slipped her finger in the waistband of Luca's shorts. "I can't tell you how many times I've imagined this moment," she said.

Luca smiled and glanced away, unable to bear the intense scrutiny in Marissa's eyes, and even less able to believe her words. But she wasn't listening to her rational mind and didn't want to hear the questions it asked.

Luca's shorts joined the rest of their clothes on the floor, and Marissa climbed on top of her before she rested on her stomach. Luca let out a short breath when the heat of Marissa's core pressed against her naked skin. She placed her hands on Marissa's thighs and took in the vision of beauty straddling her. "You're so gorgeous."

Marissa leaned back slightly, and the curls between her legs parted to reveal her clit. She moved one hand up Marissa's thigh and pressed her thumb between Marissa's lower lips.

Marissa moaned. "That isn't taking it slow."

"Compared to what my body wants, this is slow."

Marissa smiled and pushed back against the pressure of Luca's thumb, gasping again. "If that's the case, you can take all the time you need."

Luca briefly closed her eyes and made a wish that they could have the time Luca needed. All the time in the world. She moved her thumb in circles, pressing harder and softer to find Marissa's sweet spot. Somewhere in between, Marissa began to rock against Luca's hand, mesmerizing her with the sensual way her hips swayed in time with Luca's rhythm. And all the time, Marissa kept her gaze locked on Luca, never leaving her for a second. As the speed of her movement increased and her eyes half-lidded, Marissa somehow became more stunning, more desirable. And Luca's desperation to please her grew stronger.

"Perfect...so perfect," Marissa whispered, her voice husky.

Marissa's heat on Luca's stomach turned to molten lava, and Luca thrust her hips, longing for a deeper connection. She inched her other hand further up Marissa's thigh, the need to be inside her too powerful to deny any longer.

"Don't move," Marissa said.

Luca gripped Marissa's leg and kept the rhythm of her thumb steady. Marissa pushed harder against her and threw her head back as she cried out and rocked against Luca's hand. When she'd finished, she dropped against Luca's chest, breathing hard. Luca sat up slowly and laid Marissa on her back. She leaned over her and placed soft kisses on her neck before she slowly worked her way down between Marissa's breasts and along the line of her stomach to between her legs. She inhaled deeply and softly blew on Marissa's clit.

Marissa jumped and swatted at Luca's shoulder. "Tease," she whispered hoarsely.

Luca slipped her hands under Marissa's thighs and rested her hands on Marissa's hips. "It's not teasing when you follow through." Luca lowered her mouth and sucked her in gently.

Marissa moaned and lifted her hips higher, pressing herself closer to Luca's lips. "Dios mío."

Luca pulled Marissa further into her mouth and flicked her tongue around her clit firmly.

Marissa grasped Luca's hair and held her in place. "That's so fucking perfect."

Luca glanced along the soft plains of Marissa's body and met her gaze. She was sure she'd never done anything perfectly in her life, but now seemed like the best time to have started. The drowsy look of wild abandon in Marissa's eyes sent shivers that felt like tiny kisses down her spine. She throbbed hard against the crease of the comforter that pressed between her legs. She began to pull her hand from Marissa's hips to take care of that need.

"That hand better not be going anywhere near your pussy, Luca. You're mine to take care of."

The possessiveness of Marissa's words only made her pulse stronger and her need greater. Luca still moved her hand but not to between her own legs. She ran her finger along Marissa's soft, wet folds as she sucked.

Marissa cursed and tightened her grip in Luca's hair. "What are you doing to me?" she rasped.

Luca didn't answer. She didn't want to break the rhythm that had Marissa circling her hips beneath her. She could feel Marissa's pleasure building, and she slipped her finger inside.

"Oh, fuck, Luca. Fuck."

Luca didn't move inside her but she kept the pressure against her as she continued to make circles with her tongue. Marissa's thrusting grew faster and more forceful until she cried out, and Luca tasted the full force of her explosion. Marissa pressed Luca's face harder between her legs and ground her hips against her until she slowly stilled, and her breathing evened out.

Luca raised her head. Marissa's chest heaved deeply, and she was murmuring something Luca couldn't catch. She moved up beside her, maintaining the contact inside, and took Marissa's nipple in her mouth.

"Jesus, Luca. You want more?"

Luca released Marissa's breast and laughed. She looked deep into Marissa's eyes, swimming with desire. "I want all of you," she whispered. Because she had to accept that this might be the one and only time that she'd have the chance to play out the fantasy of them together. And though holding Marissa was like holding a hot coal that would hurt for ages afterward, Luca wouldn't let go.

"Look at me. Only me." Marissa held her hand to Luca's face, her expression serious. "I know what this means."

Luca swallowed against the ball of emotion that surged up her throat. Could Marissa really know what this meant? How they were creating a memory Luca would cherish until her final breath? She held Marissa's gaze for as long as she dared. Any longer and she feared her love would betray her and turn into tears. She pressed her lips to Marissa's. She deepened the kiss, and Marissa responded, wrapping her hand around Luca's neck. She released her, breathless and wanting.

Marissa tipped Luca's chin and kissed her nose gently. "Make love to me."

She didn't have to make the plea more than once. Luca began a slow, sensual rhythm, still wanting this dream to last as long as it possibly could. She watched Marissa's body, mesmerized by the hypnotic movement of her hips.

"Luca," Marissa whispered. "Please."

Luca had wanted this closeness for so long, but she could never have imagined how powerful it would be. She'd known it wouldn't be just sex, but she hadn't anticipated this depth, the desire to laugh and to cry at the same time, to celebrate and to grieve. She stared deep into Marissa's eyes and willed the Universe to set something in motion that would keep them together.

Marissa's softness and vulnerability, her absolute willingness to release herself to Luca melted her. They kissed again, never breaking their gaze, as their bodies rose and fell in perfect synchronicity. Luca moved gently, taking her cues from the subtle changes in Marissa's body. Her expression never changed. There was absolute connectivity between them, and Luca almost found it hard to concentrate on what her hand was supposed to be doing.

She slipped a second finger inside Marissa, and she moaned lightly. She drove deeper and harder, following Marissa's lead, and all the time, they looked into each other's eyes. Luca willed herself not to weep. Crying wasn't something she did, under normal circumstances. But this wasn't normal. Whatever *this* was, it surpassed every hope and expectation Luca had ever had. This was everything.

Marissa's eyes half-lidded as she rocked her hips back and forth onto Luca's hand. "Make me yours, Luca."

Ay, Dios, if only she could. She would make her own deal with the devil if she could do exactly that, and if she could belong to Marissa.

Marissa tightened around Luca's fingers and she shuddered, crying out her name over and over. She felt Marissa relax, and Luca smiled as a little smugness crept in. "You're even more beautiful when you come."

"Let's see if the same applies to you." Marissa cupped between Luca's legs and squeezed. "I'm going to take care of this, but I need a minute to recover."

Luca nodded and dropped back onto the bed. Marissa placed her head on Luca's chest and sighed. As Luca lay in the aftermath of what could only be called making love, all the thoughts and warnings Luca had managed to push away flooded forward and demanded attention. She knew she wasn't good enough for Marissa. She was a worthless orphan from the barrio, and Marissa was a princess, a goddess meant for things so big Luca couldn't begin to comprehend. She didn't deserve the love and attention of a woman so perfect that it was hard to believe she hadn't been created by the gods.

The warm burn of tears engulfed her eyes, and she blinked them away. She couldn't let Marissa see her sadness, her total desolation. Marissa would never know how precious the gift of herself, even just once, was for someone like her. And like mortals and gods, Luca couldn't hope to stay in Marissa's presence for much longer.

It had been as mind-blowing as Luca had thought it would be. Their connection had been so complete, so all-consuming that for the time it lasted, Luca had been able to ignore the impossibility of their situation, and she'd immersed herself in the fantasy that they could be together, that this could be their life.

But she couldn't delude herself as the heat of their fire dissipated in the cool air and the sweat from their love-making dried from their skin. She couldn't hold onto the dream of a future any more than she could grasp a single raindrop in a thunderstorm. The rainbow had shone over them, had given her a taste of what true happiness felt like, and then it had faded, as she knew it would. Their forever love wasn't a pot of gold at its end because she would never be able to find the end of the rainbow. That was beyond the confines of this prison, in a world she was no longer part of, one she'd been torn from.

Marissa had given her love, and Luca would treasure every second of that memory for the rest of her life. And when she was gone, as she would soon have to be, Luca would eternally grieve. She would never have denied Marissa's kiss, never rejected the offer of her affection for fear of the everlasting pain of its absence. To love and to lose, while wretched, had allowed Luca to feel emotionally and physically fulfilled on a level she had never hoped to experience. People like her weren't supposed to live happily ever after. They were barely able to live at all. But she did have this one golden moment.

Chapter Twenty-Four

MARISSA HAD SPENT MUCH of her life powerless. She could do nothing when her mamá fell ill and died. She couldn't stop her father from poisoning Arturo's purity. She was unable to put an end to the enslaved workforce. And until now, she didn't have the power to change Luca's fate.

No more.

Last night had reignited the fire within her that had faded to mere embers. Luca had given herself to Marissa completely and she had done the same. Everything that Marissa had hoped joining with a woman could be had manifested as they shared themselves with no fear of judgment or reproach. It was their first time, yet it felt like they had known each other's bodies and minds for decades. The physical and emotional barriers had fallen away, and they came together as if they were always meant to be. And when Luca had allowed Marissa to touch her, to taste and enjoy her, Marissa discovered a joy she hadn't thought possible. Watching and hearing Luca orgasm gave her a sense of ecstasy she hadn't anticipated, and it had been as pleasurable, if not more so, than her own release.

But it had been so much more than a physical connection. They had communicated their desire for a life together without words, while also acknowledging how impossible it was. It was almost as if it was both the first and last time, and so they had skipped weeks and months of hesitation and deliberation and laid themselves bare. All of it without uttering a single syllable.

Her heart ached to share her experience with her mamita, to tell her how wonderful and kind Luca was, and how she wanted to spend the rest of her life with her. Which was why she had to talk to her father today and fix what Casey Soto had broken. If Marissa could take Soto off the board and get Luca in her rightful place, maybe they could have the future they both craved but were too scared to admit to since it seemed so painfully impossible.

She took one last look at Luca, sleeping hard in her bed, and smiled.

She could easily imagine waking up to her handsome face every morning and thanking God for the privilege. Marissa slipped out of the room silently, not wanting to wake her. She locked the villa door behind her, got into her cart and started toward the main house, driven by a powerful sense of purpose.

She rounded the corner of the house and saw Arturo and Teo exiting the front door struggling with something long and apparently heavy. As she drew closer, she realized what it was, and she stopped twenty feet from them. The crunch of gravel beneath the tires alerted them to her presence.

Arturo looked across the courtyard and shook his head. "You shouldn't come any closer, Marissa," he said, breathing heavily.

He and Teo continued to Arturo's car. Teo threw his end of the body into the trunk, but Arturo was more gentle. Not that it would do whoever was wrapped up in plastic any good.

"Who is it this time?" she asked, trying to sound calm but not managing it.

"It doesn't matter," Arturo said at the same time as Teo slammed the trunk and said, "Raul Aguilar."

Icy fingers crawled up Marissa's spine and gripped her neck. "My boss? Why has my father murdered Señor Aguilar?"

"He disrespected Señor Vargas," said Teo.

Marissa walked toward them. Now that the bloodied body was hidden in the trunk, she could just about handle the conversation. "When and how? I only saw Aguilar yesterday, and everything was fine."

"Get in the car, Teo." Arturo glared at him when he didn't move fast enough.

"Better be quick. We've got two more doors to knock on before siesta."

Teo got in the car, and Arturo hurried over to Marissa.

"His office phone was bugged," Arturo whispered when he was close enough for Marissa to hear. "There was something in Aguilar's conversation with you that your father didn't like. We were instructed to bring him here, and his responses didn't help his predicament."

Marissa noticed drops of blood on Arturo's cheek. She took the pocket square from his jacket and wiped it away. She tried not to think about how close he must've been to Aguilar when he was killed, or how hard Aguilar had been struck to kill him.

"It's going to take more than that to wipe the blood from my hands," he said, taking the stained silk handkerchief back and stuffing it in his trousers.

Panic seeped into Marissa's mind as she recalled the content of her conversation with Aguilar. "You're certain that it was his phone and not mine?"

"I'm positive. You don't have anything to worry about for now."

"For now? What does that mean?" She stepped closer. "Does he suspect what we're doing?"

Arturo shook his head. "If he did, I'd already be dead, and you'd be locked in your mamita's old room."

She pulled him into a hug in case anyone was watching from the windows. "Good. It won't be long now. I have a plan to get rid of Casey and free Luca."

Arturo held her at arm's length. "What plan? We were supposed to talk last night, but then you said you were busy. What happened?"

Magic happened. Marissa couldn't stop her smile. "I've worked out a way that solves Luca's problems before we leave. I'm going to talk to my father now."

Teo sounded the car horn twice, and Arturo waved him off.

"I have to go. Do I need to worry?"

"You always worry, but no." She took his hand and squeezed. She could see he had a hundred questions and a thousand reservations, but he voiced none of them. "And thank you for trusting me."

"Just be careful, Marissa. He's getting more unpredictable by the day."

"I promise." She watched him leave before she headed into the house. She'd overcomplicated matters with her original plan, but she was confident with the new iteration. It was simple, and simple was often best.

Marissa knocked on her father's office door. She wanted something from him so as much as she enjoyed irritating him, she waited for him to call before she entered.

"Mija, so good to see you of your own accord." He stood in front of his desk and held his arms open, clearly expecting a hug.

She stepped into an awkward embrace then recoiled when she looked over his shoulder and saw Aguilar's severed head mounted on plastic on the windowsill, blood congealing around his distended neck.

He followed her gaze and shrugged. "Sorry, mija. But you should get used to the ugly side of the business if you will not marry and let a man take care of these things."

She bit back one of the many retorts she would usually fire at him. She wasn't here to defend her non-interest in any part of his business, she was here for Luca. "Since you mention ugly things." She walked to the recently fixed window and took the seat facing away from her father's desk. Marissa had never like Aguilar, but she wouldn't wish for the head of her worst enemy to be kept as decoration post-mortem.

Her father poured himself a large glass of dark rum. "Something for you?"

"No, thank you, Papá." It wasn't even ten in the morning, but he knocked it back and refilled his glass before he took the seat opposite her. She noted the dark stains on the armpits of his sky-blue shirt. Surely he hadn't exerted himself and bloodied his own hands to kill Aguilar. Now that she took the time to really look at him, he wasn't looking healthy at all.

"You have ugly business to discuss?"

"It's about Casey Soto."

He leaned back in his chair and put his feet on the table. Marissa frowned. He was usually so respectful of the house and its furnishings. He respected inanimate objects far more than he respected the value of human life.

"What of her? Everything in LA was good, no? And your writer is writing, yes?"

Marissa paused before responding. Aguilar's sightless eyes were a powerful reminder of her father's violent nature, and she was about to put Soto in his sights for a similar end. Did that make her as bad as he was, that she was prepared to sacrifice someone to help another person get what they wanted? She took a cleansing breath and focused on convincing herself that she was simply redressing the balance. No one deserved the ending her father gave them, but Marissa had little choice because Luca certainly didn't deserve to be imprisoned. Soto had always known the circles she operated in and accepted the associated risks. Luca just wanted a better life, and she had earned it through her ambition and talent. Marissa was acting as the tool to right the wrongdoing, that was all.

"The last person you need to worry about is Luca, Papá, I assure you. She's busy at the villa writing the script, as ordered." Marissa twirled her hair once, then stopped. She was sure her father hadn't paid enough attention to her over the years to realize she did that when she was nervous, but she clasped her hands together and held them in her lap just in case.

He nodded and looked self-congratulatory. "I expected nothing less. It's easy to manipulate ordinary people who are not part of our business."

Marissa clenched her hands together tighter, remembering the bruising around Luca's neck. It wasn't so much manipulation as it was terrorization. And she hated him for putting his pudgy hands on Luca and for his obvious pride in doing so. Once again, she held back and focused on her reason for being there. "The meeting in LA went very well, and we secured the deal we were looking for. It's what happened after the meeting that should concern you."

He narrowed his eyes and sat forward in his chair. Marissa prepared herself for the verbal attack she knew was inevitable.

"Why have you waited to come to me with this? You've been home for nearly two days."

She steadied herself and held firm, determined not to be intimidated. "I was going to see you yesterday, but then I was called into the office to hand over my work on the Marín case. When I got back, I was so exhausted from that and the LA trip that I fell asleep and didn't wake until early this morning. I came as soon as I was clear-headed, Papá."

He gestured behind her. "You will not have to worry about being called into his office again."

He laughed at his own macabre humor, but she couldn't bring herself to play along.

"But still, if you were so concerned, I would expect you to put the business before your comfort, Marissa."

He only used her name when he was irritated with her. This wasn't going as well as she'd hoped, but she steeled herself and continued. "I *did* put the business before my comfort by completing the roundtrip in less than twenty-four hours. But what should matter is that I'm bringing this to your attention now, and you'll be able to keep it from happening."

His expression indicated that he appreciated her standing up for herself, but she knew there was only so much mileage in that approach before his admiration turned to intolerance, and he would snap.

"Very well. Tell me your concerns."

"We went for dinner once business was concluded, and Soto told me of her plan to run with all the money from the book and movie deals without honoring her deal with you." That much was true. At least she wasn't lying as she held Soto's head to the block.

His knuckles whitened around his glass. "She thinks she can double-cross me?"

Marissa nodded. "She believes your power has weakened, and you have no hold over her now that she's over the border and a thousand miles away." She noted the vein pulsing in his neck and decided to sprinkle a little untruth to play on his paranoia. "She thinks you have enough problems to cope with locally that she would be your last priority."

He got up and lumbered over to his liquor table. He poured another drink and knocked it back before he turned to her. "Did Soto tell you who I should be worried about?"

"What do you mean?" Marissa watched his transformation with morbid fascination, not able to understand where his sudden suspicion and mistrust of almost everyone around him had originated.

"The local problems she said I have. Who are they coming from?"

Marissa shrugged. "She didn't say, and I don't know what she's talking about. Aren't you more concerned about her running with your money?"

"In this business, you have to be concerned about all of it, and if you get complacent, your power can be taken away in an instant. I'll speak with her family and see what they know." He walked back to his chair but didn't sit. "I will deal with Soto, mija, but I really thought she knew better." He grunted and wandered to the stained-glass window. "Why did she tell you what she was planning to do? Seems like a suicidal decision on her part."

A flicker of guilt tugged at her conscience again, but she dismissed it. Her father was ready to act, but this additional piece of information should tip him over the edge. "It's quite embarrassing, Papá, but she told me because she wants me to go with her."

He turned and frowned at her. "Why would she want that? Why would she think that you would go anywhere with her?"

Marissa looked at him and waited for the penny to drop, but he merely stared back at her with a blank expression. "She wants us to be together," she said when it was clear he had no idea what she was saying.

His eyes narrowed and his lip curled. He was such a caricature that

Marissa might have laughed if the situation weren't so serious.

"Be together like husband and wife?"

She nodded. "Exactly. She wants me to run away with her, and she thinks this is enough money to tempt me."

Her father scoffed. "There is not enough money in the world. Has Soto always been this way?"

This wasn't the explosion of rage she'd hoped to induce. "So I hear," she said, not wanting to say anything that might incriminate herself.

"But I haven't heard. This is another thing that has been kept from me." He clenched his fist and slammed it into his other hand. "I'm sorry, mija. I would never have put you in that position if I'd known what she was. Everyone knows her kind aren't to be trusted."

Tendrils of tension crept their way up her spine at his characterization of Soto's "kind." What would he say if he found out he was talking about his own flesh and blood?

"And she dared to try to take you away from me and turn you into one of them?"

"I don't think that's how it works, Papá, but you have nothing to worry about. I despise her." More truth laced into the lie she was threading. Before all this happened, she was indifferent toward Soto. She was an irritant who always seemed to get in the way of Marissa's attempts to approach Luca, but nothing more. But everything changed after Soto's unforgivable betrayal of Luca. Marissa had been prepared to do what she could to help Luca before she and Arturo left, but after last night, she would risk everything to make sure Soto was dealt with and Luca could return to the life she deserved. Marissa only hoped that eventually, they could somehow be together. And for that, she was willing to ignore the niggling voice at the back of her mind that whispered her father would never stop searching for her until the day he died.

"Regardless, Soto will pay for her arrogance."

That was all she needed to hear. "What about Luca and the script-writing?"

He waved his hand dismissively. "I can't think about that right now. Perhaps this is a sign to tell me that I need to concentrate my efforts on my real business."

Ay, Dios, what have I done? Fix it. "Don't be too quick to think of it that way. Despite Soto's involvement, I enjoyed negotiating our deal with

FlatLine, and it's something I would like to continue my involvement in even after you've handled Soto."

He looked surprised. "This is something you would like to do for me and the family business?"

"Yes, definitely. And you've seen the numbers, Papá, on just these books and the first film. This has the potential to be very lucrative for you—Luca is young, and this is just the beginning of her writing career."

"How would you explain Soto's deception to the LA people?"

"I'm sure it would be relatively easy for Luca to prove authorship of her books." She hadn't thought of that issue, but she and Luca could figure it out. Luca's original hard drive was probably the key. The main goal for Marissa right now was to remove Soto from the picture. "And as you say, it's far easier to manipulate law-abiding citizens. I can make Luca aware of your power and reach, even in LA. I have no doubt that she'll fall in line and provide you with a steady income stream for years to come." Or until one of his paranoid delusions came true, and someone ended both him and his business dealings. It wasn't the perfect situation Luca should be enjoying, but it was the best version of reality Marissa could see with her father involved.

He nodded slowly, clearly contemplating his options. "I need time to think, mija. And I need to talk to Arturo."

It was strange to see him this indecisive, and while he had always had advisors, she had never heard him say that he needed anyone except her mamá. She recognized that she should back off to let him process, and Arturo would lead him the way she wanted. Marissa was almost certain that she'd achieved her objective, but she wouldn't share her excitement with Luca until her father had explicitly given his permission for her to continue working with Luca and everyone else in LA. She tried not to think about the implications if her father denied her. Marissa didn't know exactly what she would do in that situation, but she did know that she wouldn't let her father hurt Luca. One way or another, she was fixing Soto's mess and giving Luca her life back, no matter the cost.

Chapter Twenty-Five

CASEY CLOSED THE DOOR of her apartment in Lou's smiling face. She impressed herself that she didn't slam it, which was what she wanted to do. After helping move all the new furnishings in, Lou clearly thought she should get an invitation to share the pizza that had just arrived. But Casey wasn't in the mood to play nice anymore. It was exhausting trying to be like Luca, and once she was inside her new home, she didn't want to have to pretend. This was supposed to be her sanctuary, where she could be herself. And nobody at the agency knew who that was. The only person in this town that did was Anastasia, and she couldn't be here because she was working late.

Their joint inability to match schedules over the past couple of days was probably for the best anyway. Marissa wasn't the kind of woman who should be screwed around on, and Casey was closer than ever to finally snaring her. She wasn't about to jeopardize that with Anastasia, no matter how much fun they'd been having. The intimate dinner she'd shared with Marissa at the restaurant of one of Vargas's rescued families had been picture-perfect. Candlelight, fine wine—the waiter said so; Casey had no idea what a fine wine should taste like—and the sexiest woman on earth sitting opposite her, with all eyes in the room on Marissa, their jealousy and desire obvious. It had given Casey a glimpse of what their life in New York could be like, and it made her more determined to make it happen.

She dropped onto her suede couch, turned on the giant TV, and began to work her way through the pizza and wash it down with ice-cold beer. As she watched a game that she didn't understand the rules for, she thought about the one she was playing by double-crossing Vargas. It was a huge risk, she knew that, but she was also pretty sure that he wouldn't waste manpower coming after her as long as he didn't suspect that Marissa was with her. She downed the last dregs of a bottle and picked up her cellphone. She and Marissa needed a strategy if they were going to avoid Vargas coming after them. Granted, the full amount of money wouldn't come in for a while yet, but she still wanted a plan in place. She wanted to know Marissa was all in. If she wasn't, then she'd use the time to convince her.

Casey dialed her number. When Marissa didn't answer immediately, she tensed, worried that Vargas had somehow found out about their tentative agreement. Arturo and Teo had refused to stay in the car, but they'd sat at the far end of the restaurant by the front door. She doubted they could've overheard them. "Hey, it's me," she said when Marissa finally answered on the eighth ring.

"You shouldn't call me on this number. I told you Father is bugging phone lines."

"You think he doesn't trust his own daughter?" Casey scoffed. "He thinks the sun rises and sets with you."

"If you believe that, you're more deluded than he is," Marissa said. "He wants a perfect daughter he can control, nothing more."

"If that's the case, shouldn't you be more careful what you say?"

"You're probably right."

Marissa sighed, and Casey could imagine her eyes losing some of their fire. She'd noticed it when they were in the car and Arturo had said he couldn't leave her alone. It was like something inside her was slowly dying, and she didn't know what to do about it. Lucky for her, Casey knew *exactly* what to do about it.

She heard a raised voice in the background but didn't catch the words. "Is someone with you?" She clenched her jaw and tried to keep her tone even. Marissa had been controlled by her father all her life. She probably wouldn't react kindly to jealousy. It didn't matter who she was with now. It wouldn't be that long until they were together, and Casey would be able to keep other people away from her. She wasn't risking everything to have someone else swoop in and steal Marissa away from her.

"Why?"

"I just want to know that you're okay to talk about the same thing we talked about when we went for dinner." She chose her words carefully in case it was Arturo or another of Vargas's henchmen guarding her.

"It's Luca."

Casey checked her watch. It was already nine, which meant it was ten there. "Isn't it a little late to be checking up on her?" She hated the thought of Luca being anywhere near Marissa. Not that she'd make a move. She'd been too much of a chicken to do anything about her crush when she was free, so she definitely wouldn't find the balls to do anything about it now. She was probably just whining about how shitty her life was and how it was all Casey's fault.

"I'm staying at the villa with her while she works on the screenplay."

Casey heard Luca more clearly this time before the sound became muffled. "Your father's put her in the villa? What's wrong with the barns?"

Marissa laughed. "Think about it, Casey. She needs a desk and a laptop. If we want her to produce good work, we have to make sure she's comfortable. And the only electricity running to the barns is for lights."

Casey got up and took the vodka from the freezer. Another beer wasn't going to help her swallow this bombshell. "She doesn't have access to the internet, does she?"

"Of course not. Father may be paranoid, but he's not stupid."

Casey twisted the cap off and took a swig from the bottle. "Paranoid? About what?"

"Nothing. Never mind. You don't have to concern yourself with Luca. I'm handling her. You need to concentrate on keeping your author act going. The last thing we need is anyone getting suspicious, especially now that you've got the movie deal. That complicated everything."

"You think I should've turned it down? It's going to give me the money I need to get you out of there, like you've always wanted."

"No, of course I don't think you should have passed on it," Marissa said. "I'm just reinforcing that things are more difficult now that they want new material. When you were just selling books that were already written, it was simpler. You have to acknowledge that."

Casey blew out a long breath. "Sure, you're right." That didn't mean she had to like the idea of Luca mooning around the villa like a lost puppy desperate for Marissa's attention. But Marissa had finally seen that Casey was the right woman to make her dreams come true, and Luca had nothing to offer her. She had nothing to worry about.

"Did you call just to chat?" Marissa asked.

"No," Casey said, though she was enjoying talking to Marissa and had almost forgotten why she'd picked up the phone. "I was thinking about our plan to finally get you away from your father. I know we have time, but I want to get things started."

"Okay. Is there a problem? You haven't changed your mind, have you?"

Casey chuckled gently. "Of course not." There was no way she'd back out. Marissa was more than worth the risk, and once they were on the East Coast, they'd be free of him. "We didn't have time to discuss the finer details and timings of everything. I want to look at the schedule so we know when money is coming in. That way we have a timeline to start working with."

"You're probably right. I'm not quite sure why he agreed to this deal, but I'm glad he did now that you're doing this for me," Marissa said. "I know I wasn't able to show my feelings in the car or the restaurant, but I'm looking forward to starting this new chapter with you. I don't know how I'll be able to thank you properly."

This was more like it. Some gratitude and affection. "Oh, I'm sure we can figure out the perfect way for you to do that, don't worry."

Marissa laughed. "I'd forgotten how crude you could be. I've missed that."

"Soon enough you won't have to miss me ever again." Casey put the vodka back in the freezer and grabbed another beer before she dropped onto the couch. "You were so hard to read back home. You always acted so distant, but I could see you wanted me. You just needed the right circumstances."

"You've got to remember I always have one of father's guards close by. If I'd given them any hint that I liked you, my father would've ended you long ago."

Casey rested her hand on her crotch. "Can you go somewhere private in the villa so we can talk dirty?"

Marissa giggled. "I'm no good at that, Casey. You'd be disappointed."

"I don't think you could ever disappoint me."

"Trust me, you would be," Marissa said. "And besides, I'd rather wait until we can be together for real. Weren't you supposed to be talking about the finer details of our future?"

Casey sighed. She'd take care of herself later. "That could be a while. Are you sure you want to wait?"

"I've waited this long for you... When can you set up a meeting to talk to the people in charge of the money?"

"I'm not sure." Maybe Casey *would* be calling on Anastasia again. If Marissa was going to hold out on her, they weren't really together, and if that was the case, she could keep having no-strings sex with Anastasia, and she wouldn't be cheating on Marissa. "But I was thinking that we need to relocate you to New York at least a month before I leave LA. That way, your father doesn't think you going missing is anything to do with me. You could come for a meeting one day and just not go home. What do you think?"

"How am I supposed to get away from Arturo or whoever else he sends with me?"

"Are they totally loyal to your father?"

"Arturo certainly is. He's been with the family almost his whole life. I don't know about Teo. I get the impression this is just a job for him, and he'd go wherever the money was."

"Mm." Casey began to formulate a plan. "That could be great for us. We could offer Teo enough money to take out Arturo and make it look like an accident." She thought about the drug dealer she'd recently met through Anastasia when they'd enjoyed a night of sex while high as kites. His gang might be a better bet. Involving Teo might be too much of a risk. "I'm making some influential friends here too, and it could be they deal with both of them. Then we don't have to worry about Teo cracking under pressure when he's back home."

"My father is cleaning house right now. Teo might not survive that anyway."

Vargas was paranoid *and* cleaning house. Casey didn't like the sound of that. "What's going on with your father, Marissa? Is there something I should know about? If this isn't the right time to be doing this, I'd rather you tell me now." She didn't want to delay—she'd waited long enough to get this close to finally having Marissa—but she wasn't stupid either. She was willing to risk everything, but she had to be sure there was a hundred percent chance of success. And if Vargas was already acting cagey, he'd be quick to suspect they were up to something. With Marissa in New York, Casey didn't want to have to deal with an inquisition from her crazed father. He was quick to violence under most circumstances; if there were other things at play, he'd be way too volatile and what they were hoping to do would be way too risky. She wondered briefly if she should let her parents know. The Soto family had worked for Vargas for a long time. She shook her head. She didn't owe them anything.

"Don't panic, Casey. It's nothing new. You should know that he does this every few years. He treats it like an animal cull, trimming off the fat."

Casey wasn't fully convinced. "You said something about him being paranoid. What did you mean?"

"It was just a turn of phrase, Casey, that's all. He's always been the same. I expect most heads of major drug cartels are the same. They have to be careful who they trust, don't they?"

Casey took a long pull on her beer. Someone was always making a power play somewhere in a cartel or looking to bring down their competition. The days where everyone worked together and the authorities were the enemy were long gone. "Has your father asked when the first installment of money is going to come through?"

"Not yet, thankfully. But since we're talking about cashflow, I don't know how much money I'll be able to get hold of in the next few months."

"The loan that I've already gotten against book sales should cover that. If you can convince your father there'll be no money for six months, that should give us the time to get the money from FlatLine too. I'll tell Alyssa I'm moving, and we'll get a PO box that'll be difficult to trace. I won't give her my forwarding address, so even if your father does try to track me, no one will have any information to give him."

"Sounds like you've got it all figured out and didn't really need to call me," Marissa said.

Casey grinned, liking that Marissa recognized her talents. "It's always good to hear your voice though."

"Listen to you being sweet. That's not something I thought I would ever say about you."

"I can be anything you want me to be, Marissa. You'll soon find that out when we're living together." When they were tucked up safe in New York, Casey would have her own set of expectations, but she didn't want to talk about that now. She was pretty sure Marissa would do exactly what Casey wanted her to do once she'd freed her from her father. And if she *was* reluctant, a little reminder that she could easily be sent back to Vargas should make her more compliant. Still, the thought that she'd finally caught her prize filled her with a sense of achievement. And the fact that Luca was around to hear it firsthand was the cherry on top... which reminded her about wanting an update. "How's the script going?"

"It's going well," Marissa said. "Luca had already played with the script-writing software and done some research, so it's taking less time than I thought it would."

Casey heard Luca's voice in the background again, and she sounded angry. Casey held back her laughter, knowing Marissa wouldn't appreciate her enjoyment of Luca's situation. It had probably been character-building, something Luca could benefit from. There was laidback, and then there was spineless, and Luca fit the second box. If Vargas ever let her go, she'd be a stronger person for what she was going through. It was almost a shame that would never happen, and Luca would die in his compound.

"She says she'll have the first draft completed by the end of next week."

"That's great. I'll let Alyssa know I'm close to getting the script to FlatLine." She smiled again at the thought of being close to Elodie Fontaine. "I can't wait to be on the set."

"I don't think that's one of your best ideas, Casey. Once you double-cross my father, you won't want to risk going back to LA. You'll have to give up this charade altogether."

"Oh, of course. Listen, I've got to go. We'll talk again soon."

"Okay. We need to be careful though," Marissa said.

"I'm always careful," she said and hung up. Damn it. She couldn't believe that she hadn't thought through the consequences fully, and she really didn't want to give that opportunity up. She'd gotten caught up in the glow of charming Marissa and lost sight of the benefits of this author *charade*. She had to think of a way she could work this so that she could have Marissa *and* keep this new life. All she'd have to do was convince Marissa everything was going according to plan. She didn't have to provide new books; they'd live off the royalties of the movie and books already in motion. As soon as Marissa escaped from her father, she would have no way of knowing what was going on back home, because the break would have to be complete. Then when she was out of the way and in New York, Casey could pay Vargas what he was owed and maintain the deal. Maybe they'd manage to keep Luca working after all. Marissa wouldn't know the difference, and Casey wouldn't give her access to the money, so she'd be totally reliant on her for everything.

Yeah, she could make it happen. She could have it all, just like she deserved.

Chapter Twenty-Six

"WHAT'S GOING ON, MARISSA?" Luca dropped into her office chair as Marissa hung up on Casey. It had taken all her restraint not to pull the phone from Marissa's grasp so she could finally vent her anger at the architect of her misfortune. It wouldn't have solved anything, but it might have made her feel better to get some of it out of her system where it felt like it was eating away at her soul. Being in the villa was great. Being with Marissa was beyond words. But her fiery rage simmered below the surface, and she was struggling to keep it under control. Hearing Casey's voice made it nearly impossible.

"What do you mean?" Marissa placed her phone down and sat in the chair on the other side of the desk.

"It feels like you've been hiding something from me all day, and now that." Luca gestured toward Marissa's cellphone. "I thought we'd agreed not to pursue that plan." She'd been trying hard not to think about Marissa leaving with Arturo soon but hadn't been successful. Every moment she spent with Marissa made her want all the moments of a future life together. But she couldn't and wouldn't ask Marissa to do anything more than what she'd already done for her. Luca simply had to reconcile her new life with the one she longed for. Marissa's freedom had become more important to her than her own dreams.

Marissa leaned back in her chair and exhaled deeply. "I'm not keeping secrets, Luca, I promise."

"Then what was all that about? It sounded a lot like what we talked about, and you were very convincing." A little too convincing for her liking. She shut her ears to the demons that were calling Marissa a liar and questioning the sweet words that had fallen from her lips.

"I came up with a better plan this morning, and I spoke to my father about it." Marissa ran her finger along the arm of chair before she began to play with her ring.

Luca leaned forward, not sure how she wanted to take that news. "You didn't think it would be worthwhile talking to me about it first?"

Marissa clasped her hands together and looked at Luca, her expression soft and open. "After what we shared last night, I can't just walk away. But I knew that you'd probably try to talk me out of it, and I couldn't be sure I was strong enough not to let you. So I went before you woke up." She got up and came around to Luca's side of the desk. "My father needs some time to think about my proposal, and I didn't want to tell you about it until he said yes—which I'm sure he will."

"Say yes to what?" Luca pulled Marissa closer. "What have you done?"

"I told him about Soto's plan to run with all his money." Marissa sat on Luca's lap and stroked the back of her neck. "He's going to deal with her, and that leaves us with the opportunity to put you in LA, where you belong."

Luca took a moment to pull apart what Marissa was saying and what it meant for the three of them. What it meant for Casey. She wanted her to pay, but she didn't want her to die. "But you didn't say anything to Casey..."

Marissa bit her lip and glanced away briefly. She cupped Luca's face and sighed. "No. No, I didn't."

"Are you going to warn her, like you said you would?"

Marissa shook her head. "I don't think I am, no. If my father doesn't have closure, I don't think he'll stop looking for her. Soto is convinced he wouldn't waste his time and resources, but he's changing. There's a paranoia in him I've never seen before. He's making ill-advised decisions in one breath and not able to make a decision without Arturo's input in the next. Ending Soto means his head should be clearer to agree to my proposal."

She took Marissa's hand and kissed her fingertips. "If your father wouldn't stop looking for Casey, what chance do you have of ever being truly free?"

"I don't know. Maybe I won't be until he dies. But I have to try."

"Have you thought about how you'll feel knowing he's murdered Casey on the basis of your information?" She studied Marissa's expression for signs of uncertainty. Luca hadn't thought Marissa was capable of something like this.

"I know what you're looking for," Marissa said and ran her fingers through Luca's hair. "I don't want this to mean me becoming part of the machine that I've been running from my entire life. But I have to do this.

It's not just my father–Soto is expecting me to run away with her. If I don't go, *she* doesn't go, and you stay here." She shook her head, and tears edged her eyes. "It will haunt me forever if I don't do something about this situation. I can't just go and start a new life and leave you here. Casey played a game knowing it was with dangerous people."

"I can't put into words what it means to me that you're prepared to do something like this for me. No one has ever put me before their own needs." Luca thumbed away the tears that tracked down Marissa's cheeks. "But I don't want you to do something that changes who you are," she pressed her palm to Marissa's heart, "in here."

"It's too late. This is exactly why I had to talk to my father before telling you what I'd done." Marissa placed her hand over Luca's.

"I hate Casey for what she's done, and I want to pound my fist into her face until my arm aches, but I don't want you to share that burden. I don't want you to stop being the extraordinary person you are by taking on my fury. Being responsible for someone's death will change you, and I couldn't live with myself if I made you do that."

Marissa smiled and pressed her lips to Luca's forehead. "Last night clarified everything, Luca. My whole world came into sharp focus, and you're at the center of it all. If we can pull this off, if I can get you to LA, I can see a future for us down the line."

Luca couldn't find the words to adequately respond. Had she heard correctly? How could it be possible that Marissa was prepared to do something like this to secure a life together? Her body felt weightless, and the rest of the room melted away, leaving only Marissa.

"You don't feel the same." Marissa clasped her hand over her mouth. "I thought... after last night... It was something special, wasn't it? Didn't you feel it?"

She began to rise, but Luca held her hips in place. "Of course I felt it." The hand of doubt crept up her chest and wrapped around her throat, determined to keep her confession within. But Luca fought it, resolute that she wouldn't let this unbelievable possibility slip through her fingers. She had nothing left to lose. If there was even a remote chance that Marissa actually felt the same way, she wasn't going to let her insecurities and self-doubt get in the way.

"I want to believe that we can make this happen." She held Marissa's face in her hands and searched Marissa's eyes, desperate to see her own love reflected in them. "But are you absolutely, one hundred percent certain that you want this, that you want...me?" Even as she asked the question, the incredulity of her words struck her like a bolt of lightning. But the truth of her heart wouldn't be denied, and her heart wanted all of this to be real.

Marissa leaned in and kissed her softly. "Mi corazón es tuyo."

"And my heart has been yours from our first meeting." Luca pulled Marissa closer and put every feeling that was tearing around her heart and mind into her kiss. The feeling of weightlessness increased as Marissa returned her passion with the same intensity. Hope grew unbridled as she dared to allow herself to believe this was really happening.

Marissa took Luca's hand and placed it at the hem of her skirt, never taking her gaze from Luca. She grazed her nails along Marissa's flesh as she slid her fingers up her thigh. She pressed her fingers over Marissa's silk panties, already hot and wet.

Marissa gasped and nibbled Luca's lower lip. "I want you. I've always wanted you."

Luca let out a slow breath. The words she'd wanted to hear for so long brushed away the uncertainty of a lifetime and filled her with a light so bright, it warmed her from within. "My heart would break in two if this was just a cruel dream."

Marissa slipped her tongue into Luca's mouth and kissed her deeper. "My dreams are full of only you, mi amor."

Luca pulled the smooth material aside and slid two fingers in. Marissa exhaled sharply and swore into her mouth. She wrapped her other hand in Marissa's soft hair and kissed her harder as she pressed her fingers deeper, and Marissa raked her nails down the inside of Luca's tank top.

Luca grunted and swallowed hard. Her pussy throbbed, aching for the same attention Marissa had given her last night, when she'd rocked her world in a way no one had ever done before. Marissa cupped her hand under Luca's breast and pinched her nipple lightly. The sensation coursed down the center of her body and strengthened the pulsing between her legs. She pushed her ass up from the chair, and Marissa laughed quietly.

"Tell me what you want, Luca," she whispered.

"You. All of you. Every day," Luca said in time to the rhythm of her hand.

Marissa pushed against Luca, driving her fingers deeper inside. "I'm here now. Make me yours, Luca. Ruin me for anyone else," she whispered.

Marissa's words and the intensity in her eyes as she stared at Luca solidified everything good she felt inside. While it all seemed so dream-like and impossible, every moment she was with Marissa was so natural too. Luca was the most alive and real she'd ever felt. Something like that couldn't be faked, so she surrendered herself to it and pushed away all the logic and negativity that told her this wouldn't work out.

Luca steadied her rhythm and kept her gaze locked on Marissa, their connection deepening with each second. She held Marissa tighter, pulling her in closer, though she couldn't get close enough, and felt her tighten around her fingers. Marissa's breathing hollowed out, and she growled Luca's name into her ear, spurring her on. Marissa threw her head back and tightened her grip on Luca's neck as she shuddered with pleasure, almost crushing Luca's fingers.

Luca pressed her face against Marissa's chest, closed her eyes, and breathed in. This was all she'd ever wanted, and everything she thought she'd never have. There was no turning back now. Her heart was lost to Marissa, as it was destined to be. Luca could only pray that Marissa's new plan would work, because now that she had Marissa, she couldn't bear to lose her.

Chapter Twenty-Seven

MARISSA WOKE WITH A start and reached out to the other side of her bed. She sighed deeply when she touched Luca's warm skin. She was still there, still safe. The nightmare of her being dragged away began to fade into the ether, as dreams often do, and Marissa relaxed. A day had passed since she'd spoken to her father, and Arturo had brought no word of his decision, only that he continued to deliberate. Rather than dwell in uncertainty, Marissa immersed herself in the bubble of the alternate reality she and Luca had created, and between frequent discoveries of each other's bodies, Luca continued to work on her screenplay while Marissa curled up in a chair and read. She allowed herself to imagine that this could be like every weekend after a satisfying week of helping people with legal issues. It was the most peace she'd experienced since before her mamita had died.

She rolled onto her side and watched Luca sleeping, her breathing soft and even. Her mamá had barely spoken of the love she shared with Marissa's father, but she was sure that it couldn't have been anything like this. The thought saddened her, and she wished that she was able to talk with her about everything she was feeling. She didn't need advice; she just wanted to share what was going on in her heart and tell her that she'd found the kind of love they'd read about. The kind that infused every cell in her body and filled her soul with light. The kind that made her smile every time her thoughts drifted to Luca, which was almost exclusively where her thoughts centered. A love that made her want to make all of Luca's dreams come true and all her nightmares disappear. A love that would have her do anything to ensure Luca's happiness.

Someone knocked loudly on the front door, but it wasn't a coded Arturo signal. She slid out of the bed quickly and pulled on a silk robe, careful to tie it tightly; she'd never appreciated any attention from her father's staff. She peeked through the side glass to see Matías and Diego waiting for her. Why they always had to travel in pairs around the safety of the compound was beyond her.

She opened the door six inches. "What do you want?"

"Señor Vargas wants to see you in his office."

After Diego spoke, he seemed to force a smile. Marissa knew only too well that he didn't like the idea of her taking over from her father. As far as he was concerned, this was men's work and women had no business at the head of a cartel. She didn't agree—a woman was more than capable of running a drug organization—but she wasn't about to change her mind just to prove him wrong.

She wanted to tell Diego she was going nowhere until after she'd taken a shower and had her morning coffee, but she was hoping for good news on her proposal and didn't want to keep herself in suspense. But she did wonder why Arturo hadn't been sent to get her. She quelled the small rise of panic that suggested that her father had discovered their plan, and Arturo had already been "handled."

"I'll get dressed and be over in fifteen minutes." She tried to close the door, but Diego placed his palm against it.

"We'll wait."

She raised her eyebrow. "Then you'll wait outside," she said and pushed harder. "I'm sure Father wouldn't be happy to know you forced yourself into my home." He released his hand, and the door slammed shut. She rested her head against it briefly. If they'd come in, they might've seen Luca in Marissa's bed, and her father would never agree to anything she'd asked for. Worst of all, he would end Luca.

She pushed away from the door and headed toward the bathroom, not wanting to think about the myriad bad things that could result from her deceit. She'd said Casey knew full well the dangers of the game she was playing; Marissa knew just as well.

Luca stood in the doorway looking adorably sleepy. "That was close," she said quietly, worry clearly etched in her expression.

"Nothing I couldn't handle." She caressed Luca's cheek and kissed her gently. "I've been summoned by Father. I expect it'll be to let me know that Soto is out of the picture, and I can begin work on installing you in Hollywood, where you belong."

"I belong with you." Luca took Marissa's hand in hers and squeezed tightly. "What if this doesn't work? I don't think I can go on without you."

Marissa kissed Luca's knuckles and smiled. "It'll work, mi vida. We just have to be patient."

Luca pulled Marissa close to her. "I don't want to be patient. You've shown me what my life could be like with you, and I want it to start now." She sighed deeply. "I know we have to wait, but I've waited too long already."

"We'll work as fast as we can, Luca, but I don't want to make mistakes by rushing anything. First, we get you out of the country, and then Arturo and I will follow." She nestled her head against Luca's chest and listened to her racing heartbeat. "When everything settles, we'll be together. Forever."

"Do you think Casey is dead?"

Marissa pulled away slightly and looked into Luca's eyes. How was it possible that she could show so much compassion for someone who had wronged her so completely? "It's probably best that neither of us think about that." She kissed Luca again and disentangled herself. "I have to go. I don't want to keep Father waiting."

Luca dropped her arms from Marissa's hips. "Be careful."

Marissa smiled gently. "He's my father. As bad as he is, he would never hurt me." She went into the bedroom and quickly dressed, leaving her hair down and taking the time to apply a small amount of makeup to appease him.

Luca waited at the doorjamb, watching. "How is it possible that you get more beautiful every morning I wake up to you?"

Marissa pulled on her pumps and walked over to Luca. She hooked her finger in the waist of Luca's shorts and kissed her hard. "The same way you look more handsome every time I look at you. The lens of love will do that to a person."

Luca wrapped her arms around Marissa's waist. "You think that's what it is? That I love you?"

Marissa arched her eyebrow. "If this isn't love, it's the work of the devil himself." She placed a fingernail beneath Luca's chin and tipped it upward. "So you'd better love me, Luca Romero."

Luca grinned and kissed her. "I love you so much my heart can barely stay sealed at the seams." She bit her lip and looked hopeful. "And you love me?"

Marissa tore herself away. "I'll be back as soon as I can. You'd best get to finishing that screenplay." She opened the door to find Diego and Matías waiting, barely a step away. "I'll follow you," she said and jangled the key to her cart.

Diego shook his head. "You won't need that. Señor Vargas insisted that we drive you."

Marissa frowned but immediately figured that it was another paranoid move on his part. She dropped the key inside on the windowsill and locked the door behind her. She imagined Luca's face as the latch clanked into place. It wouldn't be long before she had control of her own door again. And her own apartment in LA. Marissa got in Diego's SUV and looked back as he drove away. Yes, she loved Luca with all her heart, and she couldn't wait for all of this to be over so they could be together.

They were at the main house in minutes. The excitement of getting to contact Alyssa Dawes to paint a picture of half-truth quickened her step, but she forced herself to walk slowly to her father's office. After she'd seen him, she would go to her room and collect the old hard drive from Luca's computer. It would be the evidence that would prove Luca was the real author of the books Alyssa wanted.

Matías knocked and opened the door when her father called. When he swung the door open, and she saw Soto on her knees in front of his desk, her own legs buckled. It was one thing to sign someone's death warrant, it was another entirely to watch the execution. Soto looked at her through bruised and swollen eyes and spat a gob of red blood onto the plastic beneath her.

Marissa backed away, but Diego's solid form blocked her escape. "I don't want to see this, Father."

Diego eased her forward and closed the door behind him.

"Are you sure, mija?" her father asked.

She recognized the cold, detached tone in his voice though he'd never used it with her before.

"This is the woman who tried to seduce you, tried to take you away from me. From here. From where you *belong*." He rose from his chair and walked toward her, each step deliberate and slow. "This is part of our business." He cuffed Soto's head as he passed her. "You need to develop your tolerance level."

He grasped her wrist and tugged her across the room. She didn't fight. Her only present ally was Arturo, and he stood behind her father's chair, arms crossed and expression blank. A long blink was his only way to communicate with her, and though she saw it, she wished she hadn't. It only meant trouble. Whatever was about to happen, she had no choice but to endure it. She closed her eyes briefly and thought of Luca. If this had to go down so that Luca could go free, so be it. She summoned the courage her mamá had instilled and imagined tendrils of titanium threading through her veins. She could do this.

"Fine."

He released her and leaned against the edge of his desk. "Is it fine, mija?" He picked up a cellphone from the top of a pile of ledgers. "Because Soto has a slightly different story to the one you told me two days ago. And despite thirty hours of *stringent* questioning, her story hasn't changed."

He turned the iPhone over and over in his hands. What did he have that was making him act this way toward her? This was a simple case of the word of a lowlife criminal against that of his daughter. What was the problem? "I don't know what lies have come out of her mouth, but surely you don't believe anything she has to say. You know that people like her will say anything to get out of a sticky situation, let alone one that ends with their death."

He nodded slowly. "You're absolutely right, mija. But it's not the words coming from her mouth that concern me. It's yours."

He unlocked the phone and pressed the screen. Marissa's throat tightened when she heard herself agreeing to leave the compound and live her life in New York with Soto. The clay crack of crockery and the metallic song of cutlery played in the background. Soto had recorded their conversation at the restaurant after the FlatLine meeting. Marissa shrugged. "I said what I had to say to maintain the charade, Father. If I'd cut her down, she would've fled with the money. *Your* money."

"Why are you doing this?" Soto yelled. "I thought you wanted to be free of this place."

She was swiftly silenced by Teo. Marissa pressed her feet to the floor to stay in place and said nothing.

"Mm, I agree." Her father stopped playback of the recording. "You would have been right to keep her on the hook on that initial occasion. And then you told me all about her sordid plan." He grimaced. "But this is where I lose your logic."

He pressed a button on the phone again.

"And besides, I'd rather wait until we can be together for real. Weren't

you supposed to be talking about the finer details of our future?"

"That could be a while. Are you sure you want to wait?"

"I've waited this long for you... How long do you think it will be before you have all the money together?"

"I'm not sure. But I was thinking that we need to relocate you to New York at least a month before I leave LA. That way, your father doesn't think you going missing is anything to do with me. You could come for a meeting one day and just not go home. What do you think?"

He hit stop and tossed the cell onto his desk. "You knew I had sent someone to deal with her, and yet you had a long conversation after that about how you were going to kill my men to secure your future together."

Marissa swallowed hard and tried to maintain a calm expression. "She called me. I was simply keeping her sweet until you dealt with her. She would've thought something was wrong and fled before you could get to her if I hadn't answered. You would have wanted me to do things differently?"

"You just wanted the money," Soto said.

Teo moved to strike her again, but Marissa's father held up his hand. "What do you mean?"

"Hearing you talk now, it all makes sense. That's all this was ever about. She's always wanted to get away from here, and I was the perfect patsy."

Her father frowned. "Explain."

"I've opened an account in her name and have already put some of the money into it. She's told you about me because she knew you'd kill me, leaving her clear to flee with all the money." Soto shook her head and half-smiled. "If I wasn't on my knees about to die, I'd be impressed. You shouldn't be a lawyer; you should be a grifter or an actress."

Her father gripped the edge of his desk and looked down at his feet. He shook his head. "I truly hoped this day would never come."

"Papá, she's a desperate woman saying desperate things. You can't—"

"Silence. It's clear to me that Soto is not the only desperate woman here. You've engineered this whole thing to get away from me. You needed the money and the means to escape, and you found both when I agreed to Soto's request. With her out of the way, you could travel to LA for a meeting one day and never come back, just like Soto said." He turned away and hunched over. "Of all the people to betray me, I hoped that you would never be one of them."

Marissa rushed to his side and placed her hand on his shoulder. "Please, Papá. This is crazy–"

He shrugged her away and turned quickly. "No. *You* are the crazy one if you think I wouldn't see through your naïve plan." He leaned closer so their noses almost touched. "You've played a deadly game with me, mija, and predictably, you have lost." He looked beyond her and jutted his chin toward Matías. "Take her away and lock her in her room. Put a guard beneath her window and at the door. If she escapes, I will flay the skin from your flesh."

Marissa trembled and placed her hands on his chest. "Papá, no. You're wrong."

He snarled and raised his hand but hesitated. "I'm never wrong about loyalty and betrayal, Marissa. You have never wanted to honor your responsibility to the family, and once your madre passed, you became more uncontrollable." He gripped her wrists tightly. "I tried to give you a little freedom and allowed you to study law, but it was never enough for you. You've always made it clear that you didn't want to be here, to be part of this family. I hoped you might grow out of your childish petulance. I've been a fool, but I won't pander to your selfishness anymore." He released her and went back to his chair. "Matías. Take her away. I can't look at her right now."

Matías grasped her elbow and pulled her away.

"No, Papá. Please don't do this." She tried to grab the desk, but Matías was too strong and pulled her away easily.

Soto laughed and spat at Marissa's feet. "I hope you rot here with Luca. Say hi for me."

Teo silenced her again, and as Marissa was manhandled out of the office, she saw the blade of her father's favorite gutting knife glint in sunlight streaming through the windows. But her concern wasn't for Soto's fate. All her plans were destroyed. Everything had seemed so easy, but now it was all gone, and their future had been obliterated.

Chapter Twenty-Eight

LUCA GLANCED AT THE time to see it had only been two minutes since the last time she'd looked. What was taking so long? Marissa left over three hours ago, and not only was Luca missing her, she had a sharp ache in the pit of her stomach telling her something had gone wrong.

She hit save on the script and went to the kitchen for water, though she considered fixing something stronger. She emptied the bottle in seconds and tossed it in the trash before leaning on the kitchen island and resting her head against the warm surface. She breathed in the scent of Marissa's cooking infused in the wood and prayed Marissa was safe.

The front door unlocked and creaked on its hinges as it opened. Luca pushed away from the worktop and rushed into the corridor. The grim expression on Arturo's face greeted her instead of Marissa's beauty.

"Let's go," he said.

If he'd been alone, she would've asked where Marissa was and if she was okay. But he was flanked by two of Vargas's goons. "Go where?" she asked instead.

One of the other guys strode toward her and grabbed her arm. "Back to the barns."

"What? Why? I haven't finished the script. What's going on?"

"Señorita Vargas is no longer at liberty to watch over you. Señor Vargas wants you working the fields while he decides what to do with you," Arturo said, standing aside to let her and the other goon exit the building.

No longer at liberty? What the hell did that mean? She was shoved into the passenger side of Marissa's cart, and Arturo climbed in the other side.

"I'll take her from here." Arturo started the engine and drove off before the other two could decide whether or not that went against their orders.

When they were over a hundred yards away, Arturo looked at her, his nostrils flaring. "Vargas has gone crazy and locked Marissa in her room," he whispered. "Soto convinced him that Marissa was planning to escape with all their money. He was going to kill you too, but I talked him into this instead by suggesting the issue was between Soto and Marissa, and you were incidental. Neither of them mentioned you."

Luca's chest constricted and her heart raced. *Kill you too*. So Vargas had killed Casey. "No. No, this can't be happening." She grabbed his forearm. "You have to get her out of there before—"

He shrugged her off. "She wouldn't be in this mess if you'd just let her be."

He may as well have punched her in the gut. She didn't need to hear that. She already knew it. "I begged Marissa to stick to the plan and leave. But giving me shit over it won't change it now. We have to do something."

"*We?* I think you've done enough. If you're lucky, you'll get to finish the script and somehow take Casey's place, just like Marissa wanted you to, but there's no predicting what Vargas will do next. Keeping you alive for now was the best I could do. I can't promise you anything else."

"I don't need you to promise me anything. I don't care what happens to me, don't you understand that? All I care about is Marissa."

Arturo's jaw clenched and his eyes narrowed. "You should've thought about that before you convinced her to run with this ridiculous plan to frame Soto."

Luca closed her eyes and counted to ten. Arguing with Arturo wasn't going to change anything and neither was panicking, though it was creeping around the edges of her consciousness, trying its damnedest to force itself out. "She did it without telling me, I swear. But we need to focus on what's happening now. Anything else is a waste of our energy."

"Well, I don't know what we can do right now other than wait for Vargas to calm down." He glanced at her and shook his head. "And you're on your own. I can't be seen down here now that Marissa won't be coming every day. I'm sure your roommates will love you for that." He neared the barns and slowed a little. "Look, just lay low. Día de los Muertos is less than a week away, and that's when we were supposed to finally get away from this hell. I'll do what I can, but you have to understand that Marissa is my priority. I don't even know you, and I won't risk everything we've worked for to help you."

"I understand, and I don't expect you to. Marissa is *my* priority too, more than you'll ever know. If you can get her out, please make it happen.

And don't let her convince you to come for me. I can take care of myself." Even as she spoke, Luca was already formulating her own plan. And her old roommates, as Arturo called them, were going to be instrumental. All she had to do was convince them to stand with her.

He pulled to a halt, and Luca jumped out. She could see Epi and Gloria organizing breakfast and strode toward them without looking back. Arturo wasn't interested in helping her, and she didn't blame him for that, but she also wouldn't trust him to ensure Marissa's safety.

Epi looked up from the fire and frowned. "Chica, what are you doing here?" She narrowed her eyes and studied Luca's expression. "What's happened? Where is Marissa? We missed her this morning."

"I need to talk to you, to everyone," Luca said, her resolve to rescue Marissa strengthening with every second that passed. She glanced across at Jorge, the only decent guard on the compound, and he nodded almost imperceptibly. If he wouldn't help, at least he wouldn't get in their way.

Epi put her hand on Luca's back and guided her toward the tables. "Gloria, take over for me, please... Sit, chica."

Luca took the bench and held Epi's hands in hers. "Vargas has gone insane. He's been getting more and more paranoid, killing more and more people, many of them allies and people close to him."

Epi looked puzzled. "Marissa mentioned he had killed Santiago." She shook her head. "So sad. He was one of Señor Vargas's most trusted confidantes. Perhaps he has finally been driven mad by his loneliness and grief."

Luca clenched her jaw. "I don't care what his reasons are. He doesn't get to treat Marissa like this."

"What? What has he done to her?"

Luca quickly reminded Epi what had brought her to the compound and told her of Marissa's plan to oust Casey and install Luca in LA. Arturo hadn't given her much detail of what had gone down that morning, but what little she did have, she relayed to Epi. She also told her of Marissa's original plans to leave with Arturo on the evening of Día de los Muertos. She didn't seem surprised by any of it.

Epi pulled her hands from Luca's and folded them together in her lap. "Your old friend will have died a painful death by now," she said.

Luca's stomach swirled and threatened to reject her breakfast. "I'm trying hard not to think about that." Despite everything, her guts roiled at the unbidden images of her suffering, and she blinked them away. She hoped that he hadn't made Marissa watch any of it.

Epi sighed deeply. "What is it you want to do, Luca?"

She remembered the words from the woman at the beach bar. "*You're in control of your own destiny.*" She'd had her dreams in the palm of her hand, and Casey had callously snatched them away. "*She's someone who could only ever fly on the wings of someone like you.*" Luca had thought it bullshit at the time, and yet Casey had flown too close to the sun on wings of Luca's making and had paid the ultimate price. *What do I want to do?* It was time for Luca to take back control of her future, a future with Marissa in it. But she needed Epi's help and her influence.

"There are fifty of us and another forty men. We outnumber Vargas's army three to one. If we attack together, we can overcome them. We can get to the house, and I can get Marissa out. Then we end Vargas once and for all, and everyone goes free. Everyone goes back to their families and loved ones, debts wiped from the face of the earth."

"A revolution?" Epi gave a small smile. "That sounds wonderful, chica, but they are violent men trained to do violent things. We are farmers, housewives, shop keepers. And we're unarmed."

"No." Luca held Epi's shoulders firmly. "We're not unarmed." She nodded toward the women preparing food. "We have fire."

Epi glanced at them and then blew out a long, troubled breath. "And they have guns." She cupped Luca's cheek. "And you. You think you have what it takes to kill people, to 'end Vargas?'" She shook her head.

"I'll do anything for Marissa." Though she had no idea how she would handle it if she had to kill someone. This was life or death. It was Vargas or her and Marissa. She'd have no choice, and she'd reconcile it when they were away from this place. "She needs us. You don't think that there are people all around you who wouldn't kill to be free again? To never have to bury another friend in an unmarked grave? To be reunited with their families?"

Epi tilted her head. "Familia *is* everything."

It hadn't been everything to Luca, but maybe it was different now. "This is your chance to get back to your family, Epi, and to help Marissa just like she's helped you all these years."

Epi grumbled, clearly recognizing the guilt card Luca had just dealt.

"From what I saw while I was here, Marissa was the reason most of you didn't starve to death. If you asked everyone, do you think they'd turn their backs on Marissa now that *she* needs *them*? She's in trouble, Epi."

Epi narrowed her eyes then looked to the sky. "Ay, Dios. Ya vámanos."

Luca rose with Epi, who called several of the gathered women to join them. Luca watched the expressions and reactions of them all carefully as Epi relayed the pertinent parts of their discussion. Luca saw the fire of freedom flame in their eyes.

"These are the women we can trust with our lives," Epi said to Luca. "Now what?"

Luca's discomfort kicked in with all eyes trained on her expectantly. She'd written galvanizing speeches for Gem to bring the Gods together; it shouldn't be so hard to do it for real, especially with so much at stake. "We have to move tonight. There's no telling what Vargas will do from one minute to the next. We need to get the message to the men you trust to gather at midnight." She looked at Epi, who nodded as if she should keep going. "You've all been here too long. You've had your lives taken away from you by a man making the devil's deals. You don't have to sacrifice your freedom anymore. It ends now... Tonight, we burn it all down."

Chapter Twenty-Nine

LUCA SLIPPED BACK INTO the leaf-picking routine with remarkable ease, though she put it down to anticipation for tonight's revolution rather than acceptance of her ever-changing fate. She had shared knowing nods and, when the guards weren't looking, excited smiles with many of the women, and her eagerness for midnight built as the day wore on. When the sun finally set the cloudy sky on fire with a bright array of ochre and gold splashes, Luca smiled. She'd see their fire dancing in this compound tonight, and her nightmare would finally come to an end.

As they headed back to the barns, Epi nudged her elbow. "Everything is set. The men we trust are ready to go. They'll spread the word twenty minutes before midnight so even if there are snitches among us, they won't be able to act before we do."

Luca nodded. "And the women?"

"The same. On the stroke of midnight, we'll emerge from the barns and attack."

"You're sure they're prepared for this? Not everyone gets their happy ending tonight." Through the haze of bravado, Luca quietly acknowledged their plan was a dangerous one. After Epi had pointed out the obvious disparity in arms, Luca hoped that they would be able to get close enough to the guards before they were able to fire on them. She had to do this, but she didn't want innocent deaths on her conscience, and she would be no use to Marissa dead either.

Epi shrugged. "There are casualties and heroes in every war, chica. We all know this, and we are all ready for it."

"We need to approach quietly and send small groups to each of the guard outposts while we descend on the main house," Luca said.

"Yes." Epi tapped her shorts' pocket. "Ángel has sketched the layout of the house on a scrap of his shirt. He strongly suspects things have stayed the same, but he can't be sure that Vargas and Marissa haven't moved rooms since he stopped working there."

"At least it gives me somewhere to start looking while you start things out here. Does he know where the guards are in the house and how many there might be?"

Epi patted her shorts again. "It's all here."

"Arturo said that Vargas's paranoia was out of control. It's possible that he'll have more guards covering the house if he thinks he's under threat." Luca ran her hand across the back of her head. There were so many moving parts, and so much that could go wrong. The freedom she'd promised all these people could disappear in a flood of bloodshed. But she really didn't have a choice. This wasn't something she could do alone and have a hope in hell of surviving. And it really would put an end to Vargas's evil, if they could pull it off.

"Anything is possible, chica." Epi put her arm over Luca's shoulder and embraced her as they walked. "Whatever happens tonight, we'll be free."

Luca didn't respond or make eye contact though she felt Epi's gaze burning into the side of her face.

"You may have galvanized us to do this now, Luca, but it's been a long time coming. The deals Vargas made with us were never truly fair, but he's gotten greedy. He's been adding on years for tiny infractions, our allocated food portions have decreased to a barely survivable amount, and now he's imprisoned Marissa against her will. It's time, Luca, so please don't feel responsible for anyone here but yourself." She stopped and tugged Luca to a halt. "I mean it, Luca. Everyone who fights tonight wants an end to this, for themselves as much as for Marissa. They want to go home to their families; they want their lives back. You've just lit the fire beneath their hatred."

Luca looked into Epi's eyes and saw the unblinking truth behind her words. "You want to see your daughter's art for real," she said.

"Yes, I do. And Gloria wants to move to San Antonio to be with her sister. And Juan wants to hold his firstborn grandson in his arms. Everyone who marches with you tonight has their own reasons for standing up to Vargas, and they're at peace with their decision. It's not yours to take on your shoulders, do you understand me?"

"I understand, and that helps. Thank you."

They walked on in silence, with Luca contemplating the enormity of what she'd initiated. She had to free Marissa from her father's clutches, and somewhere along the line, it had dawned on her that she was prepared to die trying. She had no intention of succumbing to that particular cliché—her death wouldn't mean Marissa's freedom. The only positive result would come from a successful extraction, just like she'd seen in all the ridiculous action movies where the hero beat impossible odds to rescue the hostage.

But these weren't impossible odds. They outnumbered Vargas's army, and with darkness and surprise on their side, maybe their guns wouldn't be so influential in the outcome. "I need to get a gun as soon as I can," she said, louder than intended.

Epi hushed her, and when it looked like none of the accompanying guards had heard, she gave Luca a light shove. "Don't sabotage us before we begin, chica. And yes, you will. Have you ever used one?"

"A couple of times," Luca said. "A kid at the orphanage found one, and we used to shoot bottles down by the beach."

Epi grumbled something inaudible.

"I know it was stupid." Luca rolled her eyes, feeling like a chided child.

"Were you a good shot?"

"Eventually..." She touched the crooked part of her nose where she'd broken it with the kickback from the first time she'd fired the gun.

Epi raised her eyebrow. "Killing a man will be very different from killing a bottle, chica."

"Obviously." She was planning on aiming then closing her eyes when she squeezed the trigger. "Have you ever..."

"No. But I know I have it in me. A mother's desire to protect her family is a powerful driver. I will kill if I have to, just as you will, Luca. And when you're faced with that scenario, think only of Marissa and the consequences if you hesitate or fail."

Luca blew out a long breath. Her thoughts had been only of Marissa for a few weeks now, so *that* part wouldn't be hard. But contemplating the cost of failure would be overwhelming. She'd been forced to be strong enough for herself her whole life. She had to hope that doing the same for someone else, someone as important as Marissa, wouldn't be a stretch.

"Let's eat and then we rest," Epi said when they reached the barns.

Luca nodded. "We have a big night." She prayed that, at the end of it, she and Marissa would be walking out of here and toward a new future.

Chapter Thirty

LUCA HADN'T RESTED. SHE'D tried, but visions of what would happen to Marissa if they didn't succeed tonight kept her from slipping into any kind of useful sleep. The minutes had crawled by even when she'd been helping Epi and Gloria prepare food with the remaining contents of Marissa's last basket, and the residual buzzing energy in the barn when curfew finally came around was palpable. She'd caught single words from hushed, whispered conversations, and they strengthened her conviction that they could actually pull this off. The women around her were more than ready to fight. Their resentment been building, and the scent of their freedom was clearly a powerful motivator.

At 11:57 p.m., she swung her legs out of bed, pressed her feet to the warm soil of the ground, and dug her toes in. She couldn't wait to do the exact same thing in LA on Venice Beach, one of the places on the to-do list she'd had for years. She might not even like LA. She might not even like the States. But she wanted to find out, and she wanted Marissa by her side to do that.

Luca pulled her socks and sneakers on and remembered doing the same a few weeks ago, preparing for a supposed meeting with Marissa. Her shoes had been a lot cleaner then but now they were goners. She pushed up from the bed—she'd buy new sneakers in LA. She put on her plaid shirt, hoping it would bring her the luck Veronica had promised it would. So far, it hadn't delivered, but maybe tonight would be different. She needed all the luck she could get to rescue the woman she loved, and she wanted the chance to declare her feelings to Marissa.

In the half-light, the women around her rose and moved as one unit to gather at the doors. Luca scanned the beds to see they were all empty. When it came down to it, they were all united in their chains, and they were all ready for their freedom.

Epi waited to open them, and when the last of the women joined the crowd, she hushed them and motioned to Luca. Everyone turned to look at her.

"We do this for our families and for Marissa," Luca said. "No more words. It's time for action."

Epi pushed open the doors, and they filed into the humid night air. Luca glanced toward the men's barn just as four of them bore down on the two guards posted outside the barns. They went to ground with a struggle, and it took a little time before the guards were motionless. The men stood and waved them all forward, so they merged into a blanket of black figures and, hugging the tree line on the far side of the compound, began the half-mile walk toward the main house.

Luca held onto the unexpected calmness humming through her body. Vargas's captive workers had never shown any signs of unrest, so it seemed he'd gotten blasé about ensuring they stayed in the barns overnight. Aside from the two guards at the barn, there were no other barriers against their progress.

One hundred yards from the house, Ángel motioned for them to stop, and he waved Luca forward. "You're coming with me around the back. Everyone else will attack from the front and draw Vargas's guards to them." He handed her a pistol. "The safety's already off, so be careful. You've got fifteen rounds in the gun, and another fifteen in this." He pressed a spare magazine into her hand. "Epi told me you'd never fired a gun in anger."

Luca shook her head. "But I'm ready."

He patted her shoulder. "I know you are. It's amazing what a human will do for love."

"You know?" Luca had kept her romantic feelings for Marissa to herself, not wanting to color their willingness to help.

He gave her a crooked smile. "It was obvious when we were digging Cedro's grave."

She scanned the faces of the people gathered around her, and her heart thudded against her ribs. "Does everyone know?"

"Mostly. But you've got nothing to worry about. Nobody cares who you love. We all just want out."

Epi caught Luca's wrist. "Good luck, chica. Give Marissa our love."

Luca pulled Epi into a short embrace. "Be careful, Epi. Your daughter's waiting." She released her and didn't look back as she followed Ángel toward the house, mirroring his stooped posture. They reached the edge of the gravel driveway, and Ángel stopped. He put a finger to his mouth then pointed toward a guard smoking a cigarette at the corner of the house. They went a little farther down before carefully crossing the drive fifty yards behind the smoking guard.

"Wait here," he whispered.

She crouched down behind a water fountain and watched as he moved silently toward the guard. He yanked the guy's head back with his hand clamped over his mouth and drew a blade across his neck. Then he guided him to the ground quietly. She saw him motion into the darkness and took a deep breath. When she'd learned that Ángel had worked for Vargas, it had troubled her. Now she was grateful for his expertise.

He edged along the building and waved for her to join him. "All hell's about to break loose. Are you ready?"

What was ready supposed to feel like? It wasn't like she'd trained for this. Did the white-hot electricity coursing through her veins mean she was ready? She tightened her grip on the gun. "Yeah. Let's go."

They made their way around the back, hugging the building and dodging the external spotlights until Ángel stopped again.

"This is the service kitchen." He jimmied the lock and opened the door slowly. "Watch where you're going, and don't knock anything over."

Luca closed the door quietly behind her and widened her eyes to see in the dim light as she followed Ángel through the kitchen. He squatted at the small window in the door to the next room and held up his hand to halt her progress.

"We wait here until it begins."

She watched the seconds tick by on the wall clock until smashing glass signaled their attack. She peered through the door window as tens of armed men rushed from all directions toward the front of the house, shouting and cursing.

Ángel grabbed her forearm. "Patience."

More glass smashed, gunshots sounded, and people yelled. Part of her wished she could see it happening, but most of her just wanted all of this over and Marissa safely in her arms.

"Now."

He pushed through the door, and she followed, both hands wrapped around the pistol grip. She stayed close as he wound through the corridors, checking behind every door and in each room like she'd seen cops do in TV shows.

"What the f–"

Ángel's head slammed into the doorjamb before he was yanked into the room he'd been checking.

"Run!" he yelled.

Luca's feet refused to move. She raised her gun, hands trembling, and took tentative steps toward where Ángel had disappeared. The door rattled as something heavy struck it, and she prayed it was whoever had grabbed Ángel, and that he'd already overcome his assailant. As she neared the door and reached out to open it, Ángel's face smashed against the glass inset, shattering it. He had just enough time to look up at her and mouth, "Vamos," before he disappeared.

She looked down the corridor. With the map Ángel had drawn, she could find her way to Marissa's room. But without him, Luca was vulnerable and alone, holding a gun she didn't want to fire and facing an unknown number of enemies.

She pushed the door open with one hand and led with her gun in the other. Ángel was on his hands and knees with the guard squatting over him, his knife at Ángel's throat. "Let him go," she said, pointing her pistol at the guy's chest.

The door smashed against her side and the force of the impact threw her into the wall. As she slid to her knees, winded, Ángel reached out but the guy over him drew his blade across Ángel's neck. Luca lifted her gun and pulled the trigger. The bullet ripped into the guard's chest, and the impact sent him tumbling backward. She turned quickly to her left and saw a second guy advancing on her, but before he could kick out, she squeezed a second and third round off, hitting him in the thigh and stomach. He dropped to his knees, clutching his gut, and went for the gun in his shoulder holster. She fired four more times until he dropped face first to the floor, motionless.

The ensuing silence lasted seconds before a high-pitched ringing thundered in her ears, and Luca couldn't help but focus her gaze on the pool of bright red blood that crept toward her from the dead guard a few feet away.

"Luca."

She looked up, startled. "You're alive!" She shoved the gun in the waist of her jeans and rushed over to Ángel's side, but as she lifted him, the amount of blood on the rug beneath him tore away her joy. She pressed her hand to the wound in his neck. "It's okay. You're okay."

He half-smiled and coughed, agony clear in his expression. "No, Luca. I'm not okay. You have to go before more of them come," he said between gulps and short breaths.

"I'm not leaving you." She looked around for something to wrap around his neck. "Come on. Let's go."

Ángel gripped her hand. "Luca. Stop. Look at me."

She swallowed hard and slowly met his gaze. "I'm looking."

He shook his head. "But you're not seeing. Go and get Marissa and get yourselves out of here. Do it now. I'll survive if it's meant to be."

"But–"

"There are no buts, Luca. Leave. Now."

She reached over to the dead guard behind him and tugged the bandana from his cargo pants' pocket. "Hold this to your neck, and don't let go." She waited for him to do so then got to her feet. She took the gun from her jeans, pulled the door open and left without a backward glance. Another look at him would delay her getting to Marissa, and she was Luca's only reason for doing any of this.

She closed her eyes briefly to bring Ángel's map to mind. Straight along this corridor to the grand staircase. Take the left side and turn right at the top. Marissa's door would be the final one at the end of the corridor.

Luca hurried along the route, keeping her back to the wall and her gun at shoulder height, ready to fire. Ángel said she had fifteen in the gun, but she couldn't recall how many she'd already fired. She looked back down the stairs, wishing she'd checked the two guards for more magazines. She tapped her pocket to check if she still had the one Ángel had given her and hoped that she'd remember how to reload when she had to do it under pressure. The noise of the chaos outside rose with every step. It wasn't like anything she'd heard before. People were dying out there, and she could do nothing about it except hope that Epi and the rest of them would triumph.

She peered around the final corridor and saw a guard stationed at Marissa's door. He had his back to her as he looked out the window at what she assumed was total chaos on the front of the property. Could she shoot a man in the back? Did he deserve the chance to put down his weapon and live? She inched farther along the wall, and her hip bumped a tall, freestanding table. The giant vase toppled off before she had the chance to steady it, and though she got one hand to it, she couldn't grasp it, and it fell to the solid wooden floor, shattering into sharp shards and alerting the guy outside Marissa's room.

Bullets whipped past her head, and she threw herself backward. Her head hit the edge of a heavy picture frame, and darkness closed around her vision as she fell to the floor with a thunderous thud. *No*. Luca widened her eyes and forced the pain away. All would be lost if she allowed herself to slip into the arms of unconsciousness.

Footsteps hammered down the corridor, getting louder and louder. Amazed that she'd managed to hold onto her pistol, she leveled it to chest height and pointed it at the empty space. Jorge De Léon, the guard with whom she'd carried Cedro when he was barely alive, came around the corner, eyes wide and wild.

"Romero. What the hell?"

"Walk away, Jorge," she said, mustering the kind of calmness she imbued in her written characters when they were faced with impossible situations. "You've seen what's happening out there." She jutted her chin. "All of this ends tonight, but you don't have to."

He didn't lower his weapon. "What's to stop you from killing me if I put my gun down?"

"I don't want to kill anyone, Jorge. You have to trust my word. Walk away while you can. Go out through the kitchen, get in a cart, and leave." She saw his arms waver slightly. "This doesn't have to be your life, Jorge. You can do better, *be* better." She sat up a little straighter. "But do it now."

A beat. More gunshots and screams outside.

Jorge lowered his gun. "I'm not dying for a piece of shit like Vargas." He motioned down the corridor Luca had come up. "I'm going that way."

Luca got fully to her feet and partially dropped her arms. "And I'm going that way."

They circled around each other and began to walk backward in their respective directions. When Jorge was out of sight, Luca turned quickly and sprinted to the end of the hallway. She yanked the handle, but the door didn't open. "Marissa?"

"Luca?"

The surprise in Marissa's voice matched the relief in Luca's heart. She steadied her racing heart. They weren't out of this yet. "Yeah, it's me. I don't know where they key is so I'm going to shoot the lock. Is there something solid you can hide behind?"

"Yes..."

Luca waited until Marissa called out again. She aimed the gun at the lock mechanism, shielded her eyes, and pulled the trigger. The wood splintered, and Luca kicked at the door. It flew open, and Marissa ran at her and jumped into her arms. She stumbled backward but managed to stay standing and tightened her arms around Marissa's waist, squeezing her so hard that she gasped.

"Sorry." Luca relaxed her grip and focused on Marissa's face, the face she couldn't have lived without seeing again. "God, I've missed you."

"What's happening?" Marissa asked, breathless.

Luca tilted her head. "We're getting you out of here."

Chapter Thirty-One

MARISSA'S LEGS GAVE WAY when Luca set her down, and she clasped her arms around Luca's neck. "Don't let go."

Luca caressed her cheek and smiled. "I'll never let you go." She uncurled Marissa's arms and took her hand. "Come with me. We have to get out of here before the fire."

Marissa tugged on Luca's hand. "Fire?"

"They're burning it all down, Marissa. All the people from the barns are outside battling with your father's army." Luca stroked Marissa's fingers. "There's only one way this ends."

She looked around her room frantically. Her mamá's books. She couldn't leave them. She couldn't let her whole library be destroyed. She pulled her hand from Luca's and stepped back. "No. You have to stop them."

Luca frowned. "What? Why? Is it your father?"

"No." She motioned toward the rows and rows of books her mamá had collected, the huge library Marissa had inherited. She only had to hold one of these volumes to feel her mamá's presence. "I can't let these books *burn*."

Luca moved closer and held out her hands. "Marissa, please. When you planned to leave with Arturo, were you going to leave all of this here?"

She opened her mouth to answer but stopped herself. "Most of it, yes."

"What were you going to take with you?" Luca asked softly.

She'd contemplated that decision for months. Knowing that she'd only have a purse, choosing one book from the collection of hundreds had been like choosing a favorite child to take, only to leave the rest in an unfavorable orphanage, unloved and alone. "Only our sixth edition copy of *A Christmas Carol* by Charles Dickens."

"I'm familiar with the author," Luca said with a smile. "You should get that book, and then we can go."

Luca's reasoning made sense, of course, but leaving hundreds of books behind to a fiery fate hurt beyond logical thought. She crossed the room to the classics section and retrieved the book without hesitation, its position as familiar as her heart in her chest. "This is harder than I thought it would be," she whispered, both to Luca and her mamá.

Luca wrapped her arms around Marissa's waist and held her gently. "I can't know how you're feeling, cariña, but I'm right here with you."

Marissa sank into Luca's arms, and her fears melted away for a brief moment. How was it that even when they were surrounded by chaos and inevitable destruction, a peaceful bubble enveloped them? Because it was right. Because it was her escape from the life she'd never wanted. She scanned the shelves in front of her. This was her past, and they'd contributed to making her the woman she was today, but it was time to leave them behind and move forward, taking her mamá with her in her heart. The books were only paper and inked imagination, but they'd given her memories to last a lifetime.

She turned in Luca's arms and looked into the face of her future. "I need to gather a few more things."

Luca released her. "Okay, but please be quick. We don't have much time, and I don't know if there are any guards left in the building."

Marissa got her tote bag from the closet. She carefully placed the book in the compartment at the back, then slipped in a small pile of treasured photographs and her favorite fountain pen—the first one her mamá had bought for her. She put together a change of clothes, grabbed her make-up bag and stuffed them all in the top of the bag before closing it.

She threw the bag over her shoulder and took one last scan of the room she'd spent so many happy hours in with her mamá and so many lonely days without her. "I'm ready," she said and took Luca's outstretched hand.

Luca pulled her gun from her jeans and tugged Marissa toward the door. "Stay close and stay behind me."

"Wait!" She rushed back to her desk, yanked open the bottom drawer, and retrieved the hard drive from Luca's old computer. "We need this to prove you're the real author of your books."

"Thank you." Luca took it from her and pushed it into her back pocket. "Now let's go."

Marissa followed Luca down the corridor. She wanted to ask if Luca had used the gun she was wielding so expertly, but she also knew she didn't want the answer. The people around her were being forced to do things they wouldn't normally do, things they'd never wanted to do. It had started with Arturo, and now it had reached Luca too. "Where's Arturo?"

"I don't know," Luca whispered. "But everyone knows he's helping you, so they won't harm him."

"I won't leave without him."

Luca stopped at the end of the corridor. "I know. And the people out there won't leave without ending your father's reign. Don't worry, I'm sure we'll find him."

As they descended the stairs, the noise from outside penetrated the walls of the house. Screams, gunshots, terror. Everything she was desperate to get away from.

"Where do you think you're going?"

Her father's voice rose above it all as he emerged from the darkness at the base of the staircase. In the orange glow cast through the windows from the fires burning outside, he looked like the Devil. He held a gun in each hand, pointed toward them. His eyes were wild and unfocused, his shirt tails showed beneath his vest, and his tie and shirt were tugged open. She'd never seen him so unkempt and disheveled. She looked at Luca and saw her gun was trained on her father. "Please, Father. Please let us leave." She clutched her chest, trying to steady her racing heart.

"Why do you wish to leave me so badly? I've done everything for you since your mamá died." He waved his guns. "And this is how you repay me? Trying to sneak away in the middle of the night. And you?" He gestured wildly toward Luca. "Are you responsible for what's going on out there?" He shook his head and sneered. "I should've killed you when Soto dumped you here."

"I can't be part of your world, Papá. I hate it. All of it. Mamá wanted me to follow my dreams, and I've always dreamed of escaping. This life—your life—isn't for me. It's killing my soul." Hers wasn't the only soul he was slowly killing. Where was Arturo? Surely, he hadn't gotten out and left her there.

He snorted. "Killing your soul? Don't be so dramatic. The life I've given you has made you soft and ungrateful. You don't get to choose which parts of our family you like and discard the others. You're either family," he raised his guns higher, "or you're not."

"You can't reason with him, Marissa," Luca whispered. "He's gone."

She glanced at Luca, her eyes and her gun still focused on Marissa's father. She hadn't wanted this confrontation with her father. She'd wanted to leave quietly and not face the consequences of her departure. But now there was an inkling of hope that she *could* explain why she had to get away from here and that he would understand, even let her go with his blessing. Despite all the signs that the father she'd known had disappeared still deeper into a paralyzing paranoia, she had to try.

"I'll always be your daughter, Papá." She began to descend the stairs again. "And I am grateful for what you've given me, but I have to make a new life. I have to make my own way. I'm not happy here."

"And where do you think you're going that will make you happy? America?" He touched the butt of a gun to his head. "You're loca if you think you'll find a better life there, without me, without my money."

"I have to try, Papá. Please let me try."

"Marissa," Luca whispered.

She heard Luca's tentative footsteps beside her and paused at the bottom stair, only a few feet from her father.

"No, Marissa. I've pandered to you for too long. It's time for you to put aside your childish dreams and accept your responsibility to this family. Familia is everything." He glared at Luca. "I warned you what I would do if you fucked with my daughter. I don't know what you've done to her or what your part in all of this is, but it's time for us to have the conversation I promised you."

Marissa stepped in front of Luca, aware that his guns now pointed at her chest. What good would her heart be if Luca were to die at her father's hands anyway? "My discontent was in motion long before you forced Luca to work here. She's done nothing but hear me when I've talked, which is what I need you to do now, Papá. Please hear me."

"I've listened to your nonsense long enough. She *is* the problem. Soto planted her here to turn you against me. I don't think your plan was ever to leave. I think you want me dead, and Soto was going to take my place. That's what you wanted all along, isn't it?"

Marissa frowned at his wild and unfounded accusations, unable to fathom the origin of his twisted logic. "No, Father. I would never associate myself with her." She'd used Soto, yes, but never worked *with* her.

The floor creaked from the direction of her father's office, and Arturo came into view.

"Vargas. Why are you pointing your guns at Marissa?"

"Perfect timing, Arturo," her father said. "She was trying to escape with our writer." He rolled his eyes. "And my guns weren't aimed at my daughter until she stepped in front of them to protect Romero."

Arturo pulled the gun from his holster and targeted her father. "I'm sorry, but this has to stop. You have to let her go."

Her father frowned and looked from Marissa to Arturo and back again several times as if trying to make sense of the situation. "What are you doing, Arturo? Aim your pistol at Romero immediately, or I swear you'll join Santiago."

Arturo didn't waver though Marissa saw the sadness flicker across his eyes before it was replaced with rage.

"Lower your weapon, or I'll decorate this hallway with your brains," Arturo said.

Her father swung his left arm in Arturo's direction and aimed the gun at his head. "You too? I should have known Santiago would draw his *son* into betraying me. It's all making sense now. Santiago plotted this whole thing so that you could take over. I'll bet the whole Soto family were involved too." Spittle flew from his mouth as he spat his words. "That's why you said you couldn't find them when I sent you for them." He growled and shook his head. "I saved you from a life in the gutter—this is how you choose to repay me?"

Arturo flicked the safety off his gun. "I owe you nothing but a bullet."

"No, Arturo, don't." Marissa raised her hand but didn't move. She was caught between protecting the two people in her life she loved. If she moved to protect Arturo, she left Luca vulnerable, but if she remained motionless, he was in danger. "There's no winner here. Everyone shoots, then everyone dies. Please, Father. Just let us go."

"I'd rather see you die than leave this family," he said.

His words struck her as painfully as any bullet. They echoed in her mind, obliterating her hope for his redemption. "You don't mean that. You're hurting." For perhaps the first time, Marissa considered that her mamá's death had set him on this course, drowning in his own grief. "Mamá wouldn't want this, you know that."

Her father's complexion deepened to a dark crimson, and he bared his teeth. "Don't tell me what my wife would or wouldn't have wanted, child. You know nothing. My wife was loyal, and she would never have tolerated your betrayal. She would've pulled the trigger herself."

She looked deep into his eyes and saw nothing but madness and rage. There was no coming back for him, and there was no freedom for her. "I can't leave..."

"The only way you leave this family is to be buried by it," he said.

Marissa's chest convulsed, and she sobbed with the realization that there was no way out of this situation. She was at the center of it and the only one unarmed and unable to defend herself. She glanced back at Luca, and her grief grew exponentially. She'd finally found love and was unable to fly on its wings. An inevitable dread solidified in her stomach, so heavy it almost dragged her to the ground. Her life was over.

The front door burst open, and gunshots rang out all around her. She was knocked to the floor, Luca on top of her. She raised her head slowly as people flooded in. Arturo lay on the floor, motionless. She turned to see her father on his back. He groaned and began to drag himself to his right. Marissa followed his trajectory and saw one of his pistols nearly within reach.

Footsteps thudded past her head as someone ran toward her father and kicked the gun away. A violent mob of men and women, enraged and full of hatred from years of repression and ill treatment, surrounded her father and began to circle him. Through their legs, she saw him stumble to his feet, clutching his shoulder.

"Papá," she whispered and reached out.

"Are you okay?"

Marissa caught her breath as Luca lifted herself off her and ran her hands over Marissa's body. "Yes. But Arturo...and Father."

Luca stood and pulled Marissa to her feet. "We have to get you out of here."

Marissa looked back toward her father, and a woman she didn't recognize lifted her machete and advanced. She screamed, and Luca tugged her away before she could witness the blade fall. What she lacked in vision was more than compensated for by the sounds. Wet thuds. Screaming and yelling. Inhumanity bred from cruelty and neglect. He had brought this on himself, but that didn't mean she didn't feel every strike as if it were on her own body.

Luca stooped at Arturo's body, grasped his wrist, and pulled him toward the door. Marissa closed her ears to the assault and took hold of Arturo's other wrist. He groaned when they tugged him down the wooden steps leading from the house, and relief flooded through her.

"Over there." Luca pointed to Arturo's car.

Marissa looked across the driveway, and the carnage strewn before her made her retch. In the illumination cast by the floodlights from the house, dozens of lifeless bodies marred the perfectly manicured lawns. Blood colored the white marbled gravel. She dropped Arturo's arm, turned and vomited. She felt Luca's arm around her shoulders.

"Come with me, Marissa," Luca said and moved the hair from Marissa's eyes. "Focus on getting Arturo to the car."

Marissa wiped her mouth with her shirt sleeve. "None of this was meant to happen. No one was supposed to die because of me."

Luca pulled her upright and gently caressed her cheek. "Tonight isn't because of you. This has been ready to happen for years."

She narrowed her eyes and looked directly at Luca. "You're trying to pass this off as a coincidence?"

Luca shrugged and glanced away. "These people were desperate to break their chains. You were the catalyst, that's all."

"Marissa..." Arturo said, his voice laced with agony.

She dropped to her knees and took his hand. "Everything's going to be okay, primo. Where does it hurt?" She followed his gaze to his hand, which he'd pressed against his stomach. A deep red stained his light gray suit, and she gasped.

"It looks worse than it is." His brief smiled turned to a pained grimace.

Luca knelt beside her. "Even so, we should get you to the hospital." She put his arm over her shoulder and stood, bringing him with her.

"My keys."

"Where are they?" Marissa ducked beneath his arm and helped to support his weight as they headed toward his car.

"Jacket pocket."

She patted him down and pulled the keys out. "I'll drive." Marissa opened the rear door when they reached the vehicle, and Luca bundled Arturo into the back.

"You should get in the back with him and keep pressure on the wound," Luca said.

Marissa looked down and noticed how the set of keys jangled in time with the shaking of her hand. She looked back at the house as the workers piled out the front door, cheering with their arms around each other, victorious in their revolution. Once again, she scanned the lifeless bodies across the grounds, the cost of their freedom. She closed her eyes, but the image remained imprinted on her mind. Her father's greed had caused all this needless violence in gentle people. When the police inevitably descended on the compound, she would tell them nothing. The good ones wouldn't waste their time. The ones on her father's payroll might be harder to placate. She would need to know which were which from Arturo.

Luca placed her hands on Marissa's shoulders. "It's time to go."

Marissa handed her the keys and got in the back.

Luca closed the door behind her. "I'll be back in a minute."

She watched Luca run toward the group. She wandered among them for a few moments before embracing someone. From the height and build, Marissa decided it was probably Epi, and she managed to smile, glad that she'd survived when so many of them hadn't. Luca ran back to the car and jumped in the driver's seat.

"What happened to burning it all down?" Marissa asked as Luca sped away.

"They decided it would be a waste. But they're heading to the fields to destroy them."

She swallowed, holding the question in her throat for a while, uncertain that she wanted the answer. "Father?" She met Luca's gaze in the rearview mirror.

"He's gone."

Marissa was thankful Luca said nothing more. She didn't need to hear that her father deserved his fate, to be torn apart by the people he had enslaved. She put her bag down and turned her attention to Arturo. She didn't want to focus on her unexpected desperation for her father's blessing to leave, nor did she want to dwell on the knowledge that he would rather murder her than let her go.

They were leaving the compound without the fear that he would forever hunt them down, and she had to be grateful for that. The new life she wanted so badly stretched before her. She looked down at Arturo.

"It's finally over," he said and smiled.

She returned his smile and nodded. "Yes. It's over." And now the healing could begin.

Chapter Thirty-Two

THE CHARRED, BLACKENED FIELDS smoldered in the afternoon haze, and the smoke was still visible from the house. The smell made Luca's nose twitch. She'd thought she would never have to return here, but Marissa convinced her it would be easier to face the police now than have them searching for her. The bodies of Vargas's army and the dead workers, zipped into black bags, were being individually hoisted onto stretchers and wheeled to large black vans. She wanted the families of the workers to know their sacrifice. Epi had promised she would tell them, but she was long gone. Marissa had ensured none of the surviving workers were present by the time she called the police.

Luca looked away and back at the Vargas mansion. She couldn't handle seeing the dead being handled with such nonchalance. The carnage and chaos of the previous night had faded, but the memories would live long in her mind. She'd been prepared for none of it. Not really. She couldn't wait to put all of this behind her and start fresh in the States.

Two officers wheeled another body bag out through the front doors, and Captain Ortega beckoned them over.

"Are you ready?" Luca asked.

Marissa shook her head. "But I'll do it anyway."

Luca squeezed her shoulders and held her as they slowly walked toward the house.

Ortega held out a ring in a clear evidence bag as he stood beside the gurney and its dead cargo. "Was this your father's?"

Marissa examined it without touching it. "Yes."

"Are you absolutely certain?"

Marissa twisted the ring on her own finger. "I am. It's his wedding ring. He never took it off."

Luca glanced at the body bag, which she assumed contained Marissa's father. A lot of the workers who'd burst into the house last night had been armed with machetes from the field shed. It didn't take much deduction to realize why Vargas's body bag was shorter and lumpier than the others she'd seen being loaded onto the vans.

"Then I don't need you to try to identify your father." Ortega pocketed the ring and motioned to the officers to take Vargas away. "We'll confirm with dental records."

Luca blew out the breath she'd held. She didn't know how Marissa would deal with seeing the remains of her father, but Luca felt sure she'd probably puke. When she'd pulled Marissa away from the scene last night, it was for her own preservation as well as Marissa's.

More officers with three more bodies emerged from the house.

Ortega tilted his head slightly to meet Marissa's faraway gaze. "These are more straightforward deaths. Can you try to identify them for me?"

Luca placed her hand on the small of Marissa's back to remind her she was there.

"Of course," Marissa said.

Ortega unzipped each of the bags and stepped aside. Marissa took a visibly deep breath and looked at each of them before stumbling back slightly into Luca's arms.

"It's okay, Marissa. I'm here."

"Do you recognize any of them?"

Marissa reeled off three names, but it was the last one that caused Luca to clamp her hand over her mouth. She hadn't gone back to check if Ángel was still alive. In the confusion and her preoccupation with getting Marissa to safety, she'd totally forgotten about him. If she'd remembered, could she have saved him?

Ortega looked at Luca. "Is this man your family?"

"No." She clenched her jaw to stop from saying anything else. She had to stick to their story that she was Marissa's friend and had been nowhere near any of this.

"But you recognize him?"

"I saw him around the compound when I visited, that's all. And I've never seen a dead body before." She heard her voice falter on the lie.

Ortega arched his eyebrow. "You don't recognize the other two?"

She swallowed and shook her head. "I never took much notice of the guards. I tried not to make eye contact with any of them." She shrugged. "With all their guns, they were kind of intimidating."

"These two were always assigned to the fields," Marissa said. "Luca would never have seen them. Ángel worked in the house occasionally."

Ortega pulled a cigarette and lit it. The smoke overcame the metallic odor of congealed blood, and Luca inhaled deeply. He offered her the pack.

"No, thanks. I don't smoke. It's just preferable over the smell of death."

"It's something you get used to." He gave a quick smile then looked at Marissa. "We found the heads of your law firm boss and a woman in your father's office. Do you know anything about those?"

Luca's body tensed. *Casey*. She'd started this avalanche of terror, but did she deserve to die and have her head chopped off? She closed her eyes against the image of it happening while she was still alive and fought off the urge to retch.

"My father had become paranoid and delusional over the past few weeks. He'd set up surveillance on many of his closest allies and friends, and he had several of them murdered, including Señor Aguilar. I think the woman was one of his dealers."

Ortega tapped ash onto the ground and stared at Marissa. "You seem to know a lot about your father's business even though you weren't involved in it."

"I had no choice since he operated from the house I lived in. People walked in and were carried out wrapped in plastic sheeting regularly. And it behooved me to be aware of my father's state of mind, especially when it extended to murdering my boss. For all I knew, I could have been next."

"And you say everyone's accounted for? No one survived apart from you, your friend, and your bodyguard, Arturo Castillo?"

"That's correct."

"Was he involved in any of these murders?" Ortega asked.

Luca thought of Arturo being ordered to kill his adoptive father and wondered how many other people he'd murdered during his time. Marissa believed he had no choice, but Luca wasn't sure she agreed. If she'd been Arturo, would she have run rather than be Vargas's murder puppet? It was easy for her to judge, she supposed. She'd been terrified in her one meeting with Vargas; what would she have done rather than face certain torture and death?

"No, he wasn't. Arturo has been my personal bodyguard since he came of age," Marissa said, her tone calm and even. "He didn't work directly for my father."

Her composure was beyond impressive. Luca shoved her hands in her pockets so Ortega didn't see them trembling.

"I'll need to talk to him. Which hospital is he at?"

"San Judas," Marissa said, "but he's due to be released this evening. The doctor said that the bullet didn't do any serious damage."

"And you're sure that everyone else involved died? No one else left but you two and your bodyguard, Castillo?"

Luca shrugged and stayed silent. They'd agreed for Marissa to do the talking. Less opportunity for contradiction.

"As certain as I can be, Captain Ortega. You'll find the bodies of more workers buried in the northern field—this revolt had been brewing for a long time. They fought with my father's army. Some stormed the house and murdered him. Then they burned the fields. If any of them managed to get away, I wish them luck, and I have no desire to pursue them." Marissa touched Ortega's arm. "You know what my father was, Captain. With him and his business gone from your city, we'll all be safer."

Luca's mouth went dry as she waited for Ortega's reaction. Would *he* want to pursue the case?

Ortega took a long drag on his cigarette. "He leaves a hole, Señorita Vargas. And nature will find a way to fill it. Sometimes, the devil you know is better than his inevitable replacement."

"I won't be here to find out." Marissa hugged herself. "But I'm sure you'll handle it, Captain. Arturo told me you were one of the good ones."

Ortega inclined his head. "There aren't many of us left, but I'll do my best. If you're leaving, what happens to all this?"

"I'll probably gift the land and house to the Door of Faith Orphanage." Marissa looked across the lawns to the smoking fields. "There are too many bad memories for me to stay."

He gave a tight-lipped smile as if he understood. "I'll need you both to give a statement, which I assume will match with Castillo's. I've got a board full of unsolved murders; if you're happy for this to be the end of it, I'll tie up any loose ends and close the case."

"Thank you, Captain. I'd appreciate that. I just want to get on with my life."

Ortega motioned to another cop. "You can follow Guerrero and get it done now."

"Of course."

Luca followed Marissa to Arturo's car while Ortega told Guerrero what he wanted. She waited until the doors were closed before she cursed and put her head in her hands. "I think I used up all my bravado last night."

"You did great, Luca." Marissa caressed her neck.

"You were like ice. Maybe you can teach me."

Marissa shook her head. "It's nothing to be proud of. I've just had practice." She gently squeezed Luca's neck before letting go and starting the car. "I like you exactly the way you are. Don't change a thing."

Warmth spread through Luca's body like the caress of the sun. Marissa headed down the drive, and Luca couldn't tear her gaze away. She remembered one of the orphanage staff telling her that everything happened for a reason, that God had a plan. It was ridiculous to ask a twelve-year-old to accept that she'd been abandoned because of the strategy of a higher power, and Luca never had. But as she sat beside the most amazing woman she'd ever met, driving toward a brand-new future, she questioned her lack of faith. If Casey hadn't set these events in motion, Luca and Marissa would never have gotten to know each other properly. She would never have had the chance to fall in love with her.

Luca glanced back at the house as it receded in the rearview mirror. Casey and Vargas were her past. She focused once again on Marissa. She was her future, and Luca couldn't wait to dive headlong into it.

Chapter Thirty-Three

MARISSA SMILED WIDELY AS Epi placed the last of almost twenty thousand cempasúchil marigolds onto the giant floral figure of La Catrina on the ground outside her mamá's shrine. This was supposed to have been her final visit before she escaped to a new life in Europe, a day and night full of sorrow as she said goodbye to her mamita for the last time. Instead, she was caught up in a joyful celebration with Luca, Arturo, Epi, and many of the other workers who had fought for their freedom a few nights ago. The carnage was still fresh in her mind, but she knew as with all things, it would recede with time.

She was thankful she'd been able to find Epi and the rest of them in their old neighborhood to invite them to share the Día de los Muertos. Almost all of them had family here, though their pastel rainbow shrines were far prettier and less ostentatious than her mamá's. She'd fix that soon enough.

"It's beautiful, Epi."

Epi blushed. "You think so?"

"I think it's obvious where your daughter got her artistic talent." Marissa put her arm around Epi's shoulders. "Is Liliana flying in early tomorrow? I'd love to see her before we leave."

"Yes, yes." Epi bounced under Marissa's arm. "I'm picking her up from the airport at seven."

"Perhaps we could meet at Casa Aleta for breakfast at nine? We fly out in the afternoon."

"We would love that." Epi took Marissa's hands and kissed them. "You're an angel. We wouldn't have survived without your aid all these years. We can't ever repay you, but we will pray for you and Luca always."

Marissa blinked away tears. "There was nothing to repay, but if there had been, I think that helping Luca free me cleared that debt."

Epi released her hands. "Tomorrow then." She nodded over Marissa's shoulder. "You have an admirer."

Luca touched her hip as she walked past her and handed something to Epi. "You can give your daughter this yourself now."

"No need for that." Epi tapped her chest. "Everything I want to say is in here." She tucked the paper into her pocket, gave them one last smile and walked away.

Marissa wrapped her arms around Luca's waist and kissed her. "Thank you for being willing to postpone going to LA so I could do this."

Luca ran her fingers through Marissa's hair and chuckled. "Don't you know by now that I'd do anything for you?"

"You did kind of prove that by leading a revolution to rescue me, yes." She kissed Luca again. She'd never get enough of her soft lips. "But I know you're desperate to meet Alyssa and get everything straightened out."

Luca grinned. "I'm beyond desperate, but I don't want to do any of it without you by my side."

"You're too sweet." She was just as eager to leave this place as Luca but knowing that she could now come back at any time lightened her heart.

From the far side of La Catrina, Arturo waved with his good hand. His other arm rested in a sling across his chest, the result of a final souvenir from her father. She didn't know if it was Arturo or Luca who had felled her father, but she didn't care. She was simply glad her father's aim had been so poor. She waved back and saw the young man she'd known long ago in his smile. There would be plenty of healing to come, but he already seemed lighter with the absence of her father's shadow on his soul.

Marissa refocused on Luca. "Come with me. I want you to meet my mamá."

Luca looked up at the shrine. "It stands out, doesn't it?"

She swatted Luca's shoulder. "I know it's ugly, but I'll get it changed. Mamá would've wanted it to be more colorful, less sleek." She knocked on the dark windows. "The bulletproof glass can go too."

Luca frowned and touched Marissa's lower back. "I'm glad you'll finally be able to build the right kind of resting place for your madre."

"Me too. And my tía Carolina can come visit her now too." Marissa opened the doors to find the anteroom full of the birds of the paradise flowers she'd ordered. She inhaled the mellow, earthy scent and almost immediately felt her mamá's presence. She took Luca's hand and guided her to the shrine at the rear of the building. She lit the many candles and touched one of her mamá's photographs. "I miss you."

A whisper of a wind from nowhere flickered the flames of the candles, and Marissa smiled. "Mamá, this is Luca."

"Hi." Luca lowered her head and knelt on the colored cushions.

Marissa pulled one from the pile and positioned herself close to the photographs, her back to Luca. "I suppose you'll probably already know, but Father is dead." Marissa went through the saga from meeting Luca in the barns to her final escape. When she was done, she was filled with a brightness as if it replaced the burden she'd released in retelling the story. It felt cathartic to release the dark weight of her father's influence and share it with her mamá.

She glanced over her shoulder, and Luca smiled a smile full of promise and love. That word. That emotion. Something she hadn't felt for a living person for a long time, and this was the kind of love she'd never felt for anyone. But she hadn't been able to vocalize it. It had seemed too cliché and throwaway to say during or after they'd made love. She'd suspected that Luca would think she'd gotten carried away in the physicality of the moment and wouldn't believe her words were real. And she hadn't wanted to burst their bubble of unreality in all the moments in between; how could they have talked of love when Luca's life was in danger? These were three words she'd never said to a lover, and she wanted it to be perfect when she finally declared her love for Luca.

Here, now, with the veil thinned and her mamita close by...seemed just as perfect as a moment might get. Marissa didn't want to delay further, and she needed to hear Luca say the words back to her. She wanted to savor and remember every detail of it all. To be loved and cherished for who she was... It was a notion she'd read in so many books, but for it to come alive for her seemed like the fairy tales she'd long grown out of.

Marissa turned fully and pushed her cushion up so that she could sit face to face with Luca. She ran her fingers along Luca's cheek and to her lips, then she kissed her softly and with such tenderness, it was delicately painful. She broke away but stayed close enough to feel Luca's gentle breath on her skin. She looked deep into Luca's eyes. "I love you, Luca."

Luca let out a short breath, and her smile made her eyes crinkle. "Are you sure?"

Marissa frowned. That wasn't the response she'd been hoping for. She arched her eyebrow. "I'm sure I wasn't expecting you to say that."

Luca placed her hands on Marissa's thighs. "Sorry. I know." She closed her eyes then opened them and sighed deeply. "Let me try to explain... What we've been through over the past couple of weeks has been extremely intense. We both wanted to escape for different reasons, and we were kind of smashed together. That kind of situation can lead to emotions running high...and untrue. You're the most incredible woman I've ever met, but I'm just a gutter rat. An orphan who tends bar. Under normal circumstances, you and I don't move in the same circles, let alone have the opportunity to get to know each other." She ran her hand through her hair then dropped it in her lap. "I'm so grateful to have had the chance to know you, Marissa, but," she gestured back toward the anteroom, "you're a bird of paradise and I'm a weed. We don't exist in the same space. And I don't want you to convince yourself that you can settle for me, even for a while, just because you feel obligated after I rescued you." She shrugged. "That sounds a bit grandiose. It wasn't just—"

Marissa silenced Luca with another kiss. "I love you. And weeds are simply flowers in the wrong place. You're in the wrong place, Luca, but you won't be for much longer. When we're in LA, you'll see how right this is. It was because we were meant to be together that we made the most of the extreme situation we found ourselves in, a situation others created. But now we get to create our own situation, our own environment, and it's going to be perfect." She dragged her nail across Luca's lips. "It's going to be perfect, because we're perfect together. It's going to be perfect because I love you, and no amount of your self-sabotage is going to change how I feel."

Luca's expression softened, and Marissa saw hope in her eyes.

"You really love me?" Luca asked.

She took Luca's face in her hands. "I really love you. All of you."

Luca bit her lip. "Then you won't mind if I tell you that I love you?"

She laughed gently and shook her head. "Are you asking me or telling me?"

"I'm telling you. I'm telling you that I love you. I'm telling you that I adore you, and I can't wait to see where we'll go now that we're both free to fly."

Marissa wrapped her arms around Luca and held her tight. Everything was as it should be, finally. She heard her mamá's whispered voice, and the tall flames of the candles flickered and danced in harmony with the beating of Marissa's heart. And her heart beat for Luca.

Epilogue

Eighteen months later

LUCA PULLED HER SHIRT on, but Marissa placed her hands on her elbows and stopped her. She felt Marissa's lips on her shoulders and shuddered.

"Still sore?" Marissa asked but continued to kiss her neck.

"A little, but don't stop." Luca closed her eyes and enjoyed the sensation of Marissa's lips on the tender parts of her new tattoo. She held onto the dresser when Marissa snaked her hand around Luca's hips and slipped into her shorts.

"Do you think we've got time?"

Marissa's question was clearly rhetorical. She circled her finger over Luca's clit and stroked her chest with her other hand. She pinched Luca's nipple, making her moan. Luca gripped the hard wood tighter as her pleasure rose in a wave and washed over her. "We've always got time when you make me come that quick." Luca turned and pressed her lips to Marissa's, tasting her morning coffee as a ripple of aftershock coursed through her body.

Marissa pulled away and looked over Luca's shoulder into the mirror. "I think you should always be naked so I get to look at your beautiful wings whenever I want."

"I'm pretty sure that wouldn't be considered professional behavior on set."

Marissa rolled her eyes. "People get naked on set *all the time*."

She laughed. "The actors, yes, but not the writers."

"Maybe that's where they're going wrong."

Luca thought of the dapper butch director she was about to start working with. "I don't want to see Rix in anything but her jeans, shirt, and vest combo, thanks."

Marissa made an appreciative sound. "Oh, I don't know."

Luca gasped Marissa's upper arms gently. "I do."

Marissa laughed. "You're easy. She's too old for me." She ran her fingers along Luca's spine and nibbled on her neck.

"I'm still trying to get used to you wanting to be with me. Every sexy, powerful butch woman is a threat to me and a better option for you."

Marissa slapped Luca's chest. "Stop it. Haven't you gotten used to the idea that I'm not going anywhere?"

Luca sighed and shook her head. "I don't think I'll ever get there, sorry."

"I guess I'll just have to stick around for the next five decades or so to prove it." Marissa pulled Luca's shirt over her shoulders and slowly buttoned it.

Luca squeezed her thighs together as Marissa's nails trailed over her skin. "How is it that you can dress me in just as sexual a way as you undress me?"

"Practice." She finished the last button and stepped back, tapping her watch. "Better hurry. The driver is downstairs waiting."

"What? She's here already?" Luca dropped onto the bed and pulled her jeans and shoes on. "Why didn't you say?"

Marissa licked her middle finger and wiggled her eyebrow. "Because you wouldn't have let me have you if you knew someone was waiting on us."

Luca jumped up and finished getting dressed. "We can't be late on my first day."

"We won't be." Marissa straightened Luca's collar. "You look amazing. Let's go."

Luca bit her lip and watched Marissa sway out the bedroom like a catwalk model. The light blue summer dress she wore skimmed the top of her knees, revealing her long legs, and her four-inch heels shaped her calves in a way that made Luca weak with lust. And love. All the love.

She followed Marissa downstairs and into the car Jules French had sent for them.

"Did you manage to talk to Arturo?" Luca asked.

Marissa smiled, and her eyes lit up. "Yes! He's so excited about starting his new job today. We're meeting him at Cara for dinner. I said we'd be there around nine."

"That's great." Luca glanced out the window. She'd had a few months of therapy to get her head straight once they'd settled in LA, but Arturo was still having weekly appointments. She couldn't—and didn't want to–imagine how hard it was for him to try to create a blank slate for himself after everything he'd had to do. She squeezed Marissa's hand. "He's going to be okay."

Marissa nodded, her eyes a little glassy. "I know. He's stronger than I ever thought possible." She kissed Luca's knuckles. "We've come out the other side, and he will too."

After thirty minutes at snail's pace, the driver apologized for the insane traffic, but Luca wasn't complaining. It gave her time to take in her surroundings. And she was surrounded by Los Angeles: the smog, the palm trees, the skyscrapers, the potential. Her dream made reality and made all the sweeter because of the road she'd traveled to get there.

"Where'd you go?" Marissa asked.

Luca sighed deeply and ran her hand over the soft leather of the car seat. "I can't believe this is really happening."

"It's everything you deserve."

Luca shrugged. She didn't know that she deserved any of this, but while she waited for the other shoe to drop, she was going to wring every last drop of enjoyment from life. Her book being published would have been amazing enough. Her book being made into a movie starring Elodie Fontaine, the greatest movie star of her age? That was another level she'd never dreamed of. And Marissa Luna–she'd dumped her father's last name in favor of her mamá's–by her side. Life couldn't get any better.

Marissa handed her a glossy magazine with Elodie Fontaine on the front cover. "I was going to show you this earlier, but then you were almost naked when I came into the bedroom, so I decided to show you how much I adored you instead."

Luca grinned, sure she'd never get used to being desired so intently by a woman as beautiful as Marissa. "My interview?"

Marissa nodded. "The first of many. Your story is a Hollywood sensation; they can't get enough of it. I keep hearing, 'It's like something from a movie script.' Maybe it could be the inspiration for your next book."

"Maybe." Luca flipped to her feature. A black and white photograph of her and Marissa together, their foreheads touching and eyes closed took up the entire first page of the article. Marissa looked like she belonged on the shiny pages of journals like these, but Luca looked like the beast who'd somehow captured the beauty. The next photograph was of Luca with her agent. Alyssa had been stunned by their explanation when they showed up with the original books on Luca's hard drive, proving she wrote them. *"I could tell something wasn't right with Casey Soto, but I just couldn't figure out what,"* was Alyssa's opening quote in the article. Actually, she'd taken some convincing and hadn't believed them at first. Casey had been a stellar con artist, and she'd done a fine job of playing the role of her supposed best friend. Luca didn't think Alyssa suspected a thing, but spin and appearance were all part of the business, and honestly, Luca didn't care one way or the other. Alyssa had made the arrangements, and Luca was issued with new contracts—better contracts, thanks to Marissa—for everything.

When they slowed at the barrier to FlatLine Studios, Luca grinned and squeezed Marissa's hand. This was it. Her first day on the set of a movie being made from *her* book. The driver pulled up outside studio seven, and she and Marissa climbed out. Elodie Fontaine drove up in a cart not unlike the ones at the compound, and Luca couldn't control the resultant shiver from the memory. Elodie jumped out and smiled her trademark smile that made people worldwide tingle with desire, and she had to admit, she tingled just a little herself. She heard Marissa's gulp and tamped down her jealousy. Word was that Elodie was desperately in love with an investigative reporter who had tamed her wild ways.

"It's great to see you both again." Elodie patted Luca on the back with such force it almost knocked her off her feet. "Are you ready for this?"

Luca shook her head. "Definitely not."

Elodie grinned, wrapped her arm around Luca's shoulder, and guided her toward the set door. "You are. Half the battle in Hollywood is looking like you're ready for anything even when you're not. You look the part. Now go get it." She shoved Luca inside and held out her hand for Marissa.

Luca's eyes adjusted to the half-light of the set. Zeus's office was exactly as she'd imagined it, and she caught her breath, realizing this was all truly happening. Behind the giant IMAX cameras, she saw several chairs with names emblazoned in white across the black canvas: Rix Reardon. Elodie Fontaine. Luca Romero.

She did a double-take. Her name on a chair at a movie set.

Marissa circled her arms around Luca's waist and kissed her neck. "I love you, bigshot."

She turned in Marissa's arms and cupped her face. "And I love you, Marissa Luna. For now and always."

Marissa pouted. "I'll remind you of that when you're basking in all the glory and fame."

Luca kissed her softly. "I'll never need to be reminded how much I love you. You're not just in my heart, you're in my blood."

Marissa rolled her eyes. "I suppose I'll see that line in one of your books soon enough."

Luca laughed. "Well, you *are* my muse, and every line of love is for you."

What's Your Story?

Global Wordsmiths, CIC, provides an all-encompassing service for all writers, ranging from basic proofreading and cover design to development editing, typesetting, and eBook services. A major part of our work is charity and community focused, delivering writing projects to under-served and under-represented groups across Nottinghamshire, giving voice to the voiceless and visibility to the unseen.

To learn more about what we offer, visit: www.globalwords.co.uk

A selection of books by Global Words Press:
Desire, Love, Identity: with the National Justice Museum
Aventuras en México: Farmilo Primary School
Life's Whispers: Journeys to the Hospice
Times Past: with The Workhouse, National Trust
Times Past: Young at Heart with AGE UK
In Different Shoes: Stories of Trans Lives
From Surviving to Thriving: Reclaiming Our Voices
Don't Look Back, You're Not Going That Way

Self-published authors working with Global Wordsmiths:
E.V. Bancroft
Addison M. Conley
AJ Mason
Ally McGuire
Emma Nichols
Helena Harte
Iona Kane
James Merrick
Karen Klyne
Robyn Nyx
John Edward Parsons
Simon Smalley
Valden Bush

Other Great Butterworth Books

Dead Pretty by Robyn Nyx
An FBI agent, a TV star, and a serial killer. Love hurts.
Available on Amazon (ASIN B09QRSKBVP)

An Art to Love by Helena Harte
Second chances are an art form.
Available on Amazon (ASIN B0B1CD8Y42)

Where the Heart Leads by Ally McGuire
A writer. A celebrity. And a secret that could break their hearts.
Available from 1 April 2023

Cabin Fever by Addison M Conley
She goes for the money, but will she stay for something deeper?
Available on Amazon (ASIN B0BQWY45GH)

Zamira Saliev: A Dept. 6 Operation by Valden Bush
They're both running from their pasts. Together, they might make a new future.
Available from Amazon (ASIN B0BHJKHK6S)

Of Light and Love by E.V. Bancroft
The deepest shadows paint the brightest love.
Available from Amazon (ASIN B0B64KJ3NP)

The Helion Band by AJ Mason
Rose's only crime was to show kindness to her royal mistress...
Available from Amazon (ASIN B09YM6TYFQ)

That Boy of Yours Wants Looking At by Simon Smalley
A gloriously colourful and heart-rending memoir.
Available from Amazon (ASIN B09HSN9NM8)

Judge Me, Judge Me Not by James Merrick
A memoir of one gay man's battle against the world and himself.
Available from Amazon (ASIN B09CLK91N5)

LesFic Eclectic Volume Three edited by Robyn Nyx
A little something for all tastes.
Download for free from BookFunnel - contact Butterworth Books for link.

CPSIA information can be obtained
at www.ICGtesting.com
Printed in the USA
BVHW042330150223
658633BV00012B/164